THE BRONFMAN CREDO:

"To turn $100 into $110 is work. But to turn $100 million into $110 million is inevitable."

Mr. Bronfman was not an impressive-looking man —five feet five, with a paunch and thin mats of hair—but the expressive eyes, flickering out at the world, gave off precise barometric readings of the weathers of his soul. They could change in an instant from a look of arctic fury to the delighted sparkle of a child's first glimpse of Santa Claus. A lifetime of stress and hard work had furrowed his forehead, but the softness of the skin across his cheeks and under his jaw lent him a cherubic competence. One senior vice-president likened him to a tiger. "If Mr. Sam smelled your fright, he'd jump you. But if you stood up to him, you'd gain his respect and he could be totally charming and most thoughtful."

To his staff, a more apt animal analogy might have been that of a killer whale.

Peter C. Newman

KING OF THE CASTLE

**The Making of a Dynasty:
Seagram's and the
Bronfman Empire**

PUBLISHED BY POCKET BOOKS NEW YORK

POCKET BOOKS, a Simon & Schuster division of
GULF & WESTERN CORPORATION
1230 Avenue of the Americas, New York, N.Y. 10020

Copyright © 1978, 1979 by Peter C. Newman

Published by arrangement with Atheneum Publishers
Library of Congress Catalog Card Number: 78-65198

ISBN: 0-671-83083-X

First Pocket Books printing March, 1980

10 9 8 7 6 5 4 3 2 1

POCKET and colophon are trademarks of Simon & Schuster.

Printed in the U.S.A.

For Camilla

Author's Note

This book attempts to document for the first time the controversial history and impressive influence of a supremely monied, infinitely complex, and highly neurotic family: the Bronfmans of Montreal and New York. Little known outside their own closed circles, they rank high among the non-Arab world's richest citizens, and their ascendancy grows daily.

My portrait of Samuel Bronfman, the dynasty's guiding spirit, is by no means definitive, and while I have tried to be fair and accurate, his descendants will strongly disagree with some of my assessments. Still, I believe that I have brought together as complete a profile as it will be possible to draw before the last witnesses of Mr. Sam's rise to glory have vanished and warm legend begins to be substituted for cold facts.

The mystery that has been deliberately created to shroud the Bronfman's early careers in bootlegging through Canada's West was not simple to dispel. Fortunately, I managed to track down several of the surviving associates during the Bronfman brothers' adventures in the Saskatchewan liquor trade. Now mostly in their nodding eighties and lodged in old people's homes on the outskirts of small prairie towns, but still remembering vividly how they used to "run the booze for the Bronfmans," these valiant survivors shared their memories with me. Among them was Ken John, a hale and articulate retired accountant now living in Estevan. He was there the night Paul Matoff, Sam Bronfman's brother-in-law and operator of one of Saskatchewan's busiest "boozoriums," was killed by the blast from a saw-off shotgun poked through a window.

As supporting documentation, I was able to obtain a copy of Harry Bronfman's unpublished personal account of the family's earliest days on the prairies. I was also allowed access to some papers collected by Clifford Harvison, the Royal Canadian Mounted Police corporal who arrested the Bronfman brothers in 1934 on criminal conspiracy charges and later became one of the force's most enlightened commissioners.

In the three years it took to complete this book, I interviewed a dozen Bronfmans and several dozen of their critics, confrères, and competitors, plus the usual retinue of hangers-on, platoon sergeants, and whisky-priests that a fiscal galaxy of this magnitude inevitably attracts.

The group profile that emerges of these inheritors of the great Bronfman fortune includes hot-headed dreamers with wounded eyes and hyper egos whose emotional insecurity sometimes blights even the best of their endeavors. The male members of this exotic coterie are spending their best years in the faith, making their huge corporate empires grow with inconceivable, exponential haste—then expanding them some more.

To be a Bronfman is to be special, and they know it. Restless men in Gucci loafers, they are constantly in search of themselves. This volume is a chronicle of their quest.

IT IS NOT THE BOOK I ORIGINALLY INTENDED TO WRITE.

Following publication of *The Canadian Establishment* in 1975, I began researching the second volume, which was meant to cover many of the remaining power groupings, including a chapter on the Jewish community. The notion of Jewish power has always intrigued me, because although collectively the Jews wield tremendous influence, individually they often feel themselves painfully vulnerable, at hazard with the society that surrounds them. Here is a kind of cousinhood, men and women competing fiercely with each other for authority and prestige, yet tied together in what may well be the most vital and interesting elite of them all.

As I probed deeper into the curious power structure of North America's Jewish community, so many lines of inquiry led into various branches of the Bronfman dynasty that I realized this remarkable tribe deserved a context of its own. Even among that small group of pre-eminent families who dominate world commerce, the Bronfmans are unique in terms of both the reach of their authority and the grasp of their wealth. By devoting a separate volume to them, I saw an opportunity of attempting something close to a clinical portrayal of how power can be exercised, diffused, hoarded, and abused—all within the cloak of a fiercely proud Jewish family that rose to untold riches in one generation.

Terence Robertson, the only writer known to have previously attempted a Bronfman biography (it was never published), took his own life after completing a rough draft of the manuscript. During a 1977 trial in which the Toronto publishing firm of McClelland and Stewart Ltd. sued Mutual Life Assurance Co. to collect the $100,000 for which Robertson's life had been insured, Roderick Goodman of the *Toronto Daily Star*'s editorial department testified that on January 31, 1970, the author had telephoned him from a New York hotel room to explain that he had been commissioned to write the history of the Bronfman family but that he had "found out things they don't want me to write about." Graham Murray Caney, another *Star* editor, testified that Robertson had told him his life "had been threatened and we would know who was doing the threatening but that he would do the job himself." While he was still on the telephone, Caney had the call traced and alerted the New York Police Department. Detectives burst into Terence Robertson's hotel room just minutes before he died of barbiturate poisoning. The main existing reference to the family in book form is James Gray's excellent *Booze: The Impact of Whisky on the Prairie West,* which dealt in part with the distilling empire's Saskatchewan beginnings.

IN A PROJECT OF THIS NATURE, which is about as unauthorized as a biography can be while attempting to record the intimate details of a powerful dynasty's many foibles, it is impossible to credit sources. Most of those enlightened collaborators who befriended me with information about the family did so on the condition of their own anonymity. Only by reading the pages that follow will they realize the magnitude of my debt.

The hard work and loyalty of Helen McLachlan, my assistant, in the preparation of this manuscript has earned more gratitude and respect than I can describe or repay. I thank Susan Cole, the best damned researcher in these northern latitudes, for compiling the appendices. Bev DuBrule was a conscientious transcriber of my many interviews. I am most thankful to Lloyd Hodgkinson, the publisher of *Maclean's,* for allowing me the freedom to write this book, but in neither tone nor content does it bear the sanction of Maclean-Hunter Limited.

Many kind souls—notably my mother, Wanda Brunner, Orlie McCall, Martin Lynch, Janet Craig, Abe Rotstein, and Kevin Doyle—proved to be wise, compassionate, and steadfast friends during the often painful process of researching and writing this book. Above all, I was inspired by the cheerful presence of my daughter, Ashley, who is kinder, smarter, and funnier than even the luckiest of fathers has any right to expect.

This book bears the imprint, as does everything I have written, of the long, happy apprenticeship I served under my friend and mentor, the late Ralph Allen. I will ever be indebted to my former wife, Christina, for the epiphanies of her style and character. No balance sheet of gratitudes would be complete without a mention of Stan Kenton and his music for providing the spiritual lift and sense of cadence that sustained me through the pre-dawn hours when most of these pages were written.

This volume owes its existence to many others not mentioned here; only the responsibility for its imperfections is fully my own.

July 1, 1978

P.C.N.

Contents

PART ONE

Mr. Sam

1. The Rothschilds of the New World

EXCEPT THAT they are almost certainly richer and without a doubt more secretive, the Bronfmans have become the Rothschilds of the New World. But unlike the European banking family, which has concentrated its wealth in metals, the Bronfman dynasty holds a commanding position in the two liquids that fuel the modern world: whisky and oil.

The warring members of this unusual and impassioned family live in worlds unto themselves behind the tightest curtain of privacy money can buy. In an age when the multinational corporations that dominate international business have grown far too large and much too complex to be controlled by any one individual or family, the Bronfmans have managed to retain an iron grip on the world's largest distilling business—the Seagram Company—and discovered a unique process of passing on control of their vast commercial empire from one generation to the next, intact and still compounding.

Seagram now sells $2 billions' worth of liquor a year, marketing six hundred brands in 175 countries. This amounts to almost a million and a half bottles of liquor a day. Two of its labels—Seven Crown and V.O.— are the largest- and second-largest-selling brands of whisky in the world. At any one time, some four mil-

3

lion barrels of spirits and forty-two million gallons of
wine are being aged in its many warehouses.

Away from the glare of public concern and attention
—through tier upon tier of private holding subsidiaries
listed only in the offices of the many lawyers they retain on full-time standby—the Bronfmans have amassed
wealth and power as rapidly and silently as the flowering of buds in a time-lapse movie.

While precise estimates are impossible, the aggregate
assets currently held by the various branches of the
Bronfman family total at least $7 billion. On an inter-
national scale, the Bronfmans control one of the largest
capital pools remaining in the non-Arab world. "The
Bronfman fortune," *Fortune* has reported, "rivals that
of all but a small number of North American families,
including some that gathered their strength in the
nineteenth century when taxes had no more impact on
wealth than poor boxes."

"Among financial people in North America, the
Bronfman name generates the same kind of excitement
as the Rothschilds'," says Jean de Brabant, president
of Société Financière Privée Limitée, a merchant banking operation in Montreal. "I was talking to a banker
in Texas the other day when their name came up in
connection with some new financing. He didn't gasp
exactly, but he almost did."

The Bronfman patriarch who made the decision to
lead his family to the New World in 1889 was the most
orthodox of Jews, a man who could not conceive of
making the move without a rabbi to teach his children.
But Ekiel Bronfman's wrenching efforts to establish
his family in the Canadian prairies also forged a dynastic urge within his third son, Samuel, who would push
aside brothers and sisters, nephews and nieces, to
establish a clear line of descent for the family fortune,
flowing through him and on to his sons. Few other entrepreneurs have come close to duplicating the achievement of Samuel Bronfman (1891–1971), who raised
himself from peddling firewood and frozen whitefish
around the villages of central Manitoba to creating one

of the continent's most powerful businesses. It is doubt-ful whether one man or family can ever again build a similar industrial empire or garner such wealth—certainly not through the confluence of circumstances that allowed Sam and his brothers to flourish in the whisky trade while skating to the very edge of the U.S. and Canadian prohibition laws designed to kill it.

Sam Bronfman was not physically imposing. But he was supercharged with verve and imagination, flowing with energy, making every minute count, constantly at war with his competitors, his associates, and himself. He took his greatest pleasure from calculating the infinitesimal gradations of risk in the deals and machinations that fostered the growth of the Seagram empire. Once asked what he regarded as the human mind's most significant invention, he instantly snapped back, "Interest."

For all his business acumen and boundless success, Sam was never able to fit himself harmoniously into the society that enriched him. Although some of his best friends were WASPS, he could not accustom himself to their body language, codes of behavior, or social decorum. Haunted by his past, too full of passion and authentic emotions to hide his feelings, Sam Bronfman spent the final three decades of his life in a tumultuous struggle to become a full-fledged member of Canada's business establishment. He never made it.

The Bronfmans of Sam's time defined the Canadian establishment's limits beyond which it was not prepared to go; Sam's children not only belong to that establishment, they transcend it.

The Bronfman millions have been subdivided among the eight children and twenty-nine grandchildren of Ekiel and his wife, Minnie. Most of these assets are planted in carefully nurtured gardens called investment trusts, with cadres of professional investment consultants and tax lawyers tending their growth. At least two of the younger Bronfmans—Edward and Peter, sons of Sam's brother Allan—have created an impressive commercial empire of their own worth about $2 billion.

It includes such diverse holdings as Toronto's York-dale Shopping Centre, the Coca-Cola bottling agency on the tropical island of Antigua, Atlanta's Peachtree Center Tower, a sizable collection of properties in downtown Calgary, Montreal's huge Place Ville Marie complex, and eleven thousand parking sites in mobile-home parks throughout the U.S. Southwest.

Making money long ago ceased to be a measure of Bronfman success. "To turn $100 into $110 is work," says Edgar, Sam's elder son, who runs the main Sea-gram operations out of New York. "But to turn $100 million into $110 million is inevitable."

The sophistication of the Bronfman family's life-styles has reached such refinement that it is in the trappings of ordinariness that they have taken up an un-natural pose and pretended habitat. An exception among Bronfmans (and perhaps the ultimate in sophis-tication) is Sam's younger daughter, Phyllis, who lives in a converted peanut factory in Montreal's old quarter. They fly the world in private jetliners, unfettered by the fiscal concerns that plague more ordinary mortals, safe in the assumption that almost anything and nearly everyone is for sale—and can be bought. Except for their fear of publicity, they demonstrate little compunc-tion about enjoying their money—although some mem-bers of the family's fourth generation, now reaching adulthood, have been raised in a very different tradi-tion. To teach his children the value of money, Gerald Bronfman (son of Harry, who was one of Sam's older brothers) for a time gave his teen-aged daughters a weekly cash allowance of thirty-seven and a half cents. He accomplished this by paying out thirty-eight cents one week and thirty-seven the next week.

For most of the Bronfmans, however, it is otherwise: "After all," Edgar once observed, "what's the use of having a rich father if you can't spend his money?"

To be a Bronfman is both a blessing and a curse. Most members of the family lead alluring lives, an Indian summer existence spent in the warming glow of material comforts and the sense of grandeur that comes from feeling part of a historic succession. It is only in the loneliness of the early morning hours, when they really face themselves, that male Bronfmans contemplate the darker legacy of having to try to match their achievements with those of Mr. Sam, the empire builder, and feel the stirrings of inadequacy that accompany the realization of inevitably having to fall short. "All types of things are expected of you because you're growing up in the shadow of a literally incredible guy called Sam," says Mitch Bronfman, a grandson of Harry, Sam's brother. "But as you get older it becomes less of a burden and more of a way of life."

Young Bronfmans don't mature; they hibernate. Spoiled by all that money and all that attention, they tend to view the outside world with suspicion, venturing few real contacts with their contemporaries until they're safely into their forties, and even then never feeling entirely certain of other people's motives. "As soon as you say what your name is, there's a reaction," says Peter Bronfman. "You see the cash register ring up in the person's eyes. They meet and greet you or participate with you in a certain stereotyped way. You never know how they really feel. I guess there are pros and cons to being a Bronfman, but I'm not sure what the pros are—except, I suppose, it opens certain doors and enables you to do some things faster."

No Bronfman can escape his heritage by turning away from it; he can only grow up and try to prove himself. "My children," confesses Gerald Bronfman, "find the Bronfman name a disadvantage, but I love the life I lead."

Against the onslaught of the many outsiders constantly petitioning for a share of their money and attention, the family has erected a multitude of barriers, the most effective of them being a tribal feeling that divides the world into Bronfmans and everybody else. Yet the essence of their individualities is not easily given, even to each other. Their affections often wear boxing gloves. In the early morning hours of May 30,

1970, when a squad of radical Quebec separatists threw
four sticks of dynamite into the foyer of Peter Bronfman's house, it was front-page news in Montreal. But
the only comment that Saidye, Sam Bronfman's wife,
made about it the next time she met Peter was, "Why
you?"—implying that he was hardly an important
enough member of the dynasty to have been singled out
for special treatment. The finest of gradations are precisely observed. Charles always calls Peter's father
"Uncle Allan," but Peter invariably refers to Charles's
father as "Mr. Sam."

The various branches of the family seem bound together by high-tension wires giving off a constant buzz
of gossip: about Edgar's newest exploits, Charles's
secret war against René Lévesque's separatists, Phyllis's
latest eccentricities, Edward's divorce, Mitch's last run-
in with the Royal Canadian Mounted Police, Peter's
baffling business success, and Minda's next Paris reception. They never get tired of talking about each other's
affairs, deals, victories, and defeats. At any given time,
at least one branch of the family is bound to be in
crisis. Catastrophes and emergencies of the past become a sort of litany: the day Mona (Allan's daughter)
committed suicide; how Mitch worked himself up to a
bleeding ulcer by the age of nineteen; the latest kidnap
threat that Edgar turned over to the FBI; the real story
of Edgar's marriage to Lady Carolyn Townshend; details of the drawn-out battle that deprived Peter and
Edward of their Seagram inheritance. Because of the
many family feuds, two of Montreal's best lawyers—
Lazarus Phillips and Philip Vineberg—have become ex-
officio members of the family, charged with arbitrating
among its several factions.

There's no sense of detachment about any of these
stories or events, only the shared feeling by their partic-
ipants that being a Bronfman means living in the dead
center of an emotional hurricane. The business of having constantly to establish their self-worth to themselves
has reduced most of the grandchildren of Ekiel and
Minnie to a state of nervous tension in which they have

to keep feeling their own pulses every morning, just to make certain they're still in the race.

Sam Bronfman, who dominated this combative brood, never did subscribe to any of the analogies made between his family and the Rothschilds. "No," he told one underling who had brought up the comparison. "No. I've set it up much better than the Rothschilds. They spread the children. I've kept them together." This was a reference to Sam's unswerving determination to maintain full control of the company within his branch of the family. But the comment seems faintly reminiscent of an apocryphal story about the poor Jew who sees a baby Rothschild being helped into an elegant Rolls-Royce by a uniformed chauffeur and wistfully exclaims, "So young—and already a Rothschild!"

That is the dynastic imperative. Despite the bitter feuds that his decision caused over the years, Sam ruthlessly cut off his brothers and sisters as well as all their children from any meaningful participation in running the Seagram empire. "The closeness of the family was once a wonderful thing," laments Gerald Bronfman. "All the children and the children's children are being denied that. They've lost a lot."

THE ROTHSCHILDS STARTED OUT AS COIN-CHANGERS IN THE GHETTOS OF CENTRAL EUROPE, the Barings in textiles, the Hambros in foodstuffs, the Warburgs in silver, and the Guggenheims in Swiss embroideries. The Bronfmans had the social misfortune not only of being in the liquor business but also of being in the liquor business in Canada.

Even though the average Canadian swills 1.80 gallons of pure alcohol a year—the equivalent of 28.9 bottles of rye annually—sufficient vestiges of puritanism remain within the national psyche that booze is still regarded as an invention of the devil. This ambivalence combined with the whispers about the Bronfmans' role as kingpins in the bootlegging trade that flourished along the Canadian border during U.S. Prohibition days robbed Ekiel's heirs of the legitimacy they so desperately sought.

It was this search for legitimacy, or rather *yechus,* its Jewish equivalent, that dominated Sam Bronfman's long life and remains the dynasty's major preoccupation. *Yechus* is not merely a craving for respect but rather a state of respect recognized publicly by something grand, not with perfunctory courtesies or token awards. Emperors seek *yechus* by erecting monuments to themselves. Sam Bronfman entertained more modest ambitions: he longed to be named a governor of McGill University, elected a member of Montreal's Mount Royal Club, appointed a director of the Bank of Montreal, and summoned to the Senate of Canada. While these paltry distinctions kept eluding him, he began to retreat into himself, defining his life more and more by its exclusions and adopted snobberies than by his original passions and enthusiasms.

Sam Bronfman's search for group identity outside his Jewish milieu was constantly being fouled by his family legend. The shotgun murder of Paul Matoff, Sam's brother-in-law, by a mysterious rum-runner in 1922 at Bienfait, Saskatchewan; the brief jailing of Harry Bronfman during his trial in 1930 on a charge of attempting to bribe a federal customs official; a second court action in 1930 involving Harry, this time charged with tampering with witnesses—getting them out of the country via the Bronfman hotel chain—to save Harry's brother-in-law, David Gallaman, from jail; the accusations of fraud and excise-tax evasion made against the four Bronfman brothers in Montreal during the mid-1930s; and, above all, the undeniable fact that the Bronfman fortune was squarely based on supplying American bootleggers with their wares—this was the past that haunted him.

No illegalities were proved against any of the Bronfmans. But the murmurs never ceased. Sometimes they were more than murmurs. Until recently, whenever any Bronfman died, his closest relatives would receive telegrams from Max Chechik of Vancouver, blessing the fact that the world now had one less Bronfman. He still sends out cables every March 4 to senior members of the family, commemorating the anniversary of his father's death. The roots of this particular feud go back to the early days on the prairies, when Meyer Chechik briefly became a partner in Harry Bronfman's main bottling operation at Regina. "The Bronfmans defrauded my dad and won the trials that followed on a series of technicalities," Max Chechik, who now heads Plant Maintenance Equipment Ltd. in Vancouver, maintains. "I sent out the telegrams to irk them a little bit. The Bronfman name is still anathema to me." The elder Chechik spent the last few years of his life at Montreal's Mount Royal Hotel, across Peel Street from the Seagram headquarters, constantly telephoning any Bronfman who would take his calls, and appearing at their offices. "They don't like it that I'm here," he wrote his son in one of his last letters before he died in his hotel room of a heart attack on March 4, 1947.

In any case, the intimations left Sam with his nose forever pressed against the outside windows of the establishment's bastions. His inner ear and practiced eye could detect the split-second hesitation of tone or fractional change of look that his name produced in a stranger's reaction.

At Seagram's he was king of the castle and behaved like the emperor of the world. Away from his office, he seemed lonely and alone, afraid to open up, hoping the past might recede into forgetful memory—listening always for those murmurs.

2. Mr. Sam

SAM BRONFMAN was a Russian by background, a Canadian by persuasion, a Texan by temperament—and an upper-class Englishman by aspiration. Nothing in his mature life affected him more than the years he spent during the 1920s as a junior partner to the haughty Scottish aristocrats who owned the huge Distillers Trust. On his frequent visits to London and Edinburgh, these self-composed bluebloods imbued young Sam with such a love of British pomp and baronial circumstance that he spent the next half-century vainly trying to imitate them, hoping to establish his credentials, craving to be admitted into their magic circle.

When George VI and Queen Elizabeth visited Canada in 1939, he created the prestigious Crown Royal brand of whisky in their honor, personally blending six hundred samples before he found a taste that satisfied him. He purchased the Chivas distillery in Aberdeen because, among other things, its owners operated a high-priced grocery that served the royal family during visits to Scotland as "Purveyors of Provisions to H.M. the King." But try as he might, Sam was never able to obtain a similar royal warrant for his Chivas Regal Scotch. He got immense pleasure from attending royal functions, joining Saidye and Minda at an afternoon presentation party in the garden of Buckingham Palace on May 28, 1953. He also had two tickets (in the upper gallery of the south aisle of the nave) for the coronation of Elizabeth II in Westminster Abbey on June 2 of the same year.

Because he perceived membership in the Canadian Senate as an important mark of acceptance, he waged a cynically dogged campaign for more than twenty years to get himself an appointment. But his secret longing was to achieve a British knighthood, an ambition partly inspired by the example of Sir Mortimer Davis, a fellow Montreal Jew who not only belonged to all the right clubs (the Mount Royal, the St. James's, the Montreal Hunt, the Montreal Jockey, the Royal Montreal Golf, the Forest and Stream) and was on the board of the Royal Bank but was also knighted in 1917 by George V for philanthropic contributions. Although Canada had not recommended its citizens for titles since 1935, Bronfman never really believed that he might not be an exception. "Sam bordered on being a genius and, fortunately, his wisdom outweighed his naïvety," recalls Saul Hayes, his chief mentor in Jewish affairs. "So naïve he was in his dreams of knighthood and yet so shrewd that he could encapsule a whole concept of life in one offhand comment. It was Mike Pearson who finally turned down the senatorship he so badly wanted by promising there might be something much bigger in store. Sam immediately began to dream of becoming, as he put it, Canadian Ambassador to the Court of St. James's."

Probably the main practical effect of his British experience was to transform Sam Bronfman's view of drinking. The many long, cheerful evenings he spent sipping Scotch with his mannerly fellow distillers in their private clubs—resplendent with the aroma of properly aged leather, quality cigars, tinged with a faint whiff of fox blood—made Sam determined to change the image of alcohol then prevailing in North America. Whisky was treated as "rotgut" that the customer threw back from a hastily poured shot glass slapped down on a moist bar top. Through new packaging (he personally helped design most new labels) and prestige advertising (such as the long-running Calvert's "Man of Distinction" series), Bronfman attempted to project for his products the snob appeal and understated dignity of the London clubs. He built up one of his brands— Chivas Regal—into a byword for quality, the whisky equivalent of Rolls-Royce cars or Patek Philippe watches, and then topped himself bottling an even more exclusive (and expensive) blend called Royal Salute.

But the most obvious manifestation of Sam's reverence for the British gentry was the architecture of his homes and offices. If he couldn't have the real thing, he was bound to create his own brand of manor houses —structures with false battlements, elaborate cornices, and the kind of décor that encouraged visitors to think the scratches on the library paneling might have been made by an aristocratic ancestor's careless sword thrust. His Montreal house near the summit of Westmount was a turreted Victorian pile of instant medieval splendor crammed with treasures a peer of the realm might envy. The ultimate and most public expression of his adopted refinement was the miniature feudal castle Sam built for himself in 1928 at 1430 Peel Street in Montreal to house Seagram's headquarters. It's a creation of gray granite combining the worst of Tudor and Gothic with early Disneyland. There's a phony portcullis guarding the entrance (currently reinforced with a remote-control lock system that allows the receptionist to identify visitors before allowing them inside; a similar precautionary electronic door guards the inner offices), and until fairly recently the main floor was adorned with an old suit of armor and the skin of a rangy Bengal tiger rumored to have devoured eighty-four men.

MR. SAM WAS NOT AN IMPRESSIVE-LOOKING MAN—five feet five, with a paunch and thin mats of hair—but the expressive eyes, flickering out at the world, gave off precise barometric readings of the weathers of his soul. They could change in an instant from a look of arctic fury to the delighted sparkle of a child's first glimpse of Santa Claus. A lifetime of stress and hard work had furrowed his forehead, but the softness of the skin across his cheeks and under his jaw lent him a cherubic countenance. One senior vice-president likened him to a tiger. "If Mr. Sam smelled your fright, he'd jump you. But if you stood up to him, you'd gain his respect and he could be totally charming and most thoughtful."

To his staff, a more apt animal analogy might have been that of a killer whale. Whenever he appeared, most of them scattered like pilot fish darting behind protective rock with unreasoning fright. Any given group of Seagram executives attending a meeting in Bronfman's office would be constantly shifting about, each man craning to keep the boss in direct sight, monitoring thoughts and words, trying to guess what Mr. Sam wanted him to think and comment. Only Sam Bronfman could say and do exactly as he pleased, treating his underlings with the faintly forgiving air of a Schweitzer among the incurables.

He knew how to listen to the warnings of his senses, keeping tuned in to the nuances in play around him, exercising a form of nameless power over his employees so that they felt obliged to yield a secret piece of themselves to his command. No major decisions were taken without his advice and consent; constant homage was required—and had to be seen to be paid. One problem in dealing with Sam Bronfman was his unyielding self-confidence. When a Seagram executive messed up a deal with the Quebec Liquor Board, he came back and confessed, "I should have done it your way, Mr. Sam." The reply is etched in his memory. "What do you mean, you should have done it my way? There *is* no other way."

To some, he became a paternalistic father-confessor; to others, the unsympathetic reflection of their own inadequacies. His many probing queries were answered cautiously lest a reply rouse his legendary temper. This was no tight-lipped WASP irritation, causing its sufferer to snap out words like crisp dollar bills. This was a rowdy, blasting fury that pushed an inner plunger in Sam's brain, detonating him.* It could leave men physically shaking, mentally spent, and frequently ducking the objects Sam would hurl at them. In his New York office only a metal window divider prevented a large paperweight thrown at a terrified vice-president from going right out into the street below. (A plaque was made up to commemorate the incident, and whenever Sam started to blow, nervous executives would silently point to it, hoping to curb the worst of the outburst.)

AT ONE DIRECTORS' LUNCHEON, J. ALEXANDRE PRUD'HOMME, a partner of Seagram lawyer Aimé Geoffrion and Geoffrion's successor on the board, touched off an explosion when he asked Sam about dividend policy and was supported by Allan Bronfman. Sam responded by letting fly with his bun and then his dinner plate when Prud'homme persisted in his questioning. Prud'homme said he would resign from the board unless he got an answer. That afternoon, his resignation was delivered by special messenger.

While it was less fear than fealty that allowed the huge enterprise to prosper, some Seagram executives could never accustom themselves to Bronfman's explosions. Frank Marshall, who was director of export sales during the early fifties, got so upset that he arranged his schedule to be away from Montreal whenever Sam was in town. In case Bronfman should return unexpectedly, Marshall kept a packed suitcase in his office so that he could immediately drive to Dorval Airport, where he'd buy a ticket to any of Seagram's world operations he felt might benefit from a surprise inspection. The system worked fine for a while because overseas sales were booming; but eventually Bronfman realized that he hardly ever saw his export manager, and the

---

* Dr. Abe Mayman, Sam Bronfman's physician, believes that the temper tantrums may actually have helped him live longer by causing his blood to circulate faster and acting as a safety valve to relieve tension.

word went out: "Find Marshall. Mr. Sam wants to see him."

The hunted man kept moving around the globe for a few more months, but Mr. Sam's sixtieth birthday party was coming up, and that was an obligatory occasion for all head-office executives. The staff had mounted an elaborate film presentation, complete with sound track, depicting highlights of Seagram's sales campaigns during the past year. Sam was sitting in the front row at the ballroom of the Windsor, enjoying himself hugely, laughing as he watched scenes of slightly tipsy Egyptian army officers toasting one another with Crown Royal on the terrace of Shepheard's Hotel in Cairo. This was followed by a long-shot of a Bedouin riding a camel toward the Pyramids, bottle tucked into his burnoose. The camel approached the camera. Sam suddenly sat up, peering at its swaying rider. The focus was much tighter now, and the "Bedouin," it became clear, was none other than Frank Marshall in long nightshirt with a fez on his head, brandishing a bottle of V.O.

Sam leaped out of his chair. Pointing excitedly toward the image of his errant export manager, he bellowed at the screen, "There's the son of a bitch! That's where he's been spending his time! Riding a goddamn camel!"

Once Bronfman had calmed down a little, Marshall, who had slunk into the hall after the lights were turned out, came up behind him, tapped him lightly on the shoulder, and pleadingly whispered, "That film was taken on a Sunday, Mr. Sam."

The reply goes unrecorded.

IT WASN'T SO MUCH THE LOSS OF TEMPER THAT SHOCKED HIS ASSOCIATES as the swearing that followed. "Some of Sam's language would make a longshoreman very proud indeed," Saul Hayes recalls. The salvos of curses were directed with the care of an artillery officer observing the detonations from his battery of guns. He could adjust the range and impact of his outbursts so that if calling someone a son of a bitch didn't produce the desired effect, he would move on to tagging him "a *son* of a son of a bitch" and escalate from there. His nephew Gerald once cautioned Sam to watch his temper or he'd get ulcers. "Listen," was the reply, "I don't get ulcers. I give them."

Sam Drache, a Winnipeg lawyer and old acquaintance, remembers crossing a street in Montreal sometime in the fifties and running into Eddie Gelber. "Eddie was one of the giants in our community. He was a lawyer and a rabbi, but practiced neither profession and devoted himself in the main to Jewish life. He told me what had happened at a Canadian Jewish Congress meeting that morning and the foul language Sam had used when he was annoyed by somebody. He didn't repeat the words, but he wasn't shocked. So I said, 'Eddie, how could you sit there?' and he replied, 'Well, you simply do—he has the power to hold that organization together. He uses the evil to do good. He doesn't know any other way.' I said that I thought it had nothing to do with evil and good, that Sam was just a bully who exploded when he couldn't have his way. To me it was as simple as that."

Few associates could endure such treatment for long. Among those who did were two Seagram aides, Michael McCormick, Sam's onetime special assistant, and Jack Clifford, who worked personally with Mr. Sam for years. Clifford is a big bear of an Irishman with knowing eyes and the gift of the gab whose loyalty to the Bronfman clan has survived intact many trials of faith and endurance. His initiation was not auspicious. A twenty-three-year-old radio announcer when he joined Seagram as a salesman in 1936, his first job was to provide free liquor to the hospitality suite of a baseball convention being held at Montreal's Mount Royal Hotel. The 125 attending sportswriters soon demolished his initial twelve-case allotment, and Clifford went to see Abe Bronfman, who was in charge of head-office stock. "Abe turned me down," Clifford recalls. "He told me, 'I gave you a dozen cases last night. What are they doing over there? Throwing it out the window? We're just not going to give them any more. What do you think we are? Charity?'

"Just then the door opens and a funny little guy I haven't seen before comes in and says to me, 'Who are you?'

" 'My name's Clifford and I'm in charge of the baseball convention across the street. It's going to be opening in another hour and I've no liquor left.'

" 'What do you mean you've no liquor left?'

" 'Well, they drank the first twelve cases and Mr. Bronfman here won't give me any more. . . .' At this point the little guy starts to call Abe every name under the sun and I'm saying to myself, 'He must be pretty important to be calling Abe a Jew bastard because he looks kind of Jewish himself.' But there's no let-up.

" 'Don't you realize,' he is screaming at Abe, 'you dumb son of a bitch, what this means to us? I've got every important sportswriter in the country filing his story from the Seagram Room at the first baseball convention ever held outside the States! Ford Frick is there! Judge Landis is going to be speaking tonight! He's going to be right in our bloody room! Don't you know what that means to us, for Christ's sake?' The little guy works himself to such a pitch that he finally picks up the telephone and throws it at Abe. But the cord doesn't break, and the instrument springs back and hits him in the forehead, drawing blood. He's thrashing around, blood in his eyes. Then he turns to me and shouts, 'You get out of here, you big bastard. You're fired!'

"At this point I'm ready to go back into the radio business, but the company comptroller, who tells me that the little guy was Sam, the big boss, convinces me to work out the day. Later, I'm at my desk cleaning a few things out when Sam, his head all bandages and plaster, comes over and says, 'Hey, big boy.'

" 'Yeah, you talking to me?'

" 'Jesus. What's your name again?'

" 'Jack Clifford.'

" 'Jack, first of all you got to understand something. I'm under tremendous pressure. The banks are at my throat. The shareholders are at my throat. It's nip and tuck whether we're going to survive in this whole goddamned rat race. I get a chance for some great publicity and this goddamn stupid brother of mine has to be cheap about it. You got caught in the middle, and I want to apologize.' By now he's got his arm around my shoulder, and he's smiling and asking me to see him through his troubles. So of course I agree."

Clifford served with distinction in the Royal Canadian Navy during World War II and got back to Montreal just as liquor rationing was about to be lifted. Sam called him in shortly afterward to complain that he had been in the Mount Royal Hotel the night before, ordered a Tom Collins, and there were no Seagram brands available. "For Christ's sake," he raged, "I don't know what the hell's happening around here. I'm at the Normandie Roof, the biggest outfit in Eastern Canada, and there isn't a drop of our goddamned gin there. Not a goddamned drop of Burnett's! Not a goddamned drop of White Satin!" Clifford wasn't responsible for any of these lines. He had been placed in charge of marketing Calvert's products and asked whether he'd ordered Vickers, his gin brand.

"No," was the reply, "I forgot I owned it. But if I had, I'm damned sure they wouldn't have had any either, for Christ's sake. You better get down to the Liquor Board tomorrow. I hear rumors they're going to lift rationing soon."

The following morning Clifford discovered that the government agency had already given a large order to Corby's and Melchers, rival distilling companies. When he asked about Seagram's, he was told the board was preparing a really big purchase for the next day. Back at the office he started explaining the situation, but before he could announce the good news, Mr. Sam cut him off: "How come we're not the first? Why, those goddamned ungrateful sons of bitches, after everything I did for them! I kept their goddamned shelves packed all through the war! I gave them V.O. when we hardly had any! And you know what they're doing now? They're sucking my very guts out!"

When Clifford finally interrupted this tirade to explain that Seagram's was getting an order for five thousand cases the next morning, Bronfman waved him away. "Well, why the fuck didn't you say so in the first place? I could get a goddamn heart attack dealing with guys like you."

What set Sam off swearing most frequently were the inevitable lapses of memory among his staff. He had the gift of total recall, especially with balance-sheet tabulations, and became livid whenever lesser talents had to look things up. His capacity for retaining facts and trivia was phenomenal. He remembered reams of nineteenth-century poetry, including endless quatrains from Tennyson's *In Memoriam*.* He could roll off details of decade-old production figures, depreciation allowances, per-share earnings, situations and decisions with uncanny accuracy.

"He was like a computer," says Noah Torno, one of his former associates.† "You could put in any information you wanted, and it would always come out exactly the same way. Added to that, he had unusually strong powers of Cartesian reasoning, which was a powerful combination. But one thing he could never do was just quietly relax." When the two men were on a holiday in Jamaica, Sam became so restless while visiting a

---

* Not surprisingly, his favorite verse was:
> Who breaks his birth's invidious bar,
> And grasps the skirts of happy chance,
> And breasts the blows of circumstance,
> And grapples with his evil star.

† When Bronfman was working on the text of the 1970 Seagram annual report, which summed up the company's operating history, he called Torno. "I want you to know," Sam confided, "that I've only used the word 'friend' once in the whole thing, and it's when I refer to you." In this, Sam was bending exclusivity a bit. He referred to five other men as a "friend" or a "great friend"—but Torno was the only one in the Canadian section of the eighty-four-page report.

tourist attraction—the ghost-haunted Rose Hall mansion—that he promptly purchased it. On another vacation, in Caracas, Sam suddenly decided to copy vodka's successful Bloody Mary marketing formula by devising a rum-and-tomato-juice drink called Red Devil. Artists were flown down from New York to design a label for the canned mixture, but sales were disappointing.

One of the daily rituals that occupied an inordinate amount of Bronfman's time was the planning of his office lunch. First thing each morning he'd hold long consultations with the Seagram cooks (there are elaborate boardroom kitchens at both Montreal and New York) about what he was going to eat that day. Occasionally, if he came up with a particularly pleasing menu, he would pat his stomach and say to himself: "Mary, you're going to be well fed today." He was especially fond of Winnipeg goldeye, fillet of sole, pot roast, and boiled beef.

Keeping Mr. Sam happily fed while he was away from head office wasn't always simple. During a tour of the Seagram "Cities of Canada" paintings in the fifties, he was staying at Calgary's Palliser Hotel when an emergency required his return to New York. Merle "Schneck" Schneckenburger, a former shirt account executive in a Montreal ad agency and then one of Seagram's vice-presidents, was accompanying him. As they didn't have a private plane, Schneck booked them on a Trans-Canada Air Lines North Star. "There's no meals or anything," he warned Mr. Sam, but was told, "I don't give a damn. Get me a seat."

Once the reservations had been made, Sam returned to the subject of their lunch. "Now, you tell me that there's no meal. . . ."

"It's just a little shoebox they give you with a soggy sandwich and an apple in it."

"Oh, to hell with that. Why don't we speak to that nice cook in the hotel that made the big party for us last night and ask him if he'd put together a lunch for us?"

The Palliser chef obliged with a vengeance. He sent

a runner to buy a picnic basket and filled it with a roast chicken that had a marvelously crisp white crust on it, containers of fresh salad, a thermos of *consommé madrilène au sherry,* and a selection of his most luscious desserts. Instead of plastic plates and cutlery, he put in the knives, forks, and china usually reserved for royal visits. It looked like such a feast that when he proudly presented it to him, Mr. Sam wanted to start eating right away.

On the way to the airport, Bronfman suddenly ordered the taxi to make a detour to see whether Alberta Distillers was for sale. He ran into the office and asked a baffled office manager on duty if he wanted to sell out. The confused executive didn't even know who Sam was, so Bronfman decided the owners probably didn't want to sell—not in a hurry, anyway. Accompanied by a nervous Schneckenburger, he finally climbed into the North Star just minutes before takeoff.

The first stop was Regina, and the stewardess came through with the box lunches; but Mr. Sam waved her away. "No. No, we have a lunch of our own and plenty for any mothers with little children, too. Okay, Schneck, get out our lunch."

At this point Schneck realized that in all the rush he'd forgotten the picnic basket at the Palliser. It was still on top of the hotel-room dresser. Mr. Sam went berserk. Speechless, too angry even to yell or curse at his forgetful vice-president, he wouldn't sit with him either. The dream of that crisp roast chicken was too strong. He moved up the aisle and sat down beside an elderly farmer, on the theory that only someone with the wisdom of age would understand his plight.

"I'm surrounded by lunatics," he complained loudly enough for all the passengers to hear, explaining the details of his predicament. "I don't know what you do in your business, how you get along with people. But in my business I'm surrounded by lunatics. Come on, I'll show you one." So the two of them stood at the front of the aircraft's aisle, and Mr. Sam kept pointing out to his new friend poor old Schneck, who was trying to slide lower into his seat. But Bronfman wouldn't relent. "See him, there he is," he kept announcing to the North Star at large, "there, seven rows back, there's the goddamned fool. . . ."

Finally the plane landed in Winnipeg and Sam rushed to the airport restaurant for a plate of scrambled eggs. But he wouldn't speak to Merle Schneckenburger for the rest of the flight.

SUCH OUTBURSTS REINFORCED SAM BRONFMAN'S TYRANNICAL REPUTATION, but they did little to explain his success. His fits of temper made him appear self-destructive and petty. But the volcanic side of his nature was more than offset by a deep inner balance, a sure instinct about how far he could push each new situation for his own—and Seagram's—benefit. To this was added a well-tuned sixth sense for making favorable financial deals. Asked about the secret of his success, Sam would invariably reply, "My nose—I can detect good deals and bad deals." Sam once told Edgar Cohen, a Montreal real-estate executive and author, "In business I play the jockey, not the horse," presumably meaning that it's not the deal or the company that's important but the people running it.

What made the mixture of Bronfman's characteristics so potent was the energy with which he applied them. "A conservatively Orthodox Jew, Sam believed implicitly in the Protestant Ethic of long hours and hard work," recalls Mark Shinbane, a Winnipeg lawyer who fought many of his early legal battles. "I knew and liked him for more than fifty years. He was an unusual, complex, and contradictory character. He could be hard and ruthless, mean and generous. To a few close friends he could be financially helpful, but only when they came as supplicants. He was given to horrendous outbursts of rage, was acquisitive on the grand scale, and to get what he wanted could be charming as well as considerate."

Another Winnipeg lawyer, Sam Drache, provides a different view of Sam. Drache refers to the announce-

ment in 1962 of plans to build the Toronto-Dominion
Centre, a project that partnered the Toronto-Dominion
Bank with Cemp, the trust set up by Sam Bronfman
for his four children. "The Good Housekeeping seal
was put on what many up to that time considered
'tainted' money, and with that Sam reached the end of
his program of trying to launder his money and his
past. Rewriting life stories is a common enough game
by business tycoons. In his case, repeating his myths
so often without challenge from his brothers gave the
ring of truth to the romantic side of his rags-to-riches
career."

One reason Bronfman was able to accomplish so
much more than anyone around him was that he found
it difficult to recognize any systematic boundaries between work and play. He seldom set aside time for re-
laxation, managing to expand his periods of intense
application by combining them with intermittent bouts
of kibitzing, tenuously relevant storytelling, and just
plain dozing.

But nearly everything he did, said, or thought had to
do with business. "His was an overpowering motivation," recalls Philip Vineberg, the Bronfman family
lawyer. "Some people walk and some people run, but
Sam was like an Olympic champion, extending himself
to the utmost limits. His most distinguishing character-
istic was the intensity of that drive, his persistence, the
unquestioning and unquestioned devotion to his ultimate objective. In his thinking and in his actions, he embodied a unique blend of imagination, innovation, and
entrepreneurial energy." Although he liked to give the
impression of making grand, quixotic gestures, Bronfman seldom operated by instinct alone and almost
never made snap judgments. He was not a risk-taker.
Every aspect of each upcoming decision was analyzed
to exhaustion, in relation not only to all the facts available but also to his own moods, so that the final resolution would be as hermetically objective as possible.
This was an interminable process. Choices that had to

be made by any given year-end were usually taken late on the evening of December 31.

During these extended deliberations, Sam seldom took anything for granted. Instead of subscribing to modern management principles of delegation, he crossed lines of authority with a careless abandon that made him constantly question (and extract valuable information from) junior receptionists and senior vice-presidents. He was continually on the telephone direct-ly to the people who did things (as opposed to the people who *told* others to do things) and loved visiting his distilleries to watch the bottling machines—he was familiar with every detail of their operation, including the fact that his machines used up ten thousand miles of black-and-gold ribbon a year to drape around V.O. bottles—test the new blends, and gossip with the line foremen. He never wrote memos and seldom dictated letters, preferring to root about for himself among the various Seagram hierarchies, getting everybody's ad-vice, trying to reconcile the bewildering array of con-flicting opinions.

This could be a chaotic process. "It made working conditions very difficult," recalls Maxwell Henderson, who was Seagram's secretary-treasurer for ten years before being appointed Auditor-General of Canada.* "Sam would sniff all the whiskies in his office, have a marketing team in to decide on a run of new labels, then haul off to do a tax problem with me, and in the middle of it get one of his lawyers on the phone, give him hell for dragging his feet in some upcoming litiga-tion, meanwhile getting ready to receive a deputation from the Jewish community. I had great difficulty get-ting action on decisions and usually had to wait around until half past six, seven, or later, by which time he'd

---

* Henderson was one of the very few Seagram executives to resign instead of being fired. He quit in 1956, mainly because he was being paid less than the treasurer of the company's U.S. subsidiary, but also because he realized that real power would always remain with the Bronfmans instead of being distributed to non-family executives, no matter how able.

have had a number of snorts and would usually go to sleep in the middle of our discussion."

Sam's curiosity had no limits. Abe Mayman, the Bronfmans' physician, recalls that when he was dying, Sam interrupted one of his medical tests suddenly to inquire precisely why mountain ranges are so often found on the edges of continents. Mayman had recently read a *National Geographic* description of the phenomenon and tried to explain it between blood tests, but Bronfman persisted in his questioning until he had read the article himself.

Another example: Bound for lunch at Montreal's Montefiore Club, Sam once found himself beside a talkative cab driver. "What kind of tires do you use?" he casually inquired. The taxi owner launched into a protracted lecture on the subject, going into tiresome detail, all of which Bronfman absorbed with bemused fascination. But as the cab turned off Peel Street, one of the tires blew. The car bucked and shuddered as the driver negotiated the corner. He just made it to the curb in time to have a second tire go. Sam heaved himself out of the taxi and later told his luncheon companion, "Imagine that damned fool giving me advice about tires!"

Sam's management approach was a peculiar mixture of paternalism and oppression. Some employees were never fired or retired. Harold Nelles, a senior grain buyer stationed in Winnipeg, was still on Seagram's full-time payroll on his ninety-third birthday. Sam's favorite trick was to test subordinates by asking them questions to which he already knew the answers. He judged them not so much by whether they could come up with the right facts as by how they handled themselves if they couldn't. He was brutally harsh with any executive who tried to fool him, while those few brave souls who confessed they didn't know the right answer sometimes found themselves being promoted. Members of his immediate staff were categorized as either villains or heroes, their status being switched from one to the other often with devastating results. "When Mr. Sam

first met someone and if certain sparks flew in the right
direction, he was inclined to see in that person qualities
far greater than were really there," says Vineberg. "Because Sam himself had certain standards of ability, he
presumed that the other fellow would have them too.
In many situations this meant he would have an expec-
tation that could not be fulfilled. Most of his relations
with people went through a predictable metamorphosis.
He'd call everybody by their first names, and people in
the most humble circumstances would think and speak
of 'my friend Sam Bronfman.' But when they came into
his employ or when he had to rely on them for some
communal or other purpose, a testing period began, and
he was often very disillusioned, not because they were
failing to achieve a reasonable standard but because his
own standard was so high that the average person
couldn't expect to achieve it."

One unfortunate Seagram auditor, who had been
sent to inspect the expense pattern of the company's
Venezuelan subsidiary, found himself out in the cold
after he returned to head office and had the following
brief corridor encounter.

"So. How's business in Venezuela?"

"I don't know, Mr. Sam. I was there to look at the
books."

Bronfman looked at the accountant with utter in-
comprehension, like a man with a head-splitting hang-
over suddenly confronted by the Grand Canyon or the
Taj Mahal. The brief exchange remained engraved in
his mind. For years afterward he would repeat the story, marveling at the poor man's stupidity. "Imagine,"
he would tell visitors to his office, grabbing them by the
elbow to underline his amazement, "imagine, going all
the way to Venezuela and never asking how business
was!"

Pleasing Mr. Sam became a head-office game that
absorbed much of the staff's energies. In 1962, Bronfman led a delegation of thirty-five Montreal executives
to Israel, and on the first leg of the flight from Montreal to Rome he sat down beside his old friend Wil-

liam Gittes, a Montreal textile manufacturer. "Billy," he said, "how would you like to make a little bet?"

"What do you have in mind, Sam?"

"I'll bet you that when we set down at the airport in Rome and go over to the bar, no matter how many bottles are there, Seagram's V.O. will be right in the middle of the display."

"I think I've got the odds there."

"All right. I'll tell you what we'll bet. Drinks for the whole group."

Gittes agreed. The plane landed, they rushed over to the bar, and, sure enough, there at dead center was an oversize bottle of V.O. Back on the aircraft, the bet paid off, Sam relaxed, secure in the knowledge that the head office was still on its toes. (Because Bronfman was a V.O. drinker, Peel Street had standing instructions that whenever he traveled, an advance man would contact the sales manager of every territory he was visiting to make certain that bottles of V.O. were displayed prominently at airport bars en route.)

Another problem was Mr. Sam's attitude toward office titles. He treated most of his employees as executive assistants; titles he regarded with a disdain only diminished by the realization that they were occasionally useful substitutes for salary increases. A former whisky blender from Scotland named John MacLean who had done well in the Seagram organization decided, during the early fifties, that he should have a title commensurate with his conception of his position in the company. MacLean asked to be named general manager and was astonished when Mr. Sam agreed with a careless wave of his hand. But without warning a few months later MacLean found himself fired. "You know what?" Sam asked a member of his office entourage. "The damn fool took it seriously and started to *act* like a general manager. We can't have that sort of thing going on. Just leads to a lot of trouble. Besides, *I* am the general manager."

MacLean ended his days living in a bachelor suite of the Union Club in Victoria, Brtish Columbia. He was moved to a rest home when it was discovered that he spent most evenings sitting in his darkened window, peering through binoculars into the windows of the nearby Empress Hotel.

It sometimes seemed that Sam's chief preoccupation in the administration of Seagram affairs was to find new methods of saving money (though he did pay himself a generous salary: in 1959, for example, Sam's salary was $351,042, which ranked him just behind Henry Ford II, the head of the world's fourth-largest industrial corporation). He pinched pennies in peculiar ways. Promptly at 10:30 some mornings his secretary would bring him a glass of gin with mix; each time he would taste his drink and declare that it needed more gin. On one occasion when the mix was Schweppes Ginger Beer, he asked one of his marketing vice-presidents to join him. They were sipping their drinks when the sales executive remarked, "You know, Mr. Sam, I bet Schweppes makes more money on this ginger beer that we do on the gin. It's thirty-five cents for that small bottle." Bronfman seemed deeply concerned by his own extravagance, and when it came time for a refill, he gravely told his secretary, "Just one bottle of mix this time. It's expensive, you know. Thirty-five cents a bottle!"

Sam Bronfman had a deep ambivalence about money. In 1922, when he was in New York with Saidye and one of his sisters, they wandered into a millinery store. He wouldn't allow his bride to buy a $55 hat she liked, but as soon as they returned to the hotel he told her to order it by telephone. When she asked him why he had balked at her intended purchase in the first place, he replied, "I don't want my sister to know I'd let you spend that much for a hat." On another occasion, when his daughter Minda was house-shopping in Paris, he kept urging her to be more modest in her demands. But when she was furnishing her new residence and expressed shock at the cost of a large Oriental carpet, he urged her to buy it. "Why not? You have all the money in the world."

He hated waste and invariably spent the last few
minutes of his long working day at Seagram's Montreal
headquarters turning off all the lights—even though
members of his staff kept explaining that the cleaning
ladies would be arriving soon to turn them all on again.
He was a sucker for giveaways. Bringing home half a
dozen newspapers and magazines, he would sit up in
bed at night laboriously filling out coupons for every
catalogue or promotional brochure available, sending
off for everything from guides on how to cultivate dahl-
ias to maps for Nevada cave-exploration jaunts and
invitations that began with the come-on "FREE LAND IN
ALASKA."

He went to the office every Saturday (besides usually working at home on Sundays) and had great difficulty understanding why he often found himself alone
in the building. It was a genuine mystery, and no
amount of explanation could satisfy him. "Why do you
suppose there's nobody here today?" one of his assistants remembers being asked on a particularly gorgeous
Saturday summer afternoon in 1968.

"Because it's Saturday, Mr. Sam, and they're all at
home."

"Now, what would they be doing there?"

"Well, cutting their grass, painting their houses, playing with their children, shopping with their wives—
maybe going for a drive somewhere."

"Why would they prefer that to being here, doing
things, happy like I am?"

"Maybe because you own the place and they don't."

"Yeah? You think so?" Bronfman mumbled dubi-
ously, with a gesture to indicate that he thought the
whole idea was an unfathomable aberration of human
behavior.

On at least one occasion his extended working hours
got him into serious trouble. Jack Clifford, then a Seagram salesman, had gone back to his office at ten
o'clock on a Friday evening to pick up a liquor order
for a friend's wedding that he'd forgotten to take home
with him. He heard faint shouts for help from the build-

ing's elevator. The lift was stuck between floors with
Mr. Sam inside. "Get me out of here!" he kept yelling.
"Do something, goddamn it!"

Clifford rushed across the street to get a Mount Royal
Hotel building engineer for help. They eventually pried
the trapdoor open, but Mr. Sam's belly wouldn't fit
through it. Finally he managed to kick off his pants and
wriggle out. Instead of thanking his rescuers, Bronfman
staged an extended tantrum, kicking the elevator doors
for five minutes, using every swear word he knew, ending with the declaration, "I'll never, till the day I die,
ever set foot in this fucking elevator again." Then he
turned his fury and curses on Clifford, who gently tried
to remind his boss that if he hadn't come in for the
liquor he'd forgotten, Mr. Sam might have been stuck
until the cleaning staff arrived Sunday at midnight.

"Ah, you guys are always forgetting things," Bronfman shouted over his shoulder as he stomped off home.
For years afterward he would murmur whenever he
passed by, "Goddamn elevator . . ."

He used it only once again. In the spring of 1970,
the year before he died, he rode down with his son
Charles, who remarked, "It's been a long time since
you took the elevator, isn't it, Dad?"

"Yeah, well, it's much better exercise to take the
staircase, and you should do that yourself."

"Oh, I thought there was another story. Didn't you
get stuck in the elevator once?"

"Never got stuck in the elevator in my whole goddamn life. Where did you get that idea?"

SAM BRONFMAN WAS S SUPREME NARCISSIST. His prime
human contact was with himself. But unlike most nar-
cissistic personalities who love and hug themselves
because they can't find more attractive alternatives,
Bronfman's retreat into himself was prompted by the
dread of possible rejection.

No matter how much he achieved, the notoriety of
his early days in the liquor trade always seemed to be
present, pulling at him like an ocean current, making

him feel vulnerable to snubs even when they were imaginary. Of course, the snubs were not always imaginary. When he was on a Montreal-Winnipeg train with Saidye in 1957, he found that their sleeping compartments were separated by someone with another reservation. It turned out to be a leading Socialist politician, M. J. Coldwell. When Bronfman introduced himself and asked Coldwell to switch compartments, he replied, "Bronfman, eh? Well, I won't have anything to do with you," and slammed his door.

His underdeveloped sense of civility and frequent betrayal of the social graces flowed out of unquenchable insecurity. He patrolled himself constantly, monitoring the unspoken WASP denials. He knew all too well how to spot the kind of forced overfriendliness that prompted the well-intentioned to try to draw outsiders like himself into a conversation as though they had no way of broaching it themselves.

He was never allowed to join the Montreal clubs that counted—the Mount Royal or the St. James's—although his friends made several discreet runs at trying to put him up. The word went out that he was not even welcome as a guest. When Donald Gordon, then chairman of Canadian National Railways, once boldly marched him into the Mount Royal Club for lunch, he was asked never to do so again.

Typical of the kind of stories that used to circulate about Bronfman was the whisper about the time Mr. Sam found himself sitting beside George VI during the royal visit to Montreal in 1939. "I understand you have a large family, Mr. Bronfman," the King was rumored to have said. "Yes," Sam was supposed to have replied, "I have four brothers. I used to have five, but the RCMP shot one." The conversation never took place and neither did the shooting. Sam had only three brothers, and it was his brother-in-law who was shot—not by the RCMP.

Just before World War II, Bronfman rented the summer residence of the Rt. Hon. Arthur Purvis at Ste.

Marguerite. When Sir Victor Sassoon* came to Canada as part of an emergency wartime trade mission, Sam invited him to visit Ste. Marguerite after his official Ottawa visit. At the time, the nearby Alpine Inn, like most other Laurentian resorts, had strict and explicit rules against registering Jewish guests. Bronfman had personally been denied access to the Alpine's golf course; he vowed revenge. Even the haughty Alpine could hardly use his Jewish origins as an excuse to reject a British baronet who had just been presented to Parliament and received by the Governor General and Prime Minister. Bronfman's secretary telephoned the Alpine's manager to make the reservation and was told, "Okay. He can come for Monday, Tuesday, and Wednesday. But, hot or cold, he's got to be out of here by Thursday morning, and I hope to God my directors never find out about it."

Even though the Bronfmans deliberately stayed out

---

* Sir Victor Sassoon, a descendant of the fabulously wealthy family of Sephardic Jews who settled in Baghdad and later in Bombay, was a fabled figure in Shanghai (where he owned luxury hotels like the Cathay, with its marble baths and silver taps, and other valuable waterfront property), India (where he built himself a £110,000 private racetrack at a time when the workers in his Bombay textile mills were on strike against starvation wages), and Engand (where thoroughbreds sporting his colors won the Derby four times and every other important race at least once). Sassoon was a bachelor until the age of seventy-seven, when he married Evelyn Barnes, a Dallas nurse, and declared that "the first seventy years of life are essential if you want to make the correct choice of a wife." The Sassoon family fortune had strong roots in Judaism: an auction in Zurich of some of the Jewish manuscripts of Rabbi Solomon David Sassoon brought $2,158,000 in 1975, and there are marriage links to the Rothschilds and Gunzburgs. But there are other links: the poet Siegfried Sassoon became a convert to Roman Catholicism in 1957, and Sir Philip Sassoon's sister, Sybil, became Marchioness of Cholmondeley, wife of the Lord Great Chamberlain of England, neighbor of the royal family at Sandringham, and chatelaine of Houghton, described by the English authority Mark Girouard as the second-finest house in England. (He rated only the Queen's main residence as finer.) "A chap who stayed at Houghton once said there were Titians in the 23rd-best bedroom," Girouard reported.

of the society pages of Montreal's newspapers, that Monday evening an item appeared in the *Gazette*: "Mr. and Mrs. Sam Bronfman are entertaining at dinner this evening at the Alpine Inn in St. Marguerite's in honor of Sir Victor Sassoon. Among the guests attending will be Mr. and Mrs. Allan Bronfman, Mr. and Mrs. Sam Steinberg, Mrs. Sam Jacobs, and Mr. and Mrs. Lazarus Phillips."

The scions of Montreal society, plumed in high-hatted snobbishness and cloaked in a self-containment that, almost four decades later, would allow René Lévesque's separatists to gain power, could hardly fail to read Sam's intended message. But it served only to strengthen their barely suppressed conviction that if the Bronfman brothers couldn't be ignored, at least they need not be condoned.

In those days the symbol denoting arrival at the summit of Montreal's Anglo society was an invitation to sit on McGill's Board of Governors. Presidencies of institutions such as the Bank of Montreal and Canadian Pacific carried with them automatic elevation to McGill governorships, and Sir Edward Beatty, who became head of the Canadian Pacific Railway in 1918 and served as McGill's chancellor from 1921 until his death in 1943, held most of the university's board meetings in his own office at Windsor Station. While McGill eschewed public acknowledgment of its unofficial quota system, Jews had severely limited access to the university's medical school; in both Arts and Science faculties, Jewish males had to have averages of at least 75 percent instead of the usual grades to be admitted. For some reason, this idiotic rule did not apply to Jewish females. The appointment of Gerald Clark, later editor of the *Montreal Star*, as editor of the *McGill Daily* in 1938 was considered a great racial breakthrough, even though he was helped not inconsiderably by his prodigious talent and the fact that his name had no Jewish connotations.

McGill's most devoted philanthropist at the time was John Wilson McConnell, publisher of the *Montreal*

Star, who made a fortune in finance and sugar refining and sat on the board of the CPR, Sun Life, Royal Trust, the Bank of Montreal, Canada Steamship Lines, Inco, Hudson's Bay Company, Dominion Bridge, and Brazilian Traction. He gave away nearly $100 million during his lifetime, yet his posthumous foundation (operated through the privately owned Commercial Trust Company) still administers an estimated $600 million.

Whenever there was a hospital or university fund drive in Montreal, Bronfman would invariably try to discover exactly how much McConnell was giving so that he could match it. For his part, McConnell became determined to keep the distiller off McGill's board.

At one point in the early fifties, Cyril James, the university's principal, had lunch with Bronfman. As dessert was being brought in, the distiller hinted that he would make a donation to McGill of a million dollars in cash, hoping that he might be appointed to its board. James was delighted. He rushed back to his office and telephoned McConnell. But the *Star* publisher cut him off with the icy comment, "Now, let's get one thing straight. It's either me or Bronfman, and don't forget I've given McGill $25 million." He swore that Bronfman would become a McGill governor only over his dead body, which was exactly what happened.

Bronfman did become a McGill governor in January 1965, fourteen months after McConnell's death, and in 1971 the university began construction (not far from the McConnell Engineering Building) of the Samuel Bronfman Building to house the faculties of management and languages. Charles Bronfman was asked to be a McGill governor after his father's death; he declined.

McConnell may also have had something to do with keeping him off the board of the Bank of Montreal, even though Seagram's was the bank's largest customer. Bronfman was turned down three times for membership on the board and was invited to become a Bank of Montreal director only in the last year of McConnell's life. At the time the Bronfman appointment was reconsidered, Seagram's was also doing a considerable business with the Royal (which already held the Morgan's and Myers's rum accounts) and the Toronto-Dominion (which had become a partner of the Bronfman-owned Cemp Investments trust).

The feud between Bronfman and McConnell probably went back to a wartime bond rally at the Montreal Forum. Bronfman happened to be sitting directly behind McConnell. Just after the rally chairman ended his appeal for pledges, he tapped the publisher on the shoulder and asked, "How much do you think we should give?" McConnell, affronted by the distiller's presumption of equality, shot back, "Why don't you take care of your business just as I'll take care of mine?"

The exchange left Sam for once genuinely humbled. "McConnell was right," he said later. "I should never have taken such a liberty. Who the hell was I to associate myself with him? I had no right to do that—I'm no friend of his."

Although his philanthropy was more generous and less self-serving than that of most tycoons of his generation, including, apart from his Jewish charities, endowments of many academic chairs, art collections, and business fellowships, Bronfman was generally assuaged with minor honors. Typical were his governorships of the National Council of the Boy Scouts of Canada, the Canadian Red Cross, the International Chamber of Commerce, and the Canadian Mental Health Association. He was awarded high rank in two orders: Companion (the highest of three degrees) of the Order of Canada in 1967, and Knight of Grace (the highest of four grades) of the Order of St. John of Jerusalem in 1969. Two of his three honorary degrees were from minor universities (Brandon and Waterloo) and the only major one was the Doctorate of Laws he received from the University of Montreal in 1948.

HAVING BEEN SUFFICIENTLY REBUFFED BY MONTREAL'S ESTABLISHMENT, Sam Bronfman turned his concern to

Jewish causes. In 1929, his brother Allan had headed
the original drive to finance construction of the Jewish
General Hospital that raised twice its intended
$800,000 objective. Five years later, Sam was recruited
to lead Montreal's Federation of Jewish Philanthropies
(a post that he held until 1950), and at the outbreak of
World War II he set up the Refugee Committee of the
Canadian Jewish Congress with the help of Saul Hayes,
a compassionate Montreal lawyer with the precise mind
of a metronome who stayed on as his chief aide-de-
camp in Jewish affairs. The Refugee Committee had its
greatest success in persuading the Canadian government to pass a special order-in-council allowing 1,200
Jewish "orphans" to enter the country from Germany,
Austria, and Czechoslovakia. Hugh Keenleyside, the
External Affairs official handling the request, recalled
being only slightly astonished when the Canadian Jewish Congress delegation returned to demand that the
parents of the "orphans" be admitted as well.

Elected to head the Congress in 1938, Bronfman retained the office for the next twenty-three years, during
which he shifted the character of the organization drastically from coordinating agency to official voice of Canadian Jewry. "It wasn't until Sam came into the
picture that a national leader was found who was not
only willing to bring a national Jewish community into
existence but had the ability and energy to do it," Hayes
recalls.

Bronfman personally underwrote life insurance policies for the Canadian pilots recruited to help Israel fight
its 1948 war of independence. "But the lack of vigor
displayed by the Canadian Jewish Congress on Jewish
matters before the war and the 'quiet diplomacy' approach on Zionist matters reflected the Bronfman tech-
nique of quiet manipulation," says Larry Zolf, a CBC
writer-broadcaster. "In a very real sense, the story of
the Bronfmans is a mini-history of Canadian Jewry.
The Canadian Jewish Congress almost became a Seagram subsidiary."

Although Sam's influence within the CJC was supreme, he did not try to penetrate the more populist Zionist Organization of Canada. Bronfman was eventually named honorary president of the Zionist Organization, but never attended any of its meetings or events. "Those of us who were early Zionists," recalls Winnipeg lawyer Sam Drache, "felt strongly that we were a movement that had to be ideologically free and not bound by an umbrella organization like Congress. That was why Sam Bronfman became the dominant power of Canadian Jewry, but never its fully accepted leader. Sam not only had the money, he knew how to use power. He understood that nearly everybody needed money to get what they needed and that this could give him the authority over people that he in turn wanted to exercise."

To help him run the Canadian Jewish Congress, in addition to expanding his personal and Seagram's influence, Bronfman recruited a small group of loyalists across the country—leading local luminaries who acted as his regional surrogates. "In order for him to be king, he had to have his ambassadors," says Drache. "As I watched him, I came to the conclusion he was so powerful a client that the lawyers he picked inevitably became his captives. He approached me, and I was very tempted. But I just didn't have the necessary personality to wear a collar."

Sam Drache was one of just two Jewish leaders in the country who dared openly to oppose any Bronfman dictates. At a Congress meeting in 1950, Sam objected to Drache's sponsorship of new sales quotas for Israeli bonds on the grounds that it was not an efficient way to raise money. When Drache wouldn't back down, Bronfman and his entire entourage walked out of the hall. The only other independent-minded community leader was Michael Garber, a Montreal lawyer who succeeded Bronfman as president of the Congress after Sam moved up to its chairmanship. During the planning of a 1958 presentation to Cabinet, Garber insisted that Lawrence Freiman, then president of the Zionist Organization of Canada, be named joint spokesman for the delegation. Bronfman strenuously objected. The tension between the two men grew so bad that when Sam's brother Abe died and the family was sitting *shiva* at Abe's house, Garber at first refused to drop in unless he received an apology, but later relented.

For thirty-five years, no Jewish fund-raising drive was mounted in Canada without Sam Bronfman's pace-setting support. "Any appeal for funds, he would meet with his friends in the basement of the Belvedere house and undertake to contribute ten percent of the total on behalf of his family," remembers Billy Gittes, a Montreal friend. "Let's say he had in mind an objective of $3 million for some campaign; he'd get the group of us together and speak to us like newborn babes. 'Now, boys,' he'd explain, 'they can use all the money they can get, but we have the prerogative of naming our own terms and I won't do anything without the backbone of the community backing me up.' He'd ask us, 'Well, what do you boys think? Should the objective be somewhere between $2 million and $5 million?' And he'd keep on until we agreed that $3 million was precisely the right amount. Then he'd immediately subscribe $300,000 of it himself."

One good reason why everyone went along with Bronfman's edicts so slavishly was that his family's generosity overshadowed the combined giving of everyone else. Sam Bronfman's children in Montreal, New York, and Paris together contribute about $2 million annually to various Jewish charities.*

On June 5, 1967, at the opening of Israel's Six-Day War, Sam gathered a hundred of Canada's most in-

---

* Other major donations by Sam's branch of the family include $1 million in 1962 to build a new wing for the Israeli Museum in Jerusalem; the construction nearby five years earlier of the Biblical and Archaeological Museum; and the financing and erection in Montreal of the Saidye Bronfman cultural center, designed by Sam and Saidye's daughter Phyllis. In 1948, when Michael Comay, Israel's first ambassador to Canada, found himself operating from temporary quarters in the Chateau Laurier Hotel, Sam immediately bought him a sumptuous official residence on Clemow Avenue in Ottawa.

fluential Jews at the Montefiore Club for a day-long organizing conference. "I remember that dramatic episode, when people in the Montreal Jewish community were coming to his house on Belvedere with bags of money, their pensions, savings, and everything, pushing it at him, asking him to put it to good use for Israel," says Dr. Abe Mayman, his physician. "The thing about Sam was that he never just gave money; he worked hard for every cause he made his own. If he had, as some people believed, in some way been atoning for his past, his attitude would have been quite different."

The notion of the former rumrunner with a passion to buy his way into society's good graces doesn't seem to tally with Bronfman's personality. "I resist the idea that atonement was part of Sam's motivation," says Philip Vineberg, who became his chief legal adviser. "I don't really believe Sam thought he had anything to atone for. Certainly he had a desire to rise above his origins which if he'd been to the manner born he might not have had. But as far as the early history was concerned, you must remember that all the distillers in Canada, and in the United Kingdom for that matter, sold liquor in their own country as they were entitled to do, to buyers, some of whom were transshipping to the American market. The Canadian government encouraged the practice and collected a lot of taxes in the process. In common with everybody else in the trade, and most objective viewers, he would have felt that it was better for the Americans, who were the ultimate consumers, to get proper whisky instead of the illicit and sometimes potentially very harmful stuff that existed in the United States. I don't accept the implication . . . that he spent very much time brooding."

"Why in hell should Sam atone for anything? He never thought he had done anything wrong," says Sam Drache. "Bronfman was in the liquor business, and if he hadn't had the customers he wouldn't have been a bootlegger. So apparently there was general approval that there should be somebody in it, and at least he gave people good whisky. You can't judge his actions by our so-called consumer standards of 1978."

One explanation for his generosity in Jewish causes may have been that the anti-Semitism rampant in Montreal's WASP establishment forced Bronfman to create monuments of his own devising. Unlike some fellow philanthropists, he understood the roots of Judaism and didn't attempt to use money as a surrogate religion. "His generosity," Chaim Bermant wrote of Sam Bronfman in *The Jews* (Times Books, 1977), "arose out of a sense of obligation. It was not merely that he was very rich, but he traded in a quality product in which he took some pride, and which he liked to think was consumed mainly by quality people; benefactions went with such quality. It is unlikely that he was trying to impress anyone but himself."

Traditionally Jewish, Sam Bronfman was ultra-critical of Jews who didn't live up to their obligations and tended to be comically irreverent about most rabbis and many Jewish institutions. Bert Loeb, a former Ottawa grocery wholesaler, recalls that when he was seated beside him at an Israeli bond function in Montreal during the early sixties, Mr. Sam suddenly started to pound the table, chanting, "Those goddamned Jews! Those goddamned Jews! Those goddamned Jews!"

After a long silence, Loeb found the courage to ask, "What's the matter, Sam? What are you talking about?"

Bronfman testily replied, "When I was flying to Israel, first class on El Al, the other day, I asked for some whisky, and they served me horse piss instead. Horse piss, I tell you, horse piss! Those goddamned Jews!"

After the meeting broke up, Loeb asked Sam's brother Allan what the whole angry performance had been about. It turned out that when he ordered a drink on his last trip to Israel, Sam had been served a brand he considered inferior to his beloved V.O.

In 1951, fed up with trying to make an impression on the impervious burghers of Westmount, Bronfman purchased a large estate at Tarrytown, an hour's drive north of Manhattan. Instead of braving the real and imagined chills of hostility from outsiders, he stuck closer to established routines and familiar places, taking his environment with him whenever he could.*

Here he was, one of the wealthiest entrepreneurs in history, feeling somehow incomplete, possessed by a sense of not really having made it. Sam Bronfman decided there was only one way to cap off his career: an appointment to the Senate of Canada.

---

* He divided his time between Westmount and Tarrytown until 1965, when he moved back to Montreal permanently mainly because he was shaken awake one night to find himself staring into a flashlight held by a burglar. "We didn't hear him come in because we had air-conditioning and soft shag carpets," Saidye recalls. "I looked up and there was this tall black man with a black hood on his face and another man with a scarf around him pointing a revolver. After they asked me to open our safe, which I did, the man with the flashlight said, 'I'm going to take you to the bathroom and tie you up, both of you. I'll get you pillows to sit on.' And my Sam said to them, 'You know, you're gentlemen.' Imagine saying that under those circumstances. They tied us up and said we'd be released in twenty minutes, which of course we weren't."

3. *Running for the Red Chamber*

FOR A man whose intellect and energies had been devoted to a lifelong quest for power, attempting to enter the Canadian Senate seemed an astonishing and uncharacteristic ambition. "I suppose Sam was seeking public acknowledgment for what he'd accomplished," speculates Noah Torno. "The problems of his family's early history always plagued him and he probably was trying to tell the world, 'I don't want to be lumped in with my brothers!' Plus which, there was also the question of being Jewish. He always wanted to be first."

A more likely explanation was that, shrewd as he was, Bronfman never deluded himself that becoming a senator would endow him with any real influence. Instead, what he wanted, quite simply, was the title. He felt that elevation to the Red Chamber would crown his name with the mark of legitimacy, a sure sign of acceptance into the upper strata of his country's society. As evidence of his preoccupation with such things, Sam held a family council in 1948 when he received an honorary Doctorate of Laws from the University of Montreal to decide whether he should henceforth refer to himself as Dr. Bronfman. He was only half joking.

Within the international arena where he liked to operate, being able to call himself Senator Samuel Bronfman would have been something of a coup. Sam

44

once told J. M. McAvity, onetime president of the House of Seagram, "Think of what an impression it would make if I was known as Senator Bronfman in the United States." His conviction was bolstered by noting the respect that automatically accrued to his friend Senator Jacob Javits of New York, who often spoke in hushed tones of the U.S. Senate as "the most exclusive club in the world." The fact that the American and Canadian senates shared nothing except a common appellation bothered Bronfman not a whit. Who would ever know the difference if Senator Bronfman and his wife were registering at the George V in Paris or at Claridge's in London?

Having set his sights, Bronfman proceeded toward his objective in the most direct manner possible: by trying to buy a Canadian senatorship. It's difficult to calculate how much he spent in this quest, but $1.2 million is probably not an unreasonable total, because he contributed about $120,000 a year to Canadian political treasuries for more than a decade. Sam Bronfman was a Liberal. But just in case there might be a political turnover, he usually donated an amount equivalent to about 60 percent of his Liberal gifts to the Conservatives as well.

His chief agent in these transactions was Maxwell Henderson, who served as Canada's Auditor-General between 1960 and 1973. "As the treasurer of Seagram's, it was my lot to disburse the party funds," Henderson recalls, "and thereby hangs many a tale, because when you're donating the kind of money Mr. Sam was giving away, you expect something in return, and what he expected was to end up as a senator. That was his great goal." Ever the methodical accountant, Henderson not only kept records of all the donations but, to Sam's amazement, also actually managed to obtain signed receipts for the banknotes as they were changing hands. "I just wanted to keep the books right. So long as I had to distribute the haul money, as we called it, I wanted to know at least the name of the

gentleman getting it. You don't want to have any mis-
understandings later. They always signed."

Then, of course, when Henderson became Auditor-
General, "It was a fantastic situation. There were certain politicians who had risen to power on Mr. Sam's
money that I had handed across the table. Now I was
in Ottawa as Auditor-General, and here were these
characters who had been on the receiving end. I suppose they hoped I'd forgotten, but, being an accountant,
I still had the records."

The politicians welcomed his cash, but made no
move to fulfill Mr. Sam's dream. C. D. Howe, the crusty
Trade and Commerce Minister, then declining in authority but still a driving power in the Liberal Party,
claimed to be supporting him, but he got so tired of
Bronfman's assaults that he began to hint it was really
Jimmy Gardiner, the Agriculture Minister from the
prairies, who was vetoing the appointment because of
the Bronfmans' early exploits in Saskatchewan. Sol
Kanee, a Winnipeg lawyer who was a family friend
and hailed from the Saskatchewan town that sent Gardiner to Parliament, was immediately enlisted to help
sway him. "One day I marched into Gardiner's Parliament Hill office," he recalls, "and asked Jimmy if he
was really against Sam going to the Senate. When he
told me he wasn't, I dialed C. D. Howe's private number and said, 'I've got Jimmy right here, and he's not
opposing it.' But nothing ever happened; they were all
just fooling Sam to try and get more of his money."

At one point, Bronfman became so frustrated that
he confronted Howe with a direct threat: if he wasn't
made a senator, he would cut off all contributions to
the Liberal Party. The great C. D. fixed Bronfman with
a long, steely gaze through the foliage of his magnificent
eyebrows, then smiled a sweet smile. "It doesn't matter,
Sam," he said. "We'll just raise the excise tax on liquor
another ten percent and get it that way." Then he
gently asked the distiller to leave his office.

Sam Bronfman's main problem was that he never
learned to appreciate the subtlety of the process in

which he was involved. Any number of senators had purchased their appointment by contributing to party coffers. But while senatorships might well be for sale, they could not appear to be bought.

The idea of naming a Jew to the Canadian Senate first bubbled up during Prime Minister Mackenzie King's time when Archie Freiman, founder of an Ottawa department store, was quietly sounded out on an appointment. As soon as Bronfman heard about the approach, he launched such a vicious counter-lobby to have himself appointed that the Prime Minister backed off the whole idea. "If those Jews can't make up their minds, I won't appoint any of them," King told one associate at the time.

Louis St. Laurent, King's successor, wanted to celebrate the establishment of Israel as an independent state by announcing the appointment of Jews to the Superior Court of Quebec and the Quebec Court of Appeal. His choices were Harry Batshaw, a Montreal lawyer, and Lazarus Phillips, who wasn't interested in a judgeship at the time. Bronfman used the occasion to renew his lobbying efforts in Ottawa, but St. Laurent felt that Bronfman should not be named a senator for the very reason that made the Montreal distiller want the appointment so badly: because such a public elevation would, once and for all, bring down the curtain on his family's early history, displaying retroactive absolution on a scale the Prime Minister of Canada was not willing to grant.

At about this time, M. J. Coldwell, the Socialist leader, embarrassed Bronfman by demanding in the House of Commons to know why the government had invited someone with his "questionable background" to a state dinner at Government House. Worst of all, when Sam briefly tried to lobby on his own behalf by joining the Ottawa cocktail circuit, he found himself the object of some unwanted attention. Wherever he appeared, Clifford Harvison, then an assistant commissioner of the Royal Canadian Mounted Police but much earlier the RCMP corporal who had arrested Bronfman during

48   MR. SAM

the Montreal conspiracy proceedings of the middle
thirties, would noiselessly join any group of guests
that included the distiller and stand there quizzically
staring at him. When Bronfman moved on, Harvison,
would follow and repeat the treatment.

Pressure was meanwhile building up in the Liberal
Party to name Canada's first Jewish federal Cabinet
minister. The obvious choice was David Croll, who
had followed three successful terms as mayor of Windsor by becoming Ontario's first Jewish minister. Croll
resigned in 1937 in protest against the provincial
government's refusal to recognize the Oshawa automobile workers' union, declaring, "I would rather march
with the workers than ride with General Motors." His
reformist tendencies, distinguished war record, and a
decade as an effective member of the House of Commons seemed to make him the ideal choice. Afraid that
he might be shuffled off to the Senate instead, Croll
became an avid advocate of the Bronfman candidacy.
But C. D. Howe once again turned out to be pivotal
in the final decision. St. Laurent had granted him an
informal power of veto over most government appointments. When Howe came out unequivocally against
both Croll's becoming a member of the Cabinet and
Bronfman's becoming a member of the Senate, only one
solution remained: Croll would be named Canada's
first Jewish senator.

Sam Bronfman and a caucus of his senior executives
were conferring in Seagram's boardroom on the morning of July 28, 1955, when Robina Shanks, his secretary, brought in the bad news. Max Henderson, who
was there, remembers Sam exploding, parading about
the room in a kind of military mourner's slow march,
wailing, "I'm the King of the Jews! It should have been
mine . . . I bought it! I paid for it! Those treacherous
bastards did me in!"

TRYING TO TURN HIS DEFEAT BY OTTAWA'S LIBERAL
ESTABLISHMENT into only a temporary setback, Bronfman calculated that if the Liberals were willing to name

one Jew to the upper chamber, they might name another. They did, but it took thirteen years of political infighting, and Sam was not their ultimate choice.

Out of Sam Bronfman's bizarre race for the Senate grew the most bitter feud of his life, with the man who had become one of his best friends and closest associates: Lazarus Phillips. The two had first met in 1924, when Bronfman moved his operations to Montreal. It was Phillips, then the family's chief legal adviser, who masterminded the winning court strategy in the Bronfmans' greatest legal battle (detailed in Chapter 7) and set up the family trusts into which Seagram's huge profits would eventually flow. On October 10, 1945, Phillips's fiftieth birthday, the four Bronfman brothers presented their friend "Laz" with a private letter, done up as a parchment scroll, bearing this closing message:

Time is one of God's gifts. To each one he gives the same amount—twenty-four hours a day. Life's accomplishment is measured largely by the talents, aptitude and application of the individual. By dint of hard work and the use of your brilliant talents you have risen to a pre-eminent and enviable position in your profession, in which we take a pride second only to your own. . . .

Desiring to mark this occasion with something of permanency for you and your dear ones, and to adorn your lovely home, we would like the privilege of presenting you with a gift of a very personal nature—a portrait of yourself to be executed by an artist of your own selection. We do this with the fond hope that its presence in your home may add to the pleasure and enjoyment of yourself and your family for many, many years in health and happiness.

For most of three decades, Lazarus Phillips served as the Bronfmans' visible face and public voice. He was their chief go-between. He had the manners and the contacts, the social acceptability and political prestige to which the brothers could only aspire. With his brains and their money, he achieved a degree of political, legal, and corporate clout unique among Canadian lawyers.

Lazarus Phillips, now in his early eighties, was the most influential Canadian Jew of his generation. His maternal uncle, Hersh Cohen, had been a great Talmudic scholar and Canada's chief Orthodox rabbi, while another uncle, Lazarus Cohen, became one of the wealthiest Jews in Canada in the early years of the twentieth century (second only to Sir Mortimer Davis) by dredging much of the St. Lawrence for his friend Sir Wilfrid Laurier. Phillips inherited both those mantles and wore them with considerable pride. After serving briefly in World War I as a sergeant-major with the Canadian Expeditionary Force sent into Vladivostok to help quell the Russian Revolution, Phillips joined a small Montreal law firm started by Sam Jacobs, who not long before had entered politics and married Gertrude Stein's cousin from Baltimore. The second Jew to sit in the Canadian House of Commons,* Jacobs carried Montreal's Cartier riding (the equivalent of a congressional district in the United States) through five elections in campaigns organized by Phillips, who became Jacobs's equal partner in 1923. By the time Jacobs died in 1938, Phillips had emerged as the gray eminence of Montreal's Jewish community. He built up a miniature, sub-arctic Tammany Hall on Montreal Island, an organization powerful enough so that *goy* Liberals from the Prime Minister on down had to consult him about Jewish sensibilities and appointments whenever their policies or patronage touched the region's vital two dozen ridings. Phillips ventured out publicly himself only once, when he decided to run for Cartier in a 1943 by-election caused by the death of Peter Bercovitch, who had succeeded Jacobs. But what was supposed to be a walkaway turned into a political quagmire when two men, including Fred Rose, a Communist who ultimately got elected, moved in to split

* The first was Henry Nathan, elected from Victoria in 1871.

the Jewish vote. The night he was beaten, Mackenzie King telephoned Phillips from the Citadel in Quebec City, where he was quartered, to demand, "What do you regard as the basic cause of your defeat?"

"The basic cause of my defeat," Phillips replied, "was that Mr. Rose got more votes than I did." The terse summary so delighted the verbose King that he not only forgave his friend Laz's loss but granted him more influence than ever. It was Phillips who unfroze enough funds under export control from the grip of the Bank of Canada to finance Seagram's wartime expansion program in the United States.

Phillips's reputation in Ottawa flowed only partly from his political clout in Montreal. His large legal practice had turned him into the country's top tax expert. "All the doors were open to Laz," Max Henderson recalls. "He was a tremendous pleader of cases. He'd walk into the tax department and just dazzle them."

Henderson and the Phillips firm had easy access to Ottawa. Even though they were clearly representing Sam Bronfman's and Seagram's private interests, when the Department of National Health and Welfare came to draw up its food-and-drug regulations governing alcoholic beverages in the early fifties, Henderson and Philip Vineberg, Phillips's nephew and law partner, submitted draft clauses. Most of them were adopted without a change. On March 24, 1952, Henderson received a call from Paul Martin, Minister of National Health and Welfare, who said, "Max, I've got my pen in hand and these food and drug regulations are going into law. Before I sign them I just want to ask you one question: Are they good regulations and are you satisfied with them?" Henderson replied, "I am, Paul." The laws governing Canada's liquor industry have not been substantially altered since.

Phillips's most interesting dealings were with C. Fraser Elliott, who was Deputy Minister of National Revenue for Taxation from 1932 to 1946. "I remember one particular occasion in the mid-forties," Phillips recalls, "when I was retained by an accountancy firm to be associated with them in the presentation of a tax case involving the interests of an outstanding Canadian businessman who was then spending a great deal of his time in Ottawa as a so-called dollar-a-year man. When I asked the Deputy Minister for an appointment, he initially refused to see me because he felt that the client did not deserve even a hearing, having regard to the war difficulties and the nature of the work that the client was involved in. I insisted that it was my responsibility as a lawyer to present my case in association with a senior partner of the accountancy firm. The Deputy Minister was adamant in his attitude towards the taxpayer, and refused to make any concessions. Finally, after a series of conferences, he relented somewhat and said that he would consider with his officials some concession in the case provided I complied with one major condition, and that was that in the event of a settlement I would charge the client a very large fee. I told the Deputy Minister that this condition presented no insurmountable difficulty or problem, and that I would be glad to comply with this condition."

Typical of Phillips's high-level leverage was his involvement in rearranging Canada's vote at the United Nations sessions that preceded Israel's recognition as a state. "I remember one particular occasion," Phillips recalls, "when a high officer of the Zionist Organization asked me to submit certain representations to Brooke Claxton, who was acting Secretary of State for External Affairs in the absence of Lester Pearson. At that time the foreign ministers were meeting in Paris to deliberate on the issue of the recognition of Israel, and at that particular stage the Canadian government had decided not to support such recognition. I proceeded to Ottawa and met with Claxton, who invited me to his home that evening to dine, as I happened to be in Ottawa with my wife. After we had dinner our wives retired, and Claxton asked me to state my position, which I did. In the process I didn't realize how much time had elapsed. Close to midnight, Brooke rose and telephoned Louis St. Laurent, the Prime Minister, at his home. He apologized for waking him up, but explained the urgency of the matter in view of the meeting that was to be held in Paris the next morning. After listening to my case, the Prime Minister instructed Claxton to phone Pearson in Paris, even though it was five A.M. French time, and ask him to change the vote to an affirmative. Mike Pearson then spoke to me on the telephone and was less than complimentary, being in a somewhat irritable mood for my having awakened him so early. In due course he forgave me when he realized the urgency of the problem."

In the spring of 1949, when the proud and confident chieftains of the Liberal Party met in secret conclave at the Chateau Laurier to plan Louis St. Laurent's first election campaign as leader, Lazarus Phillips was there, splitting up the tasks and dividing the spoils, being consulted and heeded on all the fine points that in those distant days turned Liberal campaigns into royal processions. At one point in the proceedings, Jack Pickersgill, special assistant to the Prime Minister and then in the flowering of his incarnation as chief guru to the Liberal Party, waddled up to Phillips, placed a comradely arm on his shoulder, and asked him, "Are you feeling all right, Laz? We've been hanging around here for three hours and you haven't raised hell with us gentiles yet!"

How sweet it was. No Jew had ever before (or has since) enjoyed such intimate access to Liberal power at its very summit. Not unnaturally, Phillips hoped to press his personal priority of becoming a senator. He saw himself blocked by a unique Catch-22 situation. The Liberals by this time had abandoned what small intention they might once have had of naming Sam Bronfman to the Red Chamber; but to tell him so would have cut off their richest party-fund contributor—and the most direct way of tipping their hand would have been to appoint his friend and legal counsel, Lazarus Phillips.

"Why should Laz get it?" Sam kept asking anyone who would listen. "He was a two-bit lawyer when he started working for me, and I made him a multimillionaire." Various middlemen, notably Sol Kanee, tried persuading Sam to give up his claim. But he wouldn't hear of it. Meanwhile, Phillips was collecting other honors that had thus far eluded Sam Bronfman: on January 14, 1954, he was named a Royal Bank director, and on September 12, 1966, he was asked to join Montreal's hallowed Mount Royal Club.* He'd been a director of a number of companies before joining the Royal Bank board, but the bank board was the plume on the bonnet. Other corporate rewards followed. As his reputation grew, Phillips somehow managed to fill the difficult role of being a token Jew without becoming a token. He discovered the secret of making non-Jews feel all warm and pleased with their tolerance, a way to remain Jewish and successful without appearing threatening. Very low-key, intellectual, modest, deep, and virtuous, he lent his aura to business deals almost as if his presence were blessing them. Two of Montreal's top real-estate operators, Mac Cummings and Stan Feinberg, once cut themselves equally into a multimillion-dollar deal with only one unwritten understanding: that all disputes would be settled by Lazarus Phillips and that his word would be final. Phillips became chief tax consultant for the Canadian operations of Imperial Oil, Texaco, the House of Morgan, Cominco, and Du Pont. He embodied the very best way a Jew can prosper within the Canadian establishment. On February 15, 1968, he attained his ultimate goal: a summons from the Prime Minister, Mike Pearson, to sit in the Senate of Canada.

Time had been running out on the Bronfman candidacy. By reaching seventy-five, the upper chamber's compulsory retirement age under legislation enacted in 1965, Sam had in March 1966 been eliminated from a contest in which he had never really been a serious entrant. The Liberals felt it was now safe to proceed

---

* The Mount Royal had admitted Jewish members before Lazarus Phillips, but not since World War I days. In 1970, a Bronfman finally became a member, but it wasn't Sam. It was Charles.

with the elevation of Lazarus Phillips—who had only thirty-one months left until his own seventy-fifth birthday—but there were those who calculated that his old friend's stubbornness had cost him at least eighteen years of public life. When Lazarus Phillips retired from the Senate on the eve of Yom Kippur in 1970, one colleague called him "the greatest senator in the history of Canada," and his colleagues gave him a standing ovation.

His run for the Senate didn't break Bronfman's spirit, but it exhausted his patience with the petty concerns and niceties of Canadian society, so that he withdrew even more into his closed circle of corporate cronies. He instituted an office tradition insiders called "the White Rock Treatment" that involved getting together for drinks in his office after five o'clock with his close retainers, mixing their shots of V.O. with soda made by the White Rock company. He loved spicy office gossip ("Oh yeah? How'd it happen?") and occasionally would reminisce about his early days. But when one of his assistants brought in a rusted can labeled Seagram's Chickencock, a leftover from the Bronfmans' bootlegging days that had been sent in by a lady from Port Dalhousie, Ontario, who had found it in her basement, Mr. Sam exploded. "Where in hell did you get that? Take the goddamned thing and destroy it." After he'd calmed down, Bronfman sat in his overstuffed green chair looking at the relic of his past for a long time. "Jesus, it would be a fascinating story. If I could ever tell the truth of all that happened..."

4. Hidden Roots

BY THE time Sam Bronfman was fifty, he was a corporate giant, beyond the reach of ordinary curiosity, whose public stance could implant and sustain a belief that his great liquor empire had somehow sprung, fully formed, from his brow. There remained the problem of bringing forth a suitable corporate mythology to replace the true story of the Bronfman family and its beginnings. The family name itself (the Yiddish for "liquorman") was avoided in a string of incorporations in the early twenties, although "Bronfman Interests" was used for the office on St. James Street in Montreal. The brothers' first distillery, in the Montreal suburb of Ville La Salle, opened in 1925 under the corporate banner of Distillers Corporation Limited, strikingly close in name to Distillers Company Limited, the long-established Scottish giant of the whisky trade.

But it was the marriage of the Bronfman distilling company to Joseph E. Seagram and Sons Limited in 1928 that gave Sam Bronfman a corporate past that could be proudly cited in presidential addresses and annual reports. Speaking to a convention of his own salesmen at Lake George, New York, on July 17, 1952, for example, he declared, "Our company had its origin in 1857 in Canada, when Joe Seagram built a small

Hidden Roots

distillery on his farm and sold its products in the surrounding area." This romantic version of their genesis would be echoed by Sam's elder son, Edgar, when he in turn wrote about the firm's origins.

In fact, the Bronfmans could trace the Seagram empire to a small distillery on the Grand River at Waterloo, Ontario, and it *was* built in 1857. But the builders were William Hespeler and George Randall, who operated the distillery as a subsidiary of their Granite Mills milling operation. Joseph Emm Seagram was a lad of sixteen on the family farm in Waterloo County in 1857, and it was not until the 1860s that he joined the distillery at Waterloo. In 1869 he married Stephanie Erb, William Hespeler's niece, and by 1870 he had bought out Hespeler's interest in the distillery. Seagram became sole owner of the milling and distilling business at Waterloo in 1883, a date celebrated in a leading brand of whisky, Seagram's 83. He later turned to politics and was Conservative member of Parliament for Waterloo North from 1896 to 1908. He died in 1919, and his distillery business became a public company in 1926.

It was more difficult to avoid the early days of the Bronfman family's lucrative liquor trade in Canada and impossible to disown the bootleggers who peddled the gallonage in the United States during the American Prohibition years, 1920–1933. It was legal to produce liquor in Canada, and legal to export it, but Sam seldom placed himself in a position where he would be forced to comment on the bootlegging trade. Philip Siekman quoted Bronfman in a 1966 issue of *Fortune* as explaining, "We loaded a carload of goods, got our cash, and shipped it. We shipped a lot of goods. Of course, we knew where it went, but we had no legal proof. And I never went on the other side of the border to count the empty Seagram's bottles."

In fact, the Bronfman customers during Prohibition were an army (and navy) of bootleggers taking delivery in ships off the Atlantic and Pacific coasts, in small craft at handy crossings along the St. Lawrence–

Great Lakes system, in cars and trucks at dusty prairie towns bordering on North Dakota and Montana. After this trade became illegal, the Bronfmans served their customers from the islands of St. Pierre and Miquelon, fifteen miles off the coast of Newfoundland. In the next twelve months alone there was enough liquor landed in the tiny French colony to provide every resident—man, woman, and child—with a ration of ten gallons of booze a week.

The value of the legally produced Canadian product soared as contraband in the United States, and the profits of the illegal American trade gave birth to an underworld that meted out death as standard disciplinary action. It was on this brutish trade that the Bronfman family's fortune was squarely based.

American police forces could not wipe out the liquor trade and are still grappling with the underworld it spawned. But after Prohibition ended, Secretary of the Treasury Henry Morgenthau, Jr., calculated that the Canadian distillers owed some $60 million in excise taxes and customs duties on illegally imported alcohol and threatened to bar Canadian imports until the tax bill was paid. Secretary of State Cordell Hull was able to negotiate a settlement of 5 percent of the total through the Canadian legation in Washington. In May of 1936, the Bronfmans agreed to pay $1.5 million to settle their account with the American treasury. The payment was a tacit admission by the family that about half the liquor that poured into the United States from Canada during the Prohibition years had originated with them.

By the time Sam turned his attention to establishing a history for his empire, his brother Harry had been diverted from the mainstream of Seagram management. But it was Harry who put on paper his recollections of the early struggles of the family in the Canadian West. His personal "diary" is a homey mix of family announcements (births, deaths, and marriages) and business deals (peddling, horsetrading, hotels, interprovincial package liquor trade, wholesale drugs, liquor exports). It is disjointed and sketchy, but it does chronicle the progress of the Bronfmans, step by step, through one loophole after another in the prohibition legislation of Canada and its provinces. Harry makes only one small reference to the booming trade of the American Prohibition era: "Prohibition in the United States sent the Americans looking for liquor in Canada, and our business prospered both with the interprovincial business in Canada and many people from the United States coming to Canada to buy liquor to take back with them. . . . During all this time many buyers came to Montreal who bought liquor for shipment to St. Pierre. This became a large business which we called export business. . . ."

Harry's son Gerald celebrated his twenty-second birthday three days before repeal of Prohibition in the United States, and his family's dealings with American bootleggers are clearly within his memory. "One of the reasons why Sam and Allan were so successful with the U.S. bootleggers is that they [the bootleggers] were treated as business people," Gerald says. "They even had a special office at 1430 Peel Street [Seagram headquarters in Montreal] where they could do their business. Dad was absolutely fearless . . . the American bootleggers used to come up to buy large quantities of liquor before the repeal of Prohibition. The attitude was that as long as the [Canadian] government knew what we were doing, what difference did it make? We didn't have to decide who we should sell to. As long as there was somebody who was going to pay, why not sell it? There were no ifs, ands, or buts about the fact that they [the Bronfmans] had knowledge of where the liquor was going. . . . I truly don't think that Dad regarded that what happened on the other side of the border . . . bore any relationship to what was happening here, which was legal—just as long as he wasn't involved in the other side. Look, everyone in the Establishment didn't found their fortunes with kid gloves or by not taking chances or by living in a prescribed society. It was the adventuresome ones, the ones that were willing to take risks, as Dad did."

The children of Sam Bronfman have no memories of the bootlegging days (Minda, the first child, was born in 1925), so that Sam was able to maintain within his immediate family his public pose, ignoring the true nature of his own genesis. (Edgar, born in 1929, stated in a 1969 article in the *Columbia Journal of World Business* that the family sold its products only in Canada until repeal of Prohibition in the United States.) Sam Bronfman never told his children any of the Prohibition Era details, would not allow anyone to call his products "booze"; only very occasionally, when he was feeling particularly comfortable with one of his old cronies from the early days, would he mutter, "How long do you think it'll be before they stop calling me a goddamn bootlegger?"*

In his public pronouncements, Sam was able to describe the Prohibition Era trade as a mere survey of tastes preceding Seagram's entry into the American market following repeal. "I had observed that the American public who visited Canada had demonstrated a preference for lighter and finer whiskies and at that time we had begun to build up large inventories in anticipation of the day when we could ship to this great market." Sam's children might never know the details of their father's past, but they were well aware of his quest for legitimacy. "My father had a self-image which was terribly important to him," Edgar says. "He

---

* One of the few public reminders of Sam's early exploits was a lawsuit launched by an ex-bootlegger, James "Niggy" Rutkin, contending that the Bronfman brothers and another former bootlegger, Joseph Reinfeld, had conspired to cheat him out of his just rewards. In 1954 the jury ruled in Rutkin's favor, but awarded him $77,000; Rutkin had sued for $22 million. Two years later an appeal court overturned the verdict. On the basis of his own pre-trial statement, Rutkin was convicted of income-tax evasion. He served two years, got out on bail pending an appeal, and returned to jail when that appeal was turned down in 1956. Shortly afterward he took his own life with a borrowed razor.

always knew what he wanted to be, and when he got there, that's what he wanted to think of himself as, and for us to think of him as, so he never really wanted to talk about the days when he wasn't on the way up. After Father died, we were all very curious, and we sat down with Uncle Allan to try and find out what had gone on. All we got was some philosophical musing. He would never tell us any of the early history."

THE PATRIARCH OF THE BRONFMAN DYNASTY, YECHIEL, owned a grist mill and sizable tobacco plantation in Bessarabia, a rural province in the southwestern corner of the Russian Empire that in the late 1880s was being swept by the anti-Semitic pogroms of Alexander III. In February of 1889 he decided to join the exodus of Jews bound for North America. The family then consisted of Yechiel, his wife Minnie, and three youngsters—Abe, Harry, and Laura—but the Bronfmans were wealthy enough to bring with them a maid, a manservant, and, most important, a rabbi (with his wife and two children) to ensure the continuance of the group's Hebrew heritage. Sam was born during the ocean crossing to Canada,* and the little group took up a homestead near Wapella, a pioneer settlement northwest of Moosomin, in eastern Saskatchewan near the Manitoba border. About fifty Jewish families, acting independently, took up homestead lands at Wapella during the years from 1886 to 1907. It was one of the earliest European ethnic settlements in the Canadian prairies.

So limited was the Bronfmans' knowledge of the Canadian prairie climate that they thought they could

---

* This date and place of birth differ from the accepted version found in the standard reference works and Sam's obituaries, which give March 4, 1891, and Brandon, Manitoba. The "diary" of the family's history prepared by Harry Bronfman is the basis for the earlier date and place. A source close to the Samuel Bronfman family confirms that Sam was born two years earlier than 1891 and not in Brandon. Other references to Sam's age and the birthday celebrations described elsewhere in this book are based on the chronology used by the Seagram Company.

plant tobacco seed they had brought with them at once when they arrived in April. Instead, they found snow on the ground; Yechiel had to buy oxen to break the virgin land and prepare for planting. Although he was the richest resident in the tiny community, his instinct to help his less-well-off neighbors reduced him to near-poverty by the following spring. The Bronfmans were not granted respite to make the difficult mental adjustment from resentment at being uprooted from their homeland to satisfaction with their newly adopted country. The family instead had to be governed by one concern only: how to stay alive in the harsh environment of the Canadian prairies that had become their final refuge.

The hardship of those first few years in Canada is best caught in Harry Bronfman's reminiscences: "The first crop of wheat froze, and consequently [Father spent] that winter . . . going into the bush, cutting logs, loading them onto a sleigh and drawing them 20 miles with a yoke of oxen so that when they were sold there would probably be a sufficient amount of money to buy a sack of flour, a few evaporated apples, dried prunes and probably some tea and sugar to bring back to his family so that body and soul could be kept together."

Realizing that he would never become a successful farmer, Yechiel journeyed more than a hundred miles southeast to Brandon, Manitoba, then a town of thirty-five hundred, Anglicized his name to Ekiel, and got a laborer's job clearing the right of way for a line of the Canadian Northern Railway. Part of this preparation was removal of houses and lean-tos that stood in the way of construction on the outskirts of Brandon. As soon as he could afford it, he purchased one of the little sheds for twelve dollars as a home for his family.

Minnie, alone at Wapella and determined to have a bake oven of the type she knew from home, with only her memories and advice from neighbors to go on, used a special apron to carry the heavy stones. She built her oven four times, but in her eagerness to make use of it she burned out the wooden supporting arch on the first three tries. By the fourth attempt she had learned that it was necessary to let the structure dry so that it would hold together when the stays were burned away. In Harry's recollection, the only food that came from this oven was potatoes, cooked in every form Minnie could think of, until Ekiel was able to send her enough money to buy flour. During this time while she was caring for the children on the farm, the fifth child, Jean, was born.

Ekiel never forgot his obligation to the family rabbi. When he arranged to move his family to the lean-to he had set up in a district of Brandon known as the Johnston Estate, he provided the rabbi with a similar house. Going back to Wapella, he traded his oxen for a team of horses, and with a wagon brought his family with their scanty household goods and a cow to their new home.

During the years the Bronfmans lived in Brandon, another son and two more daughters were born. Ekiel soon got a better job at the Christie sawmill on the banks of the Assiniboine River and noticed that when the logs were sawed into lumber the outer slabs and trimmings from boards (known as blocks) accumulated as waste. Recognizing that a local market might exist for the wooden slabs as summer cooking fuel, he made a deal to purchase the leftover wood for seventy-five cents a wagonload and used his team to distribute it at $1.75 a load. For some time he continued to work at night in the mill and sell wood by day, later turning full time to the wood business. Abe and Harry left school at grades eight and six to help their father, but Sam continued in school until he was fifteen. He was the only one of the boys paid separately for his efforts: at the age of ten he struck a bargain with his father that he would work at selling wood for five cents a day.

The tiny enterprise flourished, and by 1898 the family was able to make a $200 down payment on a $1,000 two-story brick house closer to downtown Brandon. It had a barn out back and a parlor, all done up with burgundy-red plush furniture, that the children were only rarely allowed to enter.

Observance of religious duties continued even when conditions made it difficult. Harry remembered one year when Ekiel and Minnie took the whole family by train to Winnipeg and stayed ten days, from the day before Rosh Hashanah to the day after Yom Kippur. "They were willing to chance the possibility of breaking down the business which had just been built up rather than disregard the call for prayer and the reckoning with the Almighty," which they could do at the *shul* in Winnipeg.

The wood business was enough to support the family in summer, but something was needed to bring in a winter income. Ekiel built up a trade in frozen white-fish, which he bought at Westbourne, near Lake Mani-toba, and peddled on the way back to Brandon. After a summer as an apprentice in a cigar factory, Abe left for Winnipeg to contribute to the family's income as a cigar maker. He also developed an interest in playing cards. To prevent him from gambling and because he was needed to help with the fish business (in which Harry too was now working), he was called home. This winter venture operated on a minuscule profit margin, and there was always the danger of having fish left over following the spring thaw. One season the Bronf-mans had to salt-cure their remaining stock and drive from farmhouse to farmhouse, trading the fish for eggs and butter or old scraps of rubber and copper for re-sale, in order to salvage a little cash. With careful man-agement they were able to acquire two more teams of horses.

The Bronfman brothers' subsequent indulgence in luxury becomes more understandable when set against the drudgery and poverty of their youth. Besides run-ning the firewood and fish trades, the Bronfmans ob-tained a contract to work as teamsters with their horses on local road-improvement projects. Before breakfast and after dinner they sold loads of rich loam to local gardeners at seventy-five cents a wagonful.

Through it all, the family adhered to all the rigid tenets of Orthodox Judaism. They spoke only Yiddish among themselves; Ekiel established a local synagogue; all the Sabbath and dietary laws were strictly observed. When Harry took a job with Frank Lissaman, the proud owner of a steam-driven threshing machine, it was on the condition that he would be allowed to return home every Friday evening in time for lighting of the ritual candles. "On a certain Friday," Harry noted in his memoir, "we found ourselves fourteen miles from Brandon; although it looked like rain I managed to get started away from the threshing machine about three o'clock feeling that if I walked fast I would be home by six-thirty. It started to rain a short time after I was on the way. The roads were all muddy and I was drenched. I continued to walk, but made little headway because of the slippery roads. It was around ten o'clock at night when I arrived home to find Mother and Father and the rest of the children—some of them asleep, others lying with their heads on the table. No food had been touched and *kiddush* had not yet been made awaiting my arrival. If there was ever anything that impressed me with the simplicity and desire of my parents that I should really have in full measure the meaning of religious traditions, that night has always been a very definite example."

Harry's reminiscences stress how he learned to trade horses in his early teens to supply the family's cartage business. The logical step was to capitalize on the herds of wild horses free for the taking in nearby Montana. The family invested a bankroll of about $1,000 in a herd of western broncos, with Harry in charge. "I had by that time learned to throw a larlat and rope a horse, and I was daredevil enough to think I was a bronco buster." He and his father would bring the horses into Brandon and break them by hitching them, one at a time, in a team with their already trained carthorses. Then the "green-broke" animals would be sold off to local farmers.

It was not long before the connection between horse-trading and hotel bars was made. According to family legend, young Sam, watching his father complete one

of these deals and go into the bar of the nearby Langham Hotel for the ritual drink and handshake, looked
up at Ekiel and said, "The Langham's bar makes more
profit than we do, Father. Instead of selling horses, we
should be selling drinks." Hotel-keeping was an easy
trade to get into at the turn of the century, for the rush
of immigrants then flowing across the Canadian West
and the continual construction of more railway lines
kept the demand for temporary living quarters high.
Because the bar was an important part of the hotels'
business, local brewers and distillers were only too glad
to lend money to entrepreneurs willing to push their
brands.

A family conference of the Bronfmans decided that
this trade would be one in which the sons could prosper
as merchants and at the same time practice their religion with a minimum of hindrance. In the early winter
of 1902, Harry found that the Anglo American Hotel
in Emerson, Manitoba, was up for sale at $11,000,
with a down payment of $5,000 required. Patrick Shea,
who owned the McDonagh and Shea brewing company
in Winnipeg, and George Velie, who ran a Winnipeg
liquor store, were willing to lend the Bronfmans
$1,800. Ekiel obtained the $3,200 balance by mortgag-
ing his house and teams at an effective interest rate of
24 percent. Harry, with Abe to help him, took pos-
session of the Anglo American on February 4, 1903,
two months short of his seventeenth birthday. The
business turned out to be a success, greatly helped
because the construction gang working on an extension
of the Great Northern Railway adopted it as their
leisure headquarters. Harry was so anxious to repay
his father's debt that he turned the hotel's profit into
large-denomination bills and kept them sewed in the
inside pocket of his vest. As soon as he had accumulated
the necessary amount, he took a train back to Brandon
and presented his father with the cash. He recalled
later the tears running down his father's cheeks as he
paid off the mortgage on his possessions.

Harry wisely pulled out of the Anglo American while

it was still making a profit. He and his wife, who was expecting their first child, moved to Winnipeg and acquired a block of stores and flats in the downtown area. Ekiel, Minnie, and the other children left Brandon and joined them, the parents acting as caretakers for the apartments.

Harry's next move was to Yorkton, Saskatchewan, where he purchased the Balmoral Hotel, a brick building providing sixty guest rooms, just in time to cash in on a boom.

In 1899, a Russian religious sect called the Doukhobors had settled on about 400,000 acres of Saskatchewan land. The Doukhobors ("spirit-wrestlers") believed they spoke directly to God; they were opposed to alcohol and tobacco, did not believe in sending their children to school, and, as pacifists, refused to bear arms.

In 1903, the Doukhobors, who refused to take the Oath of Allegiance, staged a nude march to Yorkton, the upshot of all that being that in 1905 they forfeited about 260,000 acres to the government. The availability of this acreage for settlement brought on one of the biggest land rushes in prairie history. In 1904 Charles Saunders had produced the first kernels of Marquis wheat, an early-ripening strain that would transform the northern prairie into prime growing territory.

With the land boom came the railway builders Mackenzie and Mann, whose Canadian Northern Railway line was pushing westward across eastern Saskatchewan, and the Canadian Pacific Railway, whose Portage la Prairie–Saskatoon line, when Harry bought the Balmoral, ran as far as forty-two miles northwest of Yorkton. During the boom years Harry operated four other hotels along the CPR's Saskatoon line, and at one point had a second hotel in Yorkton. To augment the railway service, he also ran a livery stable, which started, he claims, with rental of quarters for his own horse, an unsalable creature, according to Harry's description, "too fast to be an ordinary driver and too

slow to win a race. . . ." The livery and hotel both
thrived, and after a major renovation program the
Balmoral boasted of steam heat, hot-and-cold-water
baths, electric lights and bells, and sample rooms.

The Bronfmans missed out on the boom in Saskatoon when Harry backed off from a proposal, put forward by Abe, to purchase the Western Hotel. But in
1910 the family purchased the Mariaggi in Port Arthur,
Ontario, a four-story structure that advertised itself as
having "110 comfortable and commodious rooms and
an elevator that runs to every floor." At this time,
three of the Bronfman brothers, Abe, Harry, and Sam,
were at work in the family hotels. Barney Aaron
joined the operation after marrying their sister Laura
in 1911.

By the time Sam was in his early twenties he took
charge of the family's largest investment, the $190,000
Bell Hotel in Winnipeg, purchased for a down payment
of $16,000 in 1913. There was a time during the First
World War when the family operated three hotels in
Winnipeg, with Harry at the Alberta Hotel on the other
side of Main Street from the Bell, where Sam was in
charge, and Barney Aaron at the Wolseley Hotel. The
youngest Bronfman brother, Allan, a student at the
University of Manitoba, moved into the Bell Hotel to
help Sam.

As proprietor of the Bell Hotel, Sam Bronfman was
absorbing the excitement of the big city, learning how
to make deals, dreaming big dreams, slowly asserting his
dominance. Under his astute management, the Bell
Hotel turned as much as $30,000 profit per year. He
launched himself into several other investments, including a venture in muskrat furs that netted him $50,000.

At this time none of the family had individual bank
accounts; hotel profits flowed into a joint pool, and
Ekiel apportioned the proceeds. The divisions were not
always achieved peaceably. "I remember one time in
1912," Sam once confided to a friend, "when we were
all at home and Father happened to mention that he
thought I had done more for the family than Abe and

Harry put together. Abe got mad. 'That's because the little bastard isn't happy unless he's making a buck,' he said. I told him to shut up, that all I was trying to do was save Father's money while he wasted it. Then Harry complained Father shouldn't let me run things, because he and Abe were older. I got really mad. I called them every form of goddamn S.O.B. I could think of, until Abe yelled that he'd own all the real estate in Manitoba while I was still a bum of a hotelkeeper. I just looked hard at both of them. Then I poked a finger at Abe's chest and said, 'We'll see, big brother, we'll see. . . .' "

Despite such quarrels, the Bronfmans continued to present a united front to the outside world. One of the accusations frequently made against them at the time was that because their hotels had become favorite stopovers for traveling salesmen who in turn attracted some dubious female company, they were in fact operating nothing more than a string of glorified brothels. Whenever Sam was publicly faced with this accusation, he shrugged and shot back, "If they were, then they were the best in the West!"

5. Getting into Booze

DEVELOPMENT OF the western frontier differed markedly in Canada from its corresponding evolution south of the border, where the rule of the gun created legends of desperadoes, posses and vigilantes chasing each other across Technicolor sunsets. Partly because of the bleak climate that one pioneer described as "six months of winter and six months of poor sledding," but more particularly as a result of the characteristics of the settlement process, the Canadian West was populated with a minimum of fuss and violence Dominated by the corporate ethic of the Hudson's Bay Company and the Canadian Pacific Railway, land distribution became an orderly bureaucratic procedure, while law and order were maintained by a centralized semi-military force in red tunics, the North West Mounted Police.* For all its tens of thousands of square miles of open land, the Canadian West offered little room for the legendary heroes and villains who settled the basic questions of morality and fence lines in the American plains. West of Winnipeg, the outposts of civilization tended to arrive simultaneously with the settlers, so that very often the first buildings to go up in a new

* In 1920 the force became the Royal Canadian Mounted Police.

townsite were a branch of one of the Canadian chartered banks, the local CPR land agent's office, the
preacher's or priest's house, and possibly an outpost of
the North West Mounted Police. It was the fitting
frontier approach for a country established by statute
of the Parliament of Britain in 1867, promising nothing
more (and nothing less) than "peace, order and good
government." This was in marked contrast to the American Declaration of Independence, which expressed its
purpose in terms of "life, liberty and the pursuit of
happiness."

One thing was the same on both sides of the border,
no matter the differences in climate, soil, and government. Liquor was the universal source of release. A
plague of drunkenness in the Canadian prairies undermined church, state, motherhood, and the operation
of the CPR.

The resultant clash of wills colored the history of
Canada's West for most of the two decades after the
outbreak of World War I. "For sheer intensity of conviction and staying power over the long haul no other
prairie mass movement ever equalled the Prohibition
crusade," wrote James H. Gray. "And yet the excitement and the political infighting that marked the long
assault on the demon rum was hardly more boisterous
than the uproar that developed after Prohibition became the law of the land. Then, as governments occasionally did their best to enforce the law, they were
heckled continually by the Prohibitionists. While the
Temperance spokesmen were demanding more adequate
enforcement, clutches of doctors, druggists, lawyers,
judges, and free-lance assuagers of the public thirst
were conspiring to reduce the law to absurdity. Out of
all this there developed a bootlegging industry that kept
the newspapers supplied with headlines and provided
both Wets and Drys with oratorical ammunition with
which to bombard the nearest legislature."*

* *Booze: The Impact of Whisky on the Prairie West* (Toronto: Macmillan of Canada, 1972), p. 1.

It is not easy to view this conflict with much objectivity from the perspective of the permissive 1970s. But at the time, the polarization between the Wets and Drys was vicious and complete. The boozers went to local hotels and bootleggers for the simple purpose of getting drunk as quickly as possible, their main concession to social congeniality being the rule never to abandon an unconscious drinking buddy. The prohibition movement, which dated back to a crusade by Bishop Laval and the Jesuit missionaries to keep whisky out of the Indian fur trade, freely mixed fundamentalist theology with even more primitive politics.

By coercion and conviction, the anti-drink crusaders moved to enlist the active support of federal and provincial parliamentarians in their battle to outlaw the demon rum. Being typically *Canadian* politicians, the legislators responded with a unique, if unspoken, compromise. Not really certain whether it was the Drys or Wets who might eventually garner more votes, they resolved the dilemma by condemning alcohol with rhetorical abandon and then passing prohibitory laws that were complicated and contradictory enough to provide some loophole for the really determined drinker to quench his thirst.*

Enacting unworkable legislation was not very difficult, considering the horrendously tangled jurisdictional status of the liquor trade. Much litigation and successive decisions by the Privy Council in London had by the turn of the century established that control of liquor sales at the retail level should be in provincial hands, while its manufacture, import, and export remained a federal responsibility. This administratively unrealistic split was further muddled by the fact that neither level of government was particularly anxious to enforce the Canada Temperance Act, which imposed responsibility for prohibition on any municipality where a majority

---

* Stephen Leacock, Canada's leading humorist and a Wet, put forward a more moderate view: "I wish somehow that we could prohibit the use of alcohol and merely drink beer and whisky and gin as we used to."

of the voters polled cast ballots against liquor. The effect produced was usually minimal because even if all the municipalities in one area voted to outlaw the sale of liquor, it could usually be imported from another part of the region.

Imprecise as they were, the laws seemed to serve their purpose: the vocal righteousness of the temperance advocates had yielded visible legislative results, while Canada's drinkers still found it fairly easy to get themselves properly soused. In the middle were the distillers and distributors of the booze itself, who managed to circumvent the intent of the laws without the risk of getting into much legal trouble. The most successful practitioners of this lucrative trade were the family Bronfman. Sometimes it almost seemed that the American Congress and the Canadian federal and provincial legislatures must have secretly held a grand conclave to decide one issue: how they could draft anti-liquor laws and regulations that would help maximize the Bronfman brothers' bootlegging profits.

WHILE FAMILY LEGEND CREDITS SAM BRONFMAN WITH ALL THE GENIUS and much of the impetus for the creation of the Seagram empire, it was his elder brother Harry who actually provided most of the early imagination and momentum that allowed the fragile enterprise to mature and prosper. During the fifteen years he spent in Yorkton, Saskatchewan, Harry's original stake in two of the town's hotels grew to include an automobile agency and a trust company. He bought out half a dozen stores and opened a motion-picture theater which inaugurated the sale of popcorn in western Canada.

In 1917, Harry Bronfman decided he'd make a run for Yorkton's mayoralty, but backed off when Levi Beck, the town's leading merchant, told him: "I'd give everything I own to keep you or any other Jew from ever becoming mayor of Yorkton." Stan Obodiac, the Yorkton-born author, recalls that it was this episode that soured the family on the town. "Before Sam and

Harry died, I tried to get them to build the Bronfman Slavic Theatre for Art and Culture in Yorkton. But this wasn't done. Harry left $5,000 to the Yorkton synagogue in his will; Sam left nothing."

The economic recession that hit the prairies following the outbreak of World War I cut deeply into Harry's hotel business. Despite his ambitious expansion in Yorkton, by the time prohibition of liquor sales was introduced to the province on July 1, 1915, he owed the Bank of British North America $100,000. To consolidate the family's remaining assets, Harry rented out the Saskatchewan properties and retreated to Winnipeg, where Sam was still running the profitable Bell Hotel. When prohibition came to Manitoba on June 1, 1916,* the family decided to leave the hotel business and make the pivotal move into the whisky trade.

Prohibition in the Canadian provinces (all of them except Quebec) did not close the distilleries or cut off liquor imports into the country. All the doors were left open for what came to be known as the interprovincial package trade, and the Bronfmans moved in to tap its lucrative potential. During a trip to Montreal in April of 1916, Sam purchased a small liquor outlet called the Bonaventure Liquor Store Company, conveniently located near the city's downtown railway yards, where travelers taking off for the rapidly drying up western provinces could obtain their liquid package goods. Barney Aaron, a Bronfman brother-in-law, moved east to run the Bonaventure operation, and warehouses were established across the country to trans-ship the liquor supplies. Sam went on the road, scouring the country

---

* Alberta, Nova Scotia, and Ontario went dry the same year, but Ontario exempted native wine (which could be purchased in strengths up to 28 percent). British Columbia, New Brunswick, and the Yukon went dry in 1917 (and so did Newfoundland, then a self-governing colony within the British Empire). Quebec remained an oasis throughout the wartime prohibition period: it didn't prohibit the sale of liquor until May 1, 1919, and even then exempted beer and wine. Prince Edward Island had been dry since 1901.

for enough stock to satisfy his burgeoning list of direct
and mail-order customers.

The most valuable location was at Kenora, Ontario,
which was the closest source to supply the lucrative
Manitoba market. The owner of a Kenora hotel that
Bronfman wanted to buy (because the township had
remained Wet under a local option) was six days' sled
drive away when Sam arrived to make an offer. Afraid
that one of his competitors might beat him out, Sam
hired a guide and dog team to negotiate the purchase
personally. It was only after they were nearly a day
out that Bronfman realized his guide had brought no
provisions except some coffee, a jug of liquor, and a
gun. "It was the six longest days of my life," he later
reminisced. "We ate deer meat every day. All that son
of a bitch could shoot was deer. He never found a
rabbit, a bird, or even a bear."

The business nearly collapsed in the winter of 1917–
18, when Sam was suddenly conscripted into the Canadian Army. He attended training exercises, but his flat
feet kept him out of active duty. A year later, on
Armistice Day, Minnie Bronfman succumbed to a flu
epidemic. Thirteen months after her death, Ekiel passed
away with cancer.

As World War I reached a crescendo, Ottawa came
under increasing attack for failing to halt the liquor
trade. The Rev. Sidney Lambert spoke for his frustrated
fellow prohibitionists when he thundered at a rally of
Drys in the capital, "I would rather Germany wins this
war than see these get-rich-quick liquor men rule and
damn the young men of Canada!" Whipped up by similar appeals from every region, the Cabinet passed an
Order in Council on March 11, 1918 (effective twenty-
one days later), prohibiting the manufacture and importation of liquors containing more than 2½ percent
proof spirits until one year after the end of the war.

This virtually wiped out the Bronfmans' mail-order
business. But there was always another loophole in the
prohibition legislation, and Harry hardly broke stride

as he headed off on a new career in wholesale drugs. He had noted that alcoholic liquors for medicinal purposes were excluded from prohibition in Saskatchewan (and a similar exemption appeared in all provincial prohibition legislation of the period). In his memoirs, he reports some success in peddling a medicated wine in Saskatchewan. But it was brother Sam who explained the ramifications of the medicinal trade: "A wholesale drug license . . . would permit the handling of drugs and liquors as well, that it was within the law for a druggist to sell liquors, and therefore it was quite within the law for wholesale druggists to supply those drugstores with liquor." Within twenty-four hours Harry had a wholesale drug license from the province of Saskatchewan and within ten days the Bronfmans were reincarnated as the Canada Pure Drug Company at Yorkton. Harry hired a chemist, sent him to Montreal to purchase a stock of standard drugstore supplies, and was back in business again. Meanwhile, the Hudson's Bay Company, lacking a wholesale drug license, had been forced to give up its contract to sell Dewar's whisky when the Canadian government brought in wartime prohibition. Harry picked up the Dewar's sales contract. He moved his new drug operation into a warehouse next to his Balmoral Hotel, right across the street from the CPR freight sheds, and through his Liberal friends in the government in Ottawa had no trouble getting it designated as a bonded warehouse.

As well as selling straight liquor through drugstores for patients with doctors sympathetic enough to prescribe it, the booze was sold to processors who concocted a variety of mixtures for the drugstore trade, including a Dandy Bracer—Liver & Kidney Cure, which, when analyzed, was found to contain a mixture of sugar, molasses, bluestone, and 36 percent pure alcohol—plus a spit of tobacco juice. Observing the many victims of suddenly virulent diseases heading for succor to their local pharmacists, Stephen Leacock wrote: "It is necessary to go to a drugstore . . . and lean up against the counter and make a gurgling sigh like apoplexy. One often sees these apoplexy cases lined up four deep."

THE DRUGSTORE TRADE WAS LUCRATIVE, BUT IT COULDN'T MAKE UP for the Bronfmans' previous mail-order sales volume. Just as business seemed to be settling into the doldrums, the nation's legislators once again rushed to the rescue. With the federal government's Order in Council outlawing interprovincial liquor traffic due to expire on the last day of 1919, the House of Commons passéd an amendment to the Canada Temperance Act that would continue the ban throughout the country. But under pressure from Quebec (which voted in legalized sale of beer, cider, and wine in April 1919), the Senate rejected the legislation. In due course a compromise emerged. The federal government would add the amendment to its statutes, but it would be put into force in the provinces (by federal Order in Council) only after the provinces held another series of referendums to prove popular support for the measure. There was strong support for prohibition and the ban on importation in most parts of the country at the end of 1919, but it would be more than a year before the provinces started to close their boundaries to the liquor trade. Meanwhile, there was another boom in the interprovincial package trade.

It was by exploiting this hiatus between two sets of laws that the Bronfman brothers were able to turn what had until then been a backdoor booze business into a major commercial enterprise that was the basis for one of the world's great fortunes. During those hectic ten months, the former hotelkeepers accomplished several major breakthroughs: they established the connections with American rumrunners on which would eventually hinge their expansion into the huge U.S. market, and they set up the string of "boozoriums" hugging the Saskatchewan–North Dakota border that would provide the cash flow to keep their operations growing.

Most important of all, they learned the rough art of
turning raw alcohol into palatable whisky.

BECAUSE OF HIS REMARKABLE BUSINESS RECORD AT
YORKTON, and the fact that he had paid off his debts on
schedule, Harry Bronfman was able to borrow money
from the Bank of Montreal to purchase large stocks of
liquor from Canadian and Scottish distilleries to fill the
family's warehouses in Montreal, Vancouver, Kenora,
and Yorkton. "I had established a reputation during
the period of depression when the Bank of British
North America had allowed me to owe them some hun-
dred-odd thousand dollars, and when the Bank of Montreal took it over, mine was the only account the British North America guaranteed," Harry says in his
memoirs. "The fact that I . . . paid up all my liabilities
put me in a strong position with the bank, and I was
able to get an almost unlimited credit." In fact, Harry
Bronfman initially obtained a loan of $50,000 from
the Bank of Montreal branch in Yorkton, but by calling on Sir Frederick Williams-Taylor at the bank's head
office in Montreal, he quickly got it increased to a re-
volving credit line of $300,000.

On Christmas Day of 1919, Percy Dallin, the federal
customs agent in Yorkton, reported the arrival of five
carloads of Scotch whisky. That overflowed the Bronfmans' warehouse space, but twenty-seven more box-
cars appeared, and the exasperated Dallin wired Ottawa
for instructions. He was ordered to ex-warehouse the
bonded merchandise, so that the booze could be taken
right off the railway cars for trans-shipment to the
Bronfmans' storage sheds across the country. In the
first few weeks of 1920, the Canada Pure Drug Company of Yorkton had brought in some 360,000 bottles
of booze. "The volume of the interprovincial trade that
was done out of Yorkton," James Gray notes in *Booze*,
"frequently delayed the Great West Express, the CPR'S
Winnipeg-to-Edmonton train, by as much as thirty minutes to complete the loading of Bronfman shipments to
thirsty customers in neighbouring provinces."

This proved to be too much for the conscientious Dallin. "The proportion of Scotch whisky to that of Brandy would appear to indicate that the goods in question are intended for beverage rather than for drug purposes," he wrote to his superior in Regina. "In the circumstances, responsibility for this license should be taken by some higher authority than that of a sub-collector of customs." His boss was unimpressed and told him to clear all shipments. Harry merely noted in his memoirs that "although the customs man in charge of this port was a Methodist, and strictly temperate, his fairness and responsibility to the job showed him that we were within the law, and it was his duty to carry out his responsibility as a customs officer in charge of the port."

Dallin's problems grew even more serious in June 1922, when the Saskatchewan government ordered all the province's liquor facilities to move into Regina, Saskatoon, or Moose Jaw, where their transactions could be more easily monitored. In his final inspection of the Bronfman warehouse in Yorkton, Dallin counted 205 drums of raw alcohol, reported the stocktaking to his superiors, then padlocked the premises. He diligently guarded the warehouse (at an annual stipend of $1,000) until an RCMP constable, on a routine inspection in the fall of 1926, reported a count of only 204 alcohol containers. Dallin tried valiantly to explain the loss: "The difficulty," he wrote to his division head in Ottawa, "arose this way to reflect upon my honour —that not being able to get the drums out of the warehouse or to be able to show any consumption in my books, I was left with the stock just the way it was. But there was one drum missing." He was suspended for a month without pay and shortly afterward retired from government service.

Not long before, by yet another timely coincidence, the greatest bonanza of all had appeared in the shape of possible access to the huge American market. The forces of temperance sentiment in the United States, which had been growing since the turn of the century,

were reaching their peak, with evangelists like Billy
Sunday firing popular feeling against the devil rum.
"Where the liquor traffic holds sway, children do not
laugh and women do not sing!" he thundered at his
growing audiences. "We say to the lords of liquor:
'Get out of your dirty business! This world is going to
live in sobriety instead of being a spewing, vomiting,
puking, jabbering, muttering, maudlin place!' The grog
shops and saloons have taken enough groans from
human lips to make another mountain range! They
have taken enough blood from human veins to redden
every wave of the sea!"

By January of 1919 the required three-quarters of
the states had voted in support of the Eighteenth
Amendment to ban the import, sale, and manufacture
of beverage alcohol. In October of that year Congress
passed the National Prohibition Enforcement Act,
known as the Volstead Act after the Republican lawyer
from Granite Falls, Minnesota, who was its congressional sponsor, to enforce tough anti-liquor regulations
across the United States starting January 16, 1920.
The Volstead Act defined intoxicating liquor as that
containing one-half of one percent or more of alcohol
by volume. It permitted the searching of hotels and
restaurants and the seizure of liquor. "Let the church
bells ring and let there be great rejoicing, for an enemy
the equal of Prussianism in frightfulness has been over-
thrown!" heralded the Hempstead, New York, chapter
of the Woman's Christian Temperance Union. It was
left to the Anti-Saloon League of New York to come
up with the most astounding declaration, claiming that
liquor had not only been undermining the progress of
American industry but that it had actually caused the
Russian Revolution. "Bolshevism flourishes in wet soil,"
its official bulletin trumpeted. "Failure to enforce Prohibition in Russia was followed by Bolshevism. Failure
to enforce Prohibition here will encourage disrespect
for law and invite Industrial Disaster. Radical and Bol-
shevist outbreaks are practically unknown in states

where Prohibition has been in effect for years. BOL-
SHEVISM LIVES ON BOOZE."

Prohibition turned out to be an unhappy experiment
—for both the Drys and the Wets. During the lawless
decade and more that the legislation was in effect,
federal Prohibition agents arrested 577,000 suspected
offenders, seized more than a billion gallons of illegal
booze, 45,000 automobiles, and 1,300 boats presumed
to have taken part in the illicit trade. None of it made
much difference. Lincoln C. Andrews, appointed Assistant Secretary of the U.S. Treasury in charge of
Prohibition enforcement, estimated in 1926 that less
than five percent of the liquor smuggled into the United
States was being seized. Fiorello La Guardia, who became mayor of New York in 1934, calculated that
Gotham's tipplers supported 22,000 speakeasies. He
startled even hardbitten New Yorkers with his estimate
that to enforce the Volstead Act properly would re-
quire 250,000 cops—plus a further 200,000 super-
policemen to keep the first group within the law. Worst
of all, between 1920 and 1930 some 34,000 Americans
died from alcohol poisoning; 2,000 gangsters and 500
Prohibition agents were killed in the many gunfights
triggered by the trade's excesses.

In retrospect, it seems that the more the temperance
advocates tried to turn not drinking into a patriotic
gesture, the more fun it became to break what, it soon
became evident, were unenforceable laws. "I was a
teetotal until Prohibition," wisecracked Groucho Marx,
catching the mood of the times. Speakeasies became
the most popular spots in every large city, imitating the
spirit of Delmonico's in New York, which featured
martinis served in refrigerated soup bowls.

In their search for reliable sources of booze, the
speakeasy operators quickly began to look northward
at the long, undefended border with Canada, where
imports of British brands were still legal and domestic
distilleries were capable of turning out a river of quality
booze available for export.

The first, groping efforts at smuggling were confined

to amateurs using more imagination than skill. They
dressed up in special suits with deep, bottle-holding
pockets and a length of rubber tubing, stoppered at
both ends, filled with liquor, wound around their waists.
One frazzled Ukrainian housewife from Buffalo went
to all the trouble of draining two dozen eggs and re-
filling them with Canadian whisky, only to have one
break in a customs officer's hand. The group of Michigan smugglers who regularly crossed into Canada
dressed in priestly robes so that their liquor-filled cars
would be reverentially waved through customs had to
give up their jaunts when one of their Studebakers got
a flat tire right beside the border station. The driver-
cleric, furious at this earthly interference with his mission, began to kick the punctured tire, shouting, "God
damn this son of a bitch!" The ensuing search quickly
revealed his secular cache of liquid contraband.

It very soon became apparent that the demand was
too urgent and much too profitable to be left to the
amateurs. But before more professional conduits could
be organized, a constant and reliable source of supply
had to be assured. Even before Prohibition came to the
United States, Harry Bronfman, wholesale druggist of
Yorkton, had secured a supply line from the Scottish
distillers and was nicely organized to make major purchases of American liquor stocks offered at bargain
prices in the pre-Prohibition sell-off. Even *after* Prohibition began, Harry, with another in the Bronfman
line of bonded drug companies, was importing alcohol
from the United States.* Canada Drugs Limited of
Yorkton, during its four-month existence in 1921, imported from the United States about 300,000 gallons
of alcohol—enough to make 800,000 gallons of whisky.

The Bronfmans' early distilling formula was nothing
if not simple. To make Scotch, for example, they reduced the sixty-five-overproof white alcohol to re-

---

* This was a considerable step up from a similar operation
run by Isaac and Jacob Sair of Oxbow, Saskatchewan. Their
raw material came directly from an undertaker in Minneapolis:
embalming fluid at a dollar a gallon.

quired bottling strength by mixing it with water, then adding some real Scotch plus a dash of burnt sugar (caramel) for coloring. The Bronfmans' primitive mixing equipment, purchased from the Brewers' and Bottlers' Supplies Company in Winnipeg, consisted of ten 1,000-gallon redwood vats and a machine that could fill and label a thousand bottles an hour.

The final and most important part of the process was bottling and affixing an appropriate label. Their initial products carried such innocuous names as Old Highland Scotch, Parker's Irish Whisky, and Special Vat Old Scotch—Sole Proprietors D. Macgregor & Company, Glasgow. Bulman Brothers, who produced these labels in Winnipeg, once committed a slight geographical error by calling one of the brands "Old Highland Malt Whisky—Bottled by Buchanan & Co., Porto, Scotland"—apparently forgetting the fact that Porto, known generally in English as Oporto, is in northwestern Portugal. Portobello might have been better, because it is on the Firth of Forth close to Edinburgh, but the distilling firm that produces Black & White—James Buchanan & Co. Ltd.—hasn't a plant there *either*. (Its locations are all in the west of Scotland.)

But gradually the Bronfman operation acquired a touch of class. Though the booze was all being poured out of the same vats, imitation Black & White, Dewar's, Glen Levitt, and Johnny Walker labels were freely used to raise the mixture's value. (Johnny Walker, a variant on the name of the well-known Johnnie Walker, fetched $45 a case; Dewar's, $42; the unlabeled "no fame" whisky went for $35. Glen Levitt presumably was a look-alike for Glenlivet, the greatest name in Highland malt whiskies.) Each day's production run depended strictly on which labels were most readily available.

The Royal Commission on Customs and Excise reported that the Bronfman operation "bottled liquors and applied to the bottles labels indicating that they contained Scotch whisky of a certain brand, whereas in fact it was not Scotch whisky, and was not manufactured by the firm whose name appeared on the labels.

In most cases these names of firms were fictitious. In our view this labelling was done for the sole purpose of misleading the customers and would appear to be in contravention of section 186 of the Excise Act . . . apparently the limitations respecting prosecutions for such offences would bar convictions, and in view of that we make no recommendations but merely cite the facts as part of the history of the various concerns owned or controlled by members of the Bronfman family."

"A Mounted Police officer who took part in a raid on the Bronfmans' Yorkton distillery once told me how they made the liquor," recalls John W. Mack, who lived in a local apartment complex known as the Yorkton Club in 1920. "They had large galvanized vats which were lined with oak. Into these they poured distilled water and alcohol, to which was added some caramel and sulphuric acid. The theory was that the acid would attack the oaken lining until it was burnt out. This completed the 'aging process' while the caramel lent the required color. After a chemist had sampled the brew with an hydrometer to pronounce it safe, the taps were turned on and the bottles filled. . . . I remember one Saturday night buying a crock of so-called J. & T. Bell, which five of us consumed out on the prairie in a Model T. About an hour later all of us were paralyzed to a certain degree, and by Sunday noon the ends of my fingers were still numb."

Harry's career as an expert distiller started badly. He had prepared the necessary ingredients for his initial run with the care of a gourmet cook:

- 382 gallons of water
- 318 gallons of sixty-five-overproof raw alcohol
- 100 gallons of aged rye whisky
- a dash of caramel
- a shot of sulphuric acid

As all great blenders know, it is proper aging that is the most essential part of the process. Not to be outdone,

Harry grandiosely decided to give this premier example of his craft a full *two days* to mellow. Forty-eight hours later, he dipped a testing beaker into one of the vats. The damn stuff had turned a dirty purple.

Not certain whether he had made some grievous error in his recipe or had been sold defective vats (actually, such discoloration can be a harmless by-product of the distillation process), Harry responded in typical Bronfman fashion. He worked off the indigo brew by mixing it with later batches of booze at ten gallons to every hundred gallons of regular, amber-colored distillate. At the same time, he refused to pay the $3,200 owing Brewers' and Bottlers' Supplies, which had sold him the vats. The company promptly sued the Bronfman brothers and won its case by bringing in an expert chemist to testify that the blue tinge had come, not from any fault in the redwood vats, but through chemical reaction with "something such as sulphuric acid." The testimony afforded a rare public look at the Bronfmans' profit margins in these formative years. Figures tabled in court showed that the cost of the materials that went into the mixture amounted to $5.25 a gallon for liquor that was being sold at the bottled equivalent of $25 a gallon. Bronfman testified that once he got the Yorkton plant running smoothly, it was processing an average of 5,000 gallons a week, which produced gross monthly revenues of $500,000 and a clear annual profit of $4,692,000.

Despite such extravagant earnings, the Bronfmans failed to file any income-tax returns until Ottawa's revenue authorities demanded an accounting in 1922. Instead of insisting on a detailing of their individual earnings, Ottawa settled for a lump-sum payment of only $200,000 to cover the 1917–1921 period on behalf of the eight Bronfman brothers and sisters. The Royal Commission on Customs and Excise recommended that the tax authorities recover any arrears, but no action followed.

While Harry kept turning out more booze, Sam traveled about the country, establishing the network of

connections with American bootleggers. He named
Harry Sokol, a former Winnipeg bartender, as his sales-
man-at-large to range the United States, negotiating
prices and delivery details. Most of the deals consisted
of whispered exchanges with Damon Runyonesque
characters in back alleys, but right from the start the
Bronfmans tried to nail down arrangements to handle
their merchandise exclusively. The most profitable long-
term arrangement was concluded with Fred Lundquist,
a pre-Prohibition liquor broker in the St. Paul–Minneapolis area, who even went to the trouble of having business cards printed that read:

Fred L. Lundquist
AGENT
YORKTON DISTRIBUTING COMPANY, LIMITED
SASKATOON, SASKATCHEWAN
WHOLESALE LIQUOR STORES
Near International Boundary
in Saskatchewan
Estevan, Bienfait, Glen Ewen, Carnduff,
Carievale, Gainsborough

What impressed Lundquist and other bootleggers
most was the Bronfman guarantee of immunity from
customs and police interference on the Canadian side
of the border. Ottawa had not only declared liquor
exports to the United States legal but also, initially at
least, tried hard to encourage them. For every gallon
of booze "exported" to the United States, the federal
treasury refunded Canadian distillers the nine-dollar-a-
gallon internal-consumption tax paid on domestically
sold liquor. In the first full year of the Volstead Act,
an estimated $23 millions' worth of bottled alcohol was
sold to American bootleggers. "Rumrunning," the *Financial Post* smugly editorialized, "has provided a tidy
bit towards Canada's favourable balance of trade."

The only sanction Ottawa exercised over this dubious
commerce was to charge a validation tax (which ran
as high as $19 a case) for issuing federal export licenses.

It was more of a revenue-producing gimmick than any attempt to police the trade, because all the applicant had to do was state any improbable destination for his shipment, as long as it was south of the United States, in order to have it freely waved through Canadian customs—presumably on its way to Cuba, Peru, or Panama. In the spring of 1923, the State Department asked Canada to refuse such licenses to ships with cargoes of liquor destined to U.S. ports. The Liberal administration of Mackenzie King took three months to reply, then coolly dismissed the request, pointing out that there existed "no provisions in the custom laws or regulations which would warrant refusal of clearance to a foreign port simply because of the fact that the entry of such liquor, without special permits, was prohibited at the foreign port in question."

"Rumrunning and border slipping broke no Canadian law, as various governments . . . repeatedly and correctly reminded the public," Ralph Allen pointed out in his history of the period.* "It took half a dozen years or more before Canada fully comprehended the impossibility of providing both an operating base and the raw materials for a multibillion-dollar criminal industry while itself remaining untouched by the crimes involved. Then the knowledge came home with savage impact, almost enough to wreck the country's most durable political dynasty."

Harry Bronfman devised some additional protection for Americans afraid of Canadian police interference by obtaining a common-carrier status for a company he formed called Trans-Canada Transportation Limited. This allowed him to hand out documents to the drivers of the Hudsons, Studebakers, Packards, and Chryslers that came north into Saskatchewan for their loads of booze, who could then wave papers to prove they were under charter to a properly accredited transport company. In the unlikely event that even this legality failed

* *Ordeal by Fire: Canada 1910–1945* (Toronto: Doubleday Canada Ltd., 1961).

to halt some over-anxious law enforcer, Harry Bronfman guaranteed the bootleggers against loss of their loads by freely replacing any liquor seized on Canadian soil. He also provided at no charge the double-duty bond required by the customs for seized vehicles.

The Studebaker "Whisky Six" was the bootleggers' favorite. Fully stripped down, with reinforced springs and upholstery removed, it could carry forty cases of whisky, worth $2,000. In case he might be missing some business, Harry opened up the City Garage next to his booze palace in Yorkton so that the American bootleggers could get their automobiles serviced while they were waiting for a new load. He also kept a stock of used cars, filled with booze, in front of his hotel and sold them "as is" to adventurous Saskatchewan farmers anxious to engage in a little moonlighting.

It was only when the cars got back onto American turf that their journeys turned illegal. They eluded American federal agents by disappearing into clouds of dust stirred up by thirty-foot chains dragged behind their speeding boozemobiles. At night, miniature searchlights mounted on rear windows would direct fierce beams into the eyes of police-car drivers. "We used to drive north and south with liquor we weren't supposed to have," recalls Jack Janpolski, a Regina resident who was in the trade. "The Bronfmans would fill in certificates for us with the amount of liquor listed, and if we were stopped driving north, we'd just say we were really going south but got lost. The permits were signed by Harry and were all quite legal. The booze was good enough, but it all came out of the same barrel, even if it had half a dozen different labels."

To shorten the bootleggers' turn-around time, the Bronfmans opened up satellite warehouses closer to the border, in Estevan, Bienfait, Carnduff, Carievale, Gainsborough, and Glen Ewen. These depots—some of them within ten miles of the international boundary—became the tension points of the operation, with Yorkton, and later Regina, being relegated to production and storage functions. R. E. A. Leech, head of the Saskatchewan Liquor Commission, told the Royal Commission on Customs and Excise: "The liquor companies built these border warehouses with the sole object of serving American bootleggers. From our point of view, these operations were quite legal providing the cars and trucks coming in were checked at customs points and again when they left. The warehouses were in pretty lonely stretches of country and might be stocked with hundreds of thousands of dollars' worth of liquor. Vulnerable to hijackers, they were generally barricaded and otherwise well protected. Windows had iron bars, padlocks were everywhere, and they were all armed with a variety of weapons, including machine guns. In fact, you could call them miniature forts."

IT WAS AT GAINSBOROUGH ON NOVEMBER 8, 1920, THAT THE GROWING TENSION between the Bronfmans and Canadian law-enforcement officers first exploded into the open. Cyril Knowles, a Conservative Party worker who had joined the Department of Customs and Excise soon after the 1911 federal election, was driving along a border road in the Manitoba-Saskatchewan corner of the international boundary with Constable A. G. Pyper of the RCMP when they spotted three Ford touring cars speeding south, swaying in the twilight under a full load of booze. Knowles discovered that the drivers—three unemployed house painters from St. Paul, Minnesota—had crossed the border the previous night without reporting their entry into Canada. This left them liable to detention until they could pay a total of $3,025 double duty on their cars, a sum that would be refunded once they returned to the States. Instead of protesting their innocence, the trio demanded to be taken to Gainsborough, where Max Heppner, the local Bronfman manager, had guaranteed their safe conduct to the U.S. border. By the time Knowles and his group got back to the boozorium, Harry Bronfman had arrived in Gainsborough to deal with the situation.

What happened next remains in dispute. Bronfman

was furious when Knowles demanded the double-duty payment on the bootleggers' cars but finally ordered Heppner to get the necessary cash out of the safe. According to Knowles's version, it was while he was filling in the formal receipt that Bronfman suggested he write it out for "a thousand dollars, twelve hundred or whatever amount he thought he could get away with with the government." Bronfman then offered to give him an extra $3,000 and promised to give him equivalent monthly payments if Knowles would guarantee immunity from further interference by the customs department.

In the testimony he gave before the Royal Commission on Customs and Excise, on February 25, 1927, Bronfman denied having made any bribe offer, but did confirm this later conversation:

> *Bronfman:* Now you've got your money. See that these fellows get their liquor and their cars back. Don't you allow anything else to happen to them. They had a bad knock.
>
> *Knowles:* They can't have the liquor. It's seized. They were in Manitoba and that liquor's been turned over to the Manitoba government.
>
> *Bronfman:* What? Do you mean to tell me you're going to take that liquor away from these men?
>
> *Knowles:* Why not? It belongs to the Manitoba government.
>
> *Bronfman:* You're no man at all. No man I know would do a thing like that.
>
> *Knowles:* I'm as good a man as you are.
>
> *Bronfman:* I'm not getting mixed up with the law. If you'll take off your badge and come outside with me as man to man, and stand up to me for ten minutes, I'll give you twice as much money.

Not unnaturally, Knowles chose to interpret the phrase "I'll give you twice as much money" as a second bribery attempt—particularly because, he testified, as Bronfman mentioned it, he pointed at the sheaf of banknotes Max Heppner had just counted out to give the customs department. Bronfman claimed that he had only meant that he was so angry it would have been worth the money just to give Knowles a beating. The commission chose to believe Knowles, concluding that "strong corroborative evidence was adduced before us in support of the testimony given by Inspector Knowles, and in our view a *prima facie* case was made out sufficient to warrant prosecution being entered against Harry Bronfman for his alleged offence."

The Gainsborough case was the first in a series of legal battles between Knowles and Harry Bronfman. Soon after Knowles captured the Gainsborough smugglers, he seized a white Cadillac engaged in the border traffic whose driver had shot at him, then fled into the bush. Hoping to flush out some inquiries, Knowles drove the impounded automobile around Winnipeg. Harry saw him and recognized the car as belonging to Harry Sokol, who worked for the family as chief salesman for the northern United States.

Using his Ottawa connections, Bronfman not only managed to get the vehicle released but somehow prompted the Department of Customs and Excise to reprimand Knowles because he had been driving a seized vehicle for personal use. Knowles immediately sent back a full explanation, concluding with this sad protest: "While I am pleased that I have the opportunity of stating the above facts, I regret this explanation was required. I have been alternately threatened and cajoled during my investigations by parties in the smuggling traffic. Efforts have been made to bribe me, and an attempt was made to bribe my brother to get me to leave certain territory uncovered. My apartment here has been burgled and documents stolen and everything possible done to embarrass the progress of investigations. If complaint has been made in the Sokol car case, it is but another effort to hamper the cleaning up of the illicit drug and liquor smuggling traffic under investigation."

BY THE END OF 1921, HARRY HAD MOVED INTO A LARGE, SPRAWLING HOUSE in Regina, and even if a few of the city's more conservative citizens frowned on the Bronfmans' activities, rumrunning was for the most part applauded rather than regarded as any kind of criminal activity. "It was something everybody did, and nobody tried particularly to hide it," recalls Lou Kushner, who once worked at the Yorkton plant. "This town was booming as long as the Bronfmans were around."

Of the many operators who had rushed into the booze trade, only a few firms had survived. "Any slap at the liquor business in Saskatchewan I regard as a slap at me," Harry Bronfman boasted in an interview in October 1922 with the *Winnipeg Tribune*. "With the exception of two small concerns in Saskatoon which have practically run out of stock, the liquor business . . . is controlled by me."

One exception was Regina Wine and Spirits Limited, operated by a trio strange enough to make the Bronfmans appear tame by comparison: Meyer Chechik, a Winnipeg wholesale chicken merchant; Zisu Natanson, the owner of a Regina junkyard; and Harry Rabinovitch, who had jumped bail on a manslaughter charge involving the death of a Minneapolis trucker in a liquor hijacking incident. Their two main assets were a license to run a bonded liquor warehouse in Regina and Chechik's $150,000 revolving credit line with Boivin, Wilson in Montreal, then Canada's largest importers of liquor from Great Britain.

Early in 1921, with liquor imports into Saskatchewan about to be cut off, Harry Bronfman set up a syndicate with the Regina booze merchants to pool their supplies into a company called Dominion Distributors. Together they purchased the Craftsman Building, near the city's Canadian Pacific Railway depot, and set about manufacturing and selling booze on a production-line basis.

By October of that year, an internal financial crisis

blew up when Chechik arrived unexpectedly from Winnipeg and was told by two of the employees he had placed in the Regina operation that there was big trouble brewing. This was how Chechik described the encounter with his two men in his testimony to the Royal Commission on Customs and Excise:

> They look to me as I am the financial man. I had very big credit in the east in the banks where I financed myself all this money. They said to me: "Mr. Chechik, we have to go to jail."
> They are only employees. They have only one or two shares. I said, "I am not running a business for anybody to go to jail. What is wrong?" They make a statement to me what shows Rabinovitch and Natanson to syphon out by pumps or by pipes from the drums, alcohol, where they substitute water. As soon as the government finds out I am the president and this is the treasurer and this is the secretary and most of the directors will have to go to jail. . . . They told me how it was done. They took out the pins [from the door hinges]. The government lock is there. They do not move or interfere with the government lock or seal but they removed the pins [which enabled them] to [open] the door.
> The [next] thing I called a meeting of these three men, and I wrote a letter to the collector of customs in Regina not to allow any more clearing of these goods or any goods from bond. [I have] money in the Imperial Bank to cover the government interests and then I start to bring action against Rabinovitch, Natanson and Bronfman.

The drums of liquor had indeed been emptied by Chechik's less discreet partners, and the government was very much owed $37,000 in excise taxes as a result. But the Winnipeg chicken wholesaler's tactics of threatening to sue his associates and calling in government agents to confess the truth clearly was unforgivable.

Chechik told the Royal Commission that Sam Bronfman had persuaded him to call off his legal action by
explaining, "It would be better, Meyer, that you should
go and pay the duty rather than cause so much trouble." The nineteen-word summary hardly did justice to
Sam's string of threats and abuse, which climaxed in
Chechik's writing out a check himself for the defaulted
$37,000.

In the early winter of 1922, the partnership attracted
the attention of Cyril Knowles, the incorruptible civil
servant, still smarting from his last encounter with the
Bronfmans. His department had started cracking down
on compounding operations (unlike blending, which
consisted of mixing two brands of whisky or brandy,
compounding is a fancy name for diluting a brand with
water and other substances), and when Knowles, accompanied by three Mounties, unexpectedly burst into
Dominion Distributors' premises, he found not only
extensive compounding equipment but also other evidence of lawbreaking. In the adjoining junkyard there
was a strip of fifteen thousand counterfeit U.S. revenue
stamps and forged labels of well-known American rums
and whiskies. Knowles arrested Natanson on charges of
compounding liquor without a license in addition to
conspiring to forge U.S. revenue documents and wired
his department for instructions. He was told to take
no further action but asked instead to catch the next
train to Ottawa and report directly to the Hon. Jacques
Bureau, the Minister of Customs.

Knowles packed all the evidence into a carton, placed
his official seal on it, and, when it was ready for shipment to the department's enforcement branch in Ottawa, instead of taking it to the Canadian Pacific Express office himself, accepted Harry Bronfman's offer
to send it off for him. When the parcel arrived, much
of the evidence was missing. But Knowles's problems
were only beginning.

When Harry told Sam and Allan about the raid, they
decided to use their Liberal connections in the capital
to seek an immediate interview with Bureau. The hap-

less Knowles had to suffer the humiliation of being kept waiting in the Minister's reception chamber while Sam and Allan were ushered into Bureau's office ahead of him. "I simply related the facts of what had happened at the Craftsman Building to the Minister," Allan later recalled. "We complained that Inspector Knowles had behaved rather badly by showing complete lack of respect for private property. Though we didn't specifically ask disciplinary action be taken, it was probably implicit in our complaint."

Knowles had come to Ottawa with a sheaf of evidence documenting the proper execution of his raid. But he never got a chance to use it. When he was finally ushered into Bureau's presence, the Minister asked him only one question: did he have any personal spite against the Bronfman organization? "I denied this," Knowles said later, "except to explain that Harry Bronfman had tried to bribe me and that I considered the Bronfmans to be in cahoots with the big bootleggers in the United States."

All charges against Dominion Distributors were immediately dropped. The only result of Knowles's mission was his receipt on February 7, 1922, of a sharp rebuke from R. R. Farrow, the department's Deputy Minister:

As explained to you when in Ottawa recently on official business the Department is unable under present conditions, namely those caused by your lack of discretion and judgment in connection with the recent Inland Revenue cases at Regina, to continue your assignment to duty in excise work.

You are therefore instructed that until otherwise ordered, your duties are to be confined to Customs work, at the Port of Winnipeg only and performed under the direction and control of Mr. W. F. Wilson, Chief, Customs Preventive Service.

For the present the Department cannot authorize you to make investigations regarding Customs mat-

ters outside the Port of Winnipeg except as specially authorized by Mr. Wilson.

Cyril Knowles remained in government service, anchored to his Winnipeg desk, until his death in 1932.

WITH SUCH OBVIOUS CLOUT IN OTTAWA AND A BUR-
GEONING BUSINESS back in Saskatchewan, the Bronfmans were gradually changing from a group of pioneer-
ing hustlers to a family of wealthy entrepreneurs. Certainly, the liquor business had become a family affair.
C. W. Harvison of the RCMP once commented, "Out
West people used to call them the Bronfman boys. Sam
was the brains, Harry the muscle, and Abe the S.O.B.
They more or less ran things as they wanted in Saskatchewan." Abe had moved east to start up the Mari-
times connections with U.S. smugglers; Harry Druxerman (Bess's husband) ran the Vancouver operation;
Frank Druxerman (Harry's brother) was in charge at
Edmonton; Barney Aaron (Laura's husband) ran the
Montreal depot; Paul Matoff (Jean's husband) supervised the Bienfait warehouse; Dave Gallaman (Harry
Bronfman's brother-in-law) operated the border house
at Estevan.

Sam ranged the United States and Canada, exploiting
the present and planning the future. Although he was
almost constantly on the road and had little time for
any permanent home life,* Sam had been sporadically
courting Saidye Rosner, whose father, Samuel, a fellow
immigrant from Bessarabia, had briefly been mayor of
Plum Coulee, Manitoba. A lively and beautiful brunette,
she had been elected president of the Girls' Auxiliary
of the Winnipeg Jewish Orphans' Home at eighteen and
had attracted swarms of suitors. Sam, then in his early
thirties, had won her heart by sending a telegram from
Vancouver, asking her for a dance date in Winnipeg.
They were married on June 20, 1922. Two days later,

* The family home had been sold after their father's death.
Rose, Allan, and Sam lived in separate suites at Winnipeg's
Fort Garry Hotel.

Sam's sister Rose married Maxwell Rady, a Winnipeg physician. Then both couples journeyed to Ottawa, where they celebrated Allan's marriage to Lucy Bilsky on June 28.

"Sam and Allan took their brides to Vancouver . . . as a combined honeymoon and business trip," Harry recorded, adding the unromantic postscript: "They spent many days ironing out matters which had been either neglected or not properly culminated prior to their weddings."

Partly because of the Bronfmans' spectacular success, the political climate in Saskatchewan had been changing. An amendment to the Saskatchewan Temperance Act came into effect June 1, 1922, restricting liquor-export houses to cities of ten thousand or more. But it accomplished little. The Bronfman mixing and bottling operation at Regina continued at full flood, and although the border boozoriums were closed, Harry merely shipped the booze via railway express to stations near the border where American bootleggers could pick up the goods. To keep up with burgeoning demand, Harry altered the mix of his whiskies. He diluted the original Yorkton formula to forty gallons of water, ten of raw alcohol, two of malt whisky, plus the usual dash of caramel and sulphuric acid.

A resolution, declaring that the export traffic in liquor was the occasion for great disorders and urging the federal government to put an end to the situation, had been passed in the Saskatchewan legislature early in the year. But it was not until November 13 that the response of Mackenzie King's Liberal government in Ottawa was announced, ordering an end to the export trade by December 15. That gave the Bronfmans a month to liquidate their Regina operations. Harry launched a giant sale, so that by deadline date all that remained at his warehouse was the actual mixing and bottling equipment. It was appropriated by Zisu Natanson, who promptly set it up in his basement and continued to turn out the booze. Natanson was arrested in 1924, fined $500, and sent to jail for two months.

When he appealed his sentence, he was given six months' hard labor in addition to the original two months in jail.

What finally precipitated the government action required for the closing of the liquor-export houses was the murder on October 4, 1922, of Paul Matoff, a Bronfman brother-in-law, at the border village of Bienfait.

6. *Murder at Beanfate*

MAIN STREET runs one dusty block north from Highway 18 to dead-end at the CPR track, and the only reason the little town doesn't give off an air of abandoned hope is that it's impossible to imagine any sense of promise or enchantment ever having been conjured up in this bleak moonscape. Old men with their good, wind-reddened faces spend hours allowing countless cups of bitter coffee to grow cold between them in the Kopper Kettle Café, trading those shattering small quips that can burn away the scrub of a hidebound life. Something seems to have leaked out from them into the dun-colored walls, the toll of small-town life gone sour.

Outside, the wind is always blowing, howling in, rainless, across the great plains of North Dakota, whipping Bienfait's unpaved main street into a perpetual dust storm. Or howling down from Lac La Ronge country, carrying angry clouds of rain that turn the town into gumbo. The farmers who drive in from the surrounding countryside walk with a practiced starboard lean to compensate for the constant wind that makes little jib sails in the vents of their jackets and tears at their nostrils. Their wives, dressed up in small crowns of afternoon hats, sit impatiently in the pick-up trucks,

99

waiting for their husbands to finish their man-talk so they can go shopping in Estevan, nine miles west.

Bienfait is a one-elevator town nestled into Saskatchewan's bleak southeast corner, a bare ten miles north of the international boundary, its modest skyline limited to a large Ukrainian Catholic church, the Plainsman Hotel, a branch of the Canadian Legion, two cafés, a general store, and the CPR station guarded by a large gray cat.

A huge black steam locomotive incongruously parked at the foot of Main Street, patrolled by the starlings nesting in its cab, remains a ghostly memorial to the men who worked in nearby strip coalfields that flourished early in the century—heaving the surrounding landscape into ugly spillpiles of abandoned overburden. The other monument to the town's grim lignite-mining past is the tombstone in the local cemetery marking the grave of three young miners, killed by police fire in Estevan on September 29, 1931. The three were among three hundred striking miners who gathered at Bienfait and moved on to Estevan for a protest parade that ended in a bloody riot, the first violence of the so-called Dirty Thirties on the prairies. The tombstone was decorated with a red star and engraved with the words "Murdered by the RCMP." The star was later whitewashed and the initials RCMP have been chipped away.

Bienfait had originally claimed its name in 1895 from the oath of a French-Canadian railway spiker who is supposed to have put down his hammer on this particular section of the Canadian Pacific Railway and exclaimed, *"C'est vraiment bien fait!"* Ottawa's earnest policies on bilingualism notwithstanding, it's been known as Beanfate ever since.

Less than a hundred farmers live in and around Bienfait now. What little nightlife exists is transacted in the cramped beverage room of the Plainsman Hotel, which boasts eleven bedrooms at six to nine dollars a night and closes half-days every Wednesday. Back in the twenties, when it was the King Edward Hotel but more widely known as White's Hotel, this was the center of the booze trade, the place where American bootleggers stayed while picking up their loads from Harry Bronfman's boozorium around the corner. Part of the legend of the rumrunning days recounted by oldtimers is the story of a week-long visit by Harry's most famous customer, Arthur Flegenheimer—better known as Dutch Schultz.*

The local celebrity—and Bienfait's chief revenue producer—was Paul Matoff, who had married Jean, the second of the four daughters of Ekiel and Minnie Bronfman. Mrs. Gordon White, widow of the man who owned Bienfait's hotel in the early twenties, remembers

---

* For those unfamiliar with the legend, Arthur Flegenheimer (who changed his name to "Dutch Schultz" because it sounded tougher) was one of Prohibition's most colorful and dangerous characters. Originally a Bronx bartender, he got into the booze trade and eventually ended up owning New York's flashy Embassy Club. He would host a front table most evenings, entertaining various gangsters, listening to Helen Morgan sing backed by the Yacht Club Boys. The Park Avenue crowd that frequented the luxurious speakeasy got a vicarious thrill dancing shoulder to shoulder with killers with chromatic suits and stainless-steel faces. By 1930, Schultz had established friendly trade relations with such leading powers as Owney Madden and Frank Costello and had become the beer baron of New York, but he soon had to deal with troublesome rivals in the gang wars. When Vincent "Mad Dog" Coll (also known as "the Mad Mick") kidnapped Madden's partner and started interfering with Schultz's beer drops, Owney and Dutch had Coll killed (he was machine-gunned in a Manhattan phone booth). After Jack "Legs" Diamond (a notorious killer whose real name was John T. Noland) hijacked a cider cargo, he was found in Albany by the Dutchman's men and dispatched. (Diamond's wife, Alice, was the only mourner to turn up at Legs's funeral; she was gunned down in Brooklyn two years later.) Schultz himself was taken by surprise while dining in the Palace Bar, a Newark chop house, on October 23, 1935. Two hoods came through the door firing .38's, killed three of his bodyguards (Lulu Rosenkrantz, Abbadabba Berman, and Abe Landau), and ventilated Dutch so thoroughly that he expired twenty-four hours later. Among his last words: "Mother is the best bet."

Matoff as "a man of average height with dark brown
hair and glasses. He dressed very smartly and always
had a beautiful diamond tie pin and a huge diamond
ring. It was quite rare to see Paul wear the same suit
two days in a row."

Jack Janpolski, who drove for the Bronfmans in those
days, has less fond memories. "Paul was a big showoff.
He used to arrive in Regina with big satchels of money
and stand on the sidewalk outside the Bank of Montreal, making us guess how much was in it. If you said,
'Maybe $10,000,' he'd do a little dance and shout,
'No. It's $100,000!' " Harry Zellickson, who worked
for Matoff, recalls that in 1922, at the peak of bootleg
traffic out of Bienfait, the little boozorium was taking
in $500,000 a month.

Ken John, a resident of Bienfait in the twenties,
roomed at White's Hotel at the time. He claims clear
memory of the events that took place at Bienfait on the
night of October 4, 1922:

> Most of the bootleggers who came up from the
> States didn't want to advertise what business they
> were in. But they did wear guns, with their shoul-
> der holsters hanging on every other bedpost at
> White's hotel. There was lots of money around. I
> remember one poker game in my room, when a
> guy stuck ten-dollar bills into the lamp chimney to
> light his cigar. They used to play snooker at
> $1,000 a game.

> Beanfate was quite populated at the time, be-
> cause of all the deep-seam coal mines around it.
> But there were no sidewalks, no street lights, or
> anything like that. Harry Bronfman opened up one
> of his liquor warehouses—the boozorium, we
> called it—and put his brother-in-law, Paul Matoff,
> in charge. He used to import the booze from Que-
> bec by CPR express, so Earl Goddard, the local
> station agent, always made a lot of money. He was
> my brother-in-law, and he'd help unload the

whisky that arrived aboard the local, which then ran from Brandon to Estevan once a day. It would get in about eight in the evening. Earl and Colin Rawcliffe, the telegraph operator, would store the stuff in the freight shed and about midnight Matoff would come over with his dray to pick up the night's load.

The rumrunners who came in from the States would arrive in their big cars with bulletproof gas tanks and stay at White's hotel until Matoff came over to tell them it was time to load up. They would pull into town during the afternoon, do their dickering for the whisky, then go over and eat at White's. The dining room was run by a stout character called Frank "Fat" Earl. There used to be all kinds of silver dollars and fifty-cent pieces around in those days, and if the supper bill came to a couple of bucks or something, Fat would challenge his guests to throw the coins at a crack in the floor, double or nothing. Old Fat, he was doing it all the time, so he usually won. But I remember when Dutch Schultz was throwing with him, and they kept at it all one afternoon. By the time they got through, Dutch could hardly get up off his knees and Fat couldn't get down.

Anyway, after these guys got back to the boozorium, Matoff and his two assistants would help them pack the bottles out of the cardboard cases into burlap sacks, stow it carefully inside their cars, and they'd roar off across the border, usually heading down through what they used to call "Whisky Gap." It wasn't so much the police and American federal agents they were scared of as being taken by hijackers on the other side.

That particular night, half a carload had come in, and Earl Goddard wanted to get it out of the station as quick as he could. He phoned Matoff and said, "Well, it's ready."

We were playing poker at the time. One of the

boys came in from visiting his girl friend up at an adjacent mine and said he'd seen a couple of strange cars parked behind the grain elevator, which to him was a significant fact and a suspicious one, anyway. He told Fat Earl, "I've got a notion there's something cooking up there. Is there any whisky at the station?"

So Fat gets on the phone and tries to get Earl Goddard. It was a little country exchange—as a matter of fact, my wife's mother was running it at the time—but Earl has gone to sleep in his place on the top floor of the station, and he doesn't answer the phone. So Fat tries again, but nothing happens.

Meanwhile, down in the station's main waiting room, Matoff is paying the express charges for the night's shipment to the telegraph operator, Colin Rawcliffe, while some of the booze is being loaded by Jimmie LaCoste into Lee Dillage's Cadillac.* All of a sudden, this twelve-gauge sawed-off shotgun is poked through the station's bay window and they let Matoff have it.

Old Lee, he ducks up into the living quarters. By this time, Goddard is awake, of course. He looks out at the station platform, and there is this guy parading around who yells, "Get your head in there!"—which Earl does right away.

The man who shot Matoff goes in, takes the $6,000 he's been taking in and dealing out. Even

---

* To speed up the process, Matoff would occasionally release the shipment directly from the CPR freight shed. Lee Dillage was a North Dakota rumrunner who used Bienfait as his main supply source. (He also sponsored an outlaw baseball team that played Saskatchewan's border towns. Its roster included Swede Risberg and Happy Felsch, two of the eight "Black Sox" of the Chicago White Sox who had been barred from organized baseball in 1920 for their part in throwing the 1919 World Series to the underdog Cincinnati Reds.) Jimmie LaCoste was a garage mechanic who acted as Dillage's main Bienfait contact.

steals Paul's diamond ring. Jimmie LaCoste, who was inside the station during the shooting, rushes out, tells Dillage to take off, and runs across the tracks to tell Gordon White, who's sitting out on the balcony of his hotel, that Matoff's just been shot.

By the time somebody's got word to the police in Estevan it was a matter of half an hour. When they came down, they went to Jimmie LaCoste's house. Of course they knew about Dillage, so they asked Jimmie to lead them to where Lee is hiding the whisky. I think Jimmie had a K45 Buick at the time—that was the fastest car in those days. He led the police on a merry-go-round to give Dillage time to get across the border and finally lost them between here and Lignite [North Dakota]. They ended up charging both Jimmie and Dillage with the murder, because they thought the two of them might have arranged the whole thing, but they were both acquitted. . . . So that's the tale of the Matoff murder.

We were full of devilment in those days. I remember one night they were having a quiet party at the boozorium. Fat Earl and I got jealous that we couldn't get in on it. So we thought we'd give them a little scare. I took the butt end of a gun and pounded the door. "Go out the front and get shot!" Fat started to yell. "Go out the back, you get killed!" What a fuss there was. I let go a couple of shells, bang, bang, and then we skinned out.

Leé Dillage's cache was discovered a few days later just north of the U.S. border. It contained eighteen sacks of rye, four of cognac, one of port, and forty cases of gin. The murder remained unsolved. Speculation about motives included Harry Bronfman's contention that it was a simple case of robbery with violence. Others claimed the shot had been meant as a blunt warning to the Bronfmans by American bootleggers that they shouldn't water their whisky so much. According to a more complicated theory, the assassination had been a reprisal for Matoff's role in helping in the arrest of some U.S. gangsters who had previously hijacked a Bronfman car loaded with booze.

7. *At the Bar of Justice*

BY THE early twenties, Canada was becoming a very different country. Automobiles were the symbol of that change, but much deeper transitions were in process. Accelerating population shifts and wartime industrialization marked the decade as a watershed in the country's urbanization. After 1921, more and more Canadians would live in cities and the frontier ethic that had sustained the large land's settlers would become a nostalgic rite. Most Canadians still subscribed to the cozy rural virtues—the notion that simple living, hard work, and moral endurance would always triumph in the end. But the pace and anonymity of city life had shifted their concerns and values into drastically altered, more materialistic channels. As the rugged individualism of the frontier began to fade, Ottawa's laissez-faire attitude gave way to mild forms of social welfare. Prime Minister Mackenzie King, the Liberal necromancer who presided over most of the twenties, was content to expend his energies on political survival, accomplishing nothing much, but lulling the forces of agrarian revolt, labor unrest, and French-Canadian nationalism in the process.

It was an interim decade, a transition between the new world that would be shaped by the dark forces of

the Depression of the thirties and the brave, simpler,
pre-1914 Canada that would never be again.

The booze traffic across the U.S. border multiplied
throughout the twenties in both intensity and quantity,
becoming a great deal more violent as its profitability
reached new highs. Finding themselves harassed on the
ground, the more up-to-date bootleggers took to the
air. One amply financed squadron, under the command
of Russell "Curly" Hosler, a World War I flying ace,
ran a smoothly scheduled night airline between southern Ontario and various small airports in northern
Michigan. To help the planes land, the rumrunners
would encircle the field with their cars, flash on their
headlights to illuminate the moment of landing, then
load up and speed away. A similar fleet, organized by
Al Capone's brother Ralph, boasted twenty aircraft,
including a trimotored cabin monoplane that could load
fifty cases. Canadian imports of British liquor zoomed,
and the Quebec towns along the U.S. border became
the trade's jumping-off points. "A hundred bottles of
whisky would make the entire population of Granby,
Que., drunk, but the sale per day is now six thousand
bottles and climbing," the *Ottawa Journal* reported.

After his Saskatchewan warehouse operations were
closed by law at the end of 1922, Harry Bronfman retired briefly to Winnipeg. He wrote in his memoirs:

> I endeavoured to adjust myself to relaxation. The
> strain of the business during this period had been
> a little hard on me, and the relaxation brought
> about a nervous breakdown. I endeavoured to re-
> gain my health for a year and a half. Sam and I
> went to the coast, returned to Winnipeg and . . .
> [then] decided to go to Louisville to attend the
> Derby. . . . When we arrived there we decided,
> after much discussion with distillery people, that
> it would be profitable as far as the Bronfman fam-
> ily was concerned to establish a distillery in Can-
> ada. We immediately proceeded to purchase the
> Greenbrier Distillery, a few miles out of Louis-

ville, and engaged a distiller and a distillery engineer. We started to tear down this distillery, and I went back to Montreal in order to look the ground over and choose a proper location for the erection of this distillery. Sam, Leslie B. Abbott, the engineer, and an old-time distillery operator by the name of Pop Knebelkamp, returned to Montreal with me for the purpose of choosing a location. Barney Aaron and my brother Abe were then living in Montreal. Barney had purchased a brand-new Chrysler car which he was courteous enough to let me have and which I used for the purpose of driving through the city and its surroundings. By the time I had finished picking a location . . . [at Ville La Salle], I had registered 10,000 miles on his car.

Most of the family's combined Bank of Montreal account was sunk into this venture. The first ceremonial spade of earth was turned at the site on the western fringes of Montreal, where the Ottawa and St. Lawrence rivers flow into the Lachine Rapids, on May 20, 1924. Less than a year later, on March 31, 1925, the basic distillery was completed,* and Harry in his memoirs boasted of having 290,000 gallons of whisky in the warehouse. "I proceeded to operate the distillery while Sam and Allan busied themselves with the financing . . . because Allan had been in Scotland and had obtained agencies for the importing of their . . . goods to Canada, he already had an acquaintanceship there. We discussed the whole situation and decided on the suggestion of Sam that, because we had already installed a miniature patent Coffey-still for the purpose of pro-

---

* The Bronfmans continued to expand the Ville La Salle plant; by 1929 it had become one of the world's largest distilleries with an annual capacity of three million gallons. To keep morale high, Harry sponsored weekend picnics for employees, and his son Allan installed a company cafeteria (which sold potatoes and gravy for five cents to staff members who brought their own sandwiches), and even put in an orchestra to play during work breaks.

ducing Scotch Grains, it was possible to affiliate with
the Distillers Company of London, England. Sam and
Allan left Montreal to lay the proposition before them."

The Bronfmans had been importing Scotch in bulk
from Distillers Company Limited (DCL) of Edinburgh
and London—an 1877 amalgamation of British distilleries controlling more than half the world's Scotch market, including such well-known brands as Haig, Black &
White, Dewar's, Johnnie Walker, Vat 69, and White
Horse—since about 1920. When they sailed for London, Sam and Allan took with them a special box containing samples of their new distillate. They booked
into the Savoy Hotel and waited to be received by the
DCL directors. Three days after their arrival, they were
ushered into the firm's oak-paneled boardroom. Their
samples were tasted and passed on without comment to
expert blenders for detailed analysis. With no sign of
the diffidence even Sam must have felt in the presence
of the collective hauteur represented by Field Marshal
Earl Haig, Lord Dewar, Lord Woolavington, Lord
Forteviot, Sir Alexander Walker, Sir James Charles
Calder, and other DCL directors, the upstart Montreal
distiller expounded his case for becoming the Scottish
liquor trust's Canadian partner. "It was really an extremely brash sort of thing for anybody to suggest," Sir
Ronald Cumming, a later chairman of DCL, recalled.
"But Sam had been a good customer for many years
and had always paid his bills promptly. That sort of
thing counts." Sam wanted DCL to purchase a half-
interest in his distillery for $1 million. He also de-
manded that the assembled aristocrats sell him their
malt whiskies so that he could mix them with his own
grain alcohol, then bottle and officially market the Ville
La Salle distillate under DCL's well-known brands.

The canny Scotsmen made no decision; but six
months later Thomas Herd, a DCL executive, arrived at
Montreal's Ritz-Carlton Hotel, spent four days recov-
ering from his transatlantic voyage, then proceeded to
investigate the Bronfmans and their colonial distillery.
When Sam pressed Herd for an opinion, he found him-

self dismissed with the observation, "Mr. Bronfman, I didn't come here to deal with you, or to be cross-examined about our intentions."

Eight weeks later Sam and Allan were called back to London and told their proposition would be accepted on condition that DCL assume a 51-percent interest in the Bronfmans' distilling company, Distillers Corporation Limited. Disappointed, but anxious not to lose the whole deal, Sam telephoned Harry in Montreal. Gerald Bronfman remembers his father, Harry, pacing the floor of his study, yelling on the transatlantic phone that their distillery was a family concern and that on no account should the Scotsmen be allowed to buy more than 50 percent. That was the deal finally struck, and Sam even managed to add a rider that he could buy out DCL's interest at a mutually agreed price.

The licensing agreement with DCL, crucial to the future of the Bronfmans' distillery, was signed in 1926, the year the Seagram family's distilling business became a public company, with an offering of 250,000 shares priced at $15 a share. Joseph Emm Seagram had established the distillery as a leading Canadian rye producer, with two money-making brands, Seagram's 83 and V.O., which was introduced in 1909. A pompous aristocrat who modeled himself on Edward VII, Seagram devoted much of his time and money to his racehorses, which won fame in Canada and on the eastern seaboard of the United States. His black-and-gold racing colors (they still appear in the ribbon that graces V.O. bottles) first won the Queen's Plate in Toronto in 1891. After his death in 1919, the business was divided up among the Seagram family, with Edward, the eldest son, in nominal control.

By 1927, DCL had taken control of the Seagram company and placed in the president's chair Percy F. Chaplin, director of a British distillery, Macdonald, Greenlees & Williams, which had merged with the big Distillers group in 1925. It was DCL's hold on the Seagram stock that gave it control over the Bronfmans' distilling company, Distillers Corporation Limited, when it was teamed with Seagram's in 1928 under the yoke of Distillers Corporation–Seagrams Limited. Under the deal, 75 percent of the shares in DC-SL went to holders of Distillers Corporation Limited stock and 25 percent to the Seagram stockholders.*

The new holding company set up its head office in the Bronfmans' corporate castle in Montreal, but it was DCL'S chairman from Edinburgh, W. H. Ross, who was named president, with Sam Bronfman as vice-president and Allan as secretary. There was only one other member of the board of directors, W. B. Cleland, a transplanted Scot who (like Percy Chaplin) was a Macdonald, Greenlees man before he became a DCL man.

The Seagram and Bronfman distilleries became separate operating subsidiaries under the new regime. Ross also held the presidential post in Distillers Corporation Limited, with Sam relegated to vice-president. But Sam was the man in charge of his family's integrated liquor operations, with Allan at headquarters, Harry the on-line man at Ville La Salle, and Abe and Barney Aaron in the field, and it was the Bronfmans' bootlegging trade that provided the major share of the $2.2 million net profit reported by DC-SL for the seventeen months up to July 1929. At its first annual meeting in October that year, vice-president Sam confidently announced that there would be a $4.2 million stock offering to finance expansion in the booming export market.

As most of the land borders between Canada and the United States became increasingly dangerous and air transport remained extremely expensive, the trade gradually shifted to sea. On the east coast, the Bronf-

---

* The new company's holdings consisted of 1,250,000 shares of Distillers Corporation Limited plus 250,000 shares of Seagram's. The only parcel of treasury stock issued afterward consisted of 242,639 shares, paid out to the owners of the first two U.S. distilleries purchased in the early thirties, and a small option arrangement of 11,225 shares released to a mysterious beneficiary in 1942.

mans acquired bonded warehouses in Saint John and Halifax, bringing in British goods and shipping them out by night in fleets of schooners. Each load required a bond guarantee equal to twice the value of the cargo. A complicated document was filed with Canadian customs detailing the amount of every cargo, its consignee and destination. The exporter then had to acquire a landing certificate at the shipment's supposed point of arrival to get back his bond guarantee. (The basic documents of the rumrunning trade were somewhat simpler: dollar bills or playing cards. The Canadian supplier would give one half of a dollar bill to his skipper. The other half was sent to the American buyer, whose agent put to sea to match his half of the bill with the half held by the Canadian skipper.) The bond guarantees were an ingenious scheme meant to prevent the liquor from being smuggled back into Canada, and, like most of the country's anti-liquor regulations, were designed to be easily circumvented. The cargoes were loaded aboard the heaving schooners, bound for such romantic destinations as Cuba, Honduras, Nassau, and Lima, the Peruvian capital, which isn't even a seaport. The bills of lading were mailed to carefully briefed (and well-greased) local customs agents, who covered them with exotic-looking rubber stamps, proving that they had received cargoes they never saw, then dispatched them back to Canada, where the exporter would calmly retrieve his prepaid duty. Most of this trade was carried out through Bronfman subsidiaries called Atlantic Import and Atlas Shipping.

The Bronfmans specialized in the Cuban trade, which ran smoothly until their friendly Havana customs agent was fired for bribery. Not wishing to disturb his profitable arrangement, he conveniently forgot to mention his loss of status to his Canadian employers and continued signing the landing certificates. A Boston bootlegger, Hannibal L. Hamlin, was eventually caught in the net and delivered the following confession to agents of the U.S. government:

On or about the 30th day of August, 1922, I met one Mr. Aaron, who, I have reason to believe, is connected as a partner with the Canadian Distributing Company who have an office in Saint John, New Brunswick, and in conversation with said Aaron, which took place in the lobby of the Royal Hotel, he informed me that he could sell Scotch whisky to me with or without the duty. Being somewhat surprised at the term "with or without duty" I asked him what he meant, and he replied, "We have a way of getting the goods out without paying the duty, therefore we are able to quote a lower price for goods shipped in this manner." I inquired as to the port of destination it would be necessary for a ship loaded with liquors to clear for from Saint John, and he replied that Havana, Cuba, was the best. I then said, "It seems rather a roundabout way to do business to have to go to Havana, Cuba, in order to clear the Customs Bond." His answer was, "You don't really have to go to Havana with the load. There is an agent at Havana to whom we mail the bond, which he then takes to a certain customs official at Havana, who properly executes it and it is then mailed back to Saint John from Havana, and the cargo covered by this bond can be landed any time at any point on the United States coast."

When he was questioned about this particular transaction before the Royal Commission on Customs, Barney Aaron lapsed into a kind of patois that left his audience baffled and his own lawyer confused:

Counsel: You never had such a conversation?

Aaron: I do not know the man. No conversation like that take place by me.

Counsel: You never knew there was any question of the validity of your landing certificates at Havana?

Aaron: What I have heard is this, that the certif-

icates and all is one hundred percent okay and
all this being okay that I was doing business okay
and if anything be wrong I would not be doing
it. . . . I want to ask Your Lordship that not one
question asked of me would be in my favour and
I say surely I did things right, and I did a lot of
business.

Chairman: Never mind what counsel asks. He is
not supposed to be too much in your favour. You
have asserted you are one hundred percent sound,
and as long as you can take that position you are
all right.

Aaron: I feel that. Otherwise, why would I not
go out and boast on the street I am one hundred
percent right, but being this commission that everybody looks up to is here and it comes out with
big headlines that I do wrong, and I should show
I am right.

Chairman: Your own counsel will make the
argument for you.

Aaron: He may forget and not say anything.

Chairman: In other words you do not trust your
counsel. You should, because you will need him.

By the mid-twenties, the bulk of the direct liquor
traffic into the United States was flowing across the
Detroit River from Windsor, Ontario. It had created
a navy of small boats (as well as a temporary pipeline
and a complicated rope arrangement that pulled an
underwater sled into a houseboat anchored off the U.S.
shore) to handle the booze. U.S. Prohibition Commissioner James Doran testified before a Senate committee
in 1929 that at least $100 millions' worth of Canadian
liquor was being illegally imported through Detroit.
Under pressure from Washington, the Canadian government responded with a classic halfway measure. Ottawa
promptly ordered the immediate shutdown of thirty of
the sixty export docks on the Windsor side of the river.

As both the diplomatic arm-twisting from Washington
and the pressure from his Conservative opposition grew

stronger, Mackenzie King on March 4, 1930, finally
introduced a bill into the House of Commons amending
the Canada Export Act to place a total embargo on
liquor clearances from Canadian ports to countries
under prohibition. As one newspaper sarcastically editorialized: "After eight years of sponsoring the rumrunning business, Prime Minister Mackenzie King has
finally discovered that criminal gangs are engaged in
the same business." The new law, which came into
effect July 1, seemed once again to strangle the Bronfmans' prospects.

JUST FIFTEEN MILES SOUTH OF NEWFOUNDLAND'S FOR-
TUNE BAY, where the Atlantic wheels into the fog-
shrouded southern arm of the Gulf of St. Lawrence,
squat the little islands of St. Pierre and Miquelon. Occupied by the French for most of the years since 1635
and formally in French hands since the Treaty of
Ghent in 1814, the barren outcrops traditionally provided a *pied à terre* for Basque and Breton fishermen.
With no local economy—the constant wind limits vege-
tation to lichens and moss—and immune to Canadian
law, St. Pierre and Miquelon flourished as legal trans-
shipment points for Canadian and British liquor destined for the insatiable American bootleg market.

The Bronfmans were soon the colony's largest
traders, using both Atlas Shipping and a new corporate
umbrella called the Northern Export Company. The
modest docks of St. Pierre's toy harbor were buried in
an avalanche of freight, pungent with the smell of
superior liquor. The odor grew so strong that at times
the fog that rolled up St. Pierre's steeply inclined streets
with the nightly tides would carry a distinct Scotch
flavor. Delighted by the unexpected windfall, the is-
landers promptly imposed a four-cent-a-bottle tax on
imports and used the revenues to dredge away sand-
bars across the inner harbor so that the large freighters
from British distilleries could unload straight onto the
docks.

The cargoes were transferred aboard fleets of

schooners for passage to Rum Row, as the three-mile limit* of the Atlantic between Boston and Atlantic City came to be known. The booze would then be unloaded into speedboats for the run to waiting convoys of trucks ashore. Speakeasy patrons happily paid premium prices for booze "right off the boat"—a fact not lost on the moonshiners of the Kentucky hills, who dipped filled bottles in tubs of salt water and wrapped them in burlap bags to give them that "true smuggled feeling." Another favorite trick was to add iodine to their whisky mix, presumably so that the unsuspecting customer might assume he was getting a whiff of peat smoke from the glenside pot stills of Scotland. As well as having to run the blockade of U.S. Coast Guard vessels, the trade was beset by hijackers, known as go-through guys, who roamed the coastal waters from Block Island Sound, off Rhode Island, to Montauk Point, Sandy Hook, and Cape May, south of Atlantic City, using Thompson submachine guns to steal cargoes of booze and shoot up any crews unwilling to abandon them.

The most colorful skipper engaged in this hazardous trade of rumrunning was William McCoy, a bronzed six-foot-two former merchant-marine sailor, who never touched a drop of liquor and made and lost several fortunes skippering his boats, the first of which, *Henry L. Marshall,* could accommodate 1,500 cases of Scotch, wrapped in burlap bags. By 1923 he was the nation's most famous rumrunner, and customers would be sent to his craft hovering in Rum Row who wanted only the best, "the real McCoy." In November of that year the U.S. Coast Guard cutter *Seneca* seized his boat and McCoy was sent to jail for nine months. When his time was up, McCoy went to Florida and became a prosperous real-estate investor in Miami. He died at seventy-one in 1946, protesting that "if the racket promised

---

* This became "an hour's steaming distance"—widely regarded as twelve miles—on May 22, 1924.

today half the fun I've had out of it in the past, I'd jump into it tomorrow."

IT WAS THEIR ST. PIERRE AND MIQUELON ADVENTURES THAT WOULD EVENTUALLY BRING the Bronfman brothers to a Montreal courthouse for trial, but not before some of their Saskatchewan shenanigans caught up with them and landed Harry in a jail cell. The circumstances of their brushes with the law—and they were never actually found guilty of any crime—were at least partly prompted by the politics of the day.

Canadian politicians seemed perfectly willing to turn a blind eye to the cynically simple breaching of their anti-liquor laws and quite content to let their country be turned into the smuggling center of the world. But when it came to some of the Liberal ministers and senior civil servants personally profiting from this alluring commerce, the Conservative opposition finally called a halt. The resultant imbroglio caused a deep constitutional crisis and came close to destroying Mackenzie King's personal hegemony.

By the spring of 1924, King was being confronted by increasingly angry deputations of Canadian business leaders fed up with the large-scale smuggling activities across the forty-ninth parallel. This was not so much a matter of high principle as the much more mundane discovery that the rumrunners had been maximizing their profits by returning to the northern side of the border with loads of duty-free goods. One magazine estimated that merchandise worth at least $50 million was being illegally brought *into* the country, endangering the profit margins of Canadian manufacturers. The most popular illegal imports were men's suits made by the inmates of U.S. prisons, selling at a fraction of their Canadian-made equivalents.

The businessmen had formed themselves into the Commercial Protective Association to investigate the situation and lobby for action from Ottawa. In typical fashion, King set out to do nothing, then stepped back a little and lent the group the services of Walter Duncan, a Department of Finance investigator. Duncan picked as his first target Joseph Edgar Alfred Bisaillon, chief preventive officer for the Department of Customs in Montreal, described by Ralph Allen in *Ordeal by Fire* as "one of the most incredible sitting ducks in the annals of public malfeasance."

Duncan discovered that Bisaillon had already been implicated in a narcotic-smuggling incident and reconstructed his role in the saga of the epic voyage of the barge *Tremblay* up the St. Lawrence. In November 1924, the Quebec Liquor Commission had been advised to look out for the *Tremblay,* chugging upriver from St. Pierre. Two of the commission's officers boarded the vessel after it had sailed past Quebec City and its 16,000-gallon cargo of raw alcohol was being unloaded at a cove near St. Sulpice. Because no duty had been paid, the agents arrested the crew and the two American smugglers (Benny "Chicago" Stewart and Joe "Gorilla" Campbell), who admitted owning the liquor consignment. As soon as the ship reached Montreal, it was boarded by Joseph Bisaillon, who ordered the Quebec Liquor Commission representatives ashore by virtue of his seniority as an official of the federal government. He released the Americans and impounded the *Tremblay* on behalf of the Crown. The charge of conspiracy to smuggle was dismissed for lack of evidence, but Bisaillon somehow managed to pocket at least $69,000 from the affair. At the same time, it was revealed that this unusually versatile public servant owned houses on both sides of the Quebec-Vermont boundary in a well-known smugglers' den called Rock Island and was putting them to appropriate use in the trans-border commerce.

Duncan's investigation prompted R. P. Sparks, president of the Commercial Protective Association, to inform Mackenzie King and his Minister of Customs that "at least half of the smuggling now going on could be prevented within a month by an energetic policy on behalf of the department." King's response was benign silence. Then on August 15, 1925, he called a general

election for October 29 and resolved the controversy
swirling around his Customs Minister by appointing
him to the Senate. At the session's final Cabinet meeting, Ernest Lapointe, King's Quebec lieutenant, observed that it was "like attending your own funeral."

In the campaign that followed, King was defeated
in his own riding and his party came back with only
101 seats, a loss of fifteen. Conservative Leader Arthur
Meighen now had the largest group in the Commons,
but King had the constitutional right to meet Parliament
and allow it to decide who should govern. King's continued indifference to the corruption of the customs department had meanwhile prompted Sparks, a long-time
Liberal, to hand Walter Duncan's findings to Harry
Stevens, an influential reform-minded Tory MP. On
February 2, 1926, Stevens finally exposed his time-
bomb. A gifted orator, Stevens held the Commons
spellbound with a marathon, four-hour recitation of
Liberal sins. He outlined in devastating detail how the
customs department's Quebec branch had been turned
into a support agency for the smuggling networks that
dealt in clothing, narcotics, and stolen cars coming into
Canada, while large quantities of liquor were being encouraged to flow the other way. In one of his milder
references, he described Bisaillon as "the worst of
crooks . . . the intimate of ministers, the petted favorite
of this government. The recipient of a moderate salary,
he rolls in wealth and opulence, a typical debauched
and debauching public official." He accused the former
Customs Minister of destroying nine filing cabinets full
of incriminating documents and charged his successor,
George Boivin, with defrauding the federal treasury of
at least $200,000.

When he took over the Customs Ministry, Boivin inherited the problem of trying to dispose of the 16,000
gallons of alcohol that had been taken off the *Tremblay*. He allowed a Quebec hay dealer named W. J.
Hushion, who happened to be a close friend, to buy
the cargo from the Crown at thirty-six cents a gallon
by certifying it to be "rubbing alcohol," useful only

for sale to hospitals. He then switched its official designation to "denatured alcohol" so that Hushion could sell the liquid to American bootleggers at many times his purchase price. Later evidence revealed that the substance was, in fact, a special type of alcohol susceptible to diffusing into liquor.

"I charge the government," Stevens concluded, "with knowledge for a year, or almost a year . . . including the Prime Minister, the Minister of Justice, the Minister of Marine, the ex-minister of Customs . . . with positive knowledge, with abundance of proof, that the grossest violations of the customs laws were being perpetrated in this country." Stevens demanded the setting up of a parliamentary committee to inquire into his charges, and, after a three-day delay, the Liberals agreed. The nine-man committee not only substantiated the accusations, but also outlined much more widespread corruption within the government service.

On June 29, 1926, the Commons unanimously resolved that "since the Parliamentary inquiry indicates that the smuggling evils are so extensive and their ramifications so far-reaching that only a portion of the illegal practices have been brought to light, the House recommends the appointment of a Judicial Commission with full powers to continue and complete investigating the administration of the Department of Customs and Excise and to prosecute all offenders. . . ."

During the year following the election of September 14, 1926, the Royal Commission crisscrossed the country, hearing approximately fifteen million words of evidence. Shortly after the commission started its hearings and Sam realized its report was not likely to be a whitewash, the four Bronfman brothers gathered and burned all their personal and corporate papers for the preceding ten years. At its Winnipeg hearing, Inspector Cyril Knowles finally made public Harry Bronfman's bribery attempt at Gainsborough, Saskatchewan, six years and two months earlier. He also testified about another incident that eventually led to a charge against

Harry of attempting to obstruct justice by tampering
with witnesses.

Early in 1922, Knowles had been tipped off that
Southern Exports Limited, a Bronfman subsidiary in
Moose Jaw run by David Gallaman, Harry's brother-in-
law, was not only shipping booze south of the border
but had also been selling an unusually high quota of its
wares for local consumption. Knowles persuaded the
Saskatchewan Liquor Commission to stage a raid. One
of the men involved in planning the crackdown was
William St. John Denton, who happened at that time
to be working as one of the commission's enforcement
officers, though he later joined Zisu Natanson in the
rumrunning business and, later still, turned informer
and betrayed Natanson's bootlegging activities to the
police. The raid itself was carried out by two "special
agents" of the province's liquor commission called Her-
bert Clements and Douglas Readman, recruited straight
off Saskatoon's skid row. They had little trouble persuading Gallaman to sell them four bottles of booze.
The Saskatchewan Liquor Commission inspector in
charge of the operation checked in at a Moose Jaw
hotel during the transaction and promptly fell asleep.
He was awakened two hours later by his jolly confrères,
sheepishly confessing that they had consumed most of
the evidence. Undaunted by this turn of events, he
rushed over to the offices of Southern Exports, arrested
Gallaman, and seized the $30,000 worth of liquid
merchandise in his warehouse. As soon as Gallaman
was formally charged with bootlegging, Bronfman
countersued for the return of his impounded stock.

At this point, as in all the criminal proceedings
against the Bronfmans, different versions of the events
begin to emerge. According to Denton's later testimony
(denied by Harry), Bronfman had paid him $1,500 for
a promise to keep Clements and Readman out of the
province during the period of the bootlegging trial.
Denton is then supposed to have conducted the two
worthies on a drinking spree across the West, staying
for two weeks each at various Bronfman hotels in

Winnipeg and the Mariaggi at Port Arthur. Because of their absence, the case against Gallaman collapsed, and Harry got his booze back.

Early in 1928, the interim reports of the Royal Commission on Customs recommended immediate prosecution of Harry Bronfman on a charge of attempted bribery. Nothing happened. Ernest Lapointe, Mackenzie King's Minister of Justice, explained to a frustrated Conservative opposition that some of the Crown witnesses were ill, and, anyway, the whole matter was really the responsibility of Saskatchewan's attorney-general. T. C. Davis, the province's Liberal incumbent of that office, quickly turned himself into a willing partner in this game of legal tennis by lamely dismissing the issue as "being within federal jurisdiction."

At the same time, the political climate of Saskatchewan was rapidly turning more Conservative and much more anti-Semitic. Bootlegging at the time was Saskatchewan's most profitable business. That, and the Bronfmans' prominence in the trade, had easily been transmuted by the legions of frustrated Drys into virulent antipathy to "the Jews." As far back as the 1920 plebiscite on liquor control, Archdeacon G. E. Lloyd, an Anglican Dry who became Bishop of Saskatchewan in 1922, had focused in on racial origins as being proportionately misrepresented in the booze trade. "Of the forty-six liquor export houses in Saskatchewan," he calculated, "sixteen are owned and run by Jews. When the Jews form one half of one percent of the population, and own sixteen of the forty-six export houses, it is time they were given to understand that since they have been received in this country, and have been given rights enjoyed by other white men, they must not defile the country by engaging in disreputable pursuits." Shaken by the murder of Paul Matoff and by the increasingly noisy white-supremacist ravings of the Ku Klux Klan, which had begun to seep across the border from the United States, Saskatchewan's tiny Jewish population— and especially the Bronfmans—found themselves being turned into scapegoats for most of the province's economic and social problems.

In 1929, a Tory named J. T. M. Anderson capitalized on this prejudice. A former Ontario public-school teacher, Anderson had won only three seats in the 1925 election. But by deliberately gathering unto his party most of the constituencies of discontent, his brand of Conservatism was soon attracting a significant following. It was evident in the October 1928 Arm River by-election, when the Tory candidate declared that "the Liberal Party, at its very inception, entered into an alliance with organized liquor interests. As a result, Saskatchewan was turned into a bootlegger's paradise. The king of the bootleggers was Harry Bronfman, who is many times a millionaire. By him, prices were ordained and magistrates were instructed how to decree justice. Bronfman is alleged to have offered Inspector Knowles a bribe of three thousand dollars a month. What sum do you think he paid into the Liberal campaign fund for immunity from prosecution during the whole time he operated in Saskatchewan and amassed his millions?" In response, Davis, the Liberal Attorney-General, promised he would personally guarantee the prosecution of Bronfman, a pledge that helped the Liberal candidate win a bare majority in what had been an overwhelmingly Liberal riding.

When the provincial general election was called for June 6, the *Regina Daily Star* launched an editorial campaign advocating Bronfman's prosecution, which led off with this relatively moderate salvo:

It is now six months and 23 days since Attorney-General T. C. Davis pledged his word in the town hall in Craik to the Arm River electors that the prosecution of Harry Bronfman, wealthy Regina bootlegger, as recommended by the Royal Commission on the Customs Scandals, would be "carried through to the end." On that pledge the electors gave a majority to the Liberal candidate.
      What is the explanation of this betrayal? Is it

true that the Gardiner Government dare not prosecute this case for fear of consequences to itself? Has the machine a stranglehold on justice in Saskatchewan?

Anderson's Tories won twenty-four seats—enough, with the added support of the legislature's five Progressives and six independents, to let them form a government, ending two and half decades of Liberal administration. Murdo MacPherson, the new Attorney-General, wasted little time drawing up the charges against Bronfman. On November 28, 1929, two RCMP officers arrested Harry at his Montreal home. Without allowing him time to call Sam or Lazarus Phillips, they whisked him away to a Regina courtroom, where he was formally charged with attempted bribery and tampering with witnesses. When questioned about the unusual abruptness of Bronfman's arrest, MacPherson told the Saskatchewan legislature, "Does it matter? We said we'd get him. Now we've got him!"

Released on $50,000 bail, Harry gathered a team of the country's best legal talent, booked a suite at the Hotel Saskatchewan, and anxiously watched his lawyers search for the tactics that would free him from a possible eleven-year prison sentence. Their first ploy on the Knowles bribery charge not only backfired but also landed Bronfman in jail. Alex McGillivray, who masterminded the defense strategy, decided that the Crown's charges had been incorrectly laid, and that the way around them was to institute *habeas corpus* proceedings. This would remove the issue from the jurisdiction of Saskatchewan (where Bronfman's lawyers believed he couldn't get a fair hearing) and allowed the Supreme Court of Canada (which then enjoyed original jurisdiction in the application of *habeas corpus*) to make the ruling. McGillivray appeared before Mr. Justice Lyman Duff in Ottawa, filed his petition, and instructed Bronfman to give up bail—since the applicant for *habeas corpus* must be incarcerated, so that the judge can determine whether or not there exists a valid charge for continuing to hold the prisoner.

Meticulously briefed on this complicated maneuver and assured that Harry was safely tucked into a Regina jail, McGillivray and his colleagues appeared before Duff on December 17. They seemed to be convincing him, but for technical reasons the Supreme Court judge decided to put off his verdict until the following day. Instead, Duff went on one of his periodical benders and didn't return to the bench until two weeks later, leaving Bronfman pacing his cell in the interval. When he did return, Duff appeared to reverse himself and dismissed the application. Harry reapplied for bail, cursed his lawyers, and returned to his suite at the Hotel Saskatchewan to await the trial, which was eventually set for a courtroom in Estevan.

Because Harry's legal advisers remained certain he couldn't get a fair trial in Saskatchewan's prevailing political climate, they devised an unusual ruse to challenge the jurors brought forward by the Estevan sheriff, a well-known Conservative. Mark Shinbane, one of the Winnipeg lawyers for the defense, organized a group of juniors from his office to dress up as tractor salesmen. They called on most of the prospective jurors, pretending to be trading local gossip. One of the lawyers involved remembers a typical exchange: "I'd knock on the farmer's door and ask what was doing in town— seemed pretty quiet.

" 'Not for long,' would be the usual answer. 'Haven't you heard? Big trial's coming up. Harry Bronfman.'

" 'What's that all about?'

" 'He's the big bootlegger. Goddamn crook.'

" 'What's going to happen?'

" 'What's going to happen? He's going to be sent up for as long as I can damn well send him up. That's what's going to happen!' "

When the jury was being empaneled, McGillivray would ask each candidate whether he knew anything about the case or had any preconceived notions about the accused's guilt. Having confessed his total ignorance of the man and the issue, the juror would find himself confronted by the "tractor salesman" reading an affidavit of their previous conversation. Several jurors were promptly disqualified, but the subterfuge proved to be unnecessary when Cyril Knowles's Ottawa superiors took the stand and denied that the customs inspector had ever reported the bribery attempt to his superiors. The jury took only four hours to acquit a smiling Harry.

Dealing with the charge of tampering with witnesses took a little longer. The jury could not reach a verdict when the case was first heard in February 1930, and the trial was set over to September in Regina. William Denton was called in as the prosecution's main witness. In order to discredit him as a reliable source of testimony, Bronfman's lawyers set out to trap Denton in what may qualify as the earliest case of mechanical eavesdropping in Canadian legal history. Using an acquaintance of Denton's called William Saier as bait, they arranged for the two men to meet in a specially rigged room of the Wascana Hotel in Regina. Hidden in the ventilated closet were Fred Hand, an official court reporter, and two independent witnesses operating a crude dictaphone. This was the transcript of the conversation, later read into the court records:

Saier: What evidence can you give that's to the point?
Denton: I'm not telling it here. I'm not telling you what I know unless some arrangement is made.
Saier: You mean you're not going to tell me nothing till he gives you money?
Denton: No. I could do the trick for them, but I won't if they don't do business with me.
Saier: Everything will be all right if I can get from you . . .
Denton: You won't get anything from me until I get what I want.
Saier: If I tell them what you want, will you tell me the whole thing?

Denton: Yeah. I'll give it to you then. If they co-operate with me. I wouldn't let Harry down.

Saier: Tell me what you'll say now.

Denton: If I told you, they wouldn't pay me a damn cent.

Saier: They'll want you to say what you have in mind to clear Harry.

Denton: You come back with the money and I'll tell you.

Saier: You're asking about thirty grand?

Denton: For God's sake, don't mention that. It'll do.

Saier: It's Bronfman's money, and he thinks we should get something definite.

Denton: They'll get it just as quick as you give the money.

Saier: After you get the money will you tell them?

Denton: Yeah, I'm going to come clean and give them the information they want. I could've done it at the last trial.

Saier: Will you take two thousand now and the rest after the trial is over?

Denton: No. I want it all. Harry Bronfman, he knows damn well I could put him in jail. If he knows anything at all he knows I could turn around and get him out of it.

The exchange was more than enough to convince the court of Denton's unreliability and of the accused's innocence. Finally feeling himself relieved of the burden of his booze-running past, Harry Bronfman invited the jury that had rendered the verdict at his trial to the Hotel Saskatchewan suite where he had filled a bathtub full of whisky to celebrate his freedom.

BY THE FALL OF 1930, THE BRONFMANS WERE BE-GINNING TO FEEL the pinch of the Depression. Profits for DC-SL started to slide, the company postponed its stock offering and instead the Bronfmans and DCL had to pump loans of $4 million into the enterprise. On the West Coast, however, the Bronfmans combined with the two main Vancouver liquor-exporting operations, Consolidated Exporters and the Pacific Forwarding organization, owned by Henry Reifel and his sons, Harry and George, for one last grand fling in the bootlegging trade.

The major Vancouver supplier involved with Consolidated Exporters was United Distillers Limited. The Reifels ran their own export business to handle liquor from their B.C. Distillery, and the Reifels and Consolidated Exporters were both operating out of Tahiti to supply U.S. bootleggers when they joined forces with the Bronfmans in a sales agency set up under an agreement signed April 5, 1933. Capitalization of the new company, to be established in Papeete, capital of Tahiti, under the laws of the French territory, was 10,000 shares, to be assigned to the three parties in accordance with their liquor contributions. The stocks listed in the agreement include a full range of Canadian and Scotch whiskies, gins, American bourbons, European champagnes and liqueurs, worth $1,230,396.45 at distillery prices. Shipments from Vancouver and Europe were to be warehoused at Papeete and transshipped to a mother ship, either the five-masted schooner *Malahat* or the steamer *Lillehorn,* to be maintained in position as a floating liquor-and-wine shop off California or the west coast of Mexico. The pact was to run for a year, but with Repeal it was "game over," one distiller recalls.

Prohibition ended on December 5, 1933, but the lawsuits lingered on; the Canadian distillers faced smuggling charges at home and also had to settle with the U.S. government on taxes levied on Canadian liquor sales in the United States during the Prohibition years. On the West Coast the Reifel family took the lion's share of trouble. The Bronfman liquor agent from Winnipeg, Harry Sokol, turned up to haunt them. When Henry Reifel and his son George C. made a trip to the United States in July 1934, U.S. customs officers served secret warrants on them in Seattle; smuggling charges were added before they were able to leave town on bail of $100,000 each. The case didn't go to trial. In July 1935 the Reifels, who jumped bail, settled with the U.S. authorities for $500,000 plus the $200,000 in forfeited bonds. When the Reifels were pulled into court in Seattle, their lawyer contended that "there is spite work behind these arrests," and old acquaintances of Sokol agree. They say that Harry, who received a dollar a case on all liquor sold, was mad at the Reifels for sending what he called a bad lot of booze to one of his customers, and never forgot that a Reifel official answered his complaints by calling him "a goddamn Jew."

There is one small piece of circumstantial evidence that supports this theory. On Saturday, December 29, 1934, Harry Sokol held an elegant dinner party in the Oval Room of the old Hotel Vancouver. The dinner was in honor of R. P. Bonham, Chester A. Emerick, Joseph L. Green, and Sam E. Whitaker. Bonham was a U.S. immigration officer, Emerick and Green were U.S. customs men, and Whitaker was with the U.S. Justice Department—a list of the principal players in the arrest of the Reifels in July in Seattle. The U.S. government's payoff to Sokol reportedly was $350,000.

BELIEVING THAT THE GRUBBY DETAILS OF THEIR FORMATIVE SEASONS on the prairies had been buried at last, the Bronfmans settled into the life of Montreal millionaires, subscribing to all the right charities, throwing occasional parties at the Belvedere Palace, carefully beginning to sound out the social receptiveness of Westmount's bastions of WASPdom. The Ville La Salle plant had become one of the more profitable distilleries in the country, and instead of curtailing their business, the end of American Prohibition had catapulted them into the immensely lucrative U.S. market. But just as the change in Saskatchewan's political climate had brought troubles to Harry for alleged past irregularities, the reshuffling of the federal political scene was about to entrap the entire Bronfman clan in the legal battle of their lives.

In October 1927, a Calgary lawyer and millionaire named Richard Bedford Bennett was elected to the leadership of the Conservative Party. He seemed to be the answer to the Tories' regional frustrations: born in New Brunswick and with solid political roots in the West. A tall, commanding figure with a belly conditioned by years of good eating and a manner of dress that consisted of plug hat, tail coat, striped trousers, and shoes that glistened so hard they almost gloated, he was a humorless politician caught up in the conservative litany of genuinely believing that any man who couldn't make a decent living was either lazy or stupid. This proved to be a dangerous philosophy for a politician who was swept into power with the Great Depression. But Bennett never wavered from his belief that the country must tough it out, that the dollar must be kept sound and tariffs remain high, that, as he put it to a group of Toronto university students, "one of the greatest assets any man or woman can have upon entering on life's struggle is poverty." He acted like a supremely confident corporation lawyer who had taken on the government as his client for five years, stating his views with supreme self-confidence, "smashing out his words," as one contemporary observer put it.

As opposition leader, Bennett had repeatedly taunted Mackenzie King for not following up the report of the Royal Commission on Customs with all-out prosecution of the Bronfmans. Since those charges had been cleared up by Harry's trials in Saskatchewan, one of Bennett's first decisions after he beat King in the 1930 election was to launch a government investigation into the liquor-smuggling industry, then still flourishing out of St. Pierre and Miquelon. Although exports from the French islands to the United States were legal, it soon became evident that at least some of the outward-bound booze was finding its way back into the Canadian market, thus evading customs and excise duties. At the same time, the fortunes being made on St. Pierre, while nominally going to legitimate French dealers, were actually slipping out into Canadian distillers' pockets through a complex money-laundering operation through a branch of the Canadian Bank of Commerce.

On September 10, 1934, Lazarus Phillips telephoned his friend Sam to warn him that sources in Ottawa had confirmed that the four Bronfman brothers and Barney Aaron would be included in the indictments about to be brought down in Canada's largest smuggling prosecution. On December 12, the *Montreal Star* reported that "in five provinces of the Dominion and in the United States, the R.C.M.P. were last night trailing sixty-one Canadians against whom stands a blanket warrant charging them with conspiracy to evade payment of more than $5 million in customs duties on smuggled liquor. Included in the list of accused are the four Bronfman brothers and their brother-in-law, Barney Aaron." The same day, the Montreal *Gazette* in a dispatch from Ottawa hinted that "nothing was left undone in recent weeks to call off the proceedings. Lawyers for the accused were known to be here frequently, but the issue of warrants last evening shows their representations to have been unavailing." Superintendent F. J. Mead, head of the Mounties' Quebec division, called the first press conference of his life to announce that "this affair has indications of being the biggest case in the history of the Royal Canadian Mounted Police. Its ramifications extend from Prince Edward Island to British Columbia, our investigations to date have shown."

Six days later, the Bronfman brothers and Barney Aaron were arrested—for years afterward, Seagram's competitors distributed photographs of "the Bronfman boys" being led out of the Peel Street offices—and taken to RCMP headquarters for photographing and fingerprinting by Inspector F. W. Zaneth, then driven in a police convoy to the Montreal Court of King's Bench chambers, where they were granted bail. Bail was set at $100,000 for each of the Bronfmans but at only $15,000 for Barney Aaron, their brother-in-law, who never quite recovered from this indignity. Safely back in their Westmount mansions, awaiting preliminary hearings, they began to feel the consequences. Rumors were circulating in Ottawa that the government's suit for the $5 million in unpaid customs duties was only the first of several charges against the alleged conspirators and that a further claim for evading $70 million in excise taxes was about to be launched. Dun & Bradstreet removed their credit rating. Price Waterhouse and Company, Seagram's auditors, had the rare experience of having to prepare their statements from account books seized and lodged at the local RCMP headquarters.

For their legal defense, the Bronfmans recruited what Mark Shinbane, the Winnipeg counsel who was part of it, called "a minor Bar convention." The trial got under way on January 11, 1935, with the accused, all sixty-one of them, occupying the whole of the public benches on one side of the courtroom. The two prosecutors (James Crankshaw and J. J. Penverne) with their scarlet-tunicked RCMP assistants took up the usual row of lawyers' desks, leaving the defense force (which eventually grew to an even dozen plus a lawyer charged with keeping a watching brief for the Bank of Montreal) to overflow into the usual "newspaper row," so that reporters covering the trial ended up seated in the jury box. In charge of proceedings was Judge Jules Desmarais, a former president of Montreal's Liberal-associated Reform Club.

THE BRONFMANS WERE UP FIRST. Proceedings got under way with the calling to the witness stand of Dudley Oliver, manager of the Bank of Montreal's branch at St. Catherine and Drummond streets, who filed thirty documents relating to the corporate accounts of the Atlas Shipping Company, which was listed as being simultaneously domiciled in St. Pierre and Miquelon, Bermuda, Saint John, New Brunswick, and Belize, British Honduras. Also produced were the banking transactions of Brintcan Investments, the

Bronfman family holding company. The bank documents revealed that during the preceding twelve months $3,055,166 had been transferred from Atlas Shipping's St. Pierre operations to the Brintcan account.

The Crown charged the Bronfmans with "conspiring to violate the statutes of a friendly country," which in laymen's language meant smuggling. "It would be fantastic," Bronfman lawyer Aimé Geoffrion countered, "for the courts of the province of Quebec to administer the laws of the United States. The prosecution should talk less about smuggling and prove some of it. . . . We are not prepared to permit that the court be used as a royal commission on our business in general, allowing . . . [the prosecution] to fish around among the evidence and put any and all facts before the public at their own selection."

Referring to the bank documentation, Geoffrion challenged the Crown to prove that a smuggling conspiracy had actually taken place:

> A general inquiry by the police, which may have been conducted privately, is bound to create prejudice against us, regardless of the manner in which it was conducted, and if it develops from the proof that we or others are guilty of contraband charges in Canada, that is not proof of the charges of smuggling into another country, and vice versa. . . . I cannot see how the Crown can argue that conspiracy to commit a crime in the United States is a crime in Canada. It would be strange if conspiracy to commit a crime in Berlin would be punishable here as an indictable offence. . . .

Crankshaw, for the prosecution, replied that the introduction of the bank letters was necessary to show that these large sums of money were transferred from the Atlas Shipping Company for the purpose of financing the smuggling of liquor back into Canada:

I will admit that some of these moneys were used for the purpose also of smuggling liquor into the United States. We cannot divide these moneys—the operations were so extensive that there is no way of dividing them. Some of these transactions were for shipments from Canada and back into Canada directly through the financing of these people. Some of them actually took place the same day—a shipment left the port of exportation both for Canada and for the United States.

There followed this exchange between the judge and the attending lawyers:

Judge: Can you prove there was smuggling into Canada?

Crankshaw: Yes.

Geoffrion: Then do it.

Crankshaw: In order to make our proof of conspiracy between Mrs. Carline* and the Bronfmans we have to introduce this evidence. If there were $3,000,000 sent down in one year for her to handle and from Halifax back up here, we cannot tell you whether there was $1,000,000 that went into the United States or $2,000,000, or vice versa into Canada, but we can tell you there is a large amount going into both. . . . And when it comes to the case of the Atlas company, which is entirely owned by four of the accused persons—it has an office in Halifax and it was from the Halifax office that it was managed by another person accused—they were chartering 20, 30 or 40 boats, and it was through these boats chartered by the Atlas company, and through the crews on these boats, all paid by [the] Atlas company, that smuggling was done into Canada and into the United States.

---

* Evelyn Carline, treasurer of Atlas Shipping and owner of one share in the company. The balance of the stock was held by the Bronfmans and Aaron.

It soon developed that the prosecution's case was
fatally weakened by the fact that when the RCMP had
raided the Seagram headquarters to confiscate the
books of Atlas Shipping and Brintcan, the Bronfman
family trust, no documents could be found. H. G. Norman, the Montreal manager of Price Waterhouse, who
had carried out the last audit of the two companies at
1430 Peel Street, vaguely remembered seeing entries
such as "Maude Thornhill—$1,472" (and assuming
that Maude was a schooner, rather than a lady) but
could shed no light on the present whereabouts of the
corporate records, except that they had been in charge
of David Costley, Brintcan's secretary-treasurer.

A former Bank of Montreal branch manager from
Regina, David Costley remains a mystery figure in the
Bronfman saga. A large, stout man who always acted as
if he were privy to the secrets of the deep, he hit the
bottle following the 1935 trials and eventually suffered
a serious head concussion when a streetcar hit the bus
he had been traveling on, though he continued to work
for the Bronfmans. His wife recalled her husband's
leaving home for a baseball game on September 8,
1942. She never saw him again. His body was found
floating in the St. Lawrence the following day, and
there was widespread speculation in Montreal at the
time that he had either fallen off or been pushed from
the Victoria Bridge. She was not permitted to view the
body, even for identification purposes, and told a friend
afterward, "It was a heavily guarded situation, and I
still think it has something to do with David burning
those papers in his basement."

Costley's cellar was searched, but nothing turned up.
The prosecution lawyers found themselves challenged
on nearly every point they tried to make by the Bronfman lawyers, taunting them to prove their case by
producing the figures—all contained in the missing
books. Tempers became so heated that at one point
Clifford Harvison, then an RCMP corporal who had
spent two years working on the case, barked at Philippe

Brais, "You should be in Hollywood!" The Bronfman
defense lawyer shouted back, "Go to hell, Harvison!"

At this point, the prosecution called a surprise
witness to step forward and testify. Louis Minsk, a
driver employed by the Bronfmans, recalled that one
afternoon in August 1934 he had executed an errand
at David Costley's behest: "He told me to take some
stuff from the office to his house at 3423 Oxford
Avenue. . . ." Minsk recalled that his cargo had consisted of six burlap bags, that Costley had accompanied
him in the truck, that he had left his load at the cellar
door of the house in the Montreal suburb of Notre
Dame de Grace, and that Costley had stayed at home
to carry the bags into his basement. Could he tell the
court what was in the bags? Minsk looked around the
breathless chamber and replied, "It was packages of
some sort that sounded like bundles of paper to me."

It was Harvison who produced the trial's most colorful witness in the person of Captain Alfred J. "Big
Fred" Lévesque, an ex-bootlegger who recounted the
details of his several trips up the Gulf of St. Lawrence,
smuggling booze for the Bronfmans. On one voyage he
skippered the *Tremblay* on a run from St. Pierre to
Rivière du Loup when he discovered that a thousand
gallons of his cargo of eight thousand gallons of alcohol
had turned rusty in the cast-iron drums.

> *Judge:* Were the excise duties paid?
> *Lévesque:* Not by me.
> *Judge:* How were you reimbursed for the rusty
>   alcohol?
> *Lévesque:* Abe Bronfman told me to filter it
> through a loaf of bread.

Despite such testimony linking the Bronfmans with
the smuggling operations from St. Pierre into Canada
as well as the United States, when Judge Desmarais
delivered his verdict on June 15, 1935, he threw the
case out of court.

The judgement read in part: "The Crown claims

that the accused opened agencies in Newfoundland and St. Pierre et Miquelon that were useless for any purpose other than smuggling and that sales made there to Canadians constituted proof of illegal conspiracy, yet the accused had every legal right to organize these agencies in the interest of their business. It is well known that at that time a great number of Canadian distilleries organized themselves to sell outside of Canada as many of their products as they could. This mode of action certainly contains no illegality as far as Canada is concerned. . . . The agencies sold liquor to all who would buy and these acts were legal in the countries in which they operated. They were not obliged to verify the destination of the goods they sold, nor was there any obligation upon them to inquire of the buyers what they intended to do with their goods. Once sold the goods were the property of the buyer and the accused could exercise no further control over their disposal. . . . It does not appear in the evidence that the accused did anything whatever to assist in importing liquor into Canada and the proof establishes against them the commission of no criminal act. I am of the opinion that there is not, *prima facie*, proof of conspiracy as alleged, and the accused are herewith discharged."

Lazarus Phillips, who had directed tactics for the defense, was rewarded with 1,000 free shares of Seagram's stock. The RCMP had grown so suspicious of Judge Desmarais's behavior that on the morning after the trial ended they subpoenaed his bank records and raided his safety-deposit box. No incriminating evidence was discovered. The judge later became chairman of the Quebec Liquor Commission.

8. Oh! To Be a Bronfman

WITH THE Montreal trial safely behind them, the Bronfmans exploded into activity. It was as if lightning had suddenly come sharking down from the sky, setting them free at last from the constraints of the haunting past, illuminating new spaces and potentials in their personal lives and business prospects. No longer afraid of having the revelation of some brooding secret spoil their progress, they launched Seagram's on the curve of exponential growth that during the next two decades would turn their modest Canadian distillery into a great multinational corporation.

Their business past could be construed as a series of lucky accidents, with the bounce of each experience leading to another and the angle of the bounce (or, in the Bronfmans' case, the nature of the latest twist in government anti-liquor legislation) determining the direction of their various ventures. Now that was all behind them. No longer operating at society's gritty margin as suppliers to bootleggers and their criminal allies, the brothers for the first time realized the liberating absence of guilt. At last they felt strong, proud, and ready.

By the dawn of 1933 it was becoming evident that American Prohibition, which was in any case close to becoming a legal fiction, could not last much longer.

139

In his preliminary voyages of discovery south of the border to see how he could grab the largest possible share of the market once liquor sales had again been made legal, Sam Bronfman had become enthralled by an American distiller named Lew Rosenstiel.* The largest shareholder in Schenley and its unquestioned boss, he had spent Prohibition jobbing booze out of St. Pierre and Bermuda into Cincinnati, his hometown. During his frequent visits to Montreal, Rosenstiel worked out a plan for a partnership with Sam, designed to combine his knowledge of the U.S. market with the Bronfman interests' financial clout (and aging stocks of whiskies), plus the prestige of the DCL distilleries' brands in Scotland. Foreseeing the end of Prohibition, Sam had decided in 1928, when Seagram's was merged with the Bronfman distillery holdings, that once Americans had satisfied their initial thirst, they would demand the quality of properly aged whiskies. He began curtailing his Canadian sales to lay production down in barrels to await the legal opening of the U.S. market. When Prohibition was repealed, his was the largest available stock of mellowed liquor. In the process, the Bronfmans acquired 20 percent of the stock of Schenley, whose lines included the renowned Golden Wedding brand of rye.

Late in 1933, Sam and Allan went overseas to discuss their proposed merger with Schenley's and make final preparations with the DCL board for a joint assault

---

* Lewis Rosenstiel took the name of the hometown of a distillery at Schenley, Pennsylvania, for his company and built it into a nationally known brand in much the way Sam Bronfman made the name of an Ontario distillery known the world over. Western Pennsylvania has been noted for its rye whisky since colonial days, and the Whisky Rebellion that broke out in 1791 in the early days of the American Republic had its start in the region. Farmers and other small distillers regarded the excise tax of that year as an infringement on their rights and refused to pay it. The insurrection collapsed in 1794 when its leaders fled at the approach of militia units from four states. The troops had been dispatched by President George Washington, himself a minor distiller.

on the U.S. market. Their reception by the Scots was not what they expected. After Sam had outlined the glowing prospects of American liquor consumption, William Henry Ross, speaking for the DCL board, frigidly rejected any notion that the mighty DCL needed a partner to share in the rich spoils of re-entering the U.S. market. "Besides," added Ross, "I think you should know that we will not, under any circumstances, be associated with Mr. Rosenstiel."

Recalling the real circumstances of the rejection by the Scottish distillers, which was based on the embarrassment they might have suffered in the United States by being associated with the Bronfman name, Maxwell Henderson later remarked that "the worst day's business the distillers of Edinburgh ever did was not to have gone into the American market with Sam. They thought they knew best, that their association with the likes of Bronfman was all right for a country like Canada, but not for the really big time."

The Bronfman brothers returned to Canada, raised $4 million to buy out the DCL holding in Distillers Corporation—Seagrams Limited, and launched themselves headlong into the American market. Sam heard that the Rossville Union Distillery in Lawrenceburg, Indiana, was for sale, and by November he had it—and $2,399,000 in cash—in exchange for 172,623 DC-SL treasury shares, and set up Joseph E. Seagram and Sons Incorporated to run it. Rosenstiel suggested a fifty-fifty partnership in the U.S. market, but the chances of a merger vanished when Bronfman visited the Schenley plant and discovered that Golden Wedding was being bottled "hot," right out of the stills with no aging. That might have been *de rigueur* back at the Yorkton bottling works in Saskatchewan, but Sam was playing in a different league now. Rosenstiel and Bronfman broke up in a memorable stand-up shouting match, challenging each other for dominance in the U.S. market, then parted company forever. Schenley held the top position until 1937, lost it to Seagram's

for the next seven years, briefly regained it into 1947,
and has lagged behind ever since.

The Canadian company's 1933 annual meeting was
moved up to January 31, 1934, "due to the absence
of your Directors in connection with your Company's
plans for the American market." The resignation of
Ross and the election of Samuel Bronfman to the
presidency of DC-SL were announced at the meeting,
and all that was left of the DCL connection were the
old DCL hand Billy Cleland and licensing arrangements
giving Sam the rights to several DCL brands in Canada.

From their new American headquarters in New
York's Chrysler Building, the Bronfmans established a
banking connection with Manufacturers Trust Company
(merged with Hanover Bank in 1961 to become Manufacturers Hanover Trust Company) and bought the
Calvert distillery in Relay, Maryland, for 70,016 treasury shares in 1934. The Calvert deal was handled by
Emil Schwarzhaupt, perhaps the most experienced corporate whisky trader in the United States, who later
recalled that Sam "was one of the smartest men I ever
did business with. I intended to trade Calvert for the
stiffest price I could get out of him. But he threw it
all back to me and said, 'You set the price, and whatever it is, it's a deal.'" Schwarzhaupt was left to figure
out a price that Sam couldn't refuse. Sam accepted
that price without question, and Schwarzhaupt—who
had become Schenley's second-largest shareholder by
selling his Bernheim Distilling Company in Louisville
(I.W. Harper bourbon) to Rosenstiel's company—was
ever afterward rueful about the Calvert deal. Sam
imported Seagram's aged Canadian stock to blend with
his newly acquired American distillates and introduced
his whiskies under the Five Crown and Seven Crown
labels. In the fall of 1934, a Seagram ad in the United
States proclaimed: "Thanks a million! Seagram sales
are breaking all records." Two years later the Calvert
brands were introduced with a $2.5-million advertising
campaign. The project that required the largest capital
outlay was construction of the new $5-million distillery

at Louisville, Kentucky, the showcase plant for the whole industry, which was officially opened during Derby Week in 1937. When the Bronfmans marked their fourth anniversary in the American market, they had about 60 million gallons of whisky aging in wood at their three U.S. plants.

What made the Bronfman business boom were some important differences in Sam's approach to the manufacture and marketing of his brands. Instead of selling freshly distilled, unmixed liquors like bourbon or straight rye, the Bronfman brands were well aged and carefully blended. Blending became a Seagram's hallmark. Sam had a formal description of the process ("The art of successfully combining a large number of meticulously selected, mature, high-quality whiskies, each with its own flavour and other desirable characteristics, in such a skillful and judicious manner that the whole is better than the sum of its parts and that each makes its own significant contribution to the finished blend without any one, however good, predominating"), a short definition ("Distilling is a science; blending is an art"), and a real explanation ("Look, when a man goes into a store for a bottle of Coca-Cola, he expects it to be the same today as it will be tomorrow. The same with Canada Dry ginger ale or Wrigley's chewing gum. The great products don't change. Well, goddammit, our product's not going to change either"). Seagram's maintains "blending libraries" at its offices in New York, Montreal, and Paisley, near Glasgow, where samples of the company's 1,200 different types of straight whiskies concurrently aging in various warehouses are constantly catalogued and tested.

The resultant "lightness" in taste captured the palates of American drinkers so fast that by the end of 1934, Five Crown had become the best-selling whisky in the country. At the same time, the Bronfmans were revolutionizing liquor-marketing patterns. Unlike most American distillers who sold their products to local rectifiers in barrel consignments, losing control over their final products, Seagram's followed the Scottish tradition of selling their whiskies in the bottle to consumers through a network of distributors, maintaining the kind of quality controls that build brand loyalty.

One of the important connections made by Sam in New York (on the advice of Lazarus Phillips) was with J. M. Hartfield, a partner in the law firm of White and Case. It was Hartfield who recommended a New York executive with experience in the trucking and warehousing industry, James Friel, to take charge of administration for the new distilling company. Jim Friel joined Seagram's in 1934 as treasurer, and when he moved up to chief administrative officer of the main U.S. subsidiary, Friel's son Joe, who had also started at Seagram's in 1934, took over as treasurer.

The other major presence in Seagram's U.S. launch, Frank Schwengel, simply walked in from the street. Schwengel, a brigadier general in the U.S. Army Reserve, was working as a Chicago adman when he came to pitch Sam for Seagram's advertising account. The two men took an instant liking for each other and the general found himself heading the distillery's fledgling U.S. sales organization.

Sam set a 1934 target of five million cases (about 15 percent of the total market) and Schwengel applied his army training to recruit a national distribution network in record time. He invited the 175 distributors he had picked to the ballroom of the Waldorf-Astoria Hotel just before launching the Crown brands and told them, "We're going with two blended whiskies and we're going to make them the first national brands in history!"

"It was chaotic after Repeal," Schwengel later recalled. "Whisky was being sold like a commodity. The price was whatever someone said it was. What we did was figure back from the retail price we decided was acceptable. Then we figured profits for the store owner, for the wholesaler, and what was left over was for us. We were fearful of selling direct or to department stores under any condition. We wanted to use the mom-and-pop stores to establish a reputation for our brand; the others could dictate to you. Our policy from the outset was to give liquor franchises to wholesalers that would give them a guaranteed fair margin of profit. Of course, that meant something like price-fixing."

Because Seagram's could maintain its marketing strategy only by rigidly enforcing its price-fixing policies, a Chicago retailer eventually took the company to court. Much to their competitors' amazement, Seagram's won, and the U.S. Supreme Court later reaffirmed the ruling, allowing Bronfman to set retail prices. As a result, Seven Crown became one of the most profitable products ever marketed in the United States, its margins comparable with those of Coca-Cola and Gillette razor blades.

Introduced in the summer of 1934 and backed with big-budget advertising campaigns, by the end of October, Five Crown and Seven Crown were selling so fast that Sam decided to launch a series of ads apparently designed to reduce drinking. "WE WHO MAKE WHISKEY SAY: DRINK MODERATELY" was the headline of the full-page message that appeared in 150 U.S. papers, with fine print subtly hinting that anyone who felt he had to drink ought to be sipping Seagram's products: "The real enjoyment which whisky can add to the pleasures of gracious living is possible only to the man who drinks good whiskey and drinks moderately. The House of Seagram does not want a dollar that should be spent for the necessities of life." Some 150,000 congratulatory letters and telegrams poured into Seagram's head office from Wets and Drys alike in what was the most successful advertising slogan of its day. A follow-up campaign was based on "Men of Distinction" who allowed themselves to be photographed savoring Lord Calvert whisky. They were paid a $1,000 honorarium which, it was assumed, would be sent in their names to a charity of their choice—all except for the president of a Minnesota steel company who insisted that his favorite charity was the bank account of his son-in-law.

By the end of the 1936 fiscal year, Seagram's sales, whipped along by General Schwengel, were up to $60

million, plus another $10 million in Canada. Sam
seemed to be running everything, though Harry was
still an important influence in the construction and
maintenance of the American manufacturing facilities.
Allan was being relegated to the role of senior executive assistant in Sam's office, while Abe was slowly
withdrawing from active management to desultory dealings in Montreal real estate.

Wartime restrictions on the production of grain alcohol didn't make even a temporary dent in the company's progress. By 1948, sales topped $438 million to
produce a net after-tax profit of $53.7 million. Sea-
gram's multiplied itself through a rampage of acquisitions.

One of the most significant moves was the partnership Mr. Sam established with Franz Sichel, which got
Seagram's into the wine business. The two men had
first met in Germany during a 1932 tour Sam and
Saidye had taken to celebrate their tenth wedding anniversary. Escaping from Hitler in 1942, Sichel found
himself in Montreal with no way of getting back into
his trade as a vintner. Bronfman sent him to California
in search of a small wine company. There the refugee
met Alfred Fromm, the former operator of a winery
in Bingen, Germany, who had established an association with the Christian Brothers, an internationally re-
spected religious order whose California adherents were
producing some fine local vintages. Bronfman agreed
to market their products and bought for Fromm and
Sichel a small winery called Mont Tivey. He instructed
them to be sure that their wine labels featured a mountain. When Sichel reported that the Tivey vineyards
were all in the valley, Mr. Sam ordered him to "buy
a goddamn mountain." He got one by acquiring for
Seagram's the renowned Paul Masson vineyards in the
Santa Cruz range above Saratoga, southwest of San
Jose. Seagram's sales of U.S. domestic wines have since
become a profitable sideline.

It was the restriction placed on manufacturing raw
alcohol during World War II that first pushed Mr. Sam

into a search for a major source of overseas supplies. His first small venture was to import rum from Puerto Rico and Jamaica, where he bought the Long Pond estate to produce his own sugarcane. Maxwell Henderson became Mr. Sam's chief agent in arranging the financing for acquisition of several West Indian distilleries, which eventually introduced the Captain Morgan, Myers's, Woods, and Trelawny labels into the Seagram stable. Henderson later helped negotiate the financing for the purchase of the Chivas Brothers grocery business in Aberdeen. The shops possessed a royal warrant that Mr. Sam hoped to apply to the quality, twelve-year-old Scotch being turned out in the firm's two small distilleries. By dealing with a bankrupt opera impresario who had been unsuccessfully trying to make a go of the liquor side of the business, Seagram's eventually bought out the whole operation for only £80,000. Through clever promotion and careful quality control, Chivas Regal has since become the world's largest-selling deluxe Scotch whisky.

Quintin Peter Jermy Gwyn, who was vice-president of Seagram Overseas Corporation, recalls the building up of the Chivas brand:

A few years after World War II, Seagram's acquired the ownership of Chivas Brothers for a modest sum and it was Mr. Sam's intention to make Chivas Regal the greatest name in Scotch whisky. This involved a vast plan of buildings such as warehouses, distillery, offices, etc., and above all a period of maturing for at least twelve years before the brand was ready to be put on the market. I still recall an historic meeting with Mr. Sam when we discussed the eventual world-market possibilities for Chivas Regal. I submitted my modest estimates, which were immediately set aside by him as quite inadequate, and he gave his own, which were much greater. But the eventual sales have exceeded even his estimates. This was not just a man marketing a new product—it was an artist producing his *chef-d'oeuvre*. It was this sense of dedication which characterized his work, explained his tensions and frustrations—it also explained his successes.

Other overseas acquisitions followed. In France, Seagram's bought control of Mumm's Champagne (with its twelve *miles* of cellars); Perrier-Jouët Champagne (which had been the favorite of Queen Victoria and the Emperor Napoleon and remains the official supplier of champagnes to the Vatican); Barton & Guestier, one of the world's largest wine shippers; and Augier Frères.*

While he was building up the empire, Mr. Sam carefully divided his place of official residence between Canada and the United States. Under the internal-revenue rules that then applied, an annual total of six months and a day lived within American jurisdiction would have made him liable to U.S. income tax. "Sam played both ends against the middle," Max Henderson recalls. "He used to move between New York and Montreal on the D&H trains out of Windsor Station in Montreal almost every night of the week. Sam and Allan kept the Canadian and American ends of the company separate with only the two of them straddling the fence, so that nobody could ever give evidence against them. They were strictly Canadian when there was trouble in the States and vice versa. I well remember when the U.S. Internal Revenue Alcohol Tax unit came up to Montreal complaining about the unfair competition Canadians were giving American distillers. So Mr. Sam spent two whole months living in Westmount, very much the Canadian. When the situation changed, they were all down in Washington arguing the other way. Oh, they were fantastic!"

One of Mr. Sam's favorite acquisitions in the exhilarating decade after the war was United Distillers

---

* For a list of Seagram's brands, see Appendix I.

Limited, a British Columbia company whose assets included the Harrison Hot Springs Hotel and a Royal Canadian Navy fairmile that had been converted into the luxurious cabin cruiser *Harwood*. The yacht had been sold to George and Harry Reifel, members of another distilling group, and renamed *Casa Mia* not long before Seagram's bought UDL in 1953, but Mr. Sam liked to use an incident involving the *Harwood* to bolster his bias against boats in general. He cited an accident that had occurred in the late 1940s when the *Harwood* was on a trip along the British Columbia coast: a fire broke out around the funnel, without serious threat to Charles and his uncle Allan, who were among the passengers. A year after the UDL purchase, Edgar fell and cut his thigh on a boat's propeller when he was water-skiing at Saranac Lake. That was enough for Mr. Sam. "No more boats," he declared. "They all either catch fire or they cut you up—one or the other. So no more boats."

He stayed away from all forms of water transportation until he found himself invited to board the private yacht of the Goddard family in Barbados during his seventy-ninth birthday celebrations. Constant in his determination not to venture out on the water, he had gone on board the thirty-seven-foot ketch to send the other members of the party off for a day's sail around the island when the captain unexpectedly cast off. "What the hell's going on here?" Sam demanded. "Why aren't we still tied up to the dock?"

He was finally persuaded that, since the hurricane season was well behind them, nothing was likely to disturb the outing, and agreed to remain on board. Five miles out, a sudden tropical squall came out of the western sky, deluging the sailboat with rain torrents and waves of salty spray. "To hell with this," Mr. Sam muttered to no one in particular. "I knew these goddamn fools I'm associated with would get me into trouble. Goddamn boat."

He donned two oilskin jackets, squanched down in

the aft cockpit, making a kind of waterproof Indian tepee out of himself, and didn't emerge until the boat was safely docked back in Bridgetown. The only visible sign of life was the occasional extension of an arm out of this strange apparition, jiggling an empty glass, demanding "more V.O. and soda."

9. The Death of a Titan

SAM BRONFMAN liked to think of himself as a Shakespearean actor performing in a play within a play, cast as the central character around whom the action revolves. But in the last sad decade of his long life, it became clear even to his faithful but dwindling retinue of friends and admirers that although he remained possessed of an inner force of will that could still frighten anyone who dared oppose him, he lacked those dimensions of soul that might have lent his death the poetic grandeur of a great man's passing. Finally weary of the travel and the din, tired of all the deals, the forced smiles and exaggerated handshaking, he seemed to be shrinking into himself, not trusting anybody very much, keeping to his beloved Belvedere Palace at the top of Westmount to brood about his awesome success and its slim rewards.

Anyone watching him poke about his mansion, a bent silhouette against the dusk of his days, would have found it hard to picture the Sam Bronfman of fifty years before—the lean, shrewd whisky trader out of Winnipeg who still knew the pleasures of achievement, dreamed big dreams, and felt certain that enough money would someday buy him the social legitimacy for which he even then so desperately yearned. Now he was wealthy beyond his wildest expectations, still

powerful, but somehow diminished by the very ostentation of his surroundings. Occasionally, when he felt
particularly alone, Sam would stand next to the Rembrandt self-portrait that Saidye had bought for him and
whisper to the canvas, "You dirty old man, you haven't
had a bath for a very long time."

Everything in the house was of museum quality.
There was no single object its owner might have bought
when he was young, nothing to remind him of the
wilder shores of his entrepreneurial beginnings, no
snapshots or mementoes that dated back to the rumrunning days, his time as a hotelkeeper, or the years of
struggle to turn Seagram's from a foundering distillery
into a business empire. The past went unrecorded as
if none of it had ever happened, as if he had been to this
grand manner born, as if there had always been a Monet,
a Chagall, a Degas, and a Rembrandt in his drawing
room. He would walk about, touching the fine furniture
and the valuable ornaments, looking out at the high
wall made of worn stones that separated the Bronfman
compond from the city shimmering below.

But, pretend as he might, Sam Bronfman remained
an exile in a foreign land. When a faithful retainer
brought in galleys of the official Seagram history composed for publication in the company's 1970 annual
report, Sam lashed out, "This is so much bullshit. If I
only told the truth, I'd sell ten million copies."

He spent an inordinate amount of energy studying
the life of Napoleon and could recite details of Bona-
parte's military maneuvers, particularly at the Battle of
Marengo. His most treasured historical memento was a
portfolio that had belonged to the French dictator,
given him by Joseph Davies, a former American ambassador to the U.S.S.R.

Bronfman maintained a limited social life, having deliberately cut himself off from most former business
associates, but his continued philanthropy made him
a kind of magnet for anyone in trouble. When a lion
escaped from the Belmont amusement park in the north
end of Montreal and bit a woman, Sam, who had

learned nothing at all of the incident, answered the
house telephone to hear this strange complaint: "It's
about the woman who was bitten by the lion. . . ."

"What lion? Here, in Montreal?"

"I'm from Kenya, and I was bitten by a lion too. . . ."

"Two lions? How many goddamn lions are there?
What's [Mayor] Jean Drapeau doing about it?"

"The doctors treated me badly and now I'm crip-
pled."

"Lions, on the streets of Montreal?" Sam kept asking. And then he had a terrible thought: *"Are there
any in Westmount?"*

"I've called the Jewish General Hospital, but they
won't listen."

"Madam, as far as I'm concerned, this is a matter to
be settled between you and the lions. Good day."

Click.

Most of the many calls for his help received a kinder
reception from Sam, who continued to dominate the
Canadian Jewish Congress and all its works. He was
particularly active during Israel's Six-Day War, when
he summoned Canada's Jewish leaders to the Montreal
Montefiore Club for a pep talk and set their combined
campaign target at $20 million—an unheard-of total
which they promptly exceeded. He drove himself re-
lentlessly coordinating the national effort and flew to
Ottawa with his old friend Sol Kanee of Winnipeg, the
1967 Congress president, to plead with Prime Minister
Lester Pearson for Canadian support of Israel at the
United Nations.

"Sam is looking pretty exhausted that day," Kanee
recalls. "We're in a cab on the way to the PM's office
when all of a sudden he collapses. I bend down over
him and can't feel any breath. Nothing. So I have the
taxi wheel around to where a police car is parked and
demand that an ambulance be called. I keep thinking,
'Oh, Sam, you can't do this to me. How am I going to
tell Saidye?' Then I hear this snort, and there's Sam
coming around. When the ambulance arrives, he refuses to get into it and kicks up such a fuss, calling me,

among other things, a useless son of a bitch, that we finally ride to the Riverside Hospital with me on the stretcher in the back and Sam sitting up beside the driver. When we get there, he sends an orderly out to buy a bottle of Chivas, which the three of us promptly demolish. Meanwhile, Abe Mayman, his private doctor, has flown in from Montreal, but Sam's too busy cursing everybody, especially me, for what happened.

"That night, after we've seen Mike Pearson, we go back to Montreal, and I stay at Belvedere because I'm flying to Moscow the next morning. When I try to sneak out of the house without saying goodbye to him, Saidye stops me.

" 'Aren't you saying goodbye to Sam?'

" 'No. To hell with him. I'm not saying goodbye to him ever again.'

" 'Oh,' she says, 'you're such old friends.'

" 'I don't give a damn. Not after what he did to me yesterday.'

" 'Do it for me.'

" 'Fine. For you.'

"I go upstairs and stand at the door of his bedroom, without a word. Sam is propped up in bed, reading a newspaper. He doesn't look up, but quietly says, 'We've been friends a long time, Sol.'

" 'I would have thought so.'

" 'Well, we're still friends.'

" 'Sure, but the next time you call me a son of a bitch will be the last time you have the privilege of calling me anything.'

" 'Nobody can be a friend of mine if I can't call him a son of a bitch. . . .' "

"Well," Kanee fondly concludes, "how could I stay mad at a crazy bugger like that?"

ONE OF SAM'S FEW INTERNATIONAL FORAYS IN HIS DECLINING YEARS was a brief journey to Ireland. It was Saidye who first broached the subject to Michael Mc-Cormick during an Expos' game at Jarry Park.

"Mike, you know all about Ireland, eh?"

"I know a little bit. I've been there many times."

"Well, I've never been there, and I want to go. So you work on Sammy Boy and I'll work on him, and we'll all go."

"Now, Mrs. Bronfman, I learned years ago not to tell your husband where to go or what to do. So you work on him, and if you get him convinced, that's fine. We'll all go to Ireland."

Next morning Sam was on the phone, bright and early, to McCormick. "What's all this horseshit about us going to Ireland? Why are you trying to talk my wife into this trip?"

"I'm not."

"Who is? She wants to go."

"So I understand."

"Well, we're bloody well not going. We have no business in Ireland and it's a goddamned fool place. Okay?"

But the following day a sheepish Sam returned to the subject. "Mike, if we went to Ireland, how long would we have to stay?"

Finally the trip was arranged, with both McCormick and Jack Clifford going along in Seagram's large private jet. "But," Sam insisted, "be sure that goddamned hostess isn't on the plane."

Sam's aversion to the company's stewardess dated from a night in 1962 when he was flown from New York to Montreal in a Seagram plane. When she asked him for his hat and coat, he refused to hand them over and insisted on pouring his own drinks. He kept peering at her over the top of his newspaper and finally demanded, "Tell me, Miss, are you a lady pilot?" When she explained that she was the hostess, he asked for an outline of her duties, and as soon as the plane landed, even before he got his coat on, rushed to an airport pay phone and bawled Edgar out for wasting company money by employing people to perform such useless tasks. On the Irish trip, when Sam was assured that Seagram's would be paying the stewardess whether she went along or not, he reluctantly agreed to take her.

"But," he said, "I don't want to see her, and I don't want her sitting on her ass in some hotel in Ireland with me paying for it, either."

The party's first stop in Dublin was to visit Jameson's distillery. The managing director showed them around the storage sheds in a big Rolls-Royce, and at one point, as they were climbing back into the limousine, Sam demanded, "What are you getting back into the car for?"

"Well, I'm going to show you some more warehouses."

"But you didn't turn the lights out in that one. Go back and switch them off."

"Mr. Bronfman," replied the astonished executive, "did you buy control or an interest in this company when I wasn't looking?"

"No. I don't own a goddamn share of it, but that's nothing to do with wasting electricity. Now go and turn out the lights." The Irishman went back into the warehouse, shaking his head in angry amazement at this strange, penny-pinching Canadian billionaire.

The same parsimonious instincts were roused in Sam by his visit to the set of *Ryan's Daughter,* then being filmed near Killarney by David Lean. Because Edgar was at the time still attempting to capture control of Metro-Goldwyn-Mayer, which was producing the movie, Sam and his party were granted special access. Tension began to mount when Sam was told that no footage was being shot because the tides weren't quite right to wash away the footprints of the heroine (Sarah Miles) in the sand. Down at the beach, Sam took one look at the idle crew and announced, "I'll go out and make some goddamn footprints!" Later, when he visited the reconstruction of a 1917 village classroom over which the hero (Robert Mitchum) was supposed to be presiding, he began to read off the list of pupils: "Malone, O'Toole, McKee, O'Flaherty . . . not a Jew among them. Maybe he was the teacher. Somebody had to teach these goddamn Irishmen the facts of life."

At the film's climax, the IRA was to carry its contraband weapons from the sea as a dramatic storm lashed the wild Irish coast. But there wasn't a cloud in the sky, and no storms were forecast. Meanwhile, M-G-M's payroll was mounting. Sam couldn't bear it. Finally he took David Lean aside: "You remember how you told me that you can shoot night scenes in daytime by using filters over the cameras. Well, why don't you change your storm sequence to a night scene? Go over to Glasgow and hire one of those big freighters sitting in the harbor, bring it back over here, run it up and down a mile or two out at sea, and it'll make all the goddamn waves you need. You'll have your storm and that'll be the end of it." Lean was impressed enough with the ingenious idea that he sent an agent to negotiate for the ship rental, but eventually the movie crew moved on location to Kenya.

On the way back to Dublin, Sam demanded they stop at Tralee, but fell asleep just before their rented limousine got there. When he woke up and discovered they had passed the picturesque coastal town by, he ordered McCormick to drive back, got out at the main square, and in his full falsetto baritone sang the first three verses of "The Rose of Tralee."

THE MOST IMPORTANT OCCASIONS IN THIS LATE, CA-THEDRAL STAGE OF SAM BRONFMAN'S CAREER were his birthday parties. They were celebrated within Seagram's and his family as great ceremonies of state, with each anniversary demanding the pomp and planning of a coronation. For his sixtieth birthday, Seagram's took over the entire Windsor Hotel in Montreal and presented Sam with an illuminated scroll bearing an affectionate message, complete with convocational cadence. The opening paragraph gives an idea: "We, his associates, admirers, friends, from this far-flung continent foregathered to do him honour on this the diamond day that with the facets of his talents shines, Do bring him from The House of Seagram greetings, and from the comradeship of Calvert, and from the fraternity of

Frankfort, and from the wide fellowship of the land, do
salute him and hail him, leader and Chief."

The reception for his seventy-fifth birthday at New
York's Americana Hotel filled three ballrooms, and a
Four Roses salesman called Martin Steinhardt read out
a poem that ended with the ill-matched quatrain:

> To his office he went,
> Elevator closed like clam,
> To many he'll be recalled,
> As just Mr. Sam.

Sam pretended total indifference to the planning of
all these events. Initially he asked his underlings not to
prepare anything elaborate—then engineered every cele-
bration's every detail. The one exception was his
seventy-ninth birthday, when he and Saidye were holi-
daying in Barbados with only McCormick along. There
seemed little chance of staging an extravaganza in the
customary grand style. But McCormick quietly enlisted
the aid of the Goddards, a family that played a dominant part in the island's trade and owned a rum-blend-
ing house that Sam was vaguely negotiating to buy. He
rented the Marine Hotel for the occasion, surreptitiously
sent out five hundred invitations to the upper crust of
Barbadian society, including the Governor General,
Sir Winston Scott, the Prime Minister, Errol Barrow,
and the Attorney-General, Senator Frederick "Sleepy"
Smith. Through the Goddards, who ran the airport's
catering service, half a dozen chefs were recruited, two
bands hired, and six bars stocked. On the appointed
evening, McCormick took Sam and Saidye to the Marine
for what he described as "a quiet little dinner." When
they walked out to the pool area, Sam suddenly found
himself engulfed by half a thousand well-wishers, decked
out in black tie and evening gowns, all sporting large
HAPPY BIRTHDAY, MR. SAM buttons. For perhaps the
first time in his life, he was speechless. But it didn't
last long. He climbed out on the diving board and began
to tell his unexpected guests the story of how he had

courted Saidye and that their favorite song had been "Baby Face." Then, under the frail sickle moon of the Barbadian night, with the ocean's waves breaking audibly offstage, Sam sang:

Baby face,
You've got the cutest little baby face.
There's not another one could take your place.
Baby face,
My poor heart is jumping,
You sure have started something.
Baby face,
I'm up in heaven when I'm in your fond embrace.
I didn't need a shove,
'Cause I just fell in love
With your pretty baby face.

The performance that night, singing to Saidye while swaying on the Marine Hotel's diving board, was an unusually public but not untypical expression of Sam's adoration of the woman he loved. Despite all the pressures and the absences, it was a great love-match to the end. In 1943, Saidye and the children had been spending the summer in the Laurentians when Sam was tipped off that his wife was going to be made an Officer of the Order of the British Empire for her wartime efforts with the Red Cross in Montreal. Sam called her to come into the city with the enticing words, "Something very nice has happened." When she walked into the Belvedere Palace, he curtsied gracefully before her, announcing: "George VI thinks as much of you as I do."

When Sam was working downtown at Seagram's Peel Street office, Saidye sometimes telephoned and asked him home for lunch. At first he would decline, pleading a previous engagement with a banker or some other associate. She would throw up the mock objection that he must love the bank more than he loved her. Then he would declare that he was immediately canceling his appointment and would come home. No,

she would airily reply, it was all a joke because she was
going out with "the ladies" in the cause of some Jewish
charity or other. Now he would chide her, "You love
'the ladies' more than you love me." In the end, they
would both cancel their appointments and eat happily
by themselves at the Belvedere Palace.

When they returned to Montreal from Barbados,
Sam became aware that he was seriously ill. While consulting his doctor, Abe Mayman, he complained that
he and Saidye could not really contemplate life without
each other. "When the time comes for one of us," he
said, "we'll climb up to the top of a high mountain,
hold hands, and jump off together."

Although Sam had said an unofficial goodbye to his
Peel Street staff the previous Christmas,* his eightieth
birthday was coming up on March 4, 1971. The Seagram loyalists were determined to outdo themselves.
Montreal's Chateau Champlain ballroom was leased for
the occasion, and he was hailed in the official program
as "Our Mr. Sam, The President of Presidents, The
Chief of Chiefs." The menu was one of the most
elaborate mass catering assignments ever undertaken
in Canada, and Lorne Greene was approached to recite
yet another fawning "oath of allegiance" from Seagram's staff until Sam discovered that the actor was de-

---

* Seagram's Christmas parties were always combined with
celebrations of Allan Bronfman's birthday, which fell on
December 21, and one of the prevailing customs was that all of
the girls in the office would give him a kiss and get a rose in
return. But Allan was away for Christmas in 1970, and Sam,
who had to go into the hospital the evening of the party for the
second of two serious cataract operations, decided to take his
place. Sam sang some songs and made a few jokes; then he
declared he was substituting for his absent brother and asked
the girls to line up for their kisses. The first two secretaries were
young and beautiful. Sam made a great production out of his
Christmas greeting. Next in line was a secretary who had grown
old and ill in the service of Seagram's. Sam gave her just a
quick brush with his right ear. "You didn't spend much time
kissing her," one of the attending vice-presidents remarked.
Sam riposted, "Look, I may be going blind, but I'm not out
of my mind."

manding a $4,000 fee and told Jack Clifford to read it himself.

Highlight of the eightieth birthday celebrations for Seagram insiders was the sight of Sam sitting in animated conversation with Lazarus Phillips. The two men had made personal peace shortly before when Rosalie, Phillips's wife, died and Michael McCormick urged Sam to express his sympathy in person.

A week later, in the main ballroom of Ottawa's Chateau Laurier Hotel, the liquor trade met to pay appropriate tribute. Sir Ronald Cumming, the retired chairman of the Distillers Company of Great Britain, flew over for the occasion from his home at Rothes, Scotland. No fewer than four Cabinet ministers showed up, and the former Deputy Minister of National Revenue played the accordion while the distillers sang "Happy Birthday." Max Henderson (then Auditor-General of Canada), Major-General George Kitching (Chief Commissioner of the Liquor Control Board of Ontario), and H. Clifford Hatch (president of Hiram Walker—Gooderham & Worts) paid their public respects. The chief executive officers of five of the largest distilling firms in the world jointly presented Sam with a decanter, set into a base hand-carved out of the white oak used for whisky-barrel staves, containing a symbolic mixture of their finest blends.

Sam's illness had by this time been definitely diagnosed as cancer of the prostate, and his restless vitality began to flow out of him. In one of his last visits to Dr. Mayman, he talked about needing at least two more decades to finish his self-appointed tasks, of how he wanted to launch a whole new career in the hunt for oil and diversify Seagram's in a multitude of new directions: "I've climbed the Rockies and conquered the Alps. In the next twenty years I want to encompass the world."

Such bursts of optimism grew increasingly rare as the disease began to ravage his body. He stayed at home, playing solitaire, seeing a few cronies, grumbling about his health. Billy Gittes, a frequent companion

in these final days, remembers the elaborate ritual they
evolved to ease Sam's suffering. "I'd go up to his house
on Belvedere about three o'clock in the afternoon, and
we'd play some gin. Then about a quarter to five he'd
ring for his nurse and say, 'It's the cocktail hour. The
sun's well over the yardarm. Please bring us a Scotch
and soda for Mr. Gittes, some V.O., a carafe of water,
and the milk I'm supposed to have.' She'd come back,
and he'd ask me to be bartender. I'd pour myself a little
Chivas, add some soda and ice; then a little rye and
water, the way I knew he liked it. As soon as the drink
was in his hand, he'd say, 'Okay, Billy, now give the
nurse that glass of milk,' and the two of us would have
a good laugh."

Sam died on July 10, 1971. The Seagram organization launched itself into a frenzy of preparation to make
his funeral the greatest tribute of them all. Every detail
was planned and rehearsed, right down to Leo Kolber's
precaution of buying a throwaway raincoat for every
invited mourner just in case it rained. Jewish tradition
treats death as an occasion of ultimate privacy, frown-
ing on exhibiting the deceased's body. But Mr. Sam
lay in state, with a white shroud, inside an open coffin
displayed in the rotunda of the Montreal headquarters
of the Canadian Jewish Congress that bears his name.
At the funeral, held in Shaar Hashomayim (Gates of
Heaven) Synagogue, custom was again abandoned and
two eulogies were given in addition to the words of the
rabbi. Saul Hayes called him "a giver of himself. He
cannot be replaced." Nahum Goldmann, head of the
World Jewish Congress, who arrived later, declared
that Sam was "mourned by the entire house of Israel."
And in the most moving oration of the day, Lazarus
Phillips paid a final tribute to his onetime Senate rival.

As the cortège was being ranked by strict protocol
for the short ride to Mount Royal Cemetery—with regal
limousines jockeying for position and impatient police
outriders self-importantly revving up their motorcycles
—the gawking mourners became conscious of just how
distinguished this gathering really was. From Ottawa

had come Canada's ultimate WASP, Brigadier the Hon. Charles Mills Drury, then President of the Treasury Board. Justice Minister John Turner was there in addition to four lesser ministers. From Toronto came the heads of the Bank of Nova Scotia, the Toronto-Dominion Bank, and the Commerce, and former Ontario Premier Leslie Frost. The large platoon of Montreal's elite included the chairmen of the Royal Bank, the Bank of Montreal, and the Canadian Pacific Railway, Dr. Robert Bell, principal of McGill, and Senator Hartland de Montarville Molson.

Sam Bronfman had joined the establishment at last.

PART TWO

The Inheritors

10. Growing Up in the Belvedere Palace

THE SONS and daughters of the very rich are nurtured within a meteorology all their own. Shielded from the harsher circumstances of daily existence, secluded and protected, they ripen entirely within the insulated cocoon of their families. Scraped knees, lost tempers, childhood escapades with strange dogs and hurt starlings, spats with fussy neighbors, those first crude lessons about the value of money, and, above all, the anguish of self-realization—all of the natural disturbances that come with growing up—are soothed away by a resident corps of gentle governesses, plump pantry maids, and avuncular chauffeurs. When the family itself insists on living in strict segregation from its surrounding society, the children's sequestration from reality becomes doubly confining, and they find themselves reaching maturity with all the superficiality of exotic flowers blooming in a fluorescent-lit hothouse.

Sam Bronfman's four children—born at regular intervals within a period of six years: Minda in 1925, Phyllis in 1927, Edgar in 1929, and Charles in 1931—had just such an upbringing, as did Edward, Peter, and Mona, their cousins, whose father, Allan, had bought an almost equally imposing mansion two doors along from the Westmount showplace purchased by Sam in the late twenties. In between stood the home of the

167

Coristine family. Eventually Sam and Allan acquired
and tore down this house so that they could use the
land first to lay out a children's bicycle path and baseball diamond and later to put in a large swimming pool.
One of Peter Bronfman's fondest childhood memories
is of clambering over the ruins of the old Coristine place
with Charles. ("If you got a crowbar in at just the right
angle, a whole wall would come tumbling down.")
Children who grew up in the neighborhood recall running between the Bronfman properties on a dare, but
never being allowed to play with the kids.

If the Westmount kids were shut out from the Bronfman compound at the top of the mountain, it was also
true that the Bronfman children were shut in, the Jewish customs of the two families lending a special dimen-
sion to their isolation. The young Bronfmans were
driven to school in the family limousines, and Saidye
frequently reminded Minda that because other children
might not feel comfortable approaching her, she should
take the initiative in trying to form friendships. "We
grew up almost entirely within our immediate family,"
Phyllis remembers.

The major social occasions were the children's birthday parties. Charles can still visualize the waves of
visiting kids rushing about the Belvedere Palace, counting the bathrooms, talking to each other in awed whispers. Peggy Mackenzie, who attended the Study, a
private school in Westmount, with the Bronfman girls,
recalls Minda's tenth birthday, when thirty children
from the school were invited. "We were seated in a
great, long dining room, and while there may not have
been a butler or footman behind every chair, there
certainly were an awful lot of them. We were all spread
out in these big, high-backed oak chairs and every child
was given a present. I got a hard-cover Conan Doyle
classic, enormously expensive-looking, particularly in
the middle of the Depression, and the other gifts were
of comparable splendor. The entertainment was a movie in the downstairs recreation room, the first film
most of us had ever watched because in Quebec you

weren't allowed to see movies until you were sixteen in those days. The whole thing was quite extraordinary."

What struck Peggy Mackenzie and other visitors to the Belvedere Palace was its unusual décor. Instead of adhering to any one style or even period, Sam characteristically attempted to encompass them all. "When you walked into one room, it was sort of art nouveau," she recalls. "The living room might be Louis Quinze. The dining room was, I think, Tudor. There was no cohesive relationship between different styles or tastes, no consistency, but individual areas were quite astounding."

In those days the Samuel Bronfman mansion had a full-time staff of eight to cook, garden, and tidy its more than twenty rooms. "We had a very aloof and austere butler at the time, a Dane called Jensen," Saidye recalls. "We called him the Prince of Belvedere Road, and the neighborhood kids were scared to death of him. The girls used to come home from school and ask me why I never baked a pie. I couldn't understand why they were so desperate for cakes, so I had our housekeeper get some for them. That wasn't good enough. They still kept asking me why I didn't cook the goodies myself. Years later I realized that almost every day one or another of their school chums would boast that 'Mummy made me a nice cake yesterday.' This made Minda and Phyllis wonder why *their* mummy didn't bake cakes. They thought that in some way I was inadequate. To kids of a sensitive age it all added up to the fact that they were different from their friends, and they couldn't understand why. I tried to explain, but they really needed their father to do it."

During the children's formative years, Sam was on the road so much that he maintained a permanent reservation for a sleeping compartment on the Montreal–New York express train, enabling him to hop aboard any night he wished. Preoccupied with Seagram's corporate affairs, Sam was at home less than a dozen days a month, and his direct influence on his children's upbringing was limited to herding them into the sun porch for occasional parable-spiced sermons he liked to call "lessons in life."

He would telephone every evening from his New York hotel suite, usually at the children's bath time. Saidye recalls one evening when he called and she couldn't hear him because of the youngsters' playful yelling.

"What the hell is happening up there?" Sam wanted to know. "It sounds like a crazy house."

"No. It's just a normal house. Why must you call when the children are having their baths?"

"Baths? At this time of day? Why can't they have their baths in the morning like ordinary people?"

Next time, Sam tried telephoning after ten and asked to speak to the children. He was astonished when Saidye explained that they were fast asleep.

Increasingly aware of how out of the ordinary they were and unable to communicate with a father who seemed distant even when he was in the house, the kids reacted in different ways. When he was eight years old, Edgar decided to leave home. One morning after he'd been disciplined by having to sit quietly in his room for two hours, his governess burst into Saidye's sitting room to show her a note Edgar had left on his pillow: "Dear Cutie—I didn't deserve the punishment you gave me yesterday and I am running away. Edgar." When the youngster got home from school that day, Saidye took him aside and told him he should let her know exactly when he intended running away so she'd be able to give him enough money to buy food and find shelter. "That just blew the sails right out of me," Edgar recalls.

A year later Edgar demonstrated the first signs of his business acumen in conversation with Julius Kessler, an elderly American distiller who was an occasional house guest. The visitor was showing the children the ornate musical watch he carried in his vest pocket, and when Edgar kept admiring the timepiece, he promised it to the youngster as a *bar mitzvah* present. Edgar considered the offer for a moment, then shook his head and replied, "Thanks. But you're an old man now, and you may not be here for my *bar mitzvah*." Kessler shrugged and handed over his watch on the spot.

The Bronfmans' greatest worry during the thirties was the vulnerability of the family to kidnapping, a crime then very much in vogue. In fact, at least one crew of crooks, led by Michael "Big Irish" McCardell, arrived in Montreal in 1931, determined to stage a Bronfman kidnapping. McCardell's second in command was a Chicago gangster called Abraham "Three Fingers Abe" Loew; his buddies were said to be Vincent "Vinnie" Massetti from Detroit and Dave Meisner, a gambler and bookie from Covington, Kentucky, across the river from Cincinnati. Also along for the caper were Albert Pegram and an unlikely character named Mario "The Throatman" Berchello, whose specialty was strangling people with a length of fish gut weighted at one end with a crucifix and a St. Christopher medal at the other, presumably to grant the victim a final form of benediction, if not absolution.

After registering at the Mount Royal Hotel, they kept the family under surveillance for three days and finally decided to snatch Sam himself by blocking off his car as he was driving to work down the Boulevard in Westmount, abducting their victim and holding him in a Vermont hideout for a ransom of $500,000.

They spent the evening before the intended grab in their hotel suite, drinking champagne, boasting about how they would make Sam Bronfman squirm, and regaling each other with plans of how they intended to spend his ransom. At one point Vinnie Massetti left to send a coded telegram to the local triggermen in charge of the Vermont hideout. On the way back through the hotel lobby he spotted an attractive woman and decided to follow her. A hefty blonde with billowy hair and breasts that promised highly pneumatic pleasures, she seemed to be welcoming his attentions. When she boarded the elevator, he hopped on and started a conversation. He noted her room number, then rejoined the gang for yet another round of champagne. After a few more drinks, Massetti returned to the blonde's room, knocked on the door, and when she opened it barged in, announcing he was with the Morality Squad. Following a heated argument and scuffle, Massetti raped the lady, who promptly reported him to the house detective. McCardell was getting ready to punish Massetti for jeopardizing their plans with a one-way ride down to the St. Lawrence docks when three policemen burst through the door to arrest the suspected rapist. They warned his nervous sidekicks not to leave town in case they were required to give evidence, but remained ignorant of the real purpose of their Montreal presence. Scared that Massetti would sing, the gang fled the city and the Bronfman kidnapping never took place.

But some of the gang returned to Canada in August of 1934 to kidnap John Sackville Labatt, the London, Ontario, brewer. He was held for $150,000 ransom (McCardell used the name Three-Fingered Abe in writing the ransom note) in a Muskoka cottage, but released unharmed three days after his abduction. The gangsters neglected to pick up the cash, which was supposed to have been handed over to them in, of all inconspicuous places, the lobby of Toronto's Royal York Hotel, and three members of the gang eventually served penitentiary terms for the bungled kidnapping. Meisner was sentenced to fifteen years for the Labatt kidnapping, but was freed after a second trial when McCardell testified that Meisner and another suspect, Kingdom "Piccolo Pete" Murray, had not been along on the kidnapping. McCardell was sentenced to twelve years and Russell Knowles and Jack Bannon got fifteen years each. Pegram was never found.

Unaware of the thwarted plot against them, the Bronfmans continued their life in the Belvedere Palace undisturbed. After graduating from the Study, the girls split up; Minda enrolled at Smith College while the artistically inclined Phyllis went off to study at Cornell and Vassar. Edgar and Charles, who attended Selwyn House, a Montreal private school for boys, were sent to Trinity College School in Port Hope, Ontario. They were the only two Jews attending the school at the time, and it turned out to be a devastating experience. "Often in the dorm," Charles recalls, "before we went to sleep, the kids started chanting 'King Item, King Edgar' over and over again at me, which, if you take the first four letters, spells 'kike.' When I protested, one kid told me to keep my big Jewish nose out of it. So I belted him." Edgar himself was less touched by the anti-Semitism than by the school's rigid rules. "What irritated me the most at Trinity was this crazy regulation that new boys had to button up their jackets with all three buttons. It ruined every suit I ever wore."

Charles encountered similar racial problems at McGill, where he enrolled in 1948. "I remember one guy coming up to me and saying that they'd had a big battle in his fraternity house because some people wanted me in, but they'd never had a Jew before. I was shocked because I wouldn't have joined the fraternity anyway. That's when I went through a whole lot of stuff inside myself as to my Jewishness. It was just when Israel was being born, and I kept thinking what would happen if there was ever a war between Canada and Israel. Eventually I came to peace with myself on it. In being Jewish there's this identity with what I would call our brethren, wherever they are, with Israel being their anchor. While I'm a member of the Jewish people, I'm also a Canadian and very proud of it. Since then I've never had any worries about divided loyalties and all that jazz."

Charles's McGill experience was debilitating, brutish, and short. He found his liberal-arts courses boring: "I could write papers. Anything that had a certain degree of bullshit I was all right with. But when it came to exams, I'd get panic attacks." He left in the middle of his third year, which he would have failed anyway, confessing to his disappointed father that it was like being let out of jail. On March 12, 1951, he began working full time for Seagram's.

Edgar meanwhile had gone off to Williams, a small college in northwestern Massachusetts. His chums there remember him mostly for his toys: fast cars and beautiful coeds. In one particularly daring exploit he ended up with a slightly battered brunette on the wrong side of a hedge, scratched but laughing, beside the smoking wreck of a newly acquired motorcycle. When Edgar was threatened with expulsion, Sam asked James Linen (then publisher of *Time* and a Williams graduate) for help. The intervention saved Edgar from being officially kicked out, but he transferred to a history Honors course at McGill and eventually earned his degree. Insecure, searching for himself, he briefly considered careers as a rabbi—at some point during his religious ecstasy Edgar decided that, in order to give his new calling more moral authority, he should alter his middle name from Miles to Moses—in law, and as an investment counsellor. He spent the university summers learning a bit about stocks and a lot about money. ("If you went to Father to ask for money, you had to explain why. If you earned it, you didn't have to explain anything.") While Edgar was still a teenager, Sam gave him $5,000 three summers in a row to teach him the workings of the stock market. At one point, Edgar had made a sizable profit from buying into Royalite (an Alberta oil producer Sam and Allan had acquired and held for a while) and when Charles (who had an $1,800 war-savings certificate) asked his father whether he should buy in as well, the elder Bronfman assured him that quick money could still be made. Charles followed the advice, but Edgar sold out, bought Seagram's shares instead, and made more profit when the distillery stock moved up while Royalite fell.

By the autumn of 1951, Edgar had joined his brother Charles in the royal courts of Seagram's.

11. *Phyllis*

DESCRIBED BY her family as "a talented oddball," Sam's second daughter, Phyllis, is the most interesting Bronfman extant. She is the only one of her generation possessed by that same mad magnetism that drew people so strongly to her father: the beguiling poignancy of someone who exists permanently on the edge of exile.

An intensely attractive divorcée with features that evoke the lingering beauty of a Picasso line drawing, she is seldom seen in anything except a track-layer's coveralls over a man's dress shirt with three large plastic peanuts pinned to the bib. Compellingly intelligent and as vulnerable as a homing bird with a thousand miles to fly, Phyllis has achieved a state of grace yet to be attempted by any other Bronfman—self-preservation through withdrawal into the imagination.

She communicates in bursts of epigrammatic prose that range from art to politics and back again. Her thoughts unroll in the glorious hues and jarring configurations of regimental flags in the Mexican Army. But it is the quality of Phyllis's silences that most impresses her few visitors. The pauses seem alive, counterpoints to the fireworks of her mind, like the shadows in a rock that inspire the sculptor who shapes it.

Once upon a time, back in the Belvedere Palace on

Phyllis's wedding day, Sam insisted on festooning the house with fifteen thousand lilac blooms, plucked in a nursery at Windsor, Ontario, and flown to Montreal by chartered plane. The actual ceremony took place beneath two large transplanted lilac shrubs teased to frame the bridal couple. A lifetime hardly seems long enough for an introspective girl to recover.

SHE IS IN TOUCH WITH CONTEMPORARY QUEBEC, SPECULATING SENSITIVELY ON FRENCH CANADA'S FUTURE. ("French Canada has its own myth and it will only mature economically if it's able to realize that myth. After all, Duplessis [premier of Quebec, 1936–1939, 1944–1959] brought in American industry and supported it on the bodies of the Québécois workers in order to establish the French presence. In fact, Quebec's leaders have always 'betrayed the masses' to establish their image.")

After her brother Charles's pre-election outburst against the Parti Québécois,* Phyllis was so angry that she tried avoiding him for two months in case she lost her temper. "I consider that I really don't identify especially one way or another with the Bronfmans," she says. "It's a little hard to make a monolith out of the way Charles lives, you know. It's very different from the way other people whose name is Bronfman choose to live, and if I could avoid being a Bronfman altogether . . . Actually, being a Bronfman in Montreal I avoid by having changed my name. I didn't come back to live here until I could return on my own terms."

PHYLLIS BRONFMAN FIRST LEFT MONTREAL TO ATTEND CORNELL BUT AFTER A YEAR THERE SWITCHED TO VASSAR, where she obtained her undergraduate degree in 1948. Her discipline was modern history; her thesis dealt with Henry James's moral dilemma in deciding to leave America. ("James seemed to be a most difficult writer, so I thought I'd really try to understand

* See Chapter 18.

him. Besides, I was interested in the fact that he had
to go abroad to comprehend his own culture, a process
I could appreciate.") It was in her graduation year that
Phyllis met Jean Lambert, a dark, tall, egocentric Middle European with the suave good looks of a French
matinee idol and the throaty speech inflections of a
first-rate Las Vegas impressionist pretending to be
Charles Boyer pretending to be a Resistance leader
about to die for the glory of France. Born at Saar-
brücken in 1920, Lambert escaped the Nazi occupation
of France and emigrated to the United States, where
he had a sister. It was a close thing. He left Paris on
the day the Nazis marched in and tried to get through
to London from Tangier, which had just been occupied
by Spanish troops. Because the connecting London
plane to Lisbon (in neutral Portugal) stopped off in
Madrid (which was cooperating with the Germans),
Lambert gave the French consul in Tangier enough
money to phone his Spanish counterpart in case he
didn't arrive safely in Lisbon. He happened to land in
Madrid on the day Heinrich Himmler, the Gestapo
chief, was paying a visit and as part of an anti-foreigner
dragnet was taken off the plane and thrown into an
underground dungeon at police headquarters. The
Tangier consul eventually remembered to call the
French diplomatic representative in Madrid, whose intervention set Lambert free. He spent the war years as
a clerk in the office of André Istel, who was Charles
de Gaulle's financial man in Washington.

Lambert later affected an air of mystery, acting as if
he had occupied a pivotal seat in history-making deals.
During boardroom small talk he invariably managed to
steer the conversation around so that he could mention
—however obliquely and with the proper show of deference—his backstage influence at the Bretton Woods
Conference of 1944, which set the monetary policies of
the postwar world. He was, in fact, the most junior
member of France's delegation, thanks to Pierre
Mendès-France, then Commissioner of Finance for the
French government-in-exile, who happened to spot his

name on a list of possible translators. He was intrigued
that a "Jean Lambert" actually existed among French-
men in Washington because after he escaped imprison-
ment by the Vichy French and joined the French
Resistance, Mendès-France had chosen "Jean Lambert"
as his assumed name.

In 1945, Lambert set himself up as an investment
consultant to capitalize on his wartime contacts. After
a year's courtship, he married Phyllis Bronfman on
May 17, 1949. Sam wasn't particularly pleased with
the match to the debonair banker, but as a wedding
gift he completely decorated and furnished the six-bed-
room apartment the young couple leased on New York's
fashionable Sutton Place.

Lambert enlisted the advice of Allen Dulles (then a
partner in the Wall Street law firm of Sullivan & Crom-
well and later the longtime potentate of the Central
Intelligence Agency) to persuade Phyllis that she should
invest in his business. She paid him a million dollars to
become a limited partner in Lambert and Company.
Her husband used the cash to cut himself into junior
positions on deals negotiated by André Meyer, the fabled head of Lazard Frères in New York. His First
Canadian venture was Calvan Consolidated Oil and
Gas in Calgary, followed by the acquisition of Consolidated Toronto Development Corporation, which
held five millions' worth of real estate straddling the
Humber River in the west end of Toronto. In 1960,
Lambert reorganized his Canadian properties into a
holding company called Great Northern Capital Corporation and bought Atlantic Acceptance Corporation,
then a small finance company in Hamilton, Ontario. In
1965, the same Atlantic Acceptance Corporation triggered a $75-million collapse. Jean Lambert was not
personally involved—the Ontario Royal Commission
that investigated the dramatic bankruptcy concluded:
"It is clear that the Lambert partners were deeply and
genuinely involved in the fortunes of Atlantic Acceptance"—but he had persuaded some of Wall Street's

most sophisticated investors (including the Ford Foundation, the U.S. Steel and Carnegie Pension Fund, and the Harvard Endowment Fund) to buy heavily into Atlantic's warrants, debentures, and unsecured notes.

PHYLLIS BRONFMAN'S MARRIAGE TO JEAN LAMBERT HAD BEEN DISSOLVED IN 1954, a decade before the Atlantic debacle took place. ("The marriage was just a way of winning my freedom; it hardly seems to have belonged to my life. Our interests were not the least bit common.") During the summer of 1952, she vanished into a Left Bank studio in Paris to paint, sculpt, and escape the North American curse of being a Bronfman. Two years later, Sam was planning to move Seagram's U.S. operations out of the Chrysler Building in New York and put up his own headquarters on land he'd acquired at 375 Park Avenue. The sketch of the original architectural conception he sent to Phyllis was less than exciting. She replied with a sixteen-page critique that outlined some criteria for the new structure. ("Basically, I was trying to discover what was the most significant statement the building could make. A building can't be ignored as a painting can be passed by, or a book left unread. It imposes itself on us, for we must approach it, find our way into and through it, be enveloped by it. The responsibility for superior planning and painstaking detail required to make a building's spatial intangibles pleasing to the eye and spirit falls on the architect. But the moment business organizations decide to build, they take a moral position; and it's upon the choice of architect that the quality of their statement depends.") Sam was so impressed that he asked her to plan its execution.

"Now I really have a job," she wrote to Eve Borsook, a friend from Vassar. "Certainly no one employed by Seagram's could [do it] by virtue of being employed. A daughter who is interested in seeing that her father puts up a fine building seems to have everyone's sympathy. And now I must say my prayers every day. What a unique chance I have!" Through Marie Alexander, another Vassar graduate, Phyllis met Philip Cortelyou Johnson, then chairman of the combined departments of architecture and industrial design at the New York Museum of Modern Art, who recognized the quality of her instincts and gave her introductions to the world's great architects. She toured their drafting rooms, inspected their models, probed their philosophies, and finally found herself face to face with the master: Ludwig Mies van der Rohe. "The younger, second-generation men are talking in terms of Mies or denying him," she wrote to her father. "They talk of new forms—articulating the skins or façades of buildings to get a play of light and shadow. But Mies has said: 'Form is not the aim of our work but only the result.' "

Sam agreed with Phyllis's choice and named her director of planning for the new Seagram building at $20,000 a year. Then in his sixty-eighth year and director of the architectural department at Illinois Institute of Technology, Mies van der Rohe, former master of the Bauhaus School, was given only two guidelines for the new building by Sam Bronfman: "to make this building the crowning glory of your life as well as mine" and to make sure it had half a million square feet of rentable office space.

One unexpected hold-up occurred when it turned out that the self-educated Mies had no license to practice architecture in New York, couldn't get one issued because he'd never attended high school, and flatly refused to take the prescribed examination. The problem was resolved by the appointment of Philip Johnson as Mies's collaborator.

The $41-million bronze tower opened for business three years later and was immediately acclaimed as one of the world's architectural wonders. "There is a quick but accurate way of describing the new Seagram Building," rhapsodized *The New Yorker*. "It is everything that most of the office buildings that have been going

up in the last few years are not. Almost any piece of
sober craftsmanship, however humble its pretensions,
would gain by such contrasting, and the Seagram Building, far from being humble, is perhaps the most quietly
ostentatious in the city. . . . It has emerged like a Rolls-
Royce acompanied by a motorcycle escort that gives it
space and speed. By a heavy sacrifice of profitable floor
area, Mies van der Rohe has achieved in this single
structure an effect of light and space usually created
only when a group of buildings are placed together on
a plot even larger than a city block."

Set back on a twin-fountained pink-granite-and-
marble plaza that serves as its pedestal, the thirty-eight-
story gunmetal-colored tower has become the illustrious
symbol of Seagram's predominance among the world's
distillers. One of the most expensive office buildings
ever erected, its mood is one of rich restraint rather
than ostentation. The fourteen elevators (lined with
hand-rubbed bronze mullions and spandrels) open up
into a magnificent lobby with travertine walls and ter-
razzo floors. The main floor also houses the Four Seasons, one of New York's most lavish restaurants, its
main wall decorated by a twenty-five-foot-high theater
drop created by Picasso in 1919. (Edgar Bronfman
seldom eats at the Four Seasons. "I have my own kitch-
en," he says. "The Four Seasons is good, but it doesn't
compare with my cook.")

The executive offices are paneled in English oak, and
visitors waiting to see Edgar find themselves sitting in
the original Barcelona leather chairs Mies van der
Rohe designed for the Berlin Building Exposition of
1931. On the fourth floor there's a wine museum, kept
at a constant sixty-five degrees Fahrenheit, where executives, seated around three medieval wooden tables,
can sip samples of Bernkasteler Doktor 1904, Mumm's
Cordon Rouge 1928, Château Léoville Barton 1924,
and other priceless vintages. "This building," boasts
Edgar, "is our greatest piece of advertising and public
relations. It establishes us once and for all, right around

the world, as people who are solid and care about quality."

Phyllis became so entranced by the architectural process that she enrolled at Yale's school of architecture. She stayed a year, then switched to the Illinois Institute of Technology, where she graduated with honors. ("Intellect is not intelligence. At Yale, students with a B.Sc. or a B.A. would posit: what does a wall want to be? The place was run on the star system, but it was supposed to be a school. There was only one criterion of stardom—immediately perceptible talent in design—the lesser talents were ground under heel. Instructors told students (read 'stars') to hide their designs so that they couldn't be copied, like the different divisions of General Motors, or Seagram's, or Paris *haute couture* in July. The school at Illinois Institute of Technology was a great relief. Kids with pimples from bad diets came to school by bus or subway. No positing. Everyone looked at everyone's drawings to see if things worked.") Later, Phyllis won a Massey Medal, the top Canadian architectural award, for her design of the Saidye Bronfman cultural center at the Snowdon Branch of the YM-YWHA in Montreal.

PHYLLIS NOW FINDS HERSELF HAPPILY ENSCONCED ON THE THREE FLOORS OF A CONVERTED PEANUT FACTORY in Montreal's old quarter. She sleeps in the loft, rents out part of the ground floor, and works in a large, whitewashed studio filled with books, sculptures, her collection of toy cars, and STOP THE SEAL HUNT buttons. She is a very private person, though hardly a recluse. She no longer paints or sculpts ("It was too personal; I'm more interested in social problems"). With her staff of eight assistants she is busy cataloguing, trying to preserve and restore the architectural treasures of *vieux Montréal*. Her efforts have been hailed and blessed by both the city and the province through grants and official publications.

Phyllis maintains her architectural presence in the

United States in her partnership with the American architect Gene R. Summers, whose sixteen-year career as assistant to Mies van der Rohe placed him on the job at the Bronfmans' Toronto-Dominion Centre. Their partnership, Ridgway Ltd., established in Newport Beach, California, in 1973, has an $11-million commercial and office complex in Orange County's Lake Forest community and a $4.1-million light-industry development in Los Angeles County. In 1976, Ridgway began a $30-million renovation of the Biltmore Hotel in Los Angeles, combining the original Renaissance-style ceilings and walls with new furnishings and decorations based on designs by the American artist Jim Dine.

Phyllis Lambert's most recent project is *Court House: A Photographic Document* (Horizon Press). Conceived and directed by Phyllis, the project involved commissioning twenty-four outstanding photographers to take eight thousand photographs of a third of the 3,043 courthouses in the United States. It has received high praise for its demonstration of "the richness and ingenuity of our own indigenous architecture. Even those of us who have long taken an interest in historic building will be astounded" (Wolf Von Eckhardt, *Washington Post*).

Back in Canada, Phyllis is a constant storm center in the dispute between Montreal's cultural establishment, whose leaders prefer to have Old Montreal preserved as an *objet d'art* on display mainly for tourists, and urban activists who would like to see a wider use evolve for buildings of all ages in the area. Phyllis, who has become the most articulate advocate of the latter group, has concentrated most of her rhetorical fire on the Viger Commission, the advisory body charged with the area's development. "Its members belong to a period when a couple of barons ruled the world," she charges, calling it an elitist, reactionary group "with no public accountability, created at a time when interest in conservation was still largely antiquarian."

Rollande Pager, the Viger Commission's vice-chairman, has been blasting her right back. "What does Phyllis Lambert mean calling us elitist?" Mme. Pager demands. "If only I had her millions. It's always an elite who runs things. Do you think I would let my milkman join the Viger Commission? *C'est toujours la crème.*"

12. Minda

MINDA IS the aristocrat among Sam's off-spring. She lives in understated elegance as the Baroness Alain François de Gunzburg within the closed world of France's *haut monde,* dining at Ledoyen, Tour d'Argent, or Lasserre, shopping for designer originals with that cool, appraising stare only true Parisians can cultivate in the cobbled inner courts of the Rue du Faubourg St. Honoré. Equally disdainful of Europe's frantic jet-setters and duty-laden bourgeoisie, she is ever *soignée,* smart, money-conscious, and tough. A self-educated patroness of the arts, acknowledged as one of the ranking hostesses of Paris, she spends the long, languid summers on Alain's sleek yacht in the Mediterranean.

She has poise; she is immensely rich; she leads a charmed life.

But the Baroness is not really a Bronfman any longer, having too long absented herself from the milieu where the family's neuroses bubbled up. She lacks the ennui, the cutting edge of self-approbation that mark the passage of more typical Bronfmans.

Although she now expends most of her energies on a cultural foundation called ASDA that arranges conferences of art historians in the Grand Palais, lent to her for the purpose by the French government, Minda's academic background has its roots in philosophy. Her Master's degree in the history department of Columbia University was earned for an esoteric dissertation delineating the influences of Darwinism on French thought from 1841 to 1900. One of a small group of especially promising American university students chosen for summer fellowships at Oxford, she later joined *Time* as a $60-a-week researcher.

Still more than a little world-shy, the youthful Minda continued to live in the family's New York suite, which then occupied seven rooms at the St. Regis Hotel. Uncomfortable with the family's wealth and power, she once confided to her mother, "You know, I'm embarrassed to bring my friends here, it's so big and luxurious. I wasn't meant to be a rich man's daughter."

Saidye replied that if her convictions were that strong she ought to give back everything that represented money to her, in particular the fur coat Sam had recently bought for her, and buy instead a $49.50 cloth garment with a rag collar. Minda had changed her mind by next morning and told her mother, "You know, you really hit me below the belt that time."

When a 1948 *Fortune* article ("Seagram in the Chips") first publicized the Bronfmans' wealth, Minda was suddenly engulfed by suitors and had good reason to recall the private lecture she'd received from Sam on her twenty-first birthday. "He used the *voice*," she remembers. "I suspected he wanted to discuss sex, but instead it was money." Her father outlined the true dimensions of the Seagram empire to her that night and explained how the stock was split among the family so that she would receive $120,000 that year (1946) from dividends alone. "You are an heiress," he said, "and don't ever forget it. A lot of men may seem to be interested in you but in fact will be more interested in your money. If you fall in love, make sure the man is not just a fortune hunter."

Minda enjoyed being courted, but it was Baron Alain de Gunzburg, then studying business administration at Harvard, who had caught her eye. The scion

of one of the few truly aristocratic Jewish families in
Europe, Alain de Gunzburg numbered among his an-
cestors bankers to the Czar, although the family title
was originally granted in 1830 by the Hapsburgs of the
Austrian Empire. Alain's father earned a distinguished
record as a company commander in the French Foreign Legion during World War I, and young Alain grew
up (much like a young Bronfman) within the protective environs of upper-class Paris. He served briefly as
a tank officer in Charles de Gaulle's Free French army,
participating in both the liberation of France and the
defeat of Germany. Having been assured entry at the
executive level in his family's banking business, Alain
realized that postwar commerce would probably be
dominated by the English language and American business methods. To capitalize on both trends, he enrolled
in the Harvard Business School and it was while there,
on a blind date, that he met Minda in 1947.

Six years later, amid the antique splendors of the
16th *arrondissement* Bois de Boulogne apartment of
the Baron's grandmother, the couple was married and
shortly afterward moved into a magnificent town house
on Avenue Bugeaud.

Sam Bronfman was proud of his new son-in-law,
who had all the polish and connections befitting a
French Jew with genuine Rothschild blood in his veins.
It was Gunzburg who in 1963 negotiated the complicated deal that brought G. H. Mumm & Cie, the prestige champagne house, into the Bronfman empire and
later helped to acquire Champagne Perrier-Jouët as a
Mumm's subsidiary. Baron de Gunzburg now acts as
chairman of Mumm's at an annual salary of $100,000.
He is also on the executive committee of Seagram's
and serves on the board of Cemp.

Alain de Gunzburg, now in his mid-fifties and looking every inch the cool French aristocrat, is deeply
involved in Jewish philanthropies, especially the raising
of funds for the Weizmann Institute. He dines frequently with President Valéry Giscard d'Estaing and enjoys

several game-hunting expeditions a season, especially bird shooting in the wilds of northern Spain.

His most important job is managing director of the Banque Louis-Dreyfus. The family bank, established by the Gunzburgs in 1820 as Louis Hirsch & Cie, was merged by Alain with the Seligman family's French investments in 1966 and two years later incorporated the Louis Dreyfus interests. Housed in a sedate-looking palace on Rue Rabelais, it is France's third-largest merchant bank (ranking just behind the Rothschilds and Banque Worms), with assets of more than $1 billion.*

Through the Gunzburgs' many European connections, the Bronfmans have floated most of their rapid expansion into the European liquor and wine markets. Although the Gunzburgs' blood ties with the Rothschilds are distant (Baron Guy de Rothschild's mother was the first cousin of Alain de Gunzburg's father's mother), the two families are closely associated in many business ventures. That was how they became partners in the controlling group behind the Club Méditerranée. Together they financed Gazocéan, which operates France's largest fleet of butane tankers, and own Union Française Immobilière, a real-estate promotion company.

In France, the Gunzburgs are considered to be very much a part of the Rothschild circle. The banking dynasty's current head is Baron Guy de Rothschild, who lives on a nine-thousand-acre estate at Ferrières, nineteen miles east of Paris, famous for its hunts and art collection. He breeds racehorses (his Exbury earned $240,000 a year at stud) and operates an impressive network of companies, including Peñarroya, the world's

---

* In the summer of 1978 Banque Bruxelles-Lambert, Belgium's second-largest banking establishment, announced that it was buying 40 percent of the capital of Banque Louis-Dreyfus from the minority owners, who included the Gunzburgs. In a second stage, the Belgian bank would subscribe to an increase in the French bank's capital that would give it a majority position. Banque Bruxelles-Lambert has historic connections with the Rothschilds.

largest lead producer. Along with three cousins—Alain, Elie, and Edmond—Guy de Rothschild owns the celebrated vineyards of Château Lafite, near Bordeaux, which rank first among the *premiers crus* of the still-valid 1855 classification.*

Most closely involved with the Bronfmans is Cousin Edmond, who operates out of an unmarked building at 45 Rue de Faubourg St. Honoré, guiding investments in Israel (the Beersheba-Eilat pipeline and the luxury resort at the Gulf of Caesarea), bungalow villages in Majorca, partnerships in Pan American's Intercontinental hotel chain, housing projects in Paris, banks and factories in Brazil, much of the French Alpine resort of Megève, and a big investment in the Club Méditerranée.

Like all Rothschilds, members of the French family have a marked tendency to intermarry, partly because it's good economics—dowries and bequests stay within the family. When the daughter of one of the Italian Rothschilds married a French cousin, genealogical experts confirmed that on her father's side she belonged to the fourth generation, on her mother's to the fifth, and she was marrying into the third. "It's not that we're clannish," a Rothschild bride once confided, "it's just that Rothschild men find us Rothschild women irresistible."

The Baroness Alain de Gunzburg may not be a Rothschild, but she knows how to behave like one. Her moment of glory came at her wedding reception, when Sam, glowing with the pride of the occasion, wanted to kiss the bride. "But, father," she mockingly reprimanded him, "Father, don't you know that you should *bow* to a baroness?"

---

* The better-known Château Mouton-Rothschild vineyards are owned by Philippe, a descendant of the English Rothschilds. In a 1978 U.S. wine auction, Château Lafite came off on top. A Memphis restaurateur paid $18,000 for an 1864 jeroboam, which holds the equivalent of four bottles; a jeroboam of 1929 Mouton-Rothschild brought $11,500 in 1976.

13. Edgar

EDGAR MILES Bronfman is chief honcho at Seagram's now. He's no Mr. Sam, but deep within his relaxed demeanor there is a subdued animal strength —as furtive as a leopard in the tall summer grass— that many a suddenly unemployed Seagram executive has overlooked at his peril. His easy self-confidence is reflected in the casual stance of the man as he looks down from his fifth-floor office (with its Miró tapestries and Rodin statues*) at the street below where ordinary New Yorkers in their polyester double-knits appear to be moving with all the grace of debauched kangaroos.

He stands there, looking through one of his ten office windows, and he is beautiful, the body supple and relaxed, the fingernails manicured but not polished, the face graced by just a touch of tan, the suits cut with precisely understated elegance by the bespoke tailor Douglas Hayward, of London. He is beautiful, and he knows all the tricks: how to invite attention by deliberately reducing the tempo of his limb movements; how to time and execute those throwaway gestures that

---

* The office contains two of Joan Miró's most valuable works as well as Auguste Rodin's famous nude statue of Honoré de Balzac, mounted on a specially designed pedestal chiseled out of travertine, overlooking another lifesize Rodin sculpture of Balzac posing in a cloak.

mean so much; how to dilute the punctuating chop of his right fist (which signals conviction) with the elbow-grabbing grip of his left hand (which conveys sincerity on the hoof). The camera-shutter wink. He is beautiful, but it is his star quality rather than good looks that sets him apart. He vaguely resembles a young Joseph Cotten with *chutzpah*. There is about him the aura of a Hollywood leading man at the top of his form, still secure enough that he doesn't have to keep looking deliberately unconcerned while making certain he's being recognized.

Edgar is the power center of the current generation of Bronfmans. His brother and sisters, his cousins and aunts and nephews, his associates and enemies—all keep trying to calculate his motives, to guess where he stands, to speculate on what he'll do next. If there is about him an elusive quality, a kind of subversive naïvety that frustrates the many Edgar-watchers, it's because he finds his own role confusing. His life boasts several incarnations. There was a stage in the exhilaration of the blood that came with the initial exercise of power in large dollops that prompted Edgar to act as if he alone mattered in the universe. This was his ultimate indulgence. He appeared, for a time, to be suffering from that rarely diagnosed disease that infects so many offspring of the very rich: a terminal case of immaturity.

When the waiter at a reception in Seagram's Montreal boardroom once ran out of V.O., Edgar marched over to Charles and spat out, "I'd fire him."

"It's too bad you can't condone one mistake," the younger brother replied.

Edgar considered this novel proposition. Then he demanded, "Why should I?" And walked away.

Life has imprinted few sorrow lines on Edgar Bronfman's forty-nine-year-old face, which betrays the soft, spoiled-child look of a man who has so much he thinks he should have everything. But his past roles have taken their toll, and he has arrived in his middle years wiser, more at peace with himself, aware that money can never purchase emotional protection; that what matters is not perfection but process; that the price of real love is very high. Above all, he knows that unchecked ambition can occupy a man's mind like a conquering army, displacing all of the remembered, everyday pleasures. "I'm not going to be a slave to the business like my father was," he once told Saul Hayes. He has since amply validated his own decree. The day after he dropped an estimated $10 million in an unsuccessful bid to gain control of Metro-Goldwyn-Mayer, Edgar flew to Spain with Baron Alain de Gunzburg to shoot red-leg partridge at a private hunting lodge while his father wept. He occasionally takes off to bag Cape buffalo in Africa, hunt quail in North Carolina, or stalk pheasant on Ile aux Ruaux in the St. Lawrence. He once went to Istanbul with newsman David Brinkley (who is a Presbyterian) to celebrate Yom Kippur and generally lives on a scale that Sam's conscience could not have afforded.

Edgar maintains several sumptuous New York residences, including an uptown Fifth Avenue penthouse and a $750,000 Tudor mansion on 174 acres at Yorktown Heights in Westchester County (Averell Harriman lives next door). "We have a nice house," he admits, "but it looks a lot more imposing than it is. It has a large master bedroom and a room for Adam; then there are some rooms upstairs for the maids and for the baby. There's also a guest house because I didn't have any space if the other kids wanted to come by. But it's nothing one would get enormously excited about."

With his third wife, Georgiana, Edgar moves in the rarefied company of that golden handful among New York's "beautiful people" who also possess significant national economic clout. He maintains a distant kinship with the American establishment—he is on a first-name basis with David Rockefeller; his friends include J. Paul Austin, chairman of Coca-Cola, and John L. Weinberg, one of Wall Street's most brilliant financiers —but has never tried to become one of its members.

His non-Jewish associations (the Saratoga Performing
Arts Center, the Salk Institute for Biological Studies,
the National Urban League, the American Technion
Society, the New York Council of Boy Scouts) qualify
more for their interest than as milestones of upward
social mobility. Most of his volunteer time is devoted to
Jewish philanthropies. He is North American chairman of the World Jewish Congress, collects hard for
the United Jewish Appeal, and in October of 1976 was
awarded the Weizmann Medallion, Israel's highest form
of international recognition. "I don't really spend a lot
of time thinking about being Jewish one way or the
other," he confesses. "I'm not sure there is a God, and
if there is one, whether He gives a damn, or why He
should. . . . We don't serve any pork products at home.
I occasionally go to synagogue, especially on Yom
Kippur. So I don't turn my back on it, but I'm not a
philosophically practicing Jew. Still, in terms of Jewish
heritage, Jewish plight, and the State of Israel, I'm very
Jewish. Recently I've started studying the Talmud once
or twice a week. I find it fascinating."

Although he didn't become a registered Democrat
until Jerry Ford granted the executive pardon to Richard Nixon, Edgar has long been active in American
politics and at one time briefly considered trying to
become Secretary of Health, Education and Welfare in
the Lyndon Johnson Cabinet. He helped finance the
1977 New York mayoral campaign of Mario Cuomo*
and was the first important Manhattan businessman to
back Carter's presidential campaign. "Jimmy Carter
came over to the apartment for dinner about two years
before his run, and while there wasn't a candidate I
didn't meet, I thought this was the one guy who was
going to make it," he says. "I checked a little bit and
discovered that what he claimed about the black vote

* A fellow sponsor was Edgar Bronfman's friend Jacqueline
Kennedy Onassis. Asked at a Cuomo press conference to explain her reasons for backing Cuomo, she replied, "Because he
reminds me of my husband." One wide-awake reporter stopped
her cold with the question, "Which one?"

was true. He had it. I raised a lot of money for him, especially from the Jewish community here in New York. My thesis was: 'Do you want him in the White House with us or without us? He's going to be there anyway.' " Along with Henry Ford II and J. Paul Austin of Coca-Cola, he organized the luncheon in New York City for fifty-two of the most prominent business executives in the United States that Carter later credited with being the turning point in helping bring the business community around to his candidacy. Edgar didn't attend President Carter's inaugural (he was in Dallas on Seagram oil business that weekend) but he must have been one of the very few Americans to turn down *six* separate invitations for the event. "If I ever did need to see Jimmy Carter about something serious," he says, "I would just pick up the phone, call Robert Lipshutz [a senior White House counsel who was treasurer of Jimmy Carter's campaign] and line up an appointment."

Ideologically, Edgar is a pragmatic Democrat who believes that free enterprise should police its own abuses. ("The electorate now mistrusts business when we act only as angry guardians of our endangered culture, automatically rejecting every government initiative and offering little in its place. We must stop being dragged, kicking and protesting, toward inevitable change and instead take an active and constructive part in it.") His Democratic inclination, however, did not prevent Seagram's, like most other major U.S. corporations, from getting caught up in the rush to contribute to Richard Nixon's 1972 re-election campaign. The Securities and Exchange Commission in Washington later revealed that the company had been engaged in illegal trade practices that included special discounts, the purchase of tickets, and cash contributions to politically sponsored dinners and other events. The $435,000 spent in 1970 on these activities, plus Nixon's $50,000, were repaid to the Seagram treasury by the Bronfmans during the SEC investigation through Cemp Investments Ltd.

Edgar is not a joiner. His only important social allegiance is to Westchester County's Century Country Club, which is so exclusive that until recently it consisted almost entirely of descendants of the German-Jewish investment banking families that populated Wall Street at the turn of the century, plus what a member once disdainfully described as "a few token Gimbels from the retail trade." The doors of the Century are so difficult to breach that there's another club called the Sunningdale whose members are really just waiting to get into the Century, though there also exists the Old Oaks Country Club, whose membership consists largely of Westchester Jews trying to get into Sunningdale.

Into the late sixties, Edgar and his family spent most of their vacations at his 4,480-acre estate (aptly named the V.O. Ranch) in Florida, and until recently he took his Grumman Gulfstream II—the most luxurious of the executive jets (priced at a pre-fitted $4.5 million, it costs at least another million to equip)—down to Acapulco for long weekends. He has since sold both the Grumman and the Acapulco villa and now owns a manor house in the horse country of Virginia. A few seasons ago, Edgar found that he enjoyed tennis matches with Gabino Palafox, the assistant pro at the Century, so much that he arranged for him to be interviewed and hired by Seagram's Mexican subsidiary. When his brother Charles arrived to join him in Acapulco for a January meeting, Edgar suggested they stage a tennis tournament.

"Sure," said Charles. "I'll take John Heilmann from our New York office as my partner. Who's going to be yours?"

"I don't know. I'll find one."

"Now, it's got to be a Seagram executive."

"Okay. I promise. Want to play for money? Let's make it ten dollars a set."

"That's too high. How about ten pesos?"

So Edgar naturally picked his former partner, Palafox, who by this time, without Charles's knowledge, had risen to become Mexico's third-ranking tennis player.

"After several sets," Edgar likes to recall, "Charles decided he really wasn't going to beat us. . . . The following year we all went to his winter place at Half Moon Bay in Jamaica and decided it was time for a rematch. Charles picked a guy called Richard Russell as his partner. Now, I happen to know Russell's the best of the Half Moon pros. But Charles insisted he'd put him on the Seagram payroll for a week as a consultant. So I told him, 'No, Charles. No, no, no. That's been done once before. . . .' "

AWAY FROM THE TENNIS COURTS, THERE IS LITTLE APPARENT RIVALRY BETWEEN THE BROTHERS. Their separate roles were settled when they were both juniors in Mr. Sam's Montreal office, during an informal chat one evening in the summer of 1952 on the porch off the Belvedere Palace kitchen. Charles's memories of that pivotal exchange are precise. "Edgar started off by saying: 'There's something we have to talk about.'

" 'What is it?'

" 'Well, I'd like to go to New York.'

" 'Be my guest.'

" 'Well, you know what that means. With eighty percent of the business done in the U.S., I'll be Number Two and you'll be Number Three.'

" 'Yeah, I understand all that, but I want to stay in Canada. Besides, I don't like the idea of being a crown prince.'

" 'I do. Anyway, we're both crown princes whether we like it or not. Let's tell Father that I'll take over in New York while you run Seagram's and Cemp here.'

" 'Agreed.' "

Edgar was at the time spending his days working at a small desk in Mr. Sam's office, learning the business from the top down. "I felt that my father loved me more . . . no . . . love isn't the word—*expected* more from me as the Number One son. At first, I resented the hell out of it. But when I was about twenty or twenty-one, I began to enjoy it."

His first major assignment came about by accident:

"I was working with Roy Martin, our chief blender at the Ville La Salle plant, a genius who taught me everything I know about blending. One day we were sitting in the lab and I noticed he looked green. I thought, this guy's got either jaundice, hepatitis, or something. So when I went home that night I asked Father if he'd send Roy on vacation. 'Yeah,' he said, 'that's fine, but who's going to do the blending?' I said that I'd try and then ran into one of the most agonizing times of my life.

"It was October, and we were getting ready for the big holiday deliveries when I found out that a batch of V.O.—about twenty-five thousand cases—wasn't up to standard. I called Father in New York, but he just told me to find my own way out of it. So I shut down the bottling house and started working straight through the weekend until I discovered the slip-up in blending. We got it corrected just in time, because I was near collapse."

Edgar's decision to close up the plant, which required considerable determination for a twenty-three-year-old, even if he was the owner's son, impressed Sam enough that he began to think in terms of granting his elder son some real authority. That same year, when Edgar flew into New York for a weekend on the town, Charles insisted that his brother help make up a foursome with two girls he knew. It was a blind date for Edgar, who remembers thinking, "If Charles saddles me with a dog, dinner's going to be a real drag." His date turned out to be Ann Margaret Loeb, daughter of John Langeloth Loeb, senior partner in Loeb, Rhoades and Company, one of Wall Street's most prestige-laden investment banking houses (now known, after a 1977 merger, as Loeb Rhoades, Hornblower & Co., with an estimated $600 million under private management). Ann and Edgar immediately took to each other and were married in 1953. At the reception after the ceremony, which united two of the world's wealthiest Jewish dynasties, an overdressed matron came up to Carl M. Loeb, the German-born founding patriarch of the New York banking house, and gushed on about the miraculous union of the beautiful young couple, how utterly suitable they were, and how this surely must be the most thrilling day of his life. The elderly Loeb's measured reply (which Sam later loved to repeat) was to shrug mild agreement and declare, "All true, Madam. But at my age, I'm not sure that I can adjust to the idea of being a poor relation."

John Loeb was appointed to Seagram's board and in turn invited the Bronfmans to participate (through Cemp) in most of Loeb, Rhoades's private offerings. Loeb took Cemp along with him into substantial stock positions in Cuban Atlantic Sugar, Curtis Publishing, Paramount, and Pure Oil Co. In December of 1955, Sam moved Edgar to New York as chairman of Seagram's administrative committee. "There were two factors involved in the timing of my transfer," Edgar recalls. "For one thing, I was old enough to escape the U.S. military draft and the other was that my father felt he really needed me down in New York. He obviously had more confidence in me than he should have had, but not more than I had at that age. The administrative operation in New York had to be straightened out, and he said that I should go down and do it. Also, I wanted to strike out on my own a little more, which was possible in New York because I was much more anonymous there than I could be in Montreal, bearing the Bronfman name."

Edgar built his young wife a storybook Georgian mansion in Purchase, New York, complete with a pool, pool house, and tennis court. He became an enthusiastic New Yorker overnight and applied for American citizenship as soon as he could qualify. "I remember the day I was sworn in," he says. "My father had me and the judge come up to the office for lunch. Dad was a little upset that I felt nothing. But I didn't think that emotionally I'd made any basic change. I have a feeling North America is all one country and I still can't get used to going through customs when I travel from New York to Canada. I find more difference going to Texas."

Edgar's arrival in New York launched him into a power struggle with Victor A. Fischel, a red-headed Seagram veteran who had joined the firm in 1928 as a $35-a-week salesman and quickly established himself as Mr. Sam's closest confidant. Ironically, it was Fischel who drove Saidye to the hospital on June 20, 1929— the day Edgar was born—because Sam was on one of his interminable series of out-of-town trips. During Prohibition Fischel took charge of dealing with the bootleggers who drove into Montreal from Saranac Lake, Plattsburgh, Rouses Point, and other northern U.S. towns to load up their Packards and Pierce-Arrows with Bronfman package goods. He moved across the border himself as soon as Sam decided to enter the American market more openly. It was Fischel's reputation as a gregarious belly-to-belly whisky salesman that established the dealer-and-distributor network that allowed the new company's brands so quickly to dominate the U.S. market. Victor Fischel still had Mr. Sam's ear, and damned if he was going to allow any young upstart to challenge his authority or his methods. The feud lasted through seven years of office infighting, and it was Edgar's ouster of Fischel against Sam's wishes that really marked the transfer of power between the two Bronfman generations.

Edgar lost the first round when he hired Robert Bragarnick away from Revlon, a company that Edgar at that time regarded as having the ideal mass-marketing approach. The cosmetics executive lasted only twenty months. His demise came about at a Seagram sales meeting, when Mr. Sam, with a grinning Victor Fischel by his side, looked down the boardroom table at the unfortunate Bragarnick and, turning to Edgar, asked, "Why is that guy still with the company?"

Now it was up to Edgar to reassert his authority, and three months later, in June of 1957, he confronted Sam with the news that the moment had arrived for him to be named president of Joseph E. Seagram & Sons Inc. The elder Bronfman wouldn't hear of it, pointing out that at twenty-eight, with less than two years of operating experience, Edgar was far from ready. The argument raged on, and finally Edgar stood up, deliberately creating the impression that he might be walking out. "If you're saying that the company isn't good enough for me," he said, "then I don't want to work for it."

Recalling his son's determination five years earlier in closing down the Ville La Salle distillery and realizing that he just might be headstrong enough to carry out his threat, Sam consulted Saidye, then capitulated.

Edgar's first major decision as Seagram's U.S. president was to resurrect Calvert Reserve, one of the company's most important brands, which had slipped in sales from an annual 3.3 million cases in 1952 to 1.2 million. Instead of merely lightening the Calvert blend to go along with market trends, Edgar chose to remove Calvert Reserve from liquor-store shelves altogether. This was considered a fairly daring step because the brand was still selling more than a million cases a year. Edgar replaced it with a fresh blend called Calvert Extra, backing its introduction with a $7-million advertising budget and a personal tour of the United States promoting the new product. The maneuver worked; within a year sales of Calvert Extra were up to two million cases. "It was the biggest marketing problem we had at the time," Edgar recalls. "What happened proved something to me about myself and may have proved something to my father about himself."

It also proved something to Victor Fischel. By 1962, Sam was backing away from him, supporting Edgar's decisions, expanding the boundaries of his son's autonomy. Edgar finally forced Fischel's resignation by offering him a separation settlement the old master salesman couldn't refuse. Seagram's agreed to finance (with 81 percent of the subscribed capital) a new marketing firm for Fischel that would handle U.S. sales of Carstairs whisky and Wolfschmidt vodka. The Fischel departure put the final stamp on Edgar's authority. "I became president *de jure* in 1957 and *de facto* in 1962," he maintains.

Edgar pushed the company into additional brands of rum (from new distilleries in Hawaii, Puerto Rico, and Jamaica), Scotch (100 Pipers and Passport), bottled cocktails (Manhattans, daiquiris, whisky sours, and martinis), and began to import wine on a large scale—fielding what the business section of *Time* described as "the most ambitious marketing program ever undertaken by any distiller." He expanded the firm's interests in Europe and South America, pushing everywhere, challenging his continually changing retinue of vice-presidents with surveys calling for ever-rising market targets. By the end of 1965 the Bronfmans were operating in 119 countries and Seagram's sales had burst through the magic $1-billion mark. Edgar brought an existential zest to his duties, deliberately straining himself to the very limits of endurance, daring his rivals at every turn. "I love competition," he declared. "Without it you can't be in this game. You might as well live on top of a mountain and write poetry. If you don't keep driving, you'll fall back. And that's just not in us."

As the business grew larger and more complicated, Sam's paternalistic and pragmatic decisions were increasingly being replaced by Edgar's faith in modern management methods. Harvard M.B.A.s and the Revlon mass-merchandisers moved in with their flow charts, planned operational programs, and rotational job-training schemes. Richard Goeltz, a whiz kid who was named treasurer of Joseph E. Seagram & Sons at the age of thirty, for example, altered the relatively simple business of insuring warehouses holding liquor stocks into something he called "risk management." For each new shed he would calculate whether it should be constructed of cinder block and equipped with an expensive sprinkler-alarm system so that the need for insurance could be practically eliminated. "It's my job," he explained, "to determine the net present value cost tradeoffs of additional capital investments to reduce insurance premiums while maintaining an exposure to loss which is acceptable to management." Or something. Edgar also introduced Seagram's to Madison

Avenue hype. To celebrate the twenty-fifth anniversary (1947–1972) of Seagram's Seven Crown's becoming the world's largest-selling whisky, for instance, dealers and distributors were invited to a three-day bash in Montreal, climaxed by six girls in chartreuse bikinis dancing on their hands. Sam Friedman, a wholesaler from Chicago, was so overcome by the occasion that at one particularly wet moment in the proceedings he got up and, searching for adequate praise in an ocean of superlatives, declared, "Seven Crown is just like the Statue of Liberty!"

Sam's most important legacy to Seagram's in his final decade was to take the distilling complex into the petroleum business. During the early fifties, along with his brother Allan he had invested in a medium-sized Alberta oil company called Royalite, which they eventually sold to Gulf. He later purchased the Frankfort Oil Company, a tiny Oklahoma producer, and in 1963 acquired the seventy-five-year-old Texas Pacific Coal and Oil Company for $276 million. Dating back to a tiny coal operation fueling steam engines at Thurber, Texas, the company had grown by acquiring a major stake in the Ranger oilfield and was by then the fifth-largest U.S. independent oil producer.

Mr. Sam was able to purchase Texas Pacific with a small cash outlay. On the basis of Seagram's earnings ($34 million) and working capital ($382 million) he floated a series of institutional loans for $50 million, which were turned over to Texas Pacific's former owners as a down payment. The balance of $226 million was paid off during the next twelve years as a fixed percentage of actual oil revenues. Seagram was at the same time able to claim a 22-percent cost-depletion allowance. "The deal," as Raoul Engel, then with the *Financial Post,* noted, "was the next best thing to self-levitation, or lifting yourself off the ground by your own shoelaces."

SAM EVENTUALLY PLACED HIMSELF ON HIS SON'S PAYROLL AS A $100,000-A-YEAR CONSULTANT, but his interest in Seagram's remained undiminished. "We'd argue," Edgar recalls, "but I never had enough *chutzpah* to say, 'Well, I'm president and by God we'll do it my way.' You couldn't fool him, you couldn't lie to him. If you didn't know something, it was much better to tell him, because if he'd catch you out, it could get very rough." The deeper problem was that Sam not unnaturally perceived Edgar as a symbol of his own mortality and, in order to keep demonstrating his staying power, occasionally contradicted the son's directives. "The trouble," commented *Forbes,* the U.S. business journal, "was that Mr. Sam grew old and increasingly out of touch with his industry. Like many a strongman-founder, he overstayed his time, either not listening to the unwelcome truth or not being told it by his fearful managers."

Personally, as well, the two men were close, but as more and more authority shifted to Edgar, it was the older Bronfman who had to demand attention. "I remember Father phoning one weekend from his place in Tarrytown and saying, 'Come on over for a *schmooz,*' and I told him, 'Listen, Pop, if you have specific problems, I'll come and talk to you about them. But I have a family.' "

What nobody dared tell Sam was that North American drinking habits were in the process of a fundamental change that was not being reflected in Seagram production priorities. During the last ten years of his life the overall sales of blended whiskies declined from 60 percent to 20 percent of the total market, but Sam never stopped believing that his company was basically in the business of flavoring alcohol. His unwillingness to keep pace with the industry's heavy move into vodka and gin marketing seriously threatened Seagram's dominance.

Mr. Sam admitted that he was wrong only once. Near the end of his life, during a sentimental journey to Ireland, he was relaxing in the bar of his Dublin hotel when Michael McCormick, the senior Seagram vice-president accompanying him, asked whether his fabulously successful career had been marred by any mistakes. "What do you mean, a bloody mistake?" Sam exploded, his eyes popping-mean like the peas in a frozen TV dinner. "Why would you ask a stupid question like that?"

After sputtering a few more expletives, Sam calmed down and confessed. "All right. So you ask that goddamn question. Yeah. Sure, I've made mistakes. The biggest was vodka. I never believed the public would want to buy something with no taste to it. My whole life was built on blending flavors."

Seagram's actually never stopped growing, however, in either revenues or profits, because its leading brands, notably Seven Crown, V.O., Chivas, and Crown Royal, continued to capture an increasing share of their declining markets. This trend has continued. While U.S. consumption of blended whisky declined by 30 percent between 1965 and 1977, Seven Crown increased its share of the remaining volume from 27 percent to 40 percent. "As for consumption by categories," Edgar Bronfman complained in his 1977 report to shareholders, "it's almost as if the labels were shuffled like a deck of cards and thrown at random down a flight of stairs."

The emphasis remained on trying to grab a larger share of the declining volume in blended whiskies, allowing competitors to move into the booming so-called "white goods" market. Mr. Sam was delighted when Frank Schwengel, Seagram's crusty sales manager, expressed his contempt for the new product by ostentatiously dumping a case of vodka into a swimming pool at an American Legion convention.

Frustrated by Sam's long-delayed departure and anxious to strike out on his own, Edgar Bronfman decided during the late sixties to turn at least part of his energies to the film industry. He had always been fascinated by that business's exhilarating ferment and excited by its potential as "a non-capital-intensive business with a positive cash flow." Cemp had been buying into Paramount for several years, but too many other capital pools were after the Hollywood studios to offer much hope of attaining control. In 1967, Edgar got Cemp Investments to purchase a block of 820,000 shares in Metro-Goldwyn-Mayer. Despite Sam's objections, the family eventually sank $40 million into acquiring 15 percent of Metro-Goldwyn-Mayer's outstanding stock, enough to capture voting control. The actual telephone call consisted of Edgar calling up Leo Kolber in Montreal and saying, "Listen, Leo, have you got any money? I just bought forty million dollars' worth of M-G-M stock." It was Edgar's long-term intention to merge the studio with Time Inc., which quietly acquired 315,000 (6 percent) of M-G-M's shares on its own. By 1970, *Time* reported a $14-million paper loss on its M-G-M investment.

Sam opposed any move into the film business in general and the M-G-M venture in particular for reasons that he found hard to articulate. But one day he walked into Edgar's office and after carefully closing the door, clearing his throat, and behaving with a hesitancy foreign to his usual manner, he stammered out the operative query: "Tell me, Edgar, are we buying all this stock in M-G-M just so you can get laid?"

"Oh, no, Pop," was Edgar's classic reply, "it doesn't cost forty million to get laid."

Edgar's involvement deepened in May 1969, when he gathered enough clout on the M-G-M board to replace Robert H. O'Brien as the studio's chairman. Appointed along with Bronfman to the M-G-M board were Leo Kolber, John L. Loeb, Jr., and Cemp general manager John Wanamaker. M G M lost $25 million in its 1968 fiscal year. His first important decision was to install his friend Louis F. "Bo" Polk, Jr., as president. His second major decision, taken only three months later, was to resign. By secretly putting out $100 millions' worth of tender calls, a high-roller from Las Vegas named Kirk Kerkorian had suddenly managed to accumulate 25 percent of M-G-M's stock—enough to force out the Bronfman interests. "Bo and I are out," Edgar told a friend at the time. "That ball game's over. With the kind of money Kerkorian's putting up, he can call the shots. Now we'll be in there for the ride." Edgar had wanted to fend off the Las Vegas bid by plunging into M-G-M even deeper, but for the first time the other members of the family overruled him. When Edgar told Sam about the Kerkorian offer, his only reaction was a long sigh of relief. "I'm just goddamned glad to see that someone else besides you thinks it's interesting."

It has never been clear exactly how much the Bronfmans lost in the M-G-M investment, though Cemp insiders estimate the amount at about $10 million. Edgar kept his personal shares, on which he eventually realized a profit, and his chief regret about the whole caper seems to have been his embarrassment when he walked into a Hollywood nightclub just after his ouster. Comedian Don Rickles stopped the show by welcoming him with the salute, "Hey, there's Edgar Bronfman! He was chairman of M-G-M for five whole minutes!" The M-G-M experience didn't extinguish Edgar's love of show business. He established Sagittarius Productions Incorporated in New York, which staged several Broadway hits during the late sixties.*

It was not other business but his personal life that

---

* Sagittarius is not named after Edgar's sign: he's a Gemini. The company's successes included Stuart Ostrow's *The Apple Tree* and *1776*, as well as the Obie Award-winning musical *The Me Nobody Knows*. Sagittarius moved into film production during the early seventies. Its major vehicles have been: *Jane Eyre*, featuring George C. Scott and Susannah York; *Ash Wednesday*, starring Elizabeth Taylor; *Charlotte's Web*, an adaptation of E. B. White's children's tale; and *Joe Hill*, which won a Cannes Film Festival Award. The company is now being run by Edgar's second son, Edgar, Jr., who produced a movie starring Peter Sellers (*Blockhouse*) when he was only seventeen and more recently acquired the movie rights to *Harlequin*, a Morris West novel, which, ironically enough, deals with the kidnapping of a wealthy young heir, and Robert Penn Warren's *A Place to Come To*, which will star Robert Redford. Edgar also owns Centaur Publishing and Bowman Music Corp.— Sagittarius subsidiaries that market the music from its productions.

next distracted Edgar from his Seagram's involvement. Despite the happy relationship with his five children— Sam II, Edgar, Jr., Holly, Matthew, and Adam—his marriage to Ann Loeb had by the early 1970s gone sour, and they decided to split up. "The divorce by Ann," reported *Time*, "who is wealthy in her own right as an heir to the John L. Loeb investment family, apparently stemmed from Bronfman's often open involvement with young models and society girls. It broke up what had once been a lively circle of New York's theatrical, intellectual and political personalities—like Nelson Rockefeller and Senator Jacob Javits—who enjoyed visiting the Bronfmans in their lavish Park Avenue apartment." (The only Bronfman money that remained in Loeb Rhoades was $5 million through Tortuga Investments Inc., a trust set up for the five Loeb-Bronfman children. Seagram's switched its Wall Street account to Goldman, Sachs & Co. after Edgar's divorce and early in 1978 wound up the Tortuga fund.)

Edgar's new romance blossomed with Lady Carolyn Townshend—the quintessence of blonde, British, aristocratic beauty and a direct descendant of the man whose tea tax on the British colonies had set off the American Revolution. He had first encountered her in 1968 during a visit to London, but they didn't begin seriously dating until December of 1972. By then the lively Lady Carolyn had met, married, and divorced Antonio Capellini, a patrician of Genoa, whom she described as "the man of my dreams." Twenty-eight at the time, Lady Carolyn joined Seagram's public-relations department in London, and during one of their sojourns together in Paris, Edgar proposed to her.

After much marital unhappiness, Egar found himself totally infatuated with the WASP princess. The lady seemed most receptive to his marriage offers, but constantly complained about her "financial insecurity." To calm her fears and assure his happiness, Edgar proposed an unprecedentedly generous pre-marriage agreement. In return for accepting his proposal, Lady Carolyn would (1) be granted a cash payment of $1 million; (2) be given the deed to the baronial Bronfman estate at Yorktown Heights (Edgar also agreed to sell his Park Avenue apartment with its marble dining room and magnificent vista of New York so that his new bride would not be reminded of Ann Loeb); (3) be allowed to pick out $115,000 worth of jewelry; (4) be paid an extra $4,000 a month on top of housekeeping funds for use as personal pocket money. In the court action that eventually upset this ante-nuptial settlement, Edgar testified that his magnanimous gesture had been rebuffed by the acquisitive Lady Carolyn as being inadequate. "She suggested that her family had advised her because I was a man of means, one million was a paltry sum and I should settle five million dollars on her."

The wedding took place on December 18, 1973, at New York's St. Regis Hotel. But nothing else did. On their wedding night, Lady Carolyn rudely dispatched Edgar to sleep in his Park Avenue apartment, and during their ensuing honeymoon in Acapulco she continued to repulse his approaches. "I told Edgar he was not being very affectionate with me," she later testified. She insisted that the marriage was in fact consummated later during the honeymoon, but Edgar vehemently denied this, claiming that Lady Carolyn "had a hangup about sex after the marriage," adding that this was difficult to understand because she had demonstrated no such restraint while he was courting her. Nels R. Johnson, a friend of the bride's, testified that Dr. Sheldon Glabman, a New York specialist in internal medicine, had boasted that Lady Carolyn had spent most of her wedding night with him. Johnson also told the court she had confided to him in Switzerland two months previously that Edgar had screwed a lot of people and "it gives me a lot of satisfaction to screw him without having to deliver."

Edgar's evidence won the day. An order signed December 16, 1974, by Jacob Grumet, a justice of the New York Supreme Court, annulled the marriage. Lady Carolyn was forced to return the million dollars as well as the deed to the Yorktown house; besides being allowed to keep the jewels, she was awarded only a relatively paltry annual allowance of $40,000 for eleven years. She agreed that she would "immediately and forever refrain from using the name Bronfman in identifying herself."

This bizarre episode seemed at first blush to be an aberration from Edgar's lifelong aim of proving himself worthy of the Bronfman crown; win or lose, by deliberately going to court over as delicate an issue as his sex life, his image could not help but be tarnished. But, at another level, his decision to battle Lady Carolyn was perfectly in character. "It was simply a matter of pride. I hate to be taken. I knew I was right and was determined to prove it. I went into court because the good lady didn't accept what I thought was a fair offer on my part. I knew there was going to be a lot of publicity, and I could live with that. But I thought it might be very difficult for my mother, so I called her just before I made the final, irrevocable decision to go ahead, and asked her advice. I remember saying, 'Before you answer yes or no, I just want to point out that I think Father worked a little too hard to give the money to such a bitch'—though I used a much stronger word than that—and my mother replied, 'You're goddamn right,' and that was that."

The next episode in Edgar's public life turned out to be even unhappier. On August 8, 1975, Edgar's eldest son, twenty-three-year-old Samuel II,* drove away from dinner at the family's Yorktown house in his green BMW sedan to visit friends. Two hours later José Luis, the Bronfman butler, answered the telephone, to be told by young Sam, "Call my father. I've been kidnapped!" A ransom note eventually arrived, demanding

---

* Young Sam was about to start a new job as a trainee in the promotion department of *Sports Illustrated*. He had graduated from Williams College, where he had taken an American Studies program with indifferent grades. When fellow students complained that the sidewalk in front of the $1.3-million Bronfman Science Center (donated by Edgar) at Williams was littered with junk, Sam swept the debris away himself.

$4.5 million in small-denomination bills, and the kidnapping became front-page news. Twenty FBI agents moved into the Bronfman house, two dozen extra telephone lines had to be installed, mysterious messengers arrived and departed, police helicopters hovered overhead, scores of reporters besieged the gates. "FEAR GROWS FOR KIDNAPPED HEIR" screamed a headline in the *New York Post*. The problem was not raising the ransom—which was the largest ever demanded in American kidnapping history—but finding some practical way of delivering it. The requested $4.5 million in twenty-dollar bills filled fourteen normal-sized suitcases.

Family spokesmen stressed that Edgar was eager to comply with instructions from the kidnappers, but despite several phone contacts it wasn't until four days later that an authenticated message was received, reducing the ransom demand by half and giving specific instructions about its delivery. In downtown New York on August 16, Edgar handed $2.3 million jammed into two oversized plastic garbage bags to a lone stranger, who drove off with them. The following day, police rescued young Sam, bound and blindfolded, in the Brooklyn apartment of Mel Patrick Lynch, a New York fireman, having been led there by Dominic Byrne, an airport-limousine driver who had become nervous and tipped them off.

In the thirty-five-day trial that followed, Lynch testified that he and Sam had been homosexual lovers. He told the court that young Bronfman had blackmailed him into the complicated kidnap hoax in an effort to extort money from his father. The possibility of subscribing to such a perplexing twist in the young heir's motivations proved less important to the jury than the kidnappers' tools. When William Link, one of the jurors, picked up the rope with which Bronfman had been tied and tugged at its knotted ends, it broke in three places. That such a binding could hold the six-foot-three, 185-pound Bronfman strained the jury's credence. Young Sam didn't deny that the rope was frayed, but claimed that if he had tried to free himself, the kidnappers would have killed him. The most damaging evidence was the tape of a telephone exchange between Edgar and his son during the kidnapping on which Sam emotionally begged his father to pay the ransom, then, regaining his composure, was heard remarking to his captors, "Hold it, I'll do it again."

The jury acquitted Lynch and Byrne of kidnapping, though they were convicted on the lesser charge of extortion. Surrounded by his family in an office at Seagram's headquarters, young Sam condemned the verdict. "I'm shocked and stunned, furious that people could believe I was a homosexual and an extortionist. I've had everything I ever wanted.* Where's my motive for a crime against my dad? . . . I was forced into a new world, far away from Williams College, Deerfield Academy, and the hallowed halls of the Seagram Building. I thought my best bet for survival was to stay put and wait for the ransom to be paid. And goddamn it, whatever the jury said, I played it right. I'm alive today, aren't I?"

Edgar staunchly defended his son, maintaining that the whole strange incident had only brought his family much closer together. "It was a very sloppy trial," he says. "There's no question as to how the parole officer or the FBI or anybody else felt about it. I mean, there's never been any question in anybody's mind, except the jury's, that Sam obviously had nothing to do with it. I always found it very insulting, that if he had anything to do with it, they would have done a much better job than they did. They couldn't possibly have been that inept. But that's all behind us."

On August 20, 1975, just three days after Sam had been rescued, Edgar married the former Georgiana Eileen Webb, the twenty-five-year-old daughter of the proprietor of Ye Olde Nosebag, an inn at Finchingfield, northeast of London in the Essex countryside, where

---

* Young Sam at that point in life was receiving annual pocket money of $32,000. He is slated to inherit $5 million at his thirtieth birthday plus an estimated $10 million when he reaches forty.

she had worked briefly as a barmaid. She has since fitted her life to his and turned Jewish—this when she was already expecting her first child, Sara; because her conversion required a new wedding ceremony, she was remarried to Edgar at a Park Avenue synagogue shortly before the birth of the child. In the process, she became one of New York's most-sought-after hostesses and charmed everyone she has met.

THE AVALANCHE OF BAD PUBLICITY GENERATED BY HIS SECOND DIVORCE and the kidnapping didn't materially affect Edgar's management style. Instead of attempting to perpetuate his father's imperious presence, he had from the beginning settled for casual informality ("Nobody calls me anything but Edgar, and that's the way it should be"). His word is final, but he tries to base major decisions on the consensus of Seagram's top executives. "The guys who work around with me, we all kind of like each other, and we know how to let our hair down. When you leave a meeting, you have to make everybody feel part of the decision and believe in it, otherwise these guys can kill you. At least sixty-five percent of my job is psychiatry. It's building men, watching their progress so that you've got back-up for the key guys."

He has less than a dozen top men reporting to him directly, is impatient with subordinates who indulge themselves in rambling discussions. ("I don't want anybody walking into my office with a problem that he doesn't have a solution for.") Edgar's chief handicap is his lack of expertise about the petroleum business, which has become one of Seagram's main revenue sources. Howard Hinson, the head of Texas Pacific Oil, sees Edgar four times a year and telephones him every other week, but Bronfman's input is limited to monitoring the financial decisions. Between 1957 and 1976, Edgar's chief of staff was a tough and self-assured chemical engineer and former naval officer named Jack Yogman. Handling most of the intricate negotiations that spread the Seagram empire into South America and Western Europe, he once found himself juggling fifteen separate deals at the same time. Yogman managed to persuade the seventeen major Chilean wine producers to market their products through Seagram and moved his company into the New Zealand market. By 1965 he had been named Seagram's executive vice-president and three years later became chief operating officer. In August of 1971, Yogman was promoted to president of Seagram's U.S. operations, and his salary took several dramatic leaps. For example, from an annual $250,000 in 1975 his compensation jumped to $398,000 the following year. Incongruously, this brought Yogman's annual income to $24,000 more than Edgar was paying himself, while Charles was taking out a comparatively modest $175,000 per year.

It was not a situation designed to last very long. Unfortunately for Yogman, he had made a macho pledge to the Bronfmans that under the prod of his managerial genius Seagram would hit $100 million in profits by the end of 1976. Instead, 1975 earnings slipped nine percent (to $74 million) and would have shown a far more drastic drop but for the inflow of substantial revenues from Seagram's petroleum subsidiary. Sales of Seven Crown were down 600,000 cases for the year; even the volume of the vaunted V.O. had dropped by more than 300,000 cases. When profits failed to revive significantly in 1976, Seagram shares started to slide badly, with investors who had once been prepared to pay fifteen times earnings beginning to believe a more modest ten might be more appropriate. "Suddenly there was conjecture," Amy Booth wrote in the *Financial Post*. "Although 'the boys' had been in the business since their teens, were they seasoned enough to run such a huge and far-flung concern? . . . Some Bronfman watchers attribute the company's profit drop to the succession to power of Edgar and Charles on the death of Mr. Sam. 'The boys are a far cry from their father,' they'll say. But that's a personal and emotional feeling that has little to do with statistics, because those who think they know will usually add:

'Saidye must be heartbroken over Edgar's shenani-gans.' "

In an interview with Amy Booth, Charles spelled out the company's problems: "I hadn't been satisfied for some time, but the numbers kept coming in. We were over-inventoried. There wasn't strict enough control. We had a multiplicity of brands and were losing money on too many of them. We weren't working hard enough. The heart had gone out of the business."

The Seagram empire had become moribund. Edgar and Charles were confronted with the uncomfortable option of becoming token proprietors or really plunging in and trying to turn their father's troubled empire around.

They decided the first necessary step was to revitalize the Seagram board of directors. Under Mr. Sam's stewardship, boardroom discussions were a family affair; he seldom gave serious heed to directors' opinions or suggestions. One former senior official, J. M. Mc-Avity, recalls that no time was allowed for discussion at board meetings. John L. Loeb, then Edgar's father-in-law, who was appointed to the board in 1956, at-tended one meeting and after seeing how Sam conducted affairs did not come to another. Annual shareholders' meetings were incestuous gatherings made up mostly of company employees and well-rehearsed outsiders who had been given sheets of paper from which to quote. Directors placed bets with each other to see if pro-ceedings could be terminated faster than the record set in 1961, when the whole affair had taken only twenty-nine minutes. That year, 112 of the 117 people who had shown up for the shareholders' gathering had been Seagram employees.

Late in the fall of 1975, a new board was appointed and Seagram's management structure was drastically altered. (The corporate name had been changed from Distillers Corporation–Seagrams Limited to The Sea-gram Company Limited in January.) Four senior direc-tors were retired, removing from the board Allan Bronf-man, Senator Louis P. Gélinas, Loeb, and Joseph

Edward Frowde Seagram.* Jack Yogman was unceremoniously fired in June of 1976, during a Monday-morning showdown in Edgar's office, attended by both brothers. "Charles's parting words to me were: 'You've had a great run,'" Yogman recalled later. "They were Bronfmans and I wasn't, and they wanted their company back."

The terms of Yogman's departure were among the most generous in the history of free enterprise: the Bronfmans agreed to pay him $250,000 a year, plus most of his previous benefits, provided that he stay out of the liquor and oil industries until 1986. Yogman at first became the $100,000-a-year vice-chairman of Esquire Inc., the magazine publishers and filmmakers. In February of 1978 he was named chief executive officer of Ward Foods, which makes Oh Henry chocolate bars and Dolly Madison ice cream.

Supreme command of the Seagram empire was vested in a newly established executive committee (meeting monthly, as compared with the quarterly gatherings of the full board) headed by Charles Bronfman and including Edgar, Leo Kolber, and Baron Alain de Gunzburg in addition to Bill Green, chairman of Clevepak Corporation (a large paper-converting company that is, among other things, the largest supplier of cores for toilet-paper rolls in the United States), and Harold Fieldsteel, the Seagram treasurer. As well as these continuing board members, four of Canada's most important business-establishment figures were invited to join:

1. Paul Desmarais, chairman and chief executive officer of Power Corporation of Canada, the country's most interesting conglomerate and one of its largest, with assets that include the highly profitable Investors Group (Great-West Life and Montreal Trust) and Consolidated-Bathurst, the big paper concern;
2. Ian Sinclair, chairman and chief executive officer

* The last member of his family to sit on the Seagram board, he owned Canbar Products Ltd. (the former Canada Barrels & Kegs Ltd.), which was an important Bronfman supplier.

of Canadian Pacific, which has grown from being merely
a railway system and through its various investment
arms has become Canada's most influential multinational corporation;

3. Fred McNeil, chairman and chief executive officer of the Bank of Montreal, Canada's third-largest
financial institution;

4. Ted Medland, president and chief executive officer
of Wood Gundy, the leading investment and under-
writing house in Canada.

Also confirmed on the new board were Mel Griffin,
the able head of Seagram's Canadian operations; Philip
Vineberg of Montreal, the Bronfman family lawyer;
and John Weinberg, senior partner in the influential
New York investment bank, Goldman, Sachs. "The
executive committee, since it's made up mostly of
family members, monitors such things as profitability
and capital debt ratios," Edgar explains, "but we use
the whole board to discuss general policy. For instance, when it comes to financing, we have Ted Medland, John Weinberg, Fred McNeil, and Paul Desmarais, all pretty savvy guys, specialists in the field.
So any time we want to float a new issue, we don't
just say: 'This is what we want to do.' But we tell
them: 'This is what we're thinking of. . . . What do you
guys feel?' "

The reorganized board managed to inject some badly
needed new blood into Seagram's corporate deliberations, but its members aren't exactly disinterested
strangers. The companies represented by individual
board members all conduct business transactions with
each other. During 1977, for instance, Seagram availed
itself to the maximum of CPR's many services and paid
out $3,237,415 to the Bank of Montreal in standby
fees and interest charges. Seagram bought the bulk of
its glass ($10.5 millions' worth in 1977) from Dom-
glas Limited, which is one of Paul Desmarais's holdings.
Philip Vineberg's legal bills during the year charged
to Seagram (not including the retainers he receives from
various members of the Bronfman family) totaled

$158,358. (Vineberg separately owns, through a personal holding company, 24,000 common shares of Seagram.) Bill Green's Clevepack Corporation until recently rented office quarters in New York's Seagram Building; various Seagram operations in Canada continued to rent space from Cadillac Fairview Corporation, which is thirty-seven percent owned by the Bronfman-controlled Cemp trusts administered by Leo Kolber. All of Seagram's public issues are floated through a banking syndicate headed by three directors: Medland of Wood Gundy, John Weinberg of Goldman, Sachs, and Baron Alain de Gunzburg of Banque Louis-Dreyfus. During 1977, the baron's Paris bank also earned $208,332 in Seagram interest payments. John Weinberg is a partner of Edgar's in the development of some new California vineyards through a jointly controlled company called GS Realty Incorporated.

Altogether, the Seagram boardroom remains a fairly cozy club of men well attuned to their mutual self-interest. One of the board's main concerns was to hire a top-flight marketing man more interested in increasing profits than revenues who could operate efficiently inside the supercharged atmosphere of the Bronfman dynasty. Gerard R. Roche of Heidrick and Struggles, the New York executive recruiters, came up with one name: Philip E. Beekman, then president of Colgate-Palmolive's international operations. A graduate of Dartmouth, he had moved through the soap company's various managerial levels until 1975, when he was named to the difficult $150,000-a-year job of running all Colgate-Palmolive's non-U.S. operations.

Beekman joined Seagram on February 1, 1977, with one of the most generous contracts ever negotiated in North American corporate history. On top of his basic $350,000 salary (plus pension benefits of $125,000 a year at fifty-five and a free $700,000 term life-insurance policy) he was granted an option to purchase 20,000 shares of Seagram stock and given the free use of a limousine and driver. Beekman took charge quickly and smoothly, reorganizing merchandising techniques, increasing the price of most products, doubling advertising outlays. His first year in office produced a net income of $87 million on sales of $2.2 billion—both records. Most significantly, his brief stewardship saw Seagram transformed from a net debtor to a cash generator. In 1975 the company's debt increased by $172 million; in 1977 the net corporate debt was reduced by $104 million. This remarkable turnaround was made possible mainly by reductions in inventory and higher oil revenues. The company's only major new investment during 1977 was to acquire control of Scotland's famous Glenlivet Distillers Limited.*

Beekman remains a Bronfman favorite. "There's always a certain euphoria when you begin, like the president has a honeymoon with Congress, and then it disappears," says Edgar. "But Phil just keeps getting better and better. We work together just beautifully." But there is no doubt about who runs the Seagram empire. Asked by a Montreal *Gazette* reporter at a recent shareholders' meeting where corporate control really rests, Edgar arched his eyebrows and made a swift reply: "My brother Charles and I are in charge of this company, and as long as we agree, that's that."

Edgar now runs Seagram's with the punctilious self-assurance of a man who has been tested and emerged

---

* The offer, at 510 pence ($9.75 U.S.) a share, cost Seagram about $90 million and beat a bid by Suntory, the Japanese distillers, for the prized Highland malt distillery. It was the largest single takeover ever negotiated by the Bronfmans. On the morning of November 7, 1977, a member of the British investment house of Hambros had telephoned his contact at Seagram's to inform him that Imperial Tobacco wanted to sell off its 25-percent holding in Glenlivet. Charles immediately convened an executive committee meeting in New York for the following day, and by November 12 Beekman and Fieldsteel had been dispatched to London to consummate the deal. A smaller block (470,494 shares, worth about $4,580,000 U.S.) was sold by Hudson's Bay Company, which reported in 1978 that it had made a net gain of £1,800,000 on the transaction. HBC, founded in 1670, is a partner of Seagram's in Hudson's Bay Distillers.

much the better for it. "My most important driving force," he says, "is the family heritage. My father created this enterprise, and he meant it to go on. I like the fact that we're the biggest and want to get us even bigger. Just the other day, we were talking about the future and somebody asked me, 'Exactly what do you think your fair share of the market should be?' I just looked right at him and said, 'Considering the quality we put in, *all of it!*' "

14. Leo

ERNEST LEO Kolber is the non-Bronfman Bronfman with the big brain. His assignment for the past two decades has been to manage—silently and profitably—the private fortune of Sam Bronfman's family. He has succeeded so well that Cemp Investments Limited, his main fiscal instrument, has grown from being the operator of a few suburban shopping centers to one of the Western world's most impressive capital pools. Although details of Cemp's operations remain shrouded in the nervous secrecy that is Kolber's trademark, the trust controls assets easily worth $4 billion; its influence extends far beyond its North American base.

Cemp may be the most sophisticated instrument of Canadian high finance ever put together, in the sense that it manages to perpetuate the Bronfmans' control of the Seagram empire while creating no tax liability for its beneficiaries. The family's control is exercised through tiers of holding companies (Econtech, Grandco, Rampart) whose chief asset is 11,422,540 shares of the distillery's stock, worth up to $525 million on the open market. The creative genius who planned this miracle of capitalism was Lazarus Phillips, Mr. Sam's chief legal adviser; Leo Kolber, its administrator since 1958, is a Montreal dentist's son with unlikely credentials who has risen to pivotal status within the Bronfman dynasty.

Leo's climb has been so rapid, the growth of his decision-making authority so impressive, that few outsiders are aware his power base is built squarely on the friendship he developed with Charles as an ambitious eighteen-year-old undergraduate at McGill University during the late forties. Moses, his father, had died when Leo was sixteen, and Luba, his mother, eked out an income from rentals of a tiny apartment block. The two boys had little in common, but somehow their friendship developed into mutual dependence, the shrewdness of the streetwise Leo (whose dominant childhood memory is of being chased home from Bancroft School on St. Urbain Street by kids yelling, "Go home, you dirty Jew!") offsetting Charles's overprotected upbringing. Leo knew precisely what he wanted from life and was single-mindedly confident he would achieve it. This was the quality that probably appealed most to Sam, who may have recognized a bit of his young self in the brash young visitor to the Belvedere Palace. Sam eventually grew so fond of Leo that he openly referred to him as "part of the family." Leo worshipped him as a father.

Kolber introduced both the young Bronfman boys to many previously unsampled delights. When Edgar secretly rented a bachelor apartment in downtown Montreal as a hideaway from his parents, the three youngsters would spend Saturday afternoons in corduroys and T-shirts, roaring around to the Berkley Avenue junk shops in Edgar's Chrysler convertible, buying up cheap furniture.

Leo was still at law school when he purchased a vacant lot in the north end of Montreal to put up some cottages. Charles and Edgar were willing to lend him the money, but Leo decided their terms weren't generous enough. He managed to round up alternative financing, hired his own tradesmen, helped to pour the concrete himself, nailed down shingles before going off to his law classes, and eventually realized a tidy margin on the deal. In 1953, a year after joining Mendelsohn, Rosentzveig and Shacter as a junior partner, Leo ran across sixty thousand square feet of choice Westmount real estate for sale at only $36,000. His Bronfman chums lent him the cash, and six months later he sold the plot for twice the price, distributing 80 percent of the proceeds ($14,400 each) to his proud backers. It was the first cash the Bronfman boys had earned on their own. Many similiar transactions followed. By 1957 it was Sam who decided that Leo Kolber (then twenty-eight) should head Cemp, the family's private investment arm, which had languished under a succession of ultracautious managers. Leo was hired at a salary of $12,500, plus 10 percent of any profits he produced. This was soon renegotiated to $50,000 a year plus 5 percent of profits and has been substantially increased since. An early venture, the Maisonneuve center in Montreal, was a failure, but in the next decade he turned Cemp into the country's largest real-estate operation.

Cemp had been set up in 1951 as a successor to Brintcan Investments, the first family control instrument, established in 1924. Brintcan and Brosis (the latter standing for "brothers and sisters"), which were in turn controlled by a holding company called Bromount, between them originally owned 53 percent of the outstanding stock in Distillers Corporation–Seagrams Ltd. Lazarus Phillips designed the family trusts* (Charles and Edgar each own 30 percent of Cemp; Minda and Phyllis both have 20 percent shares) to shield the Bronfman estate from the impact of succession duties—when James de Rothschild died in 1957, British inheritance taxes of $20 million had to be paid—while perpetuating family control of the Seagram empire. Earlier, Sam and his younger brother, Allan, had

---

* In 1966, *Fortune* estimated the personal wealth of Samuel Bronfman and his children, *not* including their interests in trust funds, at $46.5 million. At that time, in addition to controlling Cemp, the four trust funds also owned Canadian and U.S. securities worth $18 million.

pooled their interests in Seagram's, and this had involved segregating the holdings of their elder brothers Abe and Harry.

The family's controlling interest (33.1 percent of the issued stock) in Seagram's is divided into four unequal holdings:

Charles	3,676,437 shares
Edgar	3,237,889 shares
Phyllis	2,450,884 shares
Minda	2,057,330 shares

The four Bronfman heirs plus Lazarus Phillips, Philip Vineberg, and Leo Kolber act as trustees; the Cemp board of directors, which meets only two or three times a year, consists of Charles, Vineberg, Phillips, Kolber, and Baron Alain de Gunzburg, Minda's husband. As soon as the eldest child in any of the trusts reaches twenty-one, the trust is split in two, and half its income is divided among the members of the younger generation. (This process has already taken place in Edgar's and Minda's trusts.) When the eldest child reaches forty, all assets are transferred to that child as well as his brothers and sisters.

The trustee meetings are not always peaceful affairs. Charles and Edgar usually support all of Leo's decisions, but Phyllis constantly hounds him to make certain that only the best designs have been used in construction activities and that all of the environmental niceties are being observed in expansion planning. It's Minda who is the toughest critic, demonstrating a brusque temper that sometimes reminds her sister and brothers of Mr. Sam himself.

Cemp's most unusual feature is its immunity from income tax. Until 1972, Canadian laws provided that dividends flowing from one company to another (Seagram to Cemp) were not liable for taxation. When this provision was changed, limiting the exemptions to public corporations, the Seagram dividends remained tax-free, being funneled through a subsidiary called Seco-

Cemp Limited. It is listed on the Montreal and Toronto stock exchanges, even though all voting shares are held by Cemp and its directors are the same group of insiders: Charles, Kolber, Philip Vineberg, and Lazarus Phillips. By carrying its investments at cost rather than market value, Cemp has managed to get itself into a truly remarkable tax position.* "After writing off exchange and investment losses," noted Amy Booth in the *Financial Post,* "Cemp, which controls the world's major (and most profitable) distillery, was able to turn up a loss of $2.4 million [in 1975] and let it be known that 'future income for income-tax purposes may be reduced by the application of losses approximating $1.2 million reported in prior years' income tax returns.' Or, in the modern version of the old adage: he who has, gets tax losses too."

No wonder Charles Bronfman can boast, "Leo is such a terrific operator that I don't spend very much time worrying about Cemp."

LEO KOLBER RUNS THE CEMP OPERATION OUT OF A SQUASH-COURT-SIZED OFFICE on the top floor of a thirty-two-story building in downtown Montreal, which he has furnished like a London merchant banker's boardroom. (He also works out of a similarly furnished southeast-corner office on the fifty-fifth floor of the Toronto-Dominion Centre, graced by a gorgeous Joyce Wieland tapestry.) Cemp has a staff of only six executives, and it's Kolber's job to carry through the detailed negotiations that culminate in final investment decisions. "I can be tough," he says. "But I always try to leave something on the table for the other guy to pick up."

---

* The 33.1 percent it holds of Seagram's stock is listed on Cemp's books at a stated value of $80 million, even though the shares were quoted at more than $300 million in mid-1978 and have been worth as much as $525 million. The stock reached a high of $45.75 in 1974. Cemp is able to generate a tax loss because operating costs are deductible, and its income is already shielded from any assessments.

In recent years, more and more of the Bronfman family's funds and attention have been lavished on the booming southwest corner of the United States, but Cemp's first big plunge was the 1958 purchase of Principal Investment, a property firm developed by three reclusive Toronto brothers, Archie, Jacob, and David Bennett. They had spent the postwar years quietly buying into choice downtown and suburban shopping locations across the country, accumulating an estimated $150 millions' worth of properties. The Bennett brothers were so publicity-shy that when their Lawrence Plaza in Toronto was nearing completion in the summer of 1953, they spent so long debating which of them would cut the ribbon opening the center that the plaza had already been in business for a month and another center was waiting to be inaugurated by the time they officially nominated Archie. The Bennett brothers were eventually so overextended that Kolber was able to purchase the pick of their commercial sites for $18 million, folding them into Fairview, Cemp's umbrella real-estate subsidiary.

It was at this point that the measure of Leo's abilities could best be taken. The Fairview real-estate operation, which he had guided since its inception, showed a paper profit of $100 million, just before it was folded into the Cadillac merger.

In point of fact, Cemp was such a mysterious enterprise at the time that when Kolber applied to Canadian banks for $7 million in bridge financing for the deal, he was initially turned down because no one had ever seen a Cemp balance sheet. Noah Torno, the Toronto wine entrepreneur who was Sam Bronfman's main Toronto agent at the time, finally swung an arrangement with the Bank of Nova Scotia, which promised to advance the money if it received confirmation from Price Waterhouse that Cemp's net worth was at least twice the required advance. The Cemp account was later switched to the Toronto-Dominion Bank. "Eventually," Torno recalls, "I could just walk across the street to the TD and say I'd like thirty million or so. They'd issue the check without any questions and ask us to send an explanatory note over the next day." Kolber was appointed a director of the Toronto-Dominion Bank in 1972; Dick Thomson, the current chairman, is one of his best friends.

Kolber has since parlayed Cemp's investment income (now estimated at an annual $25 million) into an impressively diversified portfolio. By mid-1978 Cemp *owned* outright real estate worth $700 million and *controlled* properties valued at more than $2 billion. The company began with its holding of 33.1 percent in Seagram stock (which gives it effective control over the distillery company's $2 billions' worth of assets); in addition, Kolber has put together $100 millions' worth of other investments that at one time or another have included:*

- A sizable piece (417,568 shares) of Allied Chemical Corporation
- The largest Canadian interest (550,000 shares) in British American Oil Company (the main predecessor of Gulf Canada)
- Major holdings in Bell Telephone (now Bell Canada), Pure Oil, Curtis Publishing, Paramount Pictures, Metro-Goldwyn-Mayer (Leo Kolber remained a director of M-G-M for a decade following Edgar's abortive takeover attempt and cast the decisive vote when the decision was taken to build the Grand Hotel in Las Vegas. The Grand has a casino the spread of a football field, 2,100 rooms, and eight nightclubs. Kolber resigned from the Hollywood studio's board in the summer of 1977.)
- A tract of Jaffa orange groves in Israel ☐
- A Montreal leisure company called Fairway Bowling Lanes ☐
- Several major shopping centers in Germany ☐

---

* Holdings marked by ☐ are still in the Cemp portfolio.

- Majority ownership in Supersol, Israel's largest supermarket chain ☐
- A 5.5-percent interest in Club Méditerranée ☐ (The Club Méditerranée now runs seventy-six resort villages in twenty-four countries, has a million active members, employs 11,000 suntanned staffers. The ultimate in packaged vacations, it has eliminated the use of cash: there isn't any tipping. Everything is *à la maison,* including the topless bathing parties subtly hinted at in the club's glossy pamphlets. Worldwide sales first climbed over the $200-million mark in 1976, but growth is slowing, due perhaps to the ennui reflected in the remark of a sailing instructor at the Club Med Caravelle in Guadeloupe, who recently described the mindless pleasures of her job as "having to spend yet another shitty day in paradise.")
- A gas field in Texas ☐
- A thirty-six-outlet restaurant chain based in Montreal called Host House Foods
- A group of butane tankers flying the French flag, owned through a French company named Gazocéan
- Control of Warrington Products, which makes luggage, garden tools, refrigerators, electric ranges, barbecues, Kodiak boots, Hush Puppies loafers, Bauer skates, and Acme cowboy boots ☐
- A 3.8-percent interest in Panarctic Oils ☐
- A large apartment block in Palm Beach, Florida, held in conjunction with the Cummings family ☐
- Control of GM Resources (the former Giant Mascot Mines), which owns mining properties in British Columbia besides holding oil and gas interests in Alberta ☐
- Growing real-estate interests in the United Kingdom, Holland, and Germany ☐
- Control of Multiple Access, which owns Montreal's largest private television station and three of

the city's radio outlets, Champlain Productions, which makes original films and television series, and AGT Data Systems, a computer service company □

- An interest in Ticketron, the computer-based New York ticket-selling agency—sold in 1973 at break-even value to Control Data Corporation in the greatest deal of Leo's life, because by then the company had clearly established itself as a loser
- Signal Companies, a California holding company that owned Mack Trucks, a piece of the North Sea oil strike, and in addition a chain of radio stations called Golden Broadcasters on which Gene Autry used to sing
- A large chunk of Pan Ocean Oil, which in six months yielded Cemp a $10-million profit
- About 12.6 percent of Bow Valley Industries, a Calgary-based operating and holding company □, and
- Jump for Joy, a tiny trampoline operation attached to one of its Calgary shopping centers.

By 1966, through Cemp, the Bronfmans had become Canada's largest private landowners, owning properties then worth $165 million. One indication of Cemp's financial clout came to light in 1974, when Kolber made a sudden offer to buy Bantam, the largest of the U.S. paperback houses, for $62 million in cash. He was outbid by Giovanni Agnelli of the Fiat family, who bought Bantam for $75 million and then sold a 51-percent interest in the company to Bertelsmann of Germany for $36 million.

Cemp's largest single construction project was the 1964–1967 erection of the Toronto-Dominion Centre, the first of downtown Toronto's great banking towers. The triple-tower center remains Canada's largest rental unit, with 3.3 million square feet of leasable space. The Toronto-Dominion Bank and Cemp later were joined by Eaton's, the coast-to-coast department-store chain.

The three corporations first put up Vancouver's $110-million Pacific Centre and later joined forces for the $250-million Eaton Centre development in downtown Toronto.

Leo Kolber's most important coup was the way he put the Cemp-owned Fairview together with Cadillac Development Corporation and Canadian Equity and Development Company. Out of the amalgamation emerged North America's largest publicly traded real-estate operation. Launched in 1974 and completed on February 29, 1976, the complicated series of stock transfers left the Bronfman family in control (with 35 percent) of the new company, Cadillac Fairview Corporation Limited. The *Financial Post* reported that the merger, which combined Cadillac's depth of management with Fairview's easy access to money, would turn Cadillac Fairview "into the Canadian real estate industry's equivalent of IBM," but found that, typically, its executives "resisted the urge to comment with a zeal that would make Harpo Marx loquacious."

Cadillac Fairview has its headquarters in a magnificent $9-million building on Toronto's outskirts, set around a central court that has palm trees sweeping up a full four stories. It owns a grand total of more than twenty-nine million square feet of rentable space, making it the largest and most profitable of Cemp's many investments, producing a gross income during 1977 of about $1 million a working day. Besides thirty-five shopping centers in Canada, the company made its first major move into the United States in 1975, entering a joint-venture deal with Peter D. Leibowits of New York for the development of shopping centers. The partnership has opened one shopping center at Hickory, North Carolina, has another under construction and a site purchased for a third in the same state. The $70-million Galleria is being built in Edgar Bronfman's home county of Westchester, New York. The 667,000-square-foot Shannon Mall is under construction at Atlanta, Georgia. An American subsidiary has a 70-percent interest in an option on eighty-one acres for a

shopping center in Mississippi and a 70-percent holding in a site in Connecticut. The U.S. portfolio also
includes industrial parks in and near Los Angeles, an
office tower in Denver, and another under construction
in San Francisco, plus major housing developments in
Nevada, California, and Florida. In August, 1978, the
Canadian company announced it had reached agreement in principle with Texas Eastern Corporation to
become a fifty-fifty partner with the Houston-based gas
and pipeline firm in the ownership and development of
Houston Center, one of the largest integrated developments in North America. About $200 million has al-
ready been invested in the thirty-three-block downtown
project.

Its determination to move massively into the U.S.
market was demonstrated by Cadillac Fairview's 1976–
1977 bid for the 80,000-acre Irvine Ranch property
near Santa Ana, south of Los Angeles. The tract is due
to become the largest master-planned urban development in the United States. Kolber and his associates
offered $286 million, but were topped by a bid of
$337.4 million from Taubman-Allen-Irvine, a syndicate
that included Henry Ford II.

IN HIS APPROACH TO CEMP'S INTRICATE BUSINESS AF-
FAIRS, Leo Kolber is not so much secretive (in the
sense of trying to hide information) as genuinely puzzled by the idea that he should reveal anything about
himself or his various enterprises beyond the legal requirements of the Canada Business Corporations Act.
He did grant one newspaper interview in 1972 and believes this more than adequately discharged his public-
information responsibilities. He has never given a
speech, been on radio, or appeared on TV.

When he is talking business, especially while negotiating contracts, his gaze is cold, his manner forbidding.
He seems as distant as one of those plastic creatures
that permanently inhabit the glass souvenir paper-
weights sold to honeymooning couples at Niagara Falls.
You shake the bottle; the artificial snowflakes swirl

about; but the frigid figure inside glares out through
his protective shell, untouched and untouchable, unaware of the changing seasons.

At work, Kolber is obsessive and intense, trying constantly to organize life around himself, as if human
emotions (his own as well as those of the people he's
dealing with) could be ticked off the list of things he
has to get through on any given day. He has never con-
sciously been unkind to anyone, but the impression he
leaves with associates is that of a man constantly on the
verge of blowing up—vainly trying to control the many
forces in play around him, attempting to ensure the
future by endeavoring to assuage the present. Sid Breg-
man, one of the architects involved with him in construction of the Toronto-Dominion Centre, remembers
Kolber's abrupt greeting at 9:30 on a Monday morning: "And what have you done for your ten-percent fee
so far today?"

Part of the problem is that his function as chief
financial adviser to the Bronfman billions has made
Kolber a natural target for every ambitious entrepreneur
within sight or sound of him. "My wife, Sandra, has
me quite well analyzed," he says. "I'm on guard all
the time. Even when I go to something as informal as
a cocktail party, it doesn't take long before people are
pressing me for things, and that's got to be a pain in
the ass." Leo occasionally plays a silent game with himself at social functions by counting the time it will take
someone to ask him for a favor. He has yet to beat
eight seconds. He feels so strongly about not placing
himself in a debt relationship with anybody even at the
most mundane level that he's grown compulsive about
picking up restaurant checks and balks at attending
those corporate social functions that occupy the sunset
hours of most high-ranking executives.

He enjoys free access to most of the bankers and
investment men who matter on two continents, is constantly being wooed by some of the most powerful
business executives extant. He enjoys the clout of his
position, but retains within himself a large preserve of

inviolable privacy; together with his deliberately ob-
scurantist methods and tough demeanor, it has amply
earned Leo Kolber a reputation as the great mystery
man of Canadian high finance.

On May 2, 1977, however, Leo Kolber chose for the
first time to give public demonstration of the full reach
of his influence. There it was, right at the top of the
special Montreal Symphony Orchestra program for
"An Evening with Danny Kaye"—a list of honorary
patrons with only four names on it:

> **Pierre Elliott Trudeau**
> *Prime Minister of Canada*
> **René Lévesque**
> *Prime Minister of Quebec*
> **Jean Drapeau**
> *Mayor of Montreal*
> **E. Leo Kolber**
> *Chairman*

A few weeks before, Kolber had sent out 120 letters
inviting his business contacts to his office for a meeting
to organize the concert aimed at wiping out the Montreal Symphony's $200,000 deficit; 110 showed up.
They were asked to sell ten tickets at $100 each, while
Kolber paid out $32,000 for the $500 box seats that
he distributed himself. The final committee of one hundred Montrealers was drawn from the top layers of the
city's three major elites. The Jewish community's chieftains were represented in force, as were many of the
city's top French business leaders and the ambassadors
of the beleaguered WASP enclave.

The gala performance was a magical evening, a rare
moment of calm and pleasure in a province then being
torn apart by the introduction of the Parti Québécois's
bellicose language legislation. Up in the chairman's box
of the huge Place des Arts concert hall, separatist Premier René Lévesque, seated between Sandra and Leo,
gazed down at the dazzling assembly of corporate power
barons who had vainly fought his swift rise to power.

He kept peering at them as if to read their minds, staring hard at the men, gently flirting with the suave women who wore their smiles and jewels with a confidence born of long breeding.

Then, in the pre-curtain hush just before Danny Kaye was ushered on, the Quebec Premier turned to his host and said, "You know, nobody contributes as much to the cultural life of Montreal as the Jews."

At that precise instant, Leo Kolber, who had successfully negotiated the harrowing journey from St. Urbain Street to the chairman's box on that glittering evening, allowed his real feelings to bubble up. "Yeah?" he shot back. "So why are you scaring such hell out of them that they're nearly all thinking of leaving?"

15. Gerald

SAM BRONFMAN was no great respecter of differences in sex, creed, color, personality, or national origin. He fought with everybody. Especially the other members of his family. When he was preparing the first draft of *From Little Acorns,* that brief, heavily laundered history of Seagram's published with the 1970 annual report, he left out any mention of his three brothers. This was a particularly glaring gap, since the booklet listed just about everybody who'd had even the vaguest connection with the company, right down to Mathias Litshauer, chef at the La Salle staff criteria, saluted for making "the best boiled beef in the world."

Similarly, Lazarus Phillips, who had been directly responsible for Sam's ability to retain personal control over the burgeoning Seagram empire and had acted as his chief legal counsel since 1924, received no mention at all because of the two men's feud over membership in the Canadian Senate. Where he should have been listed the entry simply read: "We have been fortunate in the selection of our legal counsel. The late Honourable J. L. Perron, K.C., incorporated our Company. The late Aimé Geoffrion, K.C., one of Canada's greatest lawyers, and our counsel, was long one of our directors. For over 40 years the firm of Phillips and Vine-

berg has been our counsel and Philip Vineberg, Q.C.,
is now a director."

Michael McCormick, who was helping Bronfman
put the publication together, finally got up the nerve
to question the omission of Mr. Sam's brothers. "As
soon as I did," he recalls, "it was like Hiroshima and
Nagasaki going off at the same time. 'What did *they*
ever do?' Mr. Sam began to shout. So I told him he
had posterity to think about, their families and children.

"By next day he'd made casual references to them in
the text, mainly that Harry had built some of the
original distilleries, and when I suggested it was the
least he could have done, he exploded all over again.
'When that son of a bitch Harry went down to Kentucky I told him to build a brand-new plant, everything beautiful, and what does he do but buy a whole
lot of second-hand pipe, puts it in our fermenters and
all over the place.'

"' "Christ," he says to me, "nobody knows what's
inside those pipes." So I had to rip the whole goddamn stuff right out, and it cost a fortune.' "

This kind of treatment was especially rough on
Harry, who had not only supervised the erection of
the company's first three distilleries but whose nerve
and business acumen had also launched the enterprise
during its wild Saskatchewan phase in the first place.
In fact, it was on the basis of the credit rating Harry
had earned with the Bank of Montreal through Sir
Frederick Williams-Taylor, the bank's austere general
manager, that the Bronfmans were able to finance their
move east in the early twenties and construction of the
initial plant at Ville La Salle.

Sam reluctantly conceded that Harry and Abe along
with their brother-in-law Barney Aaron had been essential to his early success, but he felt much more strongly
that within the corporate environment of the modern
Seagram operation they had become embarrassing anach-
ronisms. Except for Allan, whose relatively sophisticated legal advice he listened to and occasionally even

sought, Sam treated his family partners as liabilities he had to drag behind him. From the late thirties until their deaths, he tucked them away inconspicuously in third-floor office suites at Seagram's Montreal headquarters, leaving them in charge of nothing much except the distribution of minor charitable donations. In response to the query of one naïve Seagram director about his brothers' opinion of a major corporate move, Sam just looked baffled and explained, "I don't remember asking them."

There was room for only one dynastic line within the Seagram empire. If there ever was any doubt about that simple declaration of Mr. Sam's governing concern, it became crystal clear on a winter's afternoon in 1951, when he convened an important family conference at the Belvedere Palace.

Originally, the Bronfman assets had been organized into a holding company (Brintcan), with Harry acting as president and Sam, on paper at least, second in command. This voting trust started to disintegrate when Sam decided to move control into his own hands, as well as transferring a greater share away from Harry and Abe to Allan. "If you want to give something away, I'm the one you should be giving it to!" Harry objected in one heated exchange. Lazarus Phillips was finally called in to arbitrate, and Allan sided with Sam to push through the dilution of Harry's and Abe's shares.

By the time the eight brothers and sisters had been called to the 1951 conclave for the express purpose of apportioning the family fortune, they knew that, if they weren't there exactly on sufferance, all the meaningful financial clout now resided in Sam.

The Bronfman assets at the time added up to about $19 million in cash, property, and investments, not counting the Seagram shares. Sam's announced division of family holdings was set out with terse severity— his branch of the family would retain control over thirty-seven percent of the Seagram stock. It would also claim $8 million of the other accumulated assets and dole out relatively minor amounts to the others. Allan was to get $3 million, Abe and Harry $2 million apiece, and the four sisters, Laura, Jean, Bessie, and Rose, $1 million each. When Abe objected that he and Harry should get at least as much as Allan, it was Rose who cut him down with the comment, "Sam is being generous to all of us. I for one am very proud of him."

Until the early forties, a semblance of extended family life had been maintained, with Jewish high holidays celebrated jointly at the Belvedere Palace and weekly Sabbath dinners convened at Harry's mansion on the Boulevard in the heart of Westmount. During the early fifties, the brothers shared investment tips, such as their joint sallies into North Canadian Oils and Royalite. But they gradually drifted apart, so that some of their descendants, now widely spread over the North American continent, are strangers to each other. Of Abe's five daughters, only Mildred remains in Montreal, where she is a major force in Jewish community work; Barney Aaron's son Mellor died in his youth; Mellor's brother, Arnold, is in plastic cups; Rose's son, Ernest, is in California real estate; Jean's family runs the Seagram distributorship in Boston;* Bea's grandson Bruce Druxerman operates a chain of six deli restaurants in Toronto.

THE MOST INTERESTING MEMBER OF THESE VARIOUS MINOR BRANCHES OF THE FAMILY is Harry Bronfman's second son, Gerald. A pixieish presence with a knotty walnut body and a deeply lined, not unkindly shepherd's face, he is a fussy man who occasionally takes his own

---

* Jean is the widow of Paul Matoff, killed at Bienfait. On July 7, 1978, Earl Pat Groper, her son, was charged in Dedham, Massachusetts, with fraud and forgery in the purchase of an $800,000 life-insurance policy on a business partner who was shot a month later. The business partner, George S. Hamilton, president of a furniture company with financial problems, was killed at three A.M., April 25, 1976, by one of five shots fired through the door of his home in Canton, Massachusetts, as he was answering the doorbell.

box of condiments along to lunch at the Ritz-Carlton's Café de Paris dining room and other restaurants.

He works out of a huge corner office on Sherbrooke Street with six windows and electronically controlled draperies. He divides his working time into three precise segments: forty percent business, forty percent communal affairs, and twenty percent personal matters (such as household bills and his children's stock portfolios). "While we're not the most dramatic branch of the Bronfman family, nor among its wealthiest members," he says, "we are an interesting group."

Unlike most of the Bronfmans, Gerald does not limit his community efforts to Jewish causes. He has been an active director of the Stratford Shakespearean Festival, the Montreal Museum of Fine Arts, the Montreal Symphony, the Quebec division of the Air Cadet League, and the YM-YWCA. He's a former president of the Quebec division of the Red Cross. Besides having the standard memberships in the Montefiore, Elm Ridge Country, and Greystone Curling clubs, he belongs to the non-Jewish Club St. Denis, but has shied away from applying to the Mount Royal. His wife, Marjorie, a graduate social worker and a daughter of the late Jacob Schechter of New York, is the Bronfman clan's most active hostess.

Their four children have followed very different paths: Joni teaches folk songs at Brandeis University; Judy helps rehabilitate drug addicts in Montreal's east end; Corinne is a successful Paris-trained photographer-artist now working out of New York (alone among the Bronfman fourth generation, Corinne seriously considered changing her name, or at least using a pseudonym to sign her works of art, but at the last minute decided against it); Jeffrey graduated *cum laude* from Choate, was accepted by Yale, Antioch, and Oberlin, but chose instead to follow the Divine Light Mission of Guru Maharaj Ji.

Although the family owns investment trusts worth at least $40 million, expenditures are carefully budgeted. Judy will accept no allowance at all from her parents;

Joni and Corinne have repeatedly turned down Gerald's offers to raise theirs. Gerald keeps himself on an incredibly tight financial rein. During a visit to Israel in the fall of 1977, he was being shown the Golan Heights when he was approached by a roadside vendor selling apples at three for £6 (sixty cents). Gerald offered £3 and was turned down. "I probably could have bought them for £4, but it was too late," he wrote in his private diary afterward. "Our guide, Albert, bought some and gave us one. It was sweeter than any apple I've ever had."

The family's attitude toward spending goes back to Gerald's terms as a Commerce freshman at McGill during the Depression when few of the other students had any money. "I used to look around carefully so I wouldn't pull more than a dollar bill at a time out of my pocket," he recalls. "I had to report every penny I spent to my father."

Unlike most of the other third-generation Bronfmans, Gerald for a time occupied a significant place within Seagram's, coordinating sales and production in New York as well as being in charge of packaging and Christmas cartons. Although he was not the originator of the Crown Royal cloth bag, he did suggest the choice of purple flannelette to give the package a quality feeling and allow purchasers to store their silver in it after the bottle had been emptied. Gerald's greatest coup was the idea of placing the black-and-gold ribbon under V.O. labels.

"When Seagram's purchased Wilson's [blended whisky] from the Reinfeld family, they decided to redesign the bottle in the shape of the shoulders of a man carrying the world on his back," Gerald remembers. "When I came back from a trip and saw the package, I immediately pointed out that Wilson's had been bought as a bar whisky and should have a plain, round bottle so that a bartender could handle it easily. They bought the concept, and Joe Reinfeld came to my office, shook my hand, and said thanks.

The litany of such details makes up the Bronfman legend.

By the late thirties, Gerald was rising comfortably in the Seagram hierarchy, with many of his fellow executives beginning to speculate that he might eventually become Sam's chosen successor. It was his very success that was his undoing: "My tenure at Seagram's expired when William Wendell Wachtel, then head of the Calvert subsidiary, introduced me to a corporate sales meeting with the comment: 'And now we'll hear from the heir apparent.' Both my uncles [Sam and Allan] were there, and I knew my days were numbered. I can still visualize myself walking down the length of that room, not knowing how to handle it, what to say or what to do."

He resolved the problem by enlisting in the Royal Canadian Air Force, spending most of World War II in Washington, helping to coordinate Canadian armed-services purchases. He was only a flight lieutenant at the time,* but even there his name got him noticed. "Whenever I was calling an American officer to negotiate the purchase of parts for an aircraft or something else in Canada, I always used to say 'Gerald Bronfman speaking,' and they'd usually answer, 'Yes, General Bronfman.'

"One time, an abrupt voice came on the telephone. 'McIntire here,' requesting some information I was able to get fairly quickly. So I wrote a reply to McIntire, who turned out to be the U.S. admiral then personal physician to Franklin D. Roosevelt, and signed it 'Gerald Bronfman.'

"A few days later, I was called on the carpet by Air Vice-Marshal George Walsh, the head of our mission, who told me, 'Don't ever do things like that; a flight lieutenant never speaks to an admiral.' So when I got some more data, I telephoned the White House and

* Gerald joined the RCAF in 1940 as an AC2, the equivalent of a private, and ended the war a squadron leader, equivalent to a major. He was decorated by the U.S. government with the Legion of Merit.

asked for Admiral McIntire's aide. I wasn't going to get into any more hassles.

"A voice came on, 'Sheldon here,' and I said, 'Before we go any further, what's your rank?'

"The answer was 'I'm an admiral.' So I told him to forget about the whole thing, and hung up."

AFTER THE WAR, GERALD RETURNED TO MONTREAL and was enlisted by his father to help look after the family investments. Harry Bronfman had by the late forties pulled his personal funds out of Seagram's and put them into Harborough Investments; his children's holdings were in a company called Grahsom (named after Gerald, Rona, and Allan; after Allan's death in 1944 his wife, later married to Dr. William Cohen, inherited Allan's share). Harborough's chief asset was a 20-percent holding in Dominion Dairies, the distributor of the Sealtest and Light n' Lively brands. Harry also owned three small Quebec milk-processing plants consolidated in a company called Kensington Industries. Gerald eventually sold them to Dominion and joined the company's board. At one point, he attempted to buy out Kraft's Canadian operations, but on January 3, 1961, Kraft announced that it had acquired 83.6 percent of Dominion Dairies' shares under an offer made in December 1960, leaving Gerald, who still sits on the board, the largest minority shareholder, with 227,392 shares—11.3 percent of the issued stock.

Ever since, Gerald has been quietly trading assets, collecting an impressive but undramatic portfolio concentrated in three holding companies: Gerin Limited, Gerbro Corporation, and Roslyn Developments. His Seagram's stake is 609,900 shares (worth about $18 million in the summer of 1978), and his only remaining link with the family's other branches is through Philip Vineberg, who acts as his chief legal adviser and is a director of Gerin.

At the base of Gerald's family holdings are half a dozen investments (worth more than $50 million), including Canada's second-largest bean processor and real-estate holdings. In the United States, Gerald (together with Edward Schechter, his brother-in-law) owns Stressteel Corporation, an important supplier of high-tensile-strength beams to the construction industry. Among Stressteel's projects have been the Freedom Arch in St. Louis, nuclear containment vessels for several major U.S. reactors, and the BART elevated rapid transportation system in the San Francisco Bay area. Less successful investments have included the manufacture of a revolutionary (but unmarketable) circular saw, an abortive attempt to market biomedical drugs out of Buffalo, New York, and trying to float the Dale Chemical Company in Palm Springs, California, to make sodium sulphate for the paper industry.

Gerald's most offbeat investment was spawned in the early sixties when Gilbert E. Kaplan, a young economist with the Securities and Exchange Commission in Washington, arrived at his office with the idea of buying out the *Institutional Investor,* then an insignificant Wall Street newsletter whose publisher had recently died. Bronfman agreed to finance the deal, and Kaplan has since built the publication into one of the financial world's most highly regarded magazines, with a circulation of twenty thousand and subscription rates of $65 a year. The *Institutional Investor* also sponsors conferences around the world (at $750 for registration alone) and puts out (at $495 annually) a separate *Wall Street Letter* for the really sophisticated insiders. Gerald cleared a profit of $1 million in 1971 by taking the magazine company public and buying back forty percent of it.

Gerald Bronfman's days gently drop away in *adagio* rhythm; he seldom relaxes, but never exerts himself. There is quiet dignity in his departures and arrivals. Of all the many Bronfmans, he seems most at peace with himself, a man who has journeyed to his soul and found little to disturb his composure.

If there is a touch of self-satisfaction about him, perhaps it could be based on the transformation of Gerin into a public company, which allowed him to channel dividend income from Seagram and Dominion Dairies, tax-free, to Gerin, which now has assets of $25 million and yields $1.2 million a year in dividends. In Gerin Limited, Gerald has found the ultimate fiscal miracle: instead of merely paying low income taxes for 1977, the company actually received a $4,889 refund.

Now, that's *chutzpah*. Even for a Bronfman.

16. Mitch

THE SETTING is early James Bond.

The reception area of the small, unmarked air terminal on the outskirts of Montreal is all smoked glass, unobtrusively mottled leather, and the kind of self-conscious anonymity that creates the deliberate impression it is camouflaging transactions of great moment. Outside, a dozen aircraft are nestled in a $3-million hangar, gleaming under roof-mounted spotlights as if they had recently been hand-polished by some mad scientist with a phobia about germs. Two police dogs strain against their enclosures, howling into the night. The underground garage lodges a powder-blue Jaguar, a tarpaulin-covered apple-red Lamborghini, the last Pontiac convertible ever built, and a brown Ford equipped with a scanning device that can detect radar and radio signals within a six-mile radius. The owner's office feels like the Hollywood reconstruction of 007's wintering quarters. It has nine telephones (equipped with switches, hot lines, hidden consoles) and a scattering of gadgets that includes a flashlight that shoots Mace and a golden fountain pen that shoots bullets.

The custodian of this strange conglomeration is Arvin Mitchell Bronfman, president of Execaire Aviation, Canada's largest private executive jet service. The family's resident black sheep, he has led a heady life crowded with dark incidents; at forty-six he is confused, hurt, bleeding into his shoes. At some point Mitch must have lost sight of the fact that every Bronfman's every private act may have its public consequences, and now, having been brought to account, the currency of his days is no longer valued by the usual order of things. His mind abounds with images of a thousand ghost riders on a thousand black horses galloping through an obscure landscape, all decked out in RCMP scarlet, tilting their lances at him. Convinced that he has, for some unaccountable reason, been picked as a victim for the Redcoats' persecution, he no longer believes in redemption, clean slates, or atonement. Only survival.

All men are the chief custodians of their own potential, and their protection (except for that which comes from God) must ultimately be derived from within themselves. It is the quality of being able to act in his own self-interest that seems to be missing from his make-up, so that even if he is innocent of all the many accusations made (but not really substantiated) against him, the question remains whether, for his own sake, Mitchell Bronfman ought to be allowed out without a keeper.

The reckoning of his life seems disordered, senseless, refusing to cohere. Not all the evidence is in, but up to now at least Mitch appears to have been seared by a hellfire of his own making. The privileged child of wonder he once was, especially during those early, blooming days in London, Ontario, when he would sneak away from his uncle's dairy and fly his own plane into the shimmering sunrise—that magic is long gone, and nothing much has taken its place.

Although he vehemently denies any venal implications in his friendships, Mitchell Bronfman was condemned in 1977 by the Quebec Police Commission inquiry into organized crime as having an "almost brotherly relationship" with Willie Obront, a convicted kingpin of Montreal's underworld. The commission went on record as exposing "the illegalities in which they mutually or jointly indulged, the 'special' kinds of favors they did for each other, and the resulting advantages of each in the fields of loansharking, gambling and illegal betting, securities, tax evasion and corruption." To his accusers, Bronfman makes a straightforward defense: "I was the victim of loansharking. If Obront is as bad as they say he was, why was he out and walking around?"

"At its best interpretation," says Ronald I. Cohen, former senior counsel to the commission that condemned him, "Mitch exhibited a careless disregard about how his name was being used. He has always been an outsider in terms of the Bronfman family and he may have been proud of the fact that he was obliged to make it on his own, and ultimately did—even if not in ways that would be approved by them. At least, he was making his own independent way."

MITCH IS THE ELDEST CHILD OF ALLAN BRONFMAN, whose father, Harry, was Sam's brother and a key influence in Seagram's early success. Allan was placed in charge of the Ville La Salle distillery but died suddenly on May 27, 1944, at thirty-seven. Because he hadn't made a will, under Quebec law a third of Allan's estate (worth about $15 million) was awarded to his widow, the former Freda Besner, with the balance split among Mitch and his two sisters, Marion and Beverly. The funds were placed in a trust that paid out interest but contained no special provisions for the eventual disbursement of capital. This meant that during his formative years Mitch, while in theory a rich man, enjoyed little access to his own inheritance. "No question about it," he says, "having the name Bronfman was something of a holdback. People didn't understand why I just couldn't go to the family and get them to write me a check."

After attending Selwyn House in Montreal, Mitch was sent to New York's Riverdale Country School and eventually graduated from Babson Institute in the Boston suburb of Wellesley with a degree in marketing. He went to work for his uncle Gerald at Dominion Dairies in London, Ontario, but flying was his first love. As well as sneaking in pre-dawn flights on most working days, he would spend many weekends going up in his private plane and eventually bought out the local flying school. By the time he was twenty-four, Mitch had set up Execaire in Montreal and was awarded his license to operate a charter airline for business aircraft. None of his planes carry Execaire markings, and Mitch refuses to disclose the names of his clients.*

Apart from flying, Mitch's lifelong preoccupation has been with policemen and the Mafia. He loves target shooting, raises police dogs at his farm in the Eastern Townships of Quebec—as well as guide dogs and dressage horses—has owned a police-model Harley-Davidson, and once told his staff that in the event an Execaire aircraft is hijacked, he should be smuggled aboard to "sort things out." As a youngster, he hung around police stations, especially the RCMP, formed friendships, became a kind of groupie, studying their ways and means. Since he wasn't allowed to become a cop himself, Mitch did the next best thing: he established his own police force. Known as Securex Safeguard Consultants, the outfit was much more than the usual "fuzz for rent" operation, offering "studies of [Quebec's] political and revolutionary climate, threats of bombs or kidnappings" and "instructions for the use of guerrilla theatre tactics." Quebec Justice Minister Marc-André Bedard withdrew Securex's license in the summer of

---

* Although Execaire initially owned its own planes, most of its jets now belong to large corporations; by registering them with Execaire, the companies can lease them to other firms while their owners aren't using them. Mitch's fleet includes a Westwind 1124 (owned by the Montreal industrialist Jean-Louis Lévesque), two Falcon 20s (owned by Seagram and Tele-Direct Ltd., which is Bell Canada's Yellow Page operation), two Lear 25s (owned by Labatt's and Weston's), seven HS-125s (owned by Ford of Canada, the Bank of Nova Scotia, the Toronto-Dominion Bank, the Bank of Montreal, Alberta Gas Trunk, Price Co., and Domtar), as well as a Gulfstream I and a Cessna Citation.

1977 on the technicality that one of its agents was
working without a permit.

Mitch's best friends among the policemen he met
were a duo of noncommissioned officers in the RCMP's
highly secret security service, Staff Sergeant Donald Mc-
Cleery and Sergeant Gilles Brunet. Mitch had owned a
restaurant near the Montreal Forum called Robin's
Delicatessen, where Brunet's wife, Anita, worked as a
waitress. She introduced Bronfman to the Mounties,
and the three men became fast friends.

It was because of this association that McCleery and
Brunet were eventually discharged from the RCMP. The
first report on them in the files of the force's National
Crime Intelligence Unit (dated June 6, 1972) notes
that the two policemen lunched with Bronfman at
Robin's, pointing out that the restaurant's meat was
supplied by Willie Obront. Their commanding officer,
Chief Superintendent Larry Forest, advised them to
steer clear of Bronfman, but they continued to see him.
"Before we met Mitch," McCleery recalls, "we carefully checked him out and discovered there was only
one entry in his file: that he was friendly with Willie
Obront. I saw the evidence against him and it was like
reading a comic book, so full of innuendos and un-
founded speculation that on November 27, 1973, Chief
Superintendent Forest, who was my boss, wrote headquarters: 'I suggest it [the evidence] had better be
stronger than that which I have seen if we want to
avoid considerable trouble and embarrassment.' Anyway, Mitch was also a great source of information for
the force. They often used him as a door-opener. In
fact, he once tipped us off that Obront was aware of a
'safe house'* we were running at the time in the Alexis
Nihon Plaza."

On November 9, 1973, Inspector Donald Wilson,
then in charge of the RCMP's legal branch, wrote a long
internal memorandum alleging that "the seeds of cor-

---

* Bugged quarters used for compromising suspects and de-
briefing criminal sources.

ruption are being sown in the force through these two members. Whether or not corruption has been initiated is really of no consequence. The potential is such that we must rid ourselves of the source of the disease. . . . Notwithstanding that A/Commr. Gorman and Supt. Marcoux did not specifically direct that our two members disassociate themselves from Bronfman (and I am not suggesting it was their responsibility to do so), the investigation should have been enough to dissuade McCleery and Brunet from further association with Bronfman. It has had no such effect."

On December 6, 1973, after a combined thirty-eight years of exemplary service, McCleery and Brunet were asked to hand in their guns and were summarily dismissed. "We were discharged," McCleery maintains, "because they claimed we had received specific instructions to disassociate ourselves from Mitch, and that we disobeyed them. The fact is that it was only recommended we do so, and no such order was ever issued. Their only concern was the image of the force. We never got a chance to clear ourselves." The two Mounties have since appealed their dismissals. Bronfman regards the dismissal of his two friends as the reason for what he considers the Mounties' persecution of him. "It's a vicious circle," he says. "They must make their dream come true in view of the fact that McCleery and Brunet were fired from the force based on their association with me. Unless they can justify that fact, then really McCleery and Brunet were wrongfully dismissed and some people obviously didn't do a very good job; that would be poor police work."

That the two sergeants' friendship with Mitchell Bronfman was enough to cost them their careers reflected the RCMP's concern over the fact that during a 1962 police raid on Salaison Alouette, a Montreal meat wholesale company, an IOU for $19,400 signed to William Obront by Mitchell Bronfman had been found. Obront, known in his milieu as Willie or Obie, had first come to the attention of the authorities following a Quebec Provincial Police raid on two nightclubs he owned, the Hi-Ho Café (later the Béret Bleu) and the Bal Tabarin, then the favorite hangouts of such Montreal underworld characters as Vincenzo (Vic) Cotroni, Nicola Di Iorio, and Joe Cocoliccio. Twenty-two police raids followed, and the seized documents gradually fleshed out the portrait of Obront as the Montreal underworld's chief money-mover. The function of the money-mover is best defined by Ralph Salerno, a former New York police officer, in his book *The Crime Confederation,* as a vital link in the spread of organized crime's influence: "Gambling, loansharking, narcotics and other activities produce a multi-billion-dollar cash flow. The money-mover solves a two-fold problem: he puts the cash to work and hides its true ownership."

The report of the Quebec Police Commission inquiry into organized crime documented the anatomy of an impressive business empire ruthlessly ruled by Obront as a front for much less legitimate activities. In 1976 Obront was charged with tax evasion, contempt of court, fraud, forgery, and conspiracy. He was sentenced to four years in prison and fined $75,000.*

Mitch Bronfman's association with Willie Obront dated from 1959, when he was desperately attempting to turn Execaire into a profitable operation. Finding that the family trust had tied up his legacy, Mitch stepped outside the regular channels of credit to begin what may well be the strangest financial arrangement ever to keep a Canadian corporation afloat. Between 1962 and 1974, he borrowed $1,417,250 from Obront. In return, he issued 1,199 checks totaling $2,473,416. On December 31, 1974, Bronfman still owed Obront

---

* Obront almost managed to get away. Angelo Lanzo, one of the key witnesses in his case, was found dead while hiding from the crime inquiry's subpoena. Obront left for Florida in August of 1974 and a year later somehow became a U.S. citizen. Instead of taking a chance on extradition proceedings, early on the morning of May 4, 1976, he flew off to San José in Costa Rica. He was expelled sixteen days later and returned to Montreal, handcuffed between two RCMP constables.

$200,000. This amount was seized from him by Quebec's Department of Revenue as part of the $1,058,000 owed by Obront in back taxes. The interest he paid isn't difficult to compute; it amounted very nearly to a straight 100 percent. At the same time, Bronfman joined Obront as a minority partner in the Pagoda North restaurant, a Miami hangout described by the FBI as the center of a continent-wide bookmaking ring financed by the Genovese crime family of New York. His friendship with Obront seemed to recognize few financial limits. The Quebec Police Commission inquiry into organized crime described one example:

Around 1971, Obront asked Bronfman to do him a favour of a rather special kind. Mitchell Bronfman was to sign a letter addressed to William Obront in which Bronfman reminded William Obront that he owed the writer the sum of $350,000, whereas in fact this debt never existed. As a precaution, the letter specified that should Mitchell Bronfman die, Obront could consider the debt automatically cancelled. Clearly, William Obront did not go purely by chance to Mitchell Bronfman with such a proposal. Given the scope of Bronfman's business activities and the prestige of this family's name in the business community, a letter from him would carry great credibility.

As to the fact that this debt never existed, it is enough to point out that the situation between Bronfman and Obront was the reverse at that time, since for three successive years (1970–1973) Bronfman paid $897,488 to Obront in capital and interest.

This Commission called on Mr. Bronfman to explain why he agreed to sign such a document and above all to tell the Commission what William Obront wanted to do with it. This seemed to the Commission to be the obvious question for Bronfman to put to his friend Obront before signing such a document. If Mr. Bronfman is to be believed, this gesture was a token of his friendship with or trust in William Obront at that time, and he does not remember William Obront's reasons for asking him this favour. It did not even cross his mind that William Obront could, for example, use it to show the income tax authorities that his personal fortune was not as large as it was believed to be, since he owed Mitchell Bronfman $350,000. In fact, documents in the possession of the Department of Revenue of Quebec prove that for 1971 William Obront presented, with his income tax return, a personal balance sheet prepared by chartered accountant Mr. Larry Smith, who recognized it. The balance sheet shows liabilities of $350,000, constituted by the debt he owed on demand to Mr. Mitchell Bronfman.

By this contrivance, William Obront suggested to the income tax authorities that the small amount he declared was his true income, and this helped lull the suspicions which the Department of Revenue might have had about the real size of his fortune and his income from all sources. From 1964 to 1972, Obront declared average annual incomes of $32,240 for income tax purposes. However, he collected $17,840,075 and deposited it in bank accounts which he controlled. During the same period, he paid an average of $10,860 in income tax each year.

This is merely a superficial examination, but it shows how one individual can, over a relatively short period, thanks to the benevolent complicity of an accomplice with few scruples, cheat on his income tax and so deprive the State of considerable amounts, money it needs in order to function.

"I knew what I was doing," Mitch insists. "When I first met Obront, he was a well-regarded person. The RCMP, which was investigating him, saw my checks and assumed I must be financing the underworld because anybody with the name Bronfman couldn't be borrowing money. My association with Obront was strictly on a friendship basis at a time there was no question about his background. The fact that I borrowed the funds at a high interest rate isn't a crime."

Between 1966 and 1969, Bronfman was finally able to claim his family inheritance (which amounted to something over $2.2 million) and promptly sold his Seagram stock. But even this infusion of capital wasn't enough.

The next money merchant to enter Mitch's life was a stock manipulator called Sydney Rosen, the former manager of a tavern in Windsor, Ontario. Rosen emerged on Toronto's Bay Street in the sixties in a series of deals that included the promotion of the worthless Wee-Gee Uranium Mines from 25 cents a share to $4.30 and the purchase (for one of his companies called Life Investors International) of land on Georgian Bay for $1.8 million more than the level at which it had been assessed a few months earlier, with the difference going to an agency that happened also to be a Rosen company. When Life Investors stock dropped from $4.14 to 12 cents, Rosen switched his interest to Valutrend Management Services, a private company that managed fifty-five smaller firms, some of them listed on the Montreal and Toronto stock exchanges. The largest of these was Milton Group, whose subsidiary, Transmil Properties, in turn owned 50.1 percent of Flemdon Limited, which actually had some hard cash (about $2.3 million) in its treasury.

Rosen persuaded Mitch to pay $1 million for a 38-percent interest in Milton, so that Bronfman might get access to the Flemdon cash, which he needed to pump into Execaire. The $1 million was lent to Bronfman by the Corporate Bank and Trust Company of Freeport in the Bahamas at an annual interest rate of 12 percent. Mitch then appointed Rosen to manage Flemdon's affairs. Not surprisingly, during the next two years Flemdon's $2.3 million quietly disappeared into the same Bahamian bank, whose owner turned out to be none other than Sydney Rosen.

In April of 1975, the Quebec Securities Commission accused Rosen of having bled $7 million from the fifty-five firms he managed through Valutrend to the Corporate Bank and Trust Company and suspended trading in all the companies involved. Sixteen months later, Mr. Justice Samuel H. Graham of the Bahamian Supreme Court ordered the Corporate Bank to close shop, and Rosen was charged with conspiring to defraud Flemdon's shareholders. Corporal Giuliano Zaccardelli of the RCMP, who was sent to investigate the case, could find no trace of the missing $7 million. Mitchell Bronfman's controlling block of Milton shares, which he had hypothecated to the Corporate Bank, was last reported to be on deposit at the Freeport branch of Barclays Bank.

Rosen was eventually charged with conspiring to defraud Life Investors of $2.25 million and was convicted of defrauding the public through the distribution of shares of Somed Mines (an obscure Quebec mining company with an abandoned shaft whose prospectus didn't even list which metal it might uncover) at prices ranging from 10 cents to $2.04 by paying stock salesmen secret under-the-table commissions for pushing it.

Despite such shenanigans, Execaire has prospered and now has facilities in Toronto and Calgary as well as Montreal. Mitch spends his days running the air service, keeping his lawyers busy, trying to forget the past. He drifts around Dorval airport, pointing out to visitors where the RCMP used to stake him out and how occasionally, just to give the Redcoats a little workout, he'd gun his Lamborghini and race them on the back roads toward Beaconsfield. He knows all the Mounties at the airport by their first names, jokes about how easy it is to get a gun past the X-ray security screens—"all you have to do is pack it standing up." (Mitch himself always carries an automatic in a shoulder holster and a stiletto strapped to his left calf.)

Mitch no longer regards being a Bronfman as a curse;

he's proud of the way the family stuck with him through all his troubles. He was invited to Saidye's eightieth birthday party at Charles's house, attended the Danny Kaye reception at Leo Kolber's. Cemp, the Bronfman family trust, signed a guarantee for part of Execaire's line of credit at the Bank of Montreal.

Perhaps the sympathy of the other Bronfmans is prompted in part because they share the roots of Mitchell's yearning. "I could have tried going to the family, or I could have lived on my trust income and done nothing," he says. Then, gazing around the movie set that he uses for an office, Mitch sings the sad Bronfman refrain. "All I wanted," he shrugs, "was to do something on my own."

17. Peter

HIS LOATHING for cocktail parties flirts with being a fixation. At those rare social occasions he does attend, Peter Bronfman sets his face in a slightly petitionary expression and stands about reverently as if he were at a church service, not saying much, sipping his glass of flat ginger ale, wishing the thing were mercifully over. "I happen," he privately confides, "to have a very low threshold for bullshit."

The most secretive of the Bronfmans, Peter, who is the younger son of Sam's brother Allan, has a personality charged with corrosive sensibilities and retroactive grievances that mark him as an outcast, even in the baroque gallery of this strange clan. There is about him none of the loose amiability of his cousin Edgar, who walks around a room with a kind of gracefully endearing lope, or of his cousin Charles, whose nourishing quest for certitude can charm all but the most hard-hearted of cynics.

Peter walks alone. Adrift in some private proving ground of the soul, he believes that what can turn a bearable existence into a sequence of wonders is standing up and becoming his own man, allowing the roaring boy deep inside him to take command and hurl damnation at the constraints of his life and upbringing.

More than a little miscast as a Bronfman, Peter is

so sensitive that after his father's house burned down in the summer of 1977 he spent the next six months trying to recover from what his doctor diagnosed as "sympathy" low-grade fever—even though he'd spent some of the unhappiest times of his life trying to grow up in that cold Victorian pile next to Sam's Belvedere Palace.

Peter's favorite prose passage accurately reflects his view of life. It is a fragment from an essay written in the nihilistic turmoil of the mid-sixties by journalist and author Gay Talese: "One must be *seen* to exist, for now there is no other proof. There is no longer an identity in craft, only in self-promotion. There are no acts, only scenes. Peace marches are masquerades. Selma was a minstrel. News is staged for camera crews. Critics dance with their eyes closed. Nothing is happening. It is a meaningless moment in history."

Peter's private theology holds that the ability to marvel at life is a gift of heaven. But he finds this power of enchantment difficult to achieve and even more difficult to share. A loner with a million complexes, his greatest joy is walking by himself through the fluorescent desolation of city streets in late-night rain, investigating the radiant miscellanies along the way. "Peter is rather anti-social," says Jacques Courtois, his Montreal lawyer. "He enjoys the company of a few personal friends but shuns large receptions or gatherings; he has a strong dislike of ties and jackets, let alone dressing in black tie. I suppose that, like other people of wealth, he may suspect the motives of some of those who approach him, and this might explain why he often appears to be on the defensive."

Except for being close to his children, Peter behaves like a hermit. Despite numerous invitations, he manages to visit Cousin Charles, who lives less than five minutes up the hillside of Westmount from him, no more than twice a year. He has seen Cousin Phyllis, whose house is twenty minutes away in the other direction, three times during the last fifteen years. "It might be better if I were more outgoing, a little more gregarious," he admits.

Peter has published none of his writings, but there exists a slim, mimeographed volume simply entitled "Poems 1969–1970," which captures many of his moods and attitudes. "The Cocktail Party" graphically screams out his hatred of empty social occasions:

> Hello! The bar's over there!
> Good-bye! Going so soon?
> Gotta go home and throw up!
> Terrific! Keep well!

"Pursuit" catches a glimpse of the hidden terrors Peter believes are constantly pursuing him:

> He stood in front of my car
> and wouldn't move
> So I got out and pushed him away
> and then I drove off
> and he started running along the side
> and jumped on
> and he was sort of clutching at the door and the
>   window
> and then he fell off
> and I was watching him in the mirror
> lying there
> hating me
> and then I went over the goddamn cliff.

Peter's solitary ways sometimes get him into trouble. Among the many assets in the $2-billion business empire over which he presides with his brother, Edward, was, until recently, 100-percent ownership of the Canadiens hockey team and the Montreal Forum. During a home game against the Bruins on May 7, 1977, Bob Wilson, a Boston radio commentator, was sitting high up in the press gondola with his technician when a person he later described as "a tall lanky fellow, very leisurely dressed, with open shirt and sports slacks" plunked himself down between them. "The guy didn't say anything, just sat down and calmly watched the game, gesturing to show his approbation or disappointment. I was looking for a way of telling him to get the hell out of there, that he had no business in the press box, but the many commercials kept me constantly 'on mike.' He left near the end of the first period before I could say a word to him, so I asked the usher on duty if he knew who this impudent guy was, acting as if he owned the place."

The guard informed the embarrassed commentator that his visitor had been Peter Bronfman and that he did, in fact, own both the place and the team. When he returned to watch the second period, Peter explained to Wilson that he could relax during games only by sitting next to somebody with an open microphone, so that he couldn't yell even when he felt like it. Occasionally he was so overcome by emotion that he had to leave his seat to watch the game on the color TV set in the directors' lounge.

Now and then Peter's determination not to display emotions in public turns in on itself. He can be sardonic in his observations of the privacies of others. This streak in his make-up was probably best documented in a description that he wrote for himself about a journey home from Israel in September of 1976:

Sitting in El Al's first-class section, the plane about to take off from Tel Aviv to New York on a recent morning, I was beside a middle-aged Israeli woman who informed me that she and her husband were flying free since he was an El Al employee. No sooner had I recovered from this mild hurt than she followed up with, "My husband is over there sitting beside Mr. Eban." Congratulating her on his good fortune, I learned that she was thankful she wasn't sitting there since she couldn't possibly imagine what she might say to the "great man."

Just then, an El Al steward came by and informed her that unfortunately she and her husband would have to move into "economy" to make room for two paying first-class customers who had just come aboard. Turning to me he asked if I wouldn't mind sitting beside Mr. Eban, as he didn't want to separate the newly arrived couple. I asked if he would consider having Mr. Eban move back to the now vacant seat beside me, since he was sitting up front near the clatter of the bar and the traffic that soon would be flowing to and from the washroom. Understandably, the steward was reluctant to ask Mr. Eban to move, so I picked up my briefcase and seated myself beside him.

Extending my hand, I introduced myself, thinking the name might possibly remind Mr. Eban of the time in 1967 when, shortly after the Six-Day War, he spent a few hours in my parents' home in Montreal prior to addressing a large audience on the Israeli-Arab conflict then being hotly debated at the UN. On that occasion, he had mumbled some phrase in reply to my attempt to exchange a few words, his gaze remaining fixed midway between the top of a small Sisley painting and the ceiling. I remember thinking at the time that I perhaps shouldn't have intruded on the thoughts of a man at stage centre of world attention. All of this flashed through my mind as I extended my hand, which he shook, mumbling a phrase very similar in tone and content to that which I had heard some nine years ago. The smile, too, was pretty much of the same vintage.

Realizing that Mr. Eban was undoubtedly pre-occupied with matters of significance—though not necessarily as critical as during the 1967 situation—I determined to let him go back to leafing through the dozen or so Hebrew and English newspapers on his lap. When breakfast was served and, some hours later, luncheon as well, I commented briefly about the meals being offered and was met inevitably with the same diplomatic smile that seemed to be his trademark. I assumed that this packaged response to queries and approaches from the unwashed masses was for the purpose of discouraging discussion so that he could be alone with his thoughts and his "people." His system was certainly effective. I only bothered him one more time to ask for a few sheets of paper from the scratch pad that he kept constantly nearby for intermittent jottings, so that I could write down these words about how we had lunched together.

Although Peter is an active chairman of the Jewish General Hospital, he frequently finds himself battling the group-thinking of Montreal's Jewish establishment. When Arthur Pascal, the unofficial dean of Quebec Jewry, once accused him of ignoring the collective views of the community, Peter exploded. "Listen, I've heard that bullshit all my life. It means nothing. People who are exposed to it at the age of twenty instead of five, they may take it seriously. But I don't care about the establishment. I won't let them get away with pulling that stuff on me!"

PETER'S RELUCTANCE TO SHARE THE HARD CORE OF HIS PRIVACY probably stems from his isolated youth. "I grew up in a castle on a hill, sensitive but not really aware of what was going on. I had no friends and no real relationship with my parents. I had a nurse from when I was about five to about ten and felt so strongly about her that when we met in Ireland eighteen years later, we just fell into each other's arms and hugged and hugged."

He was separated from his first wife, Diane Feldman, in 1973 and three years later married Theodora Reitsma, a vivacious Dutch blonde with faintly sucked-in cheeks whose face always seems to be sheltering a smile, turned like a sunflower toward the sun. His children are being educated in outstanding schools, but Peter lives in astonishing modesty. Until he moved into a downtown Montreal apartment recently, his main residence was a $90,000 town house on Trafalgar Place, seventy-five feet outside Westmount's eastern boundaries. He drives a brown Mercury. His only real luxury is a valuable art collection that includes canvases by Chagall, Lawren Harris, and Alfred Pellan, as well as some exquisite pieces of Eskimo sculpture. (The carvings so dominated the house that Jack Pierce, the president of Ranger Oil and a good friend of Peter's, once commented that the Bronfman living room reminded him of "the duty-free shop at Gander airport.")

Peter hates to spend money. Trevor Eyton, who is his Toronto lawyer and frequent representative on corporate boards, remembers once when relaxing with him in a Vancouver hotel room that Peter took his shoes off. Eyton noticed not only that he had a hole in one sock but also that the socks had been darned in several places. During a train trip (by coach) from Montreal to Toronto, when his companion bought a cheese-and-ham sandwich, Peter suggested that they might share it. When his wife, Dora, once ordered half a lobster as an appetizer for dinner at Toronto's Hyatt Regency Hotel (of which he had until recently owned about 37 percent),* Peter got so nervous that he started fidgeting with his wedding ring and finally dropped it with a loud, symbolic clang on the pewter serving plate.

"I don't think I'm secure enough to spend the kind of money my cousins do or live in houses like theirs," Peter says. "I've always sort of felt, 'Gee, look at all the money that person's spending. I guess he knows he can always make it.' A strong part of me keeps saying to myself, 'My God, the money just came to me; maybe it could all disappear someday.' "

Sharing most of these feelings as well as control of this branch of the Bronfman family's affairs is Peter's brother, Edward. Two years older than Peter, he attended Bishop's College School at Lennoxville in Quebec's Eastern Townships and graduated from Babson

---

* The Toronto Hyatt Regency has since joined the Four Seasons chain.

Institute near Boston with a Bachelor of Science degree in business administration. Recently divorced, Edward lives in a Westmount bungalow, drives a small BMW, spends much of his free time jogging, skiing, and enjoying the company of his three sons, Paul, David, and Brian. "I've never really looked back," he says. "My upbringing was all part of life's experience. It just took me a little longer to really understand myself. I don't think anybody in particular helped me. I just recognized that the world wasn't full of good guys. I'm not nearly as gullible as I once might have been."

"When the chips are down," says Jack Pierce, the head of Ranger Oil, which is one of Edward's favorite investments, "Edward demands special treatment, and he gets it. He's extremely gracious but occasionally expects the deference due a financial aristocrat."

Edward is slightly more relaxed than Peter and considerably more outgoing, but his deafness in one ear tends to create an air of quiet hurt about him, as if he were constantly waiting for some unexpected blow to fall and had to hoard his words like sapphires in case one of his unguarded comments might trigger the final catastrophe. The brothers are emotionally dependent on each other but in business do not regard themselves as being interchangeable. Their individual authority in the holding company named after them is very different. "Edper's shares are divided equally," says an investment expert who once worked for them, "but if Peter says 'no go' to something, it's definitely off. If Edward says 'no,' it still means 'maybe.' "

Peter and Edward vehemently deny any deliberate rivalry with their cousins Charles and Edgar, but it's not an easy statement to document. Charles's acquisition of the Expos was quickly followed by their purchase of the Canadiens; Cemp's rush into major real-estate investments through Fairview and Cadillac was copied by Edper's purchase of control in Trizec Corporation; both families have attempted to expand their investments in television, and in the fall of 1972 Edper outbid Cemp for control of Astral Communications, a large

Toronto-based film-and-TV distribution firm. "Peter and Edward have acted as good citizens and, on balance, do credit to the family name," says Edgar. "I think perhaps it was a mistake that after Charles did the Expos they bought the Canadiens because we don't really want the Bronfmans to dominate sports in Montreal. But they're entitled to their place in the sun."

There has been only one open clash between the two branches of the family. On June 19, 1972, in a hearing before the Canadian Radio-Television Commission in Kingston, Ontario, their interests came in direct conflict over rival bids to acquire control of Canadian Marconi Company, which then owned CFCF-TV in Montreal and three radio stations.

The British-owned company had already decided to accept the Cemp bid of $18 million, even though Edper's offer included more cash. But at the CRTC hearings, Jacques Courtois, speaking for Peter and Edward, accused Charles's and Edgar's branch of the family of shady dealings and stock manipulation. Specifically, Courtois accused several officers of Multiple Access Ltd., a computer company controlled by Cemp, of purchasing 10,000 shares of Multiple (into which Marconi was being folded) at $1.76 a share, knowing as insiders that their planned bid would drive up the value of the stock. A week later, the Multiple shares were worth $7. He also accused Cemp of trying to acquire the TV operation merely as a tax write-off. "I say that their main intention in this case is not to buy a radio-and-TV operation to better serve the community," Courtois charged, "but to take advantage of the tax laws, and I say if you're buying it for a tax loss, you're going to try and maximize profits in order to write off what could be eleven millions in four or five years; and if you're trying to maximize profits, you're not spending money for long-range return." And he accused Cemp of bypassing provisions of the Canadian restrictions on foreign ownership of broadcasting stations, because only one of the company's chief investors (Charles) was at that time a resident of Montreal. Philip Vineberg, speaking for Sam's line of the family, challenged Peter and Edward to reveal that one of *their* chief investors, Zoë Scheckman, the late Mona Bronfman's daughter, was a U.S. citizen. "I'm not going to be accused of misleading the commission," Courtois shouted at Vineberg from his seat in the audience. "Zoë Scheckman is not a trustee!" The slanging match concluded with the CRTC's approval of the Cemp bid and Vineberg's masterly summing up: "When you have a marriage, you can't expect a testimonial from the rejected suitor."

SUCH RIVALRY IS A LEGACY FROM THE MUCH MORE BITTER BATTLES FOUGHT BY AN EARLIER BROOD OF BRONFMANS during their scrubby days on the Canadian prairies. Allan, the father of Peter and Edward, was the only Bronfman of his generation to attend university; he turned himself into a lawyer and gave the family its social gloss. After working at Harry's hotel in Yorkton as a bellboy and saving his tips, Allan moved to Winnipeg, graduated in law from the University of Manitoba, and eventually articled for $75 a month with Andrews, Andrews, Burbidge & Bastedo. He moved to Montreal with Sam in 1924 and became his brother's front man. Sam and Allan worked together as a team, with Allan's greater polish and sure instincts during the early years particularly useful in business contacts.

Eventually, Sam grew jealous of Allan's presentability and education, particularly his younger brother's ability to attract friends and enthrall parties with his anecdotes and piano recitals. Probably the most unforgivable of Allan's actions was his thrust to force Seagram into its initial diversification through the purchase of Royalite, a Canadian oil company. If Sam was angry with those who gave him bad advice, he was downright enraged at anyone whose counsel he opposed who later proved to be correct.

Allan was a stubborn character. (Peter remembers once telling his father, in connection with a fairly minor corporate problem they had yet to discuss, "After all,

Dad, there are always two sides to every story . . ."
and being cut off by the old man banging his fist on the
desk, declaring, "No there aren't!") But he was no
match for Sam, gradually becoming a target for the
senior Bronfman's contempt, and was shunted off mainly
into looking after the family philanthropies, although
he remained a senior vice-president of Seagram's until
1975.

A former colleague recalls being in Sam's office just
after the outbreak of World War II when Allan came
in, decked out in the uniform of a private in the Canadian army. On his way to a ten-day reserve training
course at St. Bruno, near Montreal, he shook Sam's
hand, executed a smart about-turn, marched to the
door, saluted, and was gone. Sam could hardly contain
himself. "Ah, look at the fucking hero," he exclaimed.
"You'd think he'd just won the war. Christ, they get
a few more like him and Hitler's got a chance!"

It was one of Sam's eternal grudges against his
brother that during the immediate postwar reconstruction period, when Allan donated a boatload of flour to
a French city, he was promptly decorated with the
Legion of Honor. "How come he didn't send the flour
from both of us?" Sam asked anyone who'd listen. "He
does everything else jointly, for Christ's sake. Hell, he
doesn't know enough to get out of his own way, and
now they give him the goddamn Legion of Honor."
Allan didn't say a word, but he always wore the scarlet
pip that denotes the French decoration proudly in his
buttonhole.

Sam had his revenge. His excommunication from
Seagram's hallowed halls of Allan's sons began a primal
feud that split the family into warring camps and still
seethes not far below the surface of the superficially
pleasant (if rare) contacts between the two main
branches. Allan himself was quite content to play a
complementary role in the distilling giant's corporate
affairs, but he never stopped hoping that Edward and
Peter would be counted among its operating heirs.
Instead, Sam chose specifically to exclude them, even

before their abilities could fairly be appraised. Minda remembers being puzzled by the tension that began to build up between the neighbors on Belvedere Road. "When we were smaller, we thought our cousins would go into the company. Later, we knew how things stood." Charles's summary is more succinct: "Pop didn't want them in the business."

The actual *coup de grâce* that drove Allan's branch of the family out of contention took place in the summer of 1952, shortly after Peter graduated from Yale. "The boys came to me," Allan remembers, "Peter first. He started to cry and asked me, 'How is it that I can't get into the company?' So I told him."

Sam and Allan had placed their Seagram stockholdings in Seco Investments, a private company controlled jointly by their family trusts, Cemp and Edper. But the ownership was not evenly split; Sam had 2.2 million shares and Allan 1.1 million. This two-thirds majority allowed Sam to issue instructions barring Allan's children from joining Seagram's. Actually, the situation was very much more complicated. Allan had briefly considered challenging Sam's hegemony. The eight original Bronfman brothers and sisters then held 53 percent of Seagram's outstanding stock. By aligning all of the shares not owned by Sam's branch of the family and recruiting support from outside investors, Allan might have been able to exert enough pressure on Sam to change his mind about Peter and Edward. But he was beaten even before he could start. Because Cemp held the majority of Seco's shares, Sam could vote not only his own but also Edper's shares in any corporate showdown involving Seco's control block. Allan thus had no tangible weapon with which to change Sam's mind about his sons. The final decision to bar Allan's children was taken during a memorable shouting match between Sam and Allan. "Sam was really mad at me," Allan recalled, "and when Sam gets mad, he can go back four generations."

Even though he won, the fact that there had been some small challenge to his supreme authority made

Sam so angry that during the next twelve months he refused to exchange a single word with his younger brother. "For a whole year," Allan recalls, "he used to walk by my office, which was next door to his, and never stop to talk." No member of either family crossed the tailored lawn between the Belvedere mansions.

Eight years later, Sam struck another blow. Having ejected Allan's sons from any proprietary function in the company, he decided to strip them of half their holdings. Seagram's was at the time selling on the open market for $28 per share. Sam set out to purchase 600,000 shares of Edper's holding of 1.1 million at $26 per share, claiming that he was entitled to a "quantity discount" for such a large block. Peter and Edward accepted because the offer had been accompanied by what they read as a clear warning that their refusal would strip their father of his only remaining power base—the Seagram vice-presidency. This bold move raised Sam's holdings to 2.8 million shares, which with two subsequent two-for-one stock splits brought him to the more than 11 million his family now holds. At the same time, Edper's stake in Seagram was reduced to 500,000 shares, which, following similar splits, eventually left Allan's family with only two million shares. Peter and Edward have since sold off all of this portfolio, claiming with ill-concealed pride that "there are lots of better investments around."

The final break with Sam came in 1969, when Peter and Edward were making their first major financial move by attempting to purchase Great-West Life Assurance, the large Winnipeg-based insurance company. They drove up the quoted market value of their take-over instrument—a holding company called Great West Saddlery Limited—from 46 cents to $24, and suddenly found themselves being hailed as the new whiz kids of Canadian finance. On February 16, Sam called Peter into his office to confront him with a large pile of press clippings, praising the rise of "the other" Bronfmans.

"What the hell are all of these?" Sam demanded.

"I don't know," Peter replied. "I don't ever answer reporters' calls. What they write isn't my fault."

"Your private office still connected to the Seagram switchboard?"

"Yes. But we pay all the long-distance bills separately."

"Well, you better get off. Right now."

The last shreds of the umbilical cord between the two families had been cut.

Peter was then forty. He and Edward had accomplished little. They'd put up an office building in Montreal at 2055 Peel Street (where they still maintain their headquarters), bought a few bowling alleys, purchased an interest in a minor printing house, and sat around too frightened to take any risks lest they make a mistake. But now there could be no more excuses. Their Uncle Sam's brutal finality brought with it a flood of fresh perceptions. Suddenly they weren't nearly so afraid any more, realizing that there is no easy way out, not in the middle of a life, that the power to change and grow lies within each individual, not in his external circumstances.

GREAT WEST SADDLERY, THEIR CHOSEN INSTRUMENT, HAD BEEN ESTABLISHED IN 1869 to sell dry goods and to fashion harnesses for the horse-and-buggy age. The North West Mounted Police had commissioned the firm to manufacture its western-style saddles; during World War I, the company turned out 14,000 bridles for the Allied cavalry. Saddlery's stock had been manipulated by successive waves of greedy investors anxious to drain its treasury, and in March 1958 it fell into the hands of two fast-talking promoters called Hugh Paton and Hubert Cox. They acquired Brandon Packers, the George H. Hees Company (a Toronto-based household-furnishings manufacturer), and Chapples Limited (a small department-store chain in northwestern Ontario), announcing that they planned to turn Great West Saddlery into one of the largest merchandising organizations in the country. Paton grandly predicted that their

only competition in the field was the Eaton's retail organization and that projected sales would hit $100 million
by 1964. Instead, the company was driven close to
bankruptcy, with Paton and Cox each drawing four-
year penitentiary terms for defrauding Brandon Packers'
bondholders.

Peter and Edward Bronfman acquired control of
Saddlery, by then merely a handy investment shell, in
May of 1968 for $95,000, purchasing the balance of
its treasury shares for a further $597,000. A quick series
of investments followed, masterminded by Paul Lowen-
stein and Neil Baker, two brilliant young M.B.A.s
working for Edper at the time. They pushed the once-
dormant Saddlery into the most glamorous industries
of the buoyant sixties, including the computer business
(through the acquisition of Aquila Computer Services); interplanetary travel (through the establishment
of Space Research Corporation to take over the Space
Research Institute); hotels (through a partnership
with Western International); management consulting
(through a firm called Berthiaume, St. Pierre, Thériault
et Associés); and real estate (through a merger with
the impressive roster of properties built up by Sam
Hashman on the prairies). Each of these transactions
drove the Saddlery stock ever upward. Early in 1969,
Edper launched its takeover bid for Great-West Life,
a $1.5-billion company with business in force of more
than $8 billion. Stock in the ultra-conservative Winni-
peg insurer was widely enough dispersed that control
could be acquired on the open market. The Bronfmans
quickly gathered in 194,000 shares with an offer of six
Saddlery treasury certificates plus $30 cash per share
of Great-West Life. The total purchase price of $76
million fell easily within Edper's financial abilities. The
life-insurance company's stock, which had been selling
for $79 at the 1968 year-end, promptly shot up to
$149; trading was suspended for five days at the request
of David Kilgour, Great-West Life's president, who
was determined to prevent the Bronfmans from acquiring his company. The Saddlery bid dissolved when a

complicated counterbid maneuver entered the picture, but the Bronfmans were able to sell their accumulated Great-West Life stock at considerable profit.

The man who negotiated the deal was a Montreal lawyer called Jacques Courtois, who has since become Peter's and Edward's most important associate. Following a distinguished naval career, Courtois quickly turned his lucrative postwar legal practice into a cockpit of significant economic power, becoming a director of a dozen major corporations and mutual funds. His most visible role has been as president of the Club de Hockey Canadien. Peter and Edward attended most games when they owned the club, but they deliberately placed their man Courtois in the owner's box. Whenever the Governor General or some other celebrity visited the Forum, it was Courtois who guided him into the directors' lounge between periods, while the Bronfman brothers awkwardly skulked around, acting as if they were just passing by and happened to drop in and weren't quite sure they really belonged. Edward's son Paul caused some slight embarrassment one season, not only by becoming a rabid Toronto Maple Leaf fan but also by insisting on wearing a Leaf sweater into the Forum.

Courtois, a shrewd aristocrat with courtly manners and one of the best legal brains in Montreal's corporate meadows, spends his spare moments riding as joint master of the hounds at a hunt club on the western approaches to Montreal and serves as a director of both Edper and the private trusts that control it.

Edper itself is managed by Jack Cockwell, a tightly composed South African-born chartered accountant who combines a slide-rule approach to investment analysis with a sharply honed sixth sense that allows him to ferret out likely winners. Also important: portfolio adviser Austin Beutel, whose investment counseling firm manages $300 million in private funds, and J. Trevor Eyton, a canny Toronto lawyer who tends to whisper his legal advice and in the summertime maintains a telescope in his office permanently trained on

Olympic Island in Toronto harbor so that he can watch his daughters taking sailing lessons at the Royal Canadian Yacht Club.

Peter and Edward Bronfman conduct Edper's operation with what they call "informed intuition," perusing monthly budget sheets of their associated companies, interviewing prospective promoters trying to earn their finders' fees. Harold Milavsky, president of Trizec, a major Edper holding, says, "Peter gets good people, trusts them, and gives them their head. His secret is that once they've proven themselves, he allows them full authority as well as full responsibility. At Trizec, for example, we report to him only at quarterly directors' meetings."

The two brothers plus Courtois, Cockwell, Eyton, and Beutel have organized themselves into a platoon system which places two or three of them on the boards of each of their nine major corporate interests (the figures in parentheses represent the holding of Edper or an Edper-controlled company):

1. *Boyd, Stott & McDonald Limited,* Toronto (13 percent), which funnels funds into everything from sure-gain investments in real property to visionary technological developments. It holds 20 percent of the new Canadian Commercial and Industrial Bank, with assets of $198 million as of August 31, 1978, and its recently formed subsidiary, Boyd, Stott & McDonald Technologies, holds patents for a new cyclone-furnace combustion device; a water-jet shuttle that could double the speed of shuttle looms; a new process to restructure the starch molecule to yield new chemical products; a device to scan, digitize, memorize, and correlate human palm prints; and a new spun yarn.

2. *Ranger Oil (Canada) Limited,* Calgary (6 percent plus private holdings), an ambitious exploration outfit that has become Canada's third-largest independent, with substantial oil and gas reserves in Alberta, the North Sea, Colorado, Texas, Louisiana, Wyoming, and the Celtic Sea off Ireland.

3. *S. B. McLaughlin Associates Limited,* Missis-

sauga, Ontario (18 percent), a large land and real-estate development firm operating with $250 million in assets that include recent expansion into significant acreage in Michigan.

4. *IAC Limited,* Toronto (19.4 percent), originally Canada's largest financing company, now about to transform itself into the Continental Bank of Canada with an asset base of $2.5 billion.

5. *National Hees Enterprises Limited,* Toronto (78 percent), an investment vehicle with a portfolio worth $20 million.

6. *Mico Enterprises Limited,* Montreal (65 percent), a merchant-banking operation that manages a grab-bag of assets including bowling complexes, supermarkets, a deepwater harbor on Antigua, and loan and land-development companies.

7. *Astral Bellevue Pathé Limited,* Toronto (26 percent), one of the giants of the Canadian movie industry, with 1977 sales of $25 million.

8. *Carena-Bancorp Incorporated,* Montreal (70 percent), a holding company which is Peter's and Edward's private bank, with 1978 revenues running close to $3 million a month. Its most visible holding until recently was the Montreal Canadiens, sold in August 1978. Less visible is Carena-Bancorp's control position in a subsidiary called Carena Properties, which in turn holds 58.6 percent of the outstanding shares in Trizec Corporation, Canada's second-largest public real-estate development operation.

9. *Trizec Corporation,* Calgary (58.6 percent). Edper's most important asset; its crown jewel is the massive (sixty-seven acres of rentable space) Place Ville Marie complex in downtown Montreal, which remains one of Canada's largest and most prestigious office buildings. Trizec's portfolio includes forty-two office buildings, twelve shopping centers, thirty-four mobile-home parks, twenty-three retirement lodges or nursing homes, and three hotels.

Starting with its 1971 purchase of Detroit's huge Fisher Building, the company's most significant moves have been into the U.S. market, which now accounts for a quarter of its assets, including seven major Los Angeles office buildings, the Peachtree Center Tower in Atlanta, and Clearwater Mall in Florida. It also owns 11,000 parking sites in mobile-home parks spread through the American Southwest.

Juggling all of Edper's activities isn't easy. But Peter is very much in charge, so much so that Edward recently hired a personal investment assistant to help him swing some ventures on his own.

Peter has come to maturity very late, and it wasn't until recently that he finally managed to catch up with himself. "When I was twenty-four, I was acting like sixteen. I didn't start working until I was well over twenty, so I didn't have a very realistic view of what life was all about. At forty, I was still eight to ten years behind, doing and thinking things that people I know and respect were doing at thirty. But now I'm past my hang-ups and enjoying life."

The incident that finally began to liberate Peter Bronfman in his quest for identity was a conversation with his son, Bruce. Six years old at the time, Bruce wanted to know exactly what being a millionaire was all about. "I tried to explain it," Peter recalls vividly. "I told Bruce about our family history, our business, and asked him how he felt about being a millionaire."

Young Bruce considered the matter carefully and replied, "I'm very proud."

The answer deeply impressed Peter because it seemed such a healthy reaction. "Up in the castle where I grew up, the three things we never were allowed to talk about were money, other people, and sex. . . . What else is there?"

18. Charles

CHARLES IS the most appealing of the Bronfmans. His sweet-brown eyes reflect that quality of living at a distance from the center of things sometimes possessed by blind folk singers, gaitered Anglican bishops, and pet reindeer.

Unlike his brother and sisters, who fled home with barely decent haste, Charles stayed at the father's elbow, so dominated by Sam's strength of will that existence for him became diffracted into a series of double images—his own and his father's—as though he were hiding inside the rangefinder of a camera not quite in focus.

Mr. Sam could make boys out of men—and with Charles, his second son, he almost succeeded.

For forty (40) long years he was the senior Bronfman's willing shadow, the relief map of his personal anxieties drawn by the old man's whims and tantrums. During those four dim decades of love and fear, Charles's filial feelings turned into a form of peremptory worship, undiminished by his father's death. Charles's own sense of self survived, if not intact at least untainted by cynicism or misanthropy, so that he can view life with the bittersweet detachment of a man engaged in a series of existential errands.

Alone of Sam's children, Charles served his full

apprenticeship as a Bronfman. His intensely unhappy and academically unsuccessful sojourns at Trinity College School and McGill left him frustrated and dissatisfied with himself; a teen-age brush with death turned him into a wary introvert. He had been suffering from an abscessed throat when he was hit by a rare streptococcal germ. "I still remember being too tired to open my eyes, though it hurt too much to close them," he recalls. "I loved to play hockey and ski in those days, but I couldn't do anything. I spent a winter just sitting at my parents' house in Ste. Marguerite, hovering somewhere between life and death." He survived only because Sam used his influence to cut enough red tape so that young Charles became the first Canadian civilian to be treated with a brand-new wonder medication called penicillin.

The trauma of his sickness combined with Sam's unyielding domination turned Charles's already fragile ego into a perpetual proving ground. During a 1959 visit to Winnipeg for the opening of a Cemp shopping center, Charles was guest of honor at the official reception when some young people invited him along to a private party nearby. He declined, telling Michael McCormick, the vice-president of Cemp who had been assigned to accompany him: "They don't really want me. It isn't me they're asking, it's just a goddamn Bronfman millionaire, that's all. So to hell with them."

"No. Please, that's not good thinking," McCormick pleaded. "The trouble is you *are* a goddamn Bronfman millionaire, if that's the way you want to put it, and always will be, please God. So you can't carry on this way for the rest of your life every time people ask you any place, just because you think they might not be sincere. Please cut it out and go."

Charles was back by eleven that night, complaining, "First thing after I got there, somebody came up and wanted me to make a donation to some damn thing or other, then another guy asked to get in on Seagram's insurance business, and so it went. They didn't really want me, just the goddamn money, the social influence and all that crap. They didn't give a damn about me."

Charles never lets go. He feels himself constantly under pressure to establish his credentials, to win even in as innocent a pastime as backgammon. "After a while our games become absolute fights," says Jean-Claude Baudinet, a frequent backgammon partner. "He's a terrible loser. It's inbred that a Bronfman can't lose. He takes the board and throws it up in the air when it looks as if he might not win. We were once in Jamaica together when he lost his temper and threw the board upside down, so I told him, 'Charles, listen, if you do that again, you're going to have to run the beach for me as a punishment. Twice. Okay? And I'm going to sit there and watch you sweat.' Well, sure enough, it's not long before the board flew all over the place again, so we went down to the beach. But there was a hell of a storm that day; it was cold and windy. I had to sit there watching Charles enjoy himself, laughing as he ran and keeping warm while I froze. So in the end I really lost, and to him it proved that he never loses."

Similarly, when he attends the Expos' training camp in Daytona Beach, Florida, Charles comes to play, not to watch, wearing the club's white uniform with red-and-blue trim, looking bird-muscled and slightly stooped, but pushing himself to the limit for all that. He invariably appears in Expos' uniform number 83, after Seagram's best-selling rye, and even has had his portrait painted in it.

CHARLES'S COMPETITIVE SPIRIT WAS MOST EVIDENT DURING HIS EARLY YEARS WITH SEAGRAM'S. Three years after Charles had left McGill, Sam placed his second son in charge of the newly acquired Thomas Adams Distillers Limited.* "I was given forty salesmen, no known brands, and told to get out and work. It was

* The new name given United Distillers Ltd. of Vancouver, acquired by the Bronfmans in 1953. UDL's brands were known by many British Columbia drinkers as *U Die Later*.

pretty rough. All the brands were new, and I'd find that the salesmen were pushing one thing while the advertising department was pushing another." The big breakthrough came in 1955 when he confronted his father with a recommendation for a new bottle design for Adams Private Stock. "Dad was against what he called 'fancy design,' but I told him, 'I want this bottle.'

"He looked at me for a long time and asked, 'So you want to go into fancy packages?'

"I said, 'Yes,' and stuck to my guns. Within half an hour the whole thing was settled. It was the first time in my life I'd ever convinced Dad of anything. In two years that brand moved from 19,000 to 100,000 cases."

Three years later, at the age of twenty-seven, Charles was named to head the House of Seagram, a subsidiary responsible for the distillery empire's relatively minor markets in Canada, Jamaica, and Israel. On May 7, 1962, he married Barbara Baerwald, the beautiful granddaughter of a Wall Street banker he'd met on a blind date in New York. He was appointed to the Bank of Montreal's board of directors, joined the Mount Royal Club, played a lot of golf, became a director of the Montreal Symphony Orchestra ("even though I couldn't tell one symphony from another and didn't care whether I heard another concert at Place des Arts"). He lived in a nondescript apartment block on Maisonneuve Boulevard, walked a lot with his young son Stephen around Beaver Lake in Mount Royal Park, and seemed ready to melt invisibly into the city's financial landscape as the not-very-interesting young heir to Seagram's Canadian operations.

Then, in 1970, when Ellen Jane, his second child, was due, Charles broke out of his golden torpor with a vengeance. In an act of uncharacteristic bravado, he decided to build himself a great monument of a house on an oversized plot he'd acquired near the peak of the mountain in Westmount. Instead of merely discussing his requirements casually with potential architects, he wrote a thirty-page booklet for himself entitled "My House in the City" that spelled out its exact specifications. It was to be the twenty-first-century version of those magnificent sprawling manor houses that dominate the Cotswolds of England, complete with a granite tower and the visual inaccessibility of a latter-day fortress.

The structure took nearly three years to build and cost close to $2 million, making it the most expensive private residence in Canada at the time. No two windows are the same shape; floors, walls, and ceilings slope into each other on varied elevations so that few surfaces meet under as mundane circumstances as a ninety-degree angle. "The complex program for this house," commented Richard Weinstein, the New York architect who designed it, "contained several apparent contradictions. It called for a large number of separate, distinct spaces, and at the same time asked for intimacy: the family wanted a closeness in their own living rooms but wished to maintain private territories for children and adults. . . . The square footage of the entire program added up to 15,000 square feet, a large house by any measure. Yet the client wanted to preserve as much land as possible on an irregular site."

Weinstein, by tilting the curved bounding walls of the driveway upward, corrected any sense of the house sliding downhill. He designed the house around two major elements: a series of magnificent cabinet-embedded skylights that flood living areas with natural light, and a huge swimming-pool complex—it includes a sauna, solarium, and loggia besides the swimming- and wading-pool areas—with a sweeping canted glass roof that rolls down into the ground in summer. The master bedroom suite of the Bronfman abode is a self-contained realm with its own courtyard, private stairs, study, studio and skylit dressing room, and, all told, the house has six bathrooms, a wine cellar, a basement projection hall, and an upstairs playroom that Weinstein describes as being "skewed to suggest a private realm of fantasy—self-contained and spinning off into space."

The house is protected twenty-four hours a day by

watchmen from Garda Securities Services Ltd., the
company now run by a former Seagram vice-president,
Michael McCormick.

Charles usually lunches with his chief executives in
a third-floor private dining room at Seagram's Montreal
headquarters. Every noon hour they play a game that
involves being served an anonymous Seagram-bottled
wine. As well as trying to guess the brand, they have
score cards to rate its appearance, bouquet, and taste,
and see how close they come to each other's evaluation.
The meals are invariably terminated by Charles's pushing back his chair with the command: "Gentlemen, to
horse!" and they all troop back to work.

Unlike his father, Charles rarely upsets existing lines
of authority by personally soliciting the views of employees at all levels of the organization. He runs the
company by having only his four luncheon companions
report directly to him. Charles's office has the compulsory canvas by Jean-Paul Riopelle that denotes all
Bronfman inner sanctums.* The formality of the room's
heavy accents of glass, marble, and leather is set off by
bamboo wallpaper and a beige shag rug. The desk and
credenza are piled high with computer printouts, family
photographs, and sample whisky decanters. As well as
regular telephones, there are direct "hot lines" to John
McHale, president of the Expos, and Leo Kolber at
Cemp. The office atmosphere reflects the dichotomy of
its owner's view of business as both an exciting game
and a dour duty. When he first moved in, Charles kept
a large plastic tic-tac-toe coffee table that Barbara had
given him near his desk. In those days he was very
tense and felt that many of the people he dealt with were
too. The tic-tac-toe set was meant to create an atmosphere that would signify to callers that business was a
kind of pastime. Now that he's sure himself that it's
only a game, he doesn't need the tic-tac-toe table as
a reminder.

---

* Gerald Bronfman's Riopelle is larger; Peter Bronfman's is
the most beautiful; Edgar's is the darkest; Charles's is the most
valuable.

Charles has a complicated view of his calling. He holds business to be a mere fraction of his existence; the bottom line isn't everything: "I don't need money, so the making of money per se I don't find particularly interesting. Just to make a profit on the stock market, for example, I can't handle that. But to make money while you're doing other things that are useful is something that's very enjoyable to me. . . . The profit motive is damn important, but any worthwhile business guy has to think out his responsibilities to employees, to shareholders, to himself, and to his society."

He is one of the few Canadian businessmen who openly support environmentalist causes but is firmly opposed to government intervention in the economy because it kills competition. "If you take the competition out of business, it's no fun any more," he says. "I remember one time being absolutely thrilled when Canadian Club started really to go to town on us. Hiram Walker were doing a terrific job, and some of the guys around here were down in the dumps. When they asked me what I was looking so happy about, I said, 'It's about time somebody really threw us one.' "

UNLIKE HIS FATHER, CHARLES NEVER DID TRY TO MAKE IT INTO THE CANADIAN ESTABLISHMENT. They came to him. The elder Bronfman wanted badly to be recognized for what he had done, having come from nowhere and accomplished so much. The directorship at the Bank of Montreal and membership in the Mount Royal Club, which came easily to Charles, are of little importance to him. "I feel sort of sad that life happens this way," he says. "When you don't want it, you get it, and when you do want it so very badly, you have to have great wars and battles."

Charles's personal influence has increased with his self-confidence. He was, for example, recently promoted to the Bank of Montreal's audit committee, which indicates that his presence on that board has come to mean much more than merely acting as resident ambassador for its largest account. The clout is there, but for his own reasons Charles continues deliberately to play down the extent of his influence, even within Seagram's internal affairs—though his chairmanship of the giant conglomerate's policy-setting executive committee grants him an ultimate veto over Edgar's initiatives. In fact, Charles takes a very active hand in running the company's main business out of New York and spends two days a week, three out of every four weeks a month, in the Park Avenue headquarters.

Pleasantly naïve about the actual reach of his personal authority, he once asked Sol Kanee, a family friend of the Bronfmans, to get him an appointment with the Minister of Finance in Ottawa. Instead, Kanee handed over the man's unlisted telephone number and suggested that Charles call him himself. The young Bronfman was astounded when the Minister readily agreed to see him during a forthcoming Montreal visit. "You always wonder," Charles confides, "whether people are friendly because they like you or because they want something. But you get over it after a while. A great friend of mine used to say that one of my protections was that I happened to have a fairly healthy level of paranoia. I never really sought power. I used to do things, and people would say to me, 'Do you realize what you've said?'

"I'd say, 'Oh, I just said something.'

"And they'd say, 'Yes, but *you* said it. Don't you realize who you are?'

"And I used to say, 'Well, no, I'm just another guy.'

"And they'd say, 'No. You're not just another guy.' And then I had to start learning about how to keep myself in control, to measure my words. And I found that quite difficult for a while. Even today, in certain areas I don't realize the so-called power that's at my command. Sometimes it can be a little bit frightening. Sometimes it can be damn pleasurable."

Like most other rich individuals, he has great difficulty divining the motives of people who woo his attention. "Charles," says Lorne Webster, who should know,* "is one of the few rich men who can tell the difference between friendship motivated by his money and the real thing. He has a genuine sense of humor and appreciates finding it in others. This is an element that helps to smooth away much friction. Charles has many advisers and assistants at Seagram's, but he is very much his own man. This is not to say that he attempts to dominate—there is no megalomania about him. He is at peace with himself."

Superficially gregarious, he carefully husbands the extent of his commitments in social intercourse, so that even though he knows most of the people who count in the Canadian establishment, he seldom lets himself go, operating very much within his own closed orbit of a few trusted friends and associates. Charles's handful of true friends—carefully chosen compatibles who appreciate the sensitive creature behind those reindeer eyes—tend to sound overprotective in their evaluations. "Charles's main trouble," says Michael McCormick, his onetime chaperon, "is that he's at least five times as good a man as he thinks he is."

Hugh Hallward, the construction executive who is a partner of Bronfman's in the Expos, believes that "Charles probably feels a little like George VI—all of a sudden here's the second son thrust into enormous responsibility." Jean-Claude Baudinet, Charles's partner in Gabriel Lucas Limitée, Canada's most luxurious chain of jewelers, probably knows him best. "Charles's inheritance was an extremely heavy package," he says. "His father was not easy to get along with at all; his big brother is the star. It's only in the last decade that he has started becoming his own man."

Next to Leo Kolber, Charles's closest adviser is

---

* Although they grew up as near neighbors, Lorne wasn't invited inside the Belvedere Palace until Charles's twenty-seventh birthday party. It was Webster, now a senior partner in the Montreal Expos, who first introduced Charles to Evelyn de Rothschild, currently chairman of the British merchant bank. Lorne Webster, a scion of the huge Webster fortune, has become English Montreal's most imaginative entrepreneur.

Philip Vineberg, Lazarus Phillips's nephew, who joined
the Phillips firm as a junior in 1939. A remarkably
self-contained intellectual who speaks in perfectly
parsed paragraphs, Vineberg is the Bronfman family's
one-man clearing house. As well as being a director
of Seagram and Cemp, he sits on the boards of the holding companies that look after Allan's and Harry's shares
of the family fortune. Heavy with honors, he is the first
Jew to have been elected *bâtonnier* of the Montreal bar,
is a governor of McGill, and has headed the Canadian
Tax Foundation. Articulate, wise, responsive, and
above all sensible, Vineberg can synthesize any problem into what appears to be its inevitable solution. His
most valuable quality is that he seldom if ever panics.
When he and his wife, Miriam, were trying to furnish
their new condominium in Palm Beach, everyone was
thrown into a tizzy because it was discovered at the
last minute that the antique bed they'd bought at a
European auction had been soaked in the hold of the
freighter that had brought it across the Atlantic. Vineberg calmed everybody down with the comment, "Well,
at least we're lucky we weren't in it."

WHAT BROUGHT ABOUT CHARLES'S TRANSFORMATION
INTO FULL MANHOOD more than any other single factor
was his purchase, in 1968, of the Montreal Expos. It
was on the playing fields of Jarry Park that the younger
Bronfman was finally able to exorcise his bedeviled
youth and assume full command of himself. "I became
a vice-president of Seagram's before I really knew what
I was doing," he says. "But with the Expos I did everything on my own. Eventually, what you've got to try
and do is become a person in your own right. It was
the Expos that made me a man."

Neither Charles nor Westmount, where he grew up,
had much of a baseball tradition. A local bylaw pro-
hibits the playing of hardball, presumably in case an
uncouth home run should break a window; at private
school in Port Hope, Charles had to play cricket. He
did see an occasional home game of the Royals (the

Brooklyn Dodgers' farm club in the old International League) and vaguely remembers once watching the Dodgers beat the Yankees at Ebbets Field. But the only baseball Charles ever played was as first baseman for the Cemp team in an intercompany lob-ball (a form of softball) league.

Bronfman's involvement with the Expos began with a telephone call he received on April 3, 1968, from Gerry Snyder, a sporting-goods dealer in the Snowdon district of Montreal who as vice-chairman of the city's executive committee was then the ranking English-speaking representative in Mayor Jean Drapeau's administration. "We were down in Puerto Rico, Barbara and I, at a meeting of the Young Presidents' Organization," Charles remembers, "when Snyder called to say the Mayor wanted ten people to put up a million dollars each into major-league baseball. Well, I figured it wouldn't happen anyway, so I said, 'Okay, we'll be in if that's what the Mayor really wants.' Three weeks later, I was sitting at home with my wife listening to the late news, and the announcer said something about the franchise being awarded to Montreal. I turned to Barbara and said, 'Oh, shit! We're in the glue!' "

Faced with having to put up cash, most of the original sponsors dropped away, with only Charles, the Webster family, and Jean-Louis Lévesque, the New Brunswick-born Montreal financier, remaining to pick up the pieces. Then Lévesque backed out, and Charles had to make his big decision: "I shut myself in my office for two hours, just thinking, and told my secretary, 'Please leave me alone. Even if my father wants in, anybody wants in, tell them I'm sick, I'm dead, or anything you want.' I sat there, and I thought and thought and thought and said to myself, 'This just has to be. It's very good for the city,' and so on. I never even thought about whether it might be good for me, particularly. That didn't seem to enter my mind. But I guess it was somewhere in the background, because I don't believe that people have these great altruistic ideas. Something always says, 'There's something in it for me—as a person, or the monetary reward, or whatever.' "

Having decided to take the plunge, Charles informed his father that he intended to put his own money into the baseball club. "He just looked out from behind his newspaper," Charles recalls, "gave me one of his 'screw you' looks, and said, 'You're supposed to be selling whisky, not baseball.' " At this point Charles called Ben Raginsky, a Montreal psychiatrist he occasionally consulted, who strongly advised him to leap into the venture. The deal was painfully put together, with Charles finally putting up more than $4 million for a full 45 percent.* But for forty-eight hours the negotiations hung in the balance, with National League President Warren Giles attempting to balance the realities of Jarry Park against Jean Drapeau's dream of eventually erecting a covered stadium that would dwarf Houston's Astrodome. "The first night the decision was being made," Charles recalls, "I went home and bawled like a baby because I thought the whole thing had fallen through. The next night I went home and cried just as hard. I was so happy we had been given the franchise."

The new team had no firm arrangements for a park, no training camp, no operating personnel, no players, and no uniforms. Still, Bronfman now owned the first major-league baseball team ever awarded a franchise outside the United States. "If I goof at Seagram's, my father is still here, thank God, to help me out," he told friends at the time. "But if I goof with the Expos, there's nobody. With the team, I'm not my father's son. I'm my own man."

Drapeau invested $3 million in modernizing Jarry

---

* The other 55 percent came from: Hugh Hallward, 10 percent; Paul and Charlemagne Beaudry, 20 percent; Sydney Maislin, 5 percent; John McHale, 10 percent; and Lorne Webster, 10 percent. At one spring Expo training camp, Lorne and Charles had been tossing a baseball around when Webster asked if he could take one of the professional catcher's gloves for his son. "Listen," Bronfman replied, "for a million bucks you can take home a mitt."

Park to hold 28,000, and even though the Expos finished their charter year dead last in the league, a heavy forty-eight games out of first place, the team quickly became a Montreal institution. Charles proved that he was able to establish and maintain a smooth and eventually profitable operation all on his own.

The Expos have lost money in only three years, 1969, 1976, and 1977, but even then the year's deficit provided some handy write-offs to offset Charles's personal taxes. Bronfman's lawyers spent five years arguing with the Department of National Revenue in Ottawa about how the original $10-million investment ought to be divided between the easily depreciable players' contracts and the undepreciable cost of the franchise itself. The final settlement allowed a $6-million write-off, giving the operation tangible tax advantages.

The Expos now own four farm teams, rack up impressive attendance figures playing in the huge Olympic Stadium, and even win an occasional game. Bronfman has turned active management over to John McHale and estimates that he spends less than seven percent of his time worrying about baseball.

A much greater share of his energies goes into helping direct Montreal's Jewish community affairs. In 1973 Charles was elected president of Allied Jewish Community Services, Montreal's chief coordinating agency, and raised an unprecedented $23 million. "I've never tried to fill anybody's shoes," he says. "I'm not doing it because of my father. I know it was expected of me, so on and so forth. But that really didn't bother me a hell of a lot, because if I weren't genuinely interested, I wouldn't do it."

Unlike his father, Charles has seldom attempted to go beyond bringing the community's leaders together, imposing his leadership by example rather than edict. "I remember one time we were in Charles's office," says Arthur Pascal, the hardware-company executive who succeeded Sam as unofficial leader of Montreal's Jewish community, "and it was one of those situations where a large amount of money had to be sent to Israel. I had taken the leadership of calling the city's major families together, just before the campaign got under way, so that we could kind of prime the pump. We were sitting around Charles's office—there may have been ten or twelve of us—and the response was coming along very, very slowly. After we'd been chatting away for an hour, I asked Charles if he and I could step into another room for a minute. When we did, I said, 'Charles, we've reached an impasse here. We need big money if we're going to put this thing across. If you take the leadership and make a much larger pledge than you intended to, I'll do the same. We'll go back and tell these people that we're prepared to do it if they are.'

"Charles didn't hesitate at all, and it was a matter of an extra $500,000 on his part. It wasn't a question of 'Well, I'll have to go back and talk to Edgar,' or anything like that. We went back and were able to get the campaign off to a proper start."

By the spring of 1976, Charles had been elected associate chairman of the Canadian Jewish Congress, a position created especially for him as the final stepping-stone to Canadian Jewry's highest office. But that was all before Charles Bronfman's life and the country's perception of him were joltingly altered by his harsh attack on René Lévesque's brand of separatism on the eve of Quebec's history-making 1976 provincial election.

CHARLES BRONFMAN PRESIDES OVER HIS SATRAPY WITHIN THE BRONFMAN EMPIRE with elfin good humor, puffing his pipe, viewing visitors over a set of half-frame glasses, appearing more than a little disengaged, yet never neutral in the tone or temper of his commitments. Dispassionate he may be, but if there is one subject (apart from his father) about which he feels intensely, it's his pride in Canada. Charles Bronfman is a true believer in the notion of Canada as a country with a generous past and a great future. Even if he has trouble articulating his gospel, it is no vague valedictorian's dream. For Sam's second son, Canada is the physical setting in which his father was allowed to accumulate one of the world's great fortunes—a large and magic land where Jews need only a touch more luck to succeed than their gentile counterparts. He is proud to be Canadian, can be brought to tears by a very good (or very primitive) rendition of "O Canada," and secretly remains baffled by Edgar's and Minda's rejection of their birthplace.

It was within the context of this unrequited love of country that Charles Bronfman unexpectedly injected himself into the ferment of the 1976 Quebec election. The detailed sequence of events leading up to his intervention is worth recording because in retrospect it seemed at once totally uncharacteristic of his public image, yet very much in keeping with his inner self.

During the final, hectic week of that momentous contest, the Liberal premier, Robert Bourassa, found himself in a tough dilemma. By the end of his inept campaign, the Liberal leader was acting like the chief of a retreating army that has lived off the land for so long that its soldiers (and generals) have long since forgotten the original patriotic impulse for their war. Bewildered by signs of his impending defeat, Bourassa soiled the air with his fears. He had crisscrossed the province, hectoring his dwindling audiences with the appeal: "René Lévesque and the separatists must be unmasked! Halloween has lasted too long! The Parti Québécois is hiding its true option—it isn't talking about the economic costs of independence!"

Twice before, in 1970 and 1973, Bourassa had won resounding mandates simply by offering himself as the only viable alternative to separatism. Now, nobody was listening. On November 8, just a week before polling day, Bourassa's strategists, holed up in Montreal's Queen Elizabeth Hotel, had been handed the results of a confidential survey. It showed that 41 percent of the province's voters believed management of the economy was the prime issue of the campaign, with another 29 percent perceiving "honesty in government" as the decisive factor. Only 7 percent of those questioned even recognized separatism as the key plank in the Parti Québécois platform; its tactic of campaigning straight-out against Bourassa's ineffective economic policies and the many scandals that had tainted his administration was winning the day.

While Bourassa floundered, trying to retain power in the name of federalism, René Lévesque's campaign had about it the *élan* of those World War II films glorifying the French Resistance—all throwaway heroics and noble enunciations. As the campaign progressed, the Parti Québécois leader kept hunching over as if he were standing permanently under a low, leaky roof on a rainy day. It was at the televised press conferences that his skill as a professional performer really came through. He became a master of the art of the pause. Asked a question, he would hesitate, not, it seemed, to protect himself from careless answers, but to retreat into his own world the way a child does so that he can come up with a full and true reply. His blue eyes darting like hyperactive minnows from one camera to another, his mouth forming that tight loop of sincerity that TV can best appreciate, he kept hitting hard on the theme that only his election would assure Quebec of an honest government.

The signs of impending defeat were there for Bourassa to read. The money traders on Wall Street felt certain enough of Lévesque's victory that they started to sell their Canadian dollars short; some super-nervous money began to move quietly out of Quebec's trust and bank accounts. Most nervous of all was Montreal's Jewish community. Even though they're the most bilingual of Quebec's English-speaking population, the Jewish aristocrats of Montreal have expended so much energy attempting to make it into the fringes of the WASP establishment that they seldom bother very much

with the French society that surrounds them.* Instead
of trying to grasp power themselves, Montreal's Jews
traditionally satisfy their political aspirations by sending an ambassador to whatever government happens to
be in power in Quebec City at the time.

In the mid-seventies, that assignment fell to Dr.
Victor Goldbloom, an ambitious pediatrician named
Minister of Municipal Affairs and Environment in the
Bourassa regime. Two weeks before polling day, the
Jewish community's leaders packed Place des Arts for
a Chassidic festival under the direction of Ben Milner,
an early supporter of Menachem Begin's Likud party
in Israel. When the master of ceremonies introduced
various guests of honor to the audience, Goldbloom
was greeted by loud jeers, reflecting the audience's disdain for his support of the Liberal government's controversial Bill 22 dealing with minority language rights.
Norman Spector, co-owner of the city's largest independent fuel-oil company and one of the community's
most enlightened activists, became so concerned lest
Montreal's Jews lose their only Cabinet representative
that he arranged for Goldbloom to see Bronfman the
following morning. It was in Charles's office that two
decisions were made: a special rally to whip up support for Goldbloom would be held on November 10,
and a letter of endorsement signed by Montreal's Jewish leaders would be circulated to the community. The
rally, chaired by Spector, featured strongly worded
speeches of praise for Goldbloom by both Charles
Bronfman and Philip Vineberg, the Bronfman family
lawyer. "The people who came were initially very in-
dignant," Spector recalls, "but during the course of the

* While Sam never did learn French, he was so proud of
Charles's knowledge of the language that when his son once
made an entire speech in French at a meeting in Ville d'Anjou
the elder Bronfman kissed him on the mouth in front of the
whole crowd. Since the Parti Québécois's accession to power,
Charles has improved his pronunciation further by spending
a week of total immersion at a language institute.

evening their anger first changed to indifference and by the time they left, most of them were pledged supporters."

This proved too optimistic an assessment. On the following afternoon, thirty-six hours before polling day, Arthur Pascal called a secret emergency conclave at his apartment. In attendance, besides Pascal, Bronfman, Vineberg, and Spector, were Manny Batshaw, executive director of Montreal's Allied Jewish Community Services (AJCS), the city's most powerful Jewish institution, and five other Jewish community leaders. There was only one item on the agenda: a last-minute opinion poll indicated that Goldbloom would not retain his seat in the November 15 vote, with most of his riding's Jewish voters planning either to abstain or to cast their ballots for the Union Nationale. Vineberg pointed out that many young Jews were even swinging toward the Parti Québécois and that it would be worthwhile to stage a meeting to which some of the community's younger members would be invited.

This suggestion was quickly taken up, and those present agreed to telephone enough people to fill a hall. But which hall? With time running out and everyone present being on the AJCS executive, a consensus emerged that the association's auditorium on Côte Ste. Catherine Road would be ideal. The chief dissident was Manny Batshaw, the only professional Jewish civil servant in the group, who objected strongly to the idea of using institutionally neutral ground for a partisan rally. His objection was accepted to the extent that it was decided no actual candidates would be invited and that, instead of an election rally, the meeting would be turned into a forum where young voters could come to discuss their concerns. When the issue of who should address the gathering came up, Charles immediately offered to make the main speech. But Batshaw was still wary, warning Bronfman that the meeting shouldn't become too political. "Listen, Manny," Charles impatiently replied, "this is war. To hell with rules and regulations."

As the discussion droned on, it emerged that what was at stake here was much more than Goldbloom's re-election. These men regarded the possibility of a Parti Québécois victory not only as a potential disaster for their province and their country but also for themselves—at least in their function as essential power brokers for the Jewish community. Their private network of contacts extended deep into the province's Liberal Party; their leverage for getting things done, for negotiating the provincial government's participation in key community projects, suddenly lay in jeopardy. Of even deeper concern was their unspoken fear of the potential effects that the ultranationalists within the Parti Québécois, who had been making anti-Zionist noises, might have on the community's minority position.

CHARLES SPENT THE WEEKEND AT HIS LAURENTIAN RETREAT. It is not difficult to imagine his mental approach as he got himself worked up for the meeting ahead, guiding his Cadillac back to the city through the Sunday-morning hush. It's an attitude reminiscent of the anecdote about the man driving his car at night through a blizzard when he gets a flat tire and discovers that he doesn't have a jack. He sees a light glimmering faintly in the gloomy distance and resolves to tramp through the storm to see if the owner of the isolated farmhouse will lend him one. "Damned cold," he says to himself. "Sure hope that guy has a jack." The wind gets worse, but he keeps on trudging through the snow and thinking to himself, "What if he doesn't have a jack? Well, he lives out here all alone, he'd probably have that kind of thing around. But what if he doesn't. . . ."

He's close enough to see the outline of the house now and mutters to himself, "Okay, so he probably has a jack. But what if he doesn't want to lend it to me? Here

I've plowed through all this damn snow to this damn farmhouse for a little thing like a jack, and maybe he won't lend it to me! Just my goddamn luck." The man walks up the steps to the house and knocks angrily on the door, thinking, "I just know this bastard isn't going to lend me his goddamn jack!"

The door opens and a sleepy-looking farmer politely inquiries, "Yes, can I help you?"

"Yeah, you can help me," yells the stranded and by now totally irrational motorist. "You can take your jack and shove it!"

WHETHER OR NOT THIS WAS INDEED THE FRAME OF CHARLES BRONFMAN'S MIND, he did burst into Manny Batshaw's office with uncharacteristic rudeness. "When I asked Charles what he intended to say," Batshaw recalls, "it was his father's finger that pointed at me. 'Manny, I'm not telling anyone what I'm going to say.'"

"Charles, this is not a political meeting," Batshaw warned him one last time.

"Well, *I'm* going to be talking politics."

Word that Bronfman would be addressing the gathering had brought out a *Montreal Star* reporter hungry for a last-minute election story. ("I expected a relatively hostile young crowd," Charles recalls, "but they were mostly older and very sympathetic. I really didn't know what I was going to say. I just had a few notes. Then suddenly the audience was going with me, and I got carried away by the emotions of the day.")

As the meeting warmed up, Bronfman started by defending Bourassa as a good man but a bad politician who didn't realize "the injury, pain, and distress" his Official Language Act had caused. "I swear to God this is true," Bronfman implored his audience. "It's incredible to believe. But the Premier just didn't know. HE KNOWS NOW!"

Then he suddenly switched to René Lévesque's politics, accusing the PQ of being "unrealistic, deceptive, and dishonest" for not campaigning on a platform of separatism, the party's true ideology. He predicted economic chaos for Quebec if the PQ should win and brought the audience to hushed awe as he intoned this dire warning: "I see the destruction of my country, the destruction of the Jewish community. . . . If the PQ forms the next government, it's going to be pure, absolute hell. . . . This is a fight. It's a war—absolute war. . . . If we turn our backs on the Liberals, it will be suicide. The moment the PQ gets in, folks, it's done. All over."

Then Charles calmed down and issued a cold threat: "I have a fantasy about holding the next Seagram's annual meeting and telling the shareholders it's the last one to be held in Montreal. If, God forbid, the PQ is elected, I will make that statement."*

The reporters present rushed out to file a story that would make headlines in almost every newspaper in the country the following day, but Bronfman remained blissfully unaware that he had said anything particularly controversial. "It's funny," he remembers thinking, "but the only thing I was really horrified about was that I had referred in rather a bad way to one of the members of the Bourassa government, and I recall wondering, 'Gee, maybe I ought to call this guy up and apologize.' I was told by one person in the audience afterwards that I had gone too far in threatening to leave, but I just said, 'Let's see what happens.' The unfortunate part of it all was the way things get put in concrete. It's now popular belief that I called all French Canadians 'bastards,' which is ridiculous. Also, that I said I'd move my distillery. I don't know how you move a distillery."

The next day, Lévesque's separatists swept to power and Charles found himself abjectly apologizing for

* Charles's threat carried a dubious sanction. Seagram's Canadian headquarters had already been quietly transferred to Waterloo, Ontario, in the fall of 1971. Seco-Cemp Ltd., which holds effective stock control in Seagram, had initially moved its head office to Calgary and later to Toronto.

his outburst.* At a Parti Québécois victory banquet in the Queen Elizabeth Hotel, hastily printed cards at each table gleefully proclaimed: "Seagram's Liquor Not Being Served Here." Most upset was the Jewish community because of the anti-Semitism they were afraid Charles's threat might let loose; the mere assumption that any Jew possesses the power to threaten a government in power is not the kind of thing Jews like to hear discussed in public.

At the company's 1976 annual meeting (held only four days after the election), Jean-Charles Desroches, representing the Montreal branch of the St. Jean Baptiste Society, which held fifty shares of Seagram stock, accused Bronfman of "using blackmail." He fell short of demanding Charles's resignation, however. He was ruled out of order by Edgar and mollified by Philip Vineberg, who assured him that the company intended to cooperate unreservedly with the PQ administration.

Following this harrowing episode, Charles went into a protracted sulk, emerging six months later determined to carry on. "My grandparents on both sides had enough guts to come here. Canada has been very good to us. I'm not going to let this country go without a fight."

At the opening of the 1977 season of the Toronto Blue Jays, Charles was kibitzing with Donald Macdonald, then the federal Minister of Finance, who was his guest for the occasion. "It must have been a very traumatic time for you in Montreal this week, with the White Paper on the language bill being brought down," Macdonald remarked, referring to the bill establishing French as the official language of Quebec.

"It wasn't traumatic for me," Bronfman replied without a smile. "It might have been for others, but I didn't expect anything less."

Election of the PQ did nothing to stem the flow of Bronfman money from Quebec, so that by the summer of 1978 less than four percent of Cemp's assets and less

---

* Goldbloom was re-elected with a winning margin of about 14,000 votes compared to his margin of about 26,000 votes in 1973.

than one percent of Seagram's sales remained within the province. The other branches of the family had also been moving out, with Peter transferring the head office of Edper Investments to Toronto and the principal offices of Trizec Corporation to Calgary.

One year later, On May 18, 1978, René Lévesque was in New York to address the Council on Foreign Relations. Edgar introduced himself to the Quebec premier, who asked, "Are you one of the *Bronfman* Bronfmans? Your brother and I are almost on speaking terms again." At a private luncheon attended by both men in Montreal the week before, Lévesque had made a friendly reference to Charles's going for a French immersion course. After the meeting Lévesque had come up to Bronfman and asked him—in English—how his French was. Charles answered with a shrug. *"Ça marche."*

Epilogue

THE SEAGRAM empire continues to expand with a self-generated momentum that has moved well beyond the restrictions that govern more mundane enterprises. Few Canadians are aware of the Seagram domain's true dimensions because less than seven percent of its sales are now accounted for by its domestic market. With 15,200 employees and annual sales budgeted to reach $3 billion by 1980, it has become one of the world's largest corporate entities.

The company's basic marketing philosophy hasn't changed much from Mr. Sam's basic precepts; the fact that close to a million and a half bottles of Bronfman liquors are consumed every day (with sixty percent of sales in the United States) is partly attributable to the impressive roster of six hundred brands. Most labels make no reference to their Seagram connection: Barton & Guestier wines, Myers's rum, Wolfschmidt vodka, Mumm's champagne, Bersano wines, Burnett's gin, Captain Morgan rum, and many other apparently independent producers are nothing more than subsidiaries.

It's a highly complex operation. Because of a myriad of local regulations, V.O., for instance, is marketed in twenty different-sized bottles. Seagram's most important new marketing thrust has been into European wines. With operating assets outside North America worth $600 million by 1978, the company now owns eight large wineries in France as well as ten in other countries. Seagram's overseas operations are so large that the company has become a major short-term money-market operator, with at least $100 million in commercial paper outstanding at any one time. "It may sound arrogant," says Richard Goeltz, Seagram's corporate treasurer, "but the fact is that many banks approach us—to offer lines of credit, or to augment our present lines."

Without anyone particularly having noticed it, the Seagram Company is gradually turning itself into as much of an oil company as a distillery. Although it is deep into the petroleum business through part-ownership in several other exploration firms, its main instrument is the wholly owned Texas Pacific Oil Company, which has become the fifth-largest U.S. independent. Already producing 40,000 barrels of oil and 175 million cubic feet of gas a day, Texas Pacific is drilling for new wells in offshore Dubai and Thailand, in Spain, Kenya, the Philippines, the North Sea, and Mexico. Altogether, some 18.6 million acres are currently being explored. Morton Cohen of Montreal's Yorkton Securities has estimated that at least forty percent of annual earnings now come from oil and suggests that if Seagram's stock were to be sold only on the basis of the company's oil holdings, its shares would be worth at least $18 on the open market.

SEAGRAM'S EXISTENCE AND ENDURANCE, STRUCTURE AND PROSPECT, all are monuments to the foresight and intuition of Mr. Sam. Though he has been gone nearly a decade, the man's spirit still rules his domain. Statues and paintings of the elder Bronfman—appearing uncharacteristically calm in the artists' conceptions of him

—adorn every major reception area and executive office in the Montreal and New York Seagram edifices.

"I still not only think about Pop but dream about him," says Charles. "I keep asking myself how he would have acted in any given situation. When we did the Glenlivet deal, I sat down with Edgar after making the final decision, and he said, 'Well, this one Dad would have been happy about.'

"But I didn't agree. 'No. He'd probably be telling us, "You overpaid, you goddamned fools!" ' "

Charles has maintained Seagram's Montreal headquarters as a museum to his father. The executive floor is dominated by a large Cleeve Horne portrait of the founder, and Charles's own office has seven photographs or mentions of his beloved "Pop," including a framed copy of the company's 1970 annual report, which is inscribed: "To my dearest son, Charles. This story of the building of our company is also partly the story of my life with one of the lessons of my dear parents' blessed memory to be steadfast and true and build my life brick on brick. The symbol to the left is of a tree, firmly planted, with strong roots in the ground and growing ever upward. The branches denote our children and grandchildren. Also the people of our organization spread around the world. The trunk is your mother and I pray it also represents you and Barbara and the branches of your children and some day, please God, your grandchildren. With my love, Pappa. November 3, 1970."

The second-floor office from which Sam once ruled his empire has been preserved intact from the last day he occupied it. It's a large, low-ceilinged room lined in light American oak with artificial skylights at each end pouring down a soft glow. Behind the handsome mahogany desk—which looks as though it might have belonged to the titled partner in a London merchant banking house—is a higher-than-usual green chair that contrasts strangely with the low-cut visitors' sofas scattered through the office.

This was Mr. Sam's device for making himself look taller than he really was. (But it wasn't true, as some of his enemies believed, that he had every one of his boardroom chairs custom-designed so that each director, regardless of height, would sit no higher than at eye level with him.) Sam Bronfman didn't need to resort to such tricks. Once he was very late for a meeting of directors. Because they thought he wouldn't come at all, someone else had moved into his usual position at the head of the table. When Bronfman finally strode in, the presiding director got up to move. "Never mind. Stay where you are," Sam motioned him down. "Where I sit *is* the head of the table."

The walls of Sam's former sanctuary are decorated with dozens of mementoes of his long and crowded life. Included in the gallery of autographed photographs is a fading print of Stephen Leacock, the great Canadian humorist who also taught economics at McGill University. This is a reminder of Sam's first major venture beyond the making of whisky and money. In 1941, because he felt that the early reverses of World War II had left Canadians feeling pessimistic, Bronfman commissioned Leacock to write a cheerful history of Canada. Some 165,000 free copies of the book *(Canada: The Foundations of Its Future)* were eventually distributed. Members of the Bronfman clan still look back at this project with undiminished awe. On June 19, 1972, while urging the Canadian Radio-Television Commission to grant one of the family's companies a Montreal TV license, Philip Vineberg, the Bronfman lawyer, read out part of the book's foreword and told the commission, "It is in this spirit that we ask for your support and approval of our application."

A more practical reminder of Sam Bronfman's accomplishment is the black marble penholder that bears the unique inscription: "THANKS A BILLION, DAD. WITH LOVE, EDGAR AND CHARLES, October 19, 1965." That was the day Seagram's sales first exceeded a billion dollars and Sam's sons, then assuming control of the company, celebrated the event with a surprise party at the Ritz.

Another memento on Mr. Sam's old desk is his telephone. It sits there benignly enough, even though the visitor is told that its peculiar shape results from the reinforcement that had to be built in to withstand the frequent slamming by its owner. Mr. Sam had a peculiar relationship with this instrument, endowing it with a life of its own. Whenever a caller told him something he found difficult to believe, he'd hold out the earpiece and give it a deeply suspicious look, then hurl it back into its holder. At least once, when he heard news of a competitor's triumph, he ripped the phone from its moorings and threw it out the window into the street below.

EDGAR MAINTAINS A SIMILAR ATMOSPHERE OF HOMAGE FOR HIS FATHER at Seagram's New York headquarters. But his personal memories are a bit more earthy than Charles's. "God knows, I provoked him. I remember in my late teens or early twenties when I had done something Father didn't like. He finally looked at me kind of quizzically and said, 'Edgar, what would you do if you were a father like me who had a son like you?'

"I said, 'Well, I guess I'd spend all my money and tell him to go fuck himself.' He just shook his head. Didn't take my advice, thank God. We really had a fantastic relationship. It got difficult, of course, as he got older, but still he had a certain amount of respect for me, as well as a lot of love. . . .

"His secret? It really was a combination of things. He started off with an intense desire to succeed, but I suppose a lot of people have that. What he had—and he never took his eyes off it—was that he knew *how* he wanted to succeed. He wanted to make the very best product, and he wanted to have the pride of setting a price on it and having the consumer buy it at that price. At the same time, he was a fantastic negotiator. He had a real feel for people and, despite a lot of stories that one hears—and I was witness to a great many outbursts of his temper—he had the most ingratiating little smile and twinkle in his eye. He inspired an enormous amount of loyalty among the staff. On his eightieth birthday we had a luncheon for him, and we had the entire New York staff there, maybe a thousand people. When he walked into the room, I'll always remember the long cheer. It wasn't just the normal thing. He was really loved."

As THEY MOVE INTO MIDDLE AGE, Edgar and Charles are beginning to grapple with the problem of succession. "If Stevie, my boy, ever wanted to come into the company," says Charles, "and was competent enough to take over, the first thing I'd do would be to take my top executives as well as myself and move us all the hell out. Let him get his own management group. The generation gap has got to exist. I don't expect him to have the same values I have. Nor will he have my personality. There can be no question of split loyalties at the top, just no way."

"You can tie a family together with money," says Edgar. "That's something you can do. What you can't do is make them like each other. My brother and sisters, we're lucky. We get along pretty well. But for our children, we think they should make up their own minds."

The lines of inheritance have yet to be determined, but it was in the privacy of their massive grief over their father's death in 1971 that Edgar and Charles pledged their personal commitments to the future.

On the morning after the funeral, Moe Levine, Saidye's brother-in-law and supplier of the Crown Royal "purple bag," was alone in his apartment when the boys arrived to pay an unexpected visit. "Uncle Moe," Edgar wanted to know, "is there any law against us going to the cemetery?"

Levine explained that it was Jewish custom for close

family not to visit the graveyard for thirty days after the funeral. "I can't see any harm in it, but I'm not a rabbi," he said. "Why do you want to go?"

"We'd like to make a vow over Pop's grave," Charles replied, "that we'll always stick together as one unit."

Mr. Sam's dynasty would hold.

Appendices

Appendix One

This is a list of brands produced or marketed in North America by the Seagram organization (some are marketed by Seagram's in the United States only, others in Canada only; in some instances the Canadian distributor is different from the U.S. counterpart).

Whisky

Blended Whiskies

Adams Four Roses
Calvert Extra
Carstairs
Kessler
Paul Jones
Seagram's Seven Crown
Wilson

Bourbon

Antique Bourbon
Eagle Rare 101
Henry McKenna
Mattingly & Moore
Seagram's Benchmark
  Premium

Canadian

Adams Antique
Adams Gold Stripe
Adams Private Stock
Atlantic Special Rye
B.C. Double Distilled
B.C. Special
Canada House
Canadian Double Distilled
Canadian Masterpiece
Canadian Three Star
Gold Nugget
Harwood Canadian
Hudson's Bay Canadian
Hudson's Bay Fine Old
Hudson's Bay FOB
Hudson's Bay Royal Charter
Hudson's Bay Special
James Foxe

Lord Calvert Canadian
Pioneer
Seagram's Crown Royal
Seagram's Five Star
Seagram's V.O.
Seagram's 83
Seagram's 1776

Highland Whisky

Dunbars Special Highland

Irish Whisky

Black Bush
Irish Coffee
John Jameson
John Jameson—12 years old
Old Bushmill's Irish Whisky

Light Whisky

Four Roses
Galaxy

Scotch

Black Watch
Chivas Regal
Chivas Royal Salute
Famous Grouse, The
Glen Grant
Glenlivet, The
Highland Clan
House of Lords
Hudson's Bay Scotch
Logan De Luxe
Passport
Queen Anne
Seagram's 100 Pipers

Something Special
White Horse
William Longmore

Gin

Adams Silver Fizz
Bengal
Boodles British
Boodles London Dry
Burnett's Collins
Burnett's White Satin
Calvert
Gordon's
Hudson's Bay London Dry
Pickwick
Seagram's Extra Dry
Seagram's King Arthur
Vickers
Whitehall

Vodka

Bolshoi
Crown Russe
Gordon's
Hudson's Bay
Kolomyka
Moichev
Nasha
Natasha
Nikolai
Prince Igor
Ruska
Wolfschmidt

Rum

Captain Morgan Black Label

Captain Morgan De Luxe

Captain Morgan Gold Label

Captain Morgan White Label

Flagship Dark

Flagship Light

Flagship White

Granado Puerto Rican

Hudson's Bay Demerara

Hudson's Bay Demerara
   91.4°

Hudson's Bay Demerara
   151°

Hudson's Bay Jamaica

Hudson's Bay Treasure
   Island

Hudson's Bay Trinidad
   Light

Lord Selkirk Dark

Lord Selkirk White

Myers's Demerara

Myers's Jamaica

Myers's Light Amber

Myers's Planters' Punch

Myers's White

Palo Viejo Puerto Rican

Ron Llave Puerto Rican

Ronrico Puerto Rican

Trelawny White

Tropicana

Whistler Dark

Whistler White

Wood's Gold Anchor

Wood's Old Navy

Wood's White Sail White

**Rum-Based Cocktail—
Specialty Import**

Rumdinger

Tequila

El Charro Gold

El Charro Silve:

Olmeca Gold

Olmeca Silver

**Liqueurs, Cordials, Brandies,
Cognac, and Vermouths**

Abisante (Leroux)

Amaretto di Torino (Italy,
   Leroux)

Anesone (Leroux)

Anisette—Red (Leroux)

Anisette—White (Leroux)

Apple-Flavored Brandy
   (Lero.)

Apricot Brandy (Leroux)

Apricot Liqueur (Leroux)

Aquavit (Leroux)

Augier V.S.O.P. Cognac
   (Augier Frères)

Augier 3 Star Cognac
   (Augier Frères)

Blackberry Brandy (Leroux)

Blackberry Brandy—Polish
   Type (Leroux)

Blackberry Liqueur (Leroux)

Chemineaud Brandy

Cheri-Suisse, Cherry
   Chocolate (Switzerland)

Cherry Brandy (Leroux)

Cherry Karise, Dalmatian
   Cherry (Denmark,
   Leroux)

Cherry Liqueur (Leroux)

Chocolate Amaretto
   (Leroux)

Chocolate Banana (Leroux)

Chocolate Cherry (Leroux)
Chocolate Mint (Leroux)
Chocolate Raspberry
   (Leroux)
Claristine (Leroux)
Coffee Brandy (Leroux)
Cognac with Orange
   (France, Leroux)
Crème de Banana Liqueur
   (Leroux)
Crème de Cacao—Brown
   (Leroux)
Crème de Cacao—White
   (Leroux)
Crème de Café (Leroux)
Crème de Cassis (Leroux)
Crème de Menthe—Green
   (Leroux)
Crème de Menthe—White
   (Leroux)
Crème de Noya (Leroux)
Curaçao (Leroux)
Curaçao—Blue (Leroux)
Fraise de Bois, Strawberry
   (Austria, Leroux)
Framboise (F.E. Trimbach)
Ginger Brandy (Leroux)
Gold-O-Mint (Leroux)
Gran Torino Sweet Italian
   Vermouth
Grande Fine Champagne
   Cognac, Gaston Briand
   (Frank Schoonmaker
   Selection)
Grande Fine Champagne
   Cognac, Marcel Ragnaud
   (Frank Schoonmaker
   Selection)
Grenadine Liqueur (Leroux)

Irish Moss Crystallized Rock
   & Rye (Leroux)
Jacques Cardin Brandy
Kirsch (F. E. Trimbach)
Kirschwasser (Leroux)
Kümmel (Leroux)
Leroux Deluxe Brandy
Lochan Ora (Scotland)
Maraschino (Leroux)
Mirabelle (F. E. Trimbach)
F. de Navilly Brandy
Noilly Prat Dry Vermouth
Noilly Prat Sweet Vermouth
Ouzo (Leroux)
Pasha, Turkish Coffee
   (Turkey)
Paul Masson Double Dry
   Vermouth
Paul Masson Five Star
   Brandy
Paul Masson Liqueur
   Brandy
Paul Masson Mont Blanc
   Brandy
Paul Masson Sweet
   Vermouth
Peach Brandy (Leroux)
Peach Liqueur (Leroux)
Peppermint Schnapps
   (Leroux)
Poire William (F. E.
   Trimbach)
Raspberry Liqueur—Polish
   Type (Leroux)
Rock & Rye with Fruit
   (Leroux)
Sabra, Orange Chocolate
   (Israel)
Sambuca (Italy, Leroux)
Sambuca Originale (Italy)

312   *Appendix One*

San Mareno Italian Type
  Vermouth (Secrestat)
Sloe Gin (Leroux)
Strawberry Liqueur—Polish
  Type (Leroux)
Triple Sec (Leroux)
Tuaca, Demi-Sec Liqueur
  (Italy)
Vandermint, Minted
  Chocolate Liqueur
  (Holland)

Cocktail Mixes (Party Tyme)

Freeze-Dried

Daiquiri
Gimlet
Hot Buttered Rum
Hot Toddy
Mai Tai
Margarita
Piña Colada
Tequila Sunrise
Tom Collins
Whiskey Sour

Liquid

Apricot Sour
Banana Daiquiri
Calvert Manhattan
Calvert Martini
Daiquiri
Gimlet
Mai Tai
Manhattan
Margarita
Martini
Piña Colada

Tom Collins
Whiskey Sour

Champagne

Belle Epoque (Perrier-Jouët)
Blanc de Blancs (Gold Seal)
Brut (Gold Seal)
Brut (Heidsieck Monopole)
Brut (Henri Marchant)
Brut (Pinnacles Selection)
Brut Vintage (Heidsieck
  Monopole)
Cordon Rosé (G. H. Mumm
  & Cie)
Cordon Rouge Brut (G. H.
  Mumm & Cie)
Cordon Rouge Vintage
  (G. H. Mumm & Cie)
Côteaux Champenois (G. H.
  Mumm & Cie)
Crémant de Cramant (G. H.
  Mumm & Cie)
Cuvée Spéciale Extra Dry
  (Perrier-Jouët)
Diamant Bleu Vintage
  (Heidsieck Monopole)
Dry (Christian Bros.)
English Cuvée Brut (Perrier-
  Jouët)
English Cuvée Brut Vintage
  (Perrier-Jouët)
Extra Dry (G. H. Mumm &
  Cie)
Extra Dry (Gold Seal)
Extra Dry (Heidsieck
  Monopole)
Extra Dry (Henri Marchant)
Extra Dry (Pinnacles
  Selection)

Fleur de France (Perrier-
Jouët)
Pink (Gold Seal)
Pink (Henri Marchant)
Pink (Pinnacles Selection)
René Lalou (G. H. Mumm
& Cie)

Alsace Wines

Gewürztraminer (F. E.
Trimbach)
Riesling "Clos Ste. Hune)
(F. E. Trimbach)
Sylvaner (F. E. Trimbach)

Bordeaux Red Wines

Château Beychevelle '70
Château Calon Ségur '73
Château Cantegrive
Château Cheval Blanc '70
Château Clos d'Estournel
'70
Château de Sales '73
Château Duhart-Milon
Rothschild
Château Gazin '70
Château Grand Mazerolles
(Frank Schoonmaker
Selection)
Château Grand-Pontet
Château Greysac (Frank
Schoonmaker Selection)
Château Gruaud-Larose
Château Guiraud Cheval
Blanc
Château Haut-Brion '67
Château La Mission—
Haut-Brion

Château Lafite-Rothschild
'64, '66, '70
Château Langoa-Barton '70,
'72, '73
Château Larose-Trintaudon
Château La Tour Blanche
'70
Château La Tour—
Haut-Brion
Château Laurentan-Rouge
Château Laurette Ste.-Croix
de Mont '70
Château Léoville-Barton '70,
'72
Château Léoville-Poyferré
'73
Château Malartic-Lagravière
Château Margaux '70
Château Martinet (Frank
Schoonmaker Selection)
Château Meyney
Château Montrose
Château Mouton-Rothschild
'70
Château Pétrus
Château Pichon Longueville
'69
Château Puy Blanquet
Château Simard
Château Talbot
Château Trotanoy
Domaine de Chevalier '66
Médoc (Barton & Guestier)
Pontet Latour (Barton &
Guestier)
Prince Noir
Roi Chevalier (Barton &
Guestier)
St. Emilion (Barton &
Guestier)

St. Julien (Barton &
Guestier)

Bordeaux White Wines

Blanc de Blancs (Barton &
Guestier)
Château d'Yquem
Château Lafaurie-Peyraguey
Château Laurentan Blanc
Château Laville—
Haut-Brion
Graves (Barton & Guestier)
Pontet Latour (Barton &
Guestier)
Prince Blanc (Barton &
Guestier)
Sauternes (Barton &
Guestier)

Burgundy Red Wines

Beaujolais Propriété (Frank
Schoonmaker Selection)
Bonnes-Mares '67 (Barton &
Guestier)
Bourgogne (Barton &
Guestier)
Chambertin '64, '67 (Barton
& Guestier)
Chambolle-Musigny Amours
'70 (Barton & Guestier)
Charmes Chambertin '52,
'70 (Barton & Guestier)
Chassagne-Montrachet
(Barton & Guestier)
Chassagne-Montrachet Clos
St.-Jean (Barton &
Guestier)
Château de La Chaize,

Brouilly (Beaujolais,
Frank Schoonmaker
Selection)
Château de Lacarelle,
Beaujolais-Villages
(Frank Schoonmaker
Selection)
Château de Pizay, Beaujolais
Supérieur (Barton &
Guestier)
Château de Pizay, Morgon
Barton & Guestier)
Côte de Nuits-Villages
(Barton & Guestier)
Domaine Bonneau du
Martray-Corton
Domaine du Courcel, Pom-
mard (Frank Schoon-
maker Selection)
Domaine G. Roumier,
Chambolle-Musigny
(Frank Schoonmaker
Selection)
Domaine J. Guillemard,
Pommard (Frank Schoon-
maker Selection)
Domaine Jean Grivot,
Vosne-Romanée (Frank
Schoonmaker Selection)
Domaine L. Geoffrey
Gevrey Chambertin
(Frank Schoonmaker
Selection)
Domaine Lahaye, Pom-
mard
Domaine Marquis d'Anger-
ville, Volnay (Frank
Schoonmaker Selection)
Domaine P. de Marcilly,
Beaune

Domaine Pierre Gelin, Gevrey Chambertin (Frank Schoonmaker Selection)

Domaine R. Duchet, Beaune (Frank Schoonmaker Selection)

Domaine Tollot-Beaut, Aloxe-Corton (Frank Schoonmaker Selection)

Gevrey-Chambertin (Barton & Guestier)

Grands Echézeaux '69 (Barton & Guestier)

Latricières '67 (Barton & Guestier)

Latricières-Chambertin '69 (Barton & Guestier)

Mâcon Rouge (Barton & Guestier)

Moulin Vert '71 (Barton & Guestier)

Musigny '66, '69 (Barton & Guestier)

Nuits-St. Georges (Barton & Guestier)

Pommard Epenots '70 (Barton & Guestier)

Richebourg '67 (Barton & Guestier)

Savigny La Dominode '70 (Barton & Guestier)

St. Louis Beaujolais (Barton & Guestier)

Volnay Clos des Chênes '70 (Barton & Guestier)

Vosne-Romanée '70 (Barton & Guestier)

Vosne-Romanée Les Suchots (Barton & Guestier)

Burgundy White Wines

Bâtard-Montrachet '67 (Barton & Guestier)

Chablis (Barton & Guestier)

Chassagne-Montrachet Clos St. Marc '71 (Barton & Guestier)

Château de Pizay Blanc (Barton & Guestier)

Clos Reissier, Pouilly-Fuissé (Barton & Guestier)

Corton-Charlemagne '69 (Barton & Guestier)

Domaine A. Ropiteau-Mignon, Meursault

Domaine André Ramonet, Chassagne-Montrachet (Frank Schoonmaker Selection)

Domaine Bachelet Delagrange, Chassagne-Montrachet (Frank Schoonmaker Selection)

Domaine Bonneau du Martray, Corton-Charlemagne

Domaine Edouard Deleger, Chassagne-Montrachet (Frank Schoonmaker Selection)

Domaine Jean Chavy, Puligny-Montrachet (Frank Schoonmaker Selection)

Domaine Maurice Fevre, Chablis (Chateau & Estate Wine Co.)

Domaine P. de Marcilly, Chassagne-Montrachet

Domaine Pierre Matrot, Meursault (Frank Schoonmaker Selection)

Domaine Potinet Ampeau, Meursault (Frank Schoonmaker Selection)

Les Charmes, Mâcon-Lugny

Mâcon Blanc (Barton & Guestier)

Meursault (Barton & Guestier)

Pinot Chardonnay Mâcon (Barton & Guestier)

Pouilly Fuissé (Barton & Guestier)

Prince d'Argent (Barton & Guestier)

Puligny-Montrachet (Barton & Guestier)

Puligny-Montrachet Les Folatières (Barton & Guestier)

St. Louis Chardonnay (Barton & Guestier)

Danish Wine

Cherry Kijafa

Lambrusco

Lini Lambrusco

Loire Wines

Château de Maimbray, Sancerre (Frank Schoonmaker Selection)

Château de Tigné, Rosé d'Anjou (Frank Schoonmaker Selection)

Clos la Perrière, Sancerre

Domaine de la Batardière, Muscadet

Domaine de l'Oisellnière, Muscadet (Frank Schoonmaker Selection)

Domaine de Saint-Laurent-l'Abbaye, Pouilly-Fumé

Domaine Pabiot, Pouilly-Fumé (Frank Schoonmaker Selection)

Muscadet (Barton & Guestier)

Nectarblanc (Rémy Pannier)

Nectarosé (Rémy Pannier)

Pouilly-Fumé (Barton & Guestier)

Sancerre (Barton & Guestier)

Vouvray (Barton & Guestier)

Madeira Wines

Madeira (Gold Seal)

Paul Masson (Pinnacles Selection)

Moselle Wines

Bereich Bernkastel Riesling (Julius Kayser & Co.)

Moselle Bluemchen (Julius Kayser & Co.)

Piesporter Michelsberg Riesling (Julius Kayser & Co.)

Zeller Schwarze Katz (Julius
Kayser & Co.)

Moselle-Saar Wines

Bernkasteler Doktor u.
Graben, Wwe. Dr. H.
Thanisch
Friedrich Wilhelm Gym-
nasium, Trier (Frank
Schoonmaker Selection)
Reichsgraf von Kesselstatt,
Trier (Frank Schoon-
maker Selection)
Scharzhofberger, Egon
Müller
Wehlener Sonnenuhr, Joh.
Jos. Prüm
Weingut Le Gallais,
Wiltingen (Frank Schoon-
maker Selection)
Weingut O. Tobias, Piesport
(Frank Schoonmaker
Selection)
Weingut Otto Dünweg,
Neumagen (Frank
Schoonmaker Selection)

**Muscatel, Claret, and Tokay
Wines**

Claret (Christian Bros.)
Muscatel (Christian Bros.)
Muscatel (Paul Masson,
Pinnacles Selection)
Tokay (Christian Bros.)

Piedmontese Red Wines

Barbaresco (Bersano)

Barbera d'Asti (Bersano)
Barolo (Bersano)
Dolcetto Amaro (Bersano)
Grignolino (Bersano)
Nebbiolo d'Alba (Bersano)

Port Wines

Granada Port (Secrestat)
Port (Gold Seal)
Rare Souzao (Pinnacles
Selection)
Rare Tawny (Pinnacles
Selection)
Rich Ruby (Pinnacles
Selection)
Ruby Port (Christian Bros.)
Ruby Port (Gold Seal)
Tawny (Pinnacles Selection)
Tawny Port (Christian
Bros.)
Tawny Port (Gold Seal)
Tinta Cream Port (Christian
Bros.)
Treasure Port (Christian
Bros.)
Vintage Porto (Warre & Co.,
Frank Schoonmaker
Selection)

Puerto Rican Wine

Mardi Gras Pineapple Wine
(G. Allen Parlier Co.)

Red Wines—Domestic

Barbera (Paul Masson)
Baroque Burgundy (Paul
Masson)

Burgundy (Christian Bros.)
Burgundy (Gold Seal)
Burgundy (Paul Masson)
Burgundy Natural (Gold
  Seal)
Cabernet Sauvignon
  (Christian Bros.)
Cabernet Sauvignon (Paul
  Masson)
Catawba Red (Gold Seal)
Catawba Red (Henri
  Marchant)
Chambord (Secrestat)
Concord (Gold Seal)
Concord (Henri Marchant)
Gamay Beaujolais (Paul
  Masson)
Gamay Noir (Christian
  Bros.)
Labrusca (Gold Seal)
Labrusca Red (Henri
  Marchant)
Moulin Mouton (Secrestat)
Petite Sirah (Paul Masson)
Pineau de la Loire (Christian
  Bros.)
Pinot Chardonnay (Christian
  Bros.)
Pinot Noir (Christian Bros.)
Pinot Noir (Paul Masson)
Pinot St. George (Christian
  Bros.)
Rubion Claret (Paul
  Masson)
Ruby Cabernet (Paul
  Masson)
Zinfandel (Christian Bros.)
Zinfandel (Paul Masson)

Red Wines—Imported

Barbera Cascina Tranquillo
  (Bersano, Italian)
Bon Sol Chilean Burgundy
Chianti Classico, Palazzo al
  Bosco (Frank
  Schoonmaker Selection)
Corbières (Barton &
  Guestier, French)
Costières du Gard (Barton &
  Guestier, French)
Torchietta Mescetore Del
  700 '64 (Italian)

Rhine Wines

Bereich Niersteiner (Julius
  Kayser & Co.)
Hattenheimer Nussbrunnen,
  Langwerth von Simmern
Johannisberger Klaus Graf
  von Schönborn
Landgraf von Hessen,
  Johannisberg (Frank
  Schoonmaker Selection)
Liebfraumilch (Black
  Tower)
Liebfraumilch Glockenspiel
  (Julius Kayser & Co.)
Rüdesheimer Bischofsberg,
  Valentine Schlotter
Schloss Eltz, Eltville (Frank
  Schoonmaker Selection)
Schloss Groenesteyn,
  Rüdesheim (Frank
  Schoonmaker Selection)
Schloss Johannisberg Fürst
  von Metternich

Schloss Vollrads, Graf
Matuschka-Greiffenclau

Staatsweinguter, Eltville
(Frank Schoonmaker
Selection)

Weingut Dr. Bürklin-Wolf,
Wachenheim (Frank
Schoonmaker Selection)

Weingut H. Braun, Nierstein
(Frank Schoonmaker
Selection)

Weingut J. B. Becker,
Walluf (Frank
Schoonmaker Selection)

Rhône Red Wines

Bellicard & Cie, Côtes du
Rhône (Frank
Schoonmaker Selection)

Château d'Aigueville, Côtes
du Rhône (Frank
Schoonmaker Selection)

Château de Malijay, Côtes
du Rhône

Châteauneuf-du-Pape
(Barton & Guestier)

Côtes du Luberon (Barton &
Guestier)

Domaine Comte de Lauze,
Châteauneuf-du-Pape
(Frank Schoonmaker
Selection)

Domaine de la Meynarde
(Barton & Guestier)

Domaine de la Roquette,
Châteauneuf-du-Pape

Prince Rouge (Barton &
Guestier)

Rhône Rosé Wines

Domaine de la Meynarde
Rosé (Barton & Guestier)

Domaine de Longval, Tavel
(Perrier Jouët)

Tavel (Barton & Guestier)

Rosé Wines

Bon Sol Chilean Rosé

Catawba Pink (Gold Seal)

Catawba Pink (Henri
Marchant)

Chablis Rosé (Gold Seal)

Chateau La Salle (Christian
Bros.)

Gamay Rosé (Pinnacles
Selection)

La Salle Rosé (Christian
Bros.)

Napa Rosé (Christian Bros.)

Pica Rosé (Secrestat)

Pink (Paul Masson)

Rosé (Pinnacles Selection)

Vin Rosé (Christian Bros.)

Vin Rosé (Gold Seal)

Vin Rosé Sec (Pinnacles
Selection)

Sangria

Paul Masson California
Sangria

Sangria Red (Secrestat)

Sherries

Cocktail (Pinnacles
Selection)

Cocktail Sherry (Christian Bros.)

Cocktail Sherry (Gold Seal)

Cream Sherry (Christian Bros.)

Cream Sherry (Gold Seal)

Dry Sherry (Christian Bros.)

Golden Cream (Pinnacles Selection)

Golden Sherry (Christian Bros.)

Granada Canadian Sherry (Secrestat)

Medium Dry (Pinnacles Selection)

Meloso Cream Sherry (Christian Bros.)

Pale Dry (Pinnacles Selection)

Rare Cream (Pinnacles Selection)

Rare Dry (Pinnacles Selection)

Rare Flor (Pinnacles Selection)

Sherry (Gold Seal)

Sparkling Wines (Non-Champagne)

Asti Spumante (Bersano)

Cold Duck (Gold Seal)

Cold Duck (Henri Marchant)

Cold Duck (Secrestat)

Crackling Chablis (Pinnacles Selection)

Crackling Rosé (Pinnacles Selection)

Gratien & Mayer, Saumur Brut

Sparkling Burgundy (Gold Seal)

Sparkling Burgundy (Henri Marchant)

Sparkling Burgundy (Pinnacles Selection)

Very Cold Duck (Pinnacles Selection)

Tuscan Red Wines

Chianti (Ricasoli)

Chianti Classico (Brolio)

Riserva (Brolio)

Tuscan White Wine

Bianco (Brolio)

Veronese Red Wines

Bardolino (Bersano)

Valpolicella (Bersano)

Veronese White Wine

Soave (Bersano)

White Wines—Domestic

Catawba White (Gold Seal)

Catawba White (Henri Marchant)

Chablis (Christian Bros.)

Chablis (Gold Seal)

Chablis (Paul Masson)

Chablis Nature (Gold Seal)

Chantilly (Secrestat)

Chenin Blanc (Christian
Bros.)
Chenin Blanc (Paul Masson)
Dry Sauterne (Paul Masson)
Emerald Dry (Paul Masson)
French Colombard (Paul
Masson)
Gewürtztraminer (Christian
Bros.)
Gewürtztraminer Vintage
(Pinnacles Selection)
Grey Riesling (Christian
Bros.)
Johannisberg Riesling
(Christian Bros.)
Johannisberg Riesling (Paul
Masson)
Johannisberg Riesling
Varietal (Gold Seal)
Johannisberg Riesling
Vintage (Pinnacles
Selection)
Labrusca White (Henri
Marchant)
Napa Fumé Blanc (Christian
Bros.)
Papillon (Secrestat)
Pica White (Secrestat)
Pinot Blanc (Paul Masson)
Pinot Chardonnay (Paul
Masson)
Pinot Chardonnay Varietal
(Gold Seal)
Pinot Chardonnay Vintage
(Pinnacles Selection)
Rhine (Christian Bros.)

Rhine (Gold Seal)
Rhine (Paul Masson)
Rhine Castle (Paul Masson)
Riesling (Christian Bros.)
Riesling (Paul Masson)
Sauterne (Christian Bros.)
Sauterne (Gold Seal)
Sauvignon Blanc (Christian
Bros.)
White Burgundy (Gold Seal)

White Wines—Imported

Bianchi Borgona
(Argentina)
Bon Sol Chilean Riesling
Cantina Sociale di Soave
(Frank Schoonmaker
Selection, Italy)
Chablis Valentin Bianchi
(Argentina)
Gumpoldskirchner Doktor
Spätlese, Dr. Ernst Weigl
(Austria)
Gumpoldskirchner Eichberg
1973, Dr. Ernst Weigl
(Austria)
Kremser Pfaffenberg
Riesling Spätlese, Fritz
Salomon (Austria)
Nuesto Margaux Bianchi
(Argentina)
Schloss Kirchberg Kremser
Wachtberg Grüner
Veltliner, Fritz Salomon
(Austria)
Vin Santo (Brolio, Italy)

Appendix Two

This is a list of the holdings of the Bronfmans in the United States.

Name	Description
ARIZONA	
Real Estate	
Capri Village	mobile-home community
Central Park	mobile-home community
Catalina Park	mobile-home community
Papigo Peaks Village	mobile-home community
Mesa Village	mobile-home community
Hacienda de Valencia	mobile-home community
ARKANSAS	
Other Holdings	oil interests
CALIFORNIA	
Los Angeles and Los Angeles County	
Real Estate	
Biltmore Hotel	hotel
Encino Valley Gateway	office
Hollywood Center	office

Company Representing Bronfman Family Interest	Percentage Owned	Size/Assets
Trizec	100	281 sites
Trizec	100	293 sites
Trizec	100	379 sites
Trizec	100	279 sites
Trizec	100	199 sites
Trizec	100	364 sites
Texas Pacific Oil (*See also* Dallas)	100	135,400 gross acres
Ridgway Ltd.*	100	1,072 rooms
Trizec	100	631,000 sq. ft.
Trizec	100	481,000 sq. ft.

* Phyllis Bronfman is the half-owner of Ridgway Ltd.

Name	Description
Airport Freeway	office
Valley Center	office
Wilshire Center	office
Tristar Towers North	office
Tristar Towers South	office
Los Angeles Industrial Center	industrial (23 buildings)
Pacific Gateway Center	industrial (6 buildings)
Pacific Gateway Center	industrial (3 buildings under construction)
Los Angeles Industrial Center	serviced zone industrial
Pacific Gateway Center	serviced zone industrial
Cerritos Industrial Park	industrial

Orange County
Real Estate

Orange County Industrial Center	industrial (5 buildings)
Orange County Industrial Center	industrial (under construction) serviced zone industrial
Concorde-Cascade	mobile-home community
Lamplighter Village	mobile-home community
Rancho Valley	mobile-home community
Canada Business Center	industrial park

COLORADO
Real Estate

Holiday Hills Village	mobile-home community
Hillcrest Village	mobile-home community
Cimarron	mobile-home community
Golden Terrace Village	mobile-home community
Pueblo Grande Village	mobile-home community
Holiday Village	mobile-home community

Other Holdings

Bow Valley Industries	
Bow Valley Exploration U.S. Inc.	
Ranger Oil	
	oil interests
	oil interests
Connors Drilling Inc.	

Company Representing Bronfman Family Interest	Percentage Owned	Size/Assets
Cadillac Fairview	52.5	103 acres
Banque Louis-Dreyfus	100	
Warrington Products	100	
Louis Dreyfus Property Corp.	33⅓	335,000 sq. ft.
Louis Dreyfus Property Corp.	100	125,000 sq. ft.
Louis Dreyfus Property Corp.	100	489,000 sq. ft.
Trizec	67	876,000 sq.ft.
Cadillac Fairview	85	340 units
Cadillac Fairview	85	157 units
Cadillac Fairview	50	136 units
Trizec	100	555 sites
Trizec	100	479 sites
Trizec	100	470 sites
Trizec	100	438 sites
Trizec	100	418 sites
Trizec	100	379 sites
Trizec	100	361 sites
Trizec	100	354 sites
Trizec	100	329 sites
Trizec	100	228 sites
Trizec	100	192 sites

Name	Description
Plaza of the Americas	condominiums
Central Park Orlando	retirement lodge

GEORGIA
   Atlanta
   Real Estate

| Peachtree Center Tower | office |
| Shannon Mall | shopping center (under construction) |

KANSAS
   Real Estate

| Gaslight Lawrence | mobile-home community |

KENTUCKY
   Other Holdings

| | oil interests |

LOUISIANA
   Other Holdings

East Cameron	oil interests
Blocks #268, #303	
	oil interests
	oil interests

MICHIGAN
   Detroit
   Real Estate

First National Building	office
Fisher Building	office
New Center Building	office
	land held

MINNESOTA
   Real Estate

| Camelot Acres | mobile-home community |

MISSISSIPPI
   Jackson

Company Representing Bronfman Family Interest	Percentage Owned	Size/Assets
Cadillac Fairview	50	860 units
Trizec	100	180 capacity
Trizec	67	411,000 sq. ft.
Cadillac Fairview	75	677,000 sq. ft.
Trizec	100	421 sites
Texas Pacific Oil	100	181,800 gross acres
Bow Valley Industries	15	
Ranger Oil	100	8,703 gross acres
Texas Pacific Oil	100	132,700 gross acres
Trizec	100	951,000 sq. ft.
Trizec	100	920,000 sq. ft.
Trizec	100	290,000 sq. ft.
S. B. McLaughlin		50 acres
Trizec	100	319 sites

Name	Description
Real Estate	land option for shopping center
MONTANA	
Real Estate	
Casa Village	mobile-home community
Other Holdings	
	oil interests
NEVADA	
Real Estate	
Rancho Bonanza	mobile-home community
Bonanza Village	mobile-home community
NEW YORK	
Flushing	
Other Holdings	
Danby U.S.A. Corp.	sales division
New York	
Other Holdings	
Institutional Investor	business publication
Syracuse	
Other Holdings	
Syracuse Cablesystems	cable TV system
Westchester County	
Real Estate	
12 land parcels	multi-house residential
The Galleria	shopping center at White Plains
NORTH CAROLINA	
Hickory	
Real Estate	
Valley Hills Mall	shopping center
New Bern	

Company Representing Bronfman Family Interest	Percentage Owned	Size/Assets
Cadillac Fairview	52.5	81 acres
Trizec	100	482 sites
Texas Pacific Oil	100	258,700 gross acres
Trizec	100	182 sites
Trizec	100	182 sites
Warrington Products	100	
Gerin	40	
Canadian Cablesystems Ltd. (Edper)	67	
Louis Dreyfus Property Corp.	100	between 50 and 100 acres
Cadillac Fairview	43	860,000 sq. ft.
Cadillac Fairview	75	515,000 sq.ft.

Name	Description
Real Estate Twin Rivers Mall	shopping center (under construction)
Rocky Mount *Real Estate*	land held for shopping center
OKLAHOMA *Real Estate* Rockwood Village	mobile-home community
PENNSYLVANIA Wilkes-Barre *Other Holdings* Stressteel Corporation	manufactures steel
SOUTH DAKOTA *Other Holdings*	oil interests
TEXAS Dallas *Real Estate* River Davis Apartments	apartment
Other Holdings Texas Pacific Oil Co. Inc.*	oil company
	oil interests oil interests

---

* Not included in this list are the following subsidiaries of Texas Pacific Oil Co. Inc.: Petroleo Pacifico Inc., Texas Pacific India Inc., Texas Pacific International Inc., Texas Pacific Malaysia Inc., Texas Pacific Oil Co. of Guatemala, Texas Pacific Oil Co. of Indonesia, and Texas Pacific Oil Italia Corporation SpA.

Company Representing Bronfman Family Interest	Percentage Owned	Size/Assets
Cadillac Fairview	75	280,000 sq. ft.
Cadillac Fairview	75	750,000 sq. ft.
Trizec	100	264 sites
Gerin	100	
Texas Pacific Oil	100	457,200 gross acres
Louis Dreyfus Property Corp.	50	270 units
Joseph E. Seagram & Sons Inc.	100	owns 232 million barrels of oil (valued at $926,000,000)
Texas Pacific Oil	100	457,200 gross acres
Ranger Oil	100	11,663 gross acres

Name	Description
UTAH	
Other Holdings	
	oil interests
WYOMING	
Other Holdings	
	oil interests
	oil interests

Company Representing Bronfman Family Interest	Percentage Owned	Size/Assets
Texas Pacific Oil	100	213,200 gross acres
Texas Pacific Oil	100	347,500 gross acres
Ranger Oil	100	6,600 gross acres

Index

Company Representing Bronfman Family Interest	Percentage Owned	Size/Assets
Trizec	100	467,000 sq. ft.
Trizec	100	369,000 sq. ft.
Trizec	100	346,000 sq. ft.
Trizec	40	483,000 sq. ft.
Trizec	40	170,000 sq. ft.
Cadillac Fairview	100	1,598,000 sq. ft.
Cadillac Fairview	100	432,000 sq. ft.
Cadillac Fairview	100	275,000 sq. ft.
Cadillac Fairview	100	77.8 acres
Cadillac Fairview	100	145.5 acres
Ridgway Ltd.	100	80 acres
Cadillac Fairview	100	545,000 sq. ft.
Cadillac Fairview	100	181,000 sq. ft.
Cadillac Fairview	100	99.9 acres
Trizec	100	282 sites
Trizec	100	270 sites
Trizec	100	140 sites
Ridgway Ltd.	100	25 acres
Trizec	100	758 sites
Trizec	100	603 sites
Trizec	100	327 sites
Trizec	100	264 sites
Trizec	100	252 sites
Trizec	100	240 sites
Cemp	12.6	
Bow Valley Industries	100	
Edper	6	
Ranger Oil	100	9,533 gross acres
Texas Pacific Oil	100	330,500 gross acres
(*See also* Arkansas)		
Bow Valley Industries	100	

Name	Description

CONNECTICUT
　Danbury
　Real Estate
　　　　　　　　　　　　　　land held for
　　　　　　　　　　　　　　shopping center

　Stamford
　Real Estate
　Louis Dreyfus Property Corp.　　development
　Westport
　Other Holdings
　Weston Industries　　　　　　marketing company

DELAWARE
　Real Estate
　Georgetown Plaza　　　　　　hotel-office

DISTRICT OF COLUMBIA
　Washington
　Real Estate
　1220 19th St.　　　　　　　　office

　1801 K St.　　　　　　　　　office

FLORIDA
　Real Estate
　Clearwater Mall　　　　　　　shopping center
　Islandia　　　　　　　　　　residential
　Brandywine　　　　　　　　residential
　Sun and Surf　　　　　　　　condominium
　Holiday Parks　　　　　　　mobile-home community
　Windmill Fort Myers　　　　mobile-home community
　Windmill Sarasota　　　　　mobile-home community
　Regency Cove　　　　　　　mobile-home community
　Carriage Cove　　　　　　　mobile-home community
　Lake Haven　　　　　　　　mobile-home community
　Bay Aristocrat　　　　　　　mobile-home community
　Palm Lake Estates　　　　　mobile-home community
　East Bay Oaks　　　　　　　mobile-home community
　Eldorado　　　　　　　　　mobile-home community
　Stonehenge on the Hill　　　mobile-home community

Ross, William Henry, 112,
141-42
Rossville Union Distillery, 141
Rothschild, Baron Guy de,
188-89
Rothschild, Edmond, 189
Rothschild family, 9, 34n,
188-89
Royal Bank, 37
Royal Canadian Mounted
Police (RCMP), 132,
138, 248, 252
Royal Commission on Customs
and Excise, 85, 90, 93,
121, 124, 131
Royalite, 202, 265
Rum, 147, 201
Rum Row, 117
Russell, Richard, 196
Rutkins, James "Niggy," 60n
Ryan's Daughter (film), 156

Sagittarius Productions
Incorporated, 206
Saidye Bronfman cultural
center, 40n
Saier, William, 127-28
St. James' Club, 33
St. Laurent, Louis, 47, 48,
52-53
St. Pierre Island, 116-19,
131-33, 137, 138
Sair, Isaac, 82n
Sair, Jacob, 82n
Salerno, Ralph, 250
Saskatchewan province, 79, 97
anti-Semitism in, 123-24
conservatism in, 123-24
1929 elections in, 124-25
Saskatchewan Liquor
Commission, 122
Saskatchewan Temperance
Act, 97

Sassoon, Rabbi Solomon
David, 34n
Sassoon, Siegfried, 34n
Sassoon, Sir Victor, 34-35
Sassoon, Sybil, 34n
Saunders, Charles, 67
S. B. McLaughlin
Associates, Ltd., 272-73
Schechter, Edward, 242
Scheckman, Zoë, 265
Schenley, 140, 141
Schneckenburger, Merle,
22, 23-24
Schultz, Dutch, 101-03
Schwarzhaupt, Emil, 142
Schwengel, Frank, 143-46, 204
Seagram, Edward, 111
Seagram, Joseph Edward
Frowde, 214-15
Seagram, Joseph Emm, 57, 111
Seagram building (New
York City), 179-82
Seagram company (Joseph
E. Seagram and Sons
Inc.), 3-4, 141
board of directors of, 214-17
Bronfman family's con-
trolling interest in, 222-23
Canadian headquarters of,
295n
cooks of, 22
entrance into U.S. markets,
140-45
executive committee of,
215-16
historical background of,
56-59
marketing philosophy of,
299-300
Montreal headquarters of,
14
New York headquarters of,
203-04